House on Latimer Square

The Compass Rose Journey
Book One

WENDY MUTTON

DEMPSTER STREET
PUBLISHING

Chapter One

Edinburgh Scotland
March 1936

A Matter of Money

Laurie MacKenzie glanced at the gold engravings on his college ring that proclaimed him a graduate of the University of Edinburgh, class of 1937. If you'd told him two years ago he'd be celebrating at a classy nightclub in an expensive white tux he'd have laughed into his ale. It would have suited him better to blow off some steam at a lively pub with his mates, but Marguerite insisted they meet at the Blue Finn, an upscale place. She wasn't the pub type. He entered the crowded lobby and nodded with appreciation at the boisterous crowd. The band played a favorite American song, *Pennies from Heaven*. The singer didn't sound like Bing Crosby, but it still put Laurie in the mood to dance.

He handed his fedora and overcoat to a pretty blonde in the

cloakroom, feeling pleased at the way she smiled at him, her gaze traveling over his features. Laurie had a dusky complexion, an odd contrast to his sea-blue eyes. He raked his fingers through his auburn hair, pulling it away from his dark brows. *I can feel it, my luck has finally changed for the better.* He straightened his tie before stepping into the crowd.

Small lamps flickered from the round tables encircling the full dance floor. Couples swayed to the music, barely moving in the crush. He caught sight of Marguerite. Her pale hair shone in the soft light, making his pulse race. He recognized two classmates sitting at her table. A lad leaned forward, saying something that made her laugh. He shook off a momentary stab of jealousy. No worries. *The lass is all mine. After all, she pursued me first.*

"Pardon me. Excuse me." Laurie maneuvered past dancing couples. She hadn't noticed him yet. He shrugged his new white dinner jacket into place, congratulating himself on his decision to borrow the money for his new duds. He wanted to watch her face when she saw how he'd dressed for her.

"Mr. MacKenzie?" A young busboy stood at his elbow.

"That's me."

"A man at the bar gave me a note for you." The boy held up a folded cocktail napkin.

"Thanks." Laurie stopped to read the scribbled message before asking, "Which man?" But the lad was gone.

The note read: "*Back door. Urgent. Rab.*" Although the hand bore no resemblance to that of his grandfather, there was always the possibility the old man had sent someone. *Rab's getting so eccentric it's hard to know what to expect from him next.*

He was tempted to ignore the note, but doubtless Rab wouldn't send someone unless he really needed help. With a heavy sigh, he turned toward the kitchen. *I'll make this quick.* Marguerite had picked him, sure, but it wasn't wise to let his beautiful blonde wait with so many other suitors ready to catch her attention.

He asked a passing waiter, "Where can I find the back door?" The chap pointed down a corridor to his left. Laurie trotted down the hall and through the doorway. A hand reached out, spinning him around. He yelled, "What the hell!" and struggled to pull away. A large fist rammed into his nose. The brute held Laurie in place by the lapels of his dinner jacket. Another stunning blow landed just above his right eye. Laurie could handle himself in a fight, but now when he swung out, he couldn't connect with anything solid. The massive hulk before him wore a suit that stretched over bulging muscles. His long arms held Laurie like a rag doll. Then with surprising quickness, the bloke let go of him and landed three punches to Laurie's midsection. Breathless, Laurie slumped to the ground.

Time seemed to slow. Here in the dark alley, he noticed the clamor of a busy kitchen mingled with the hum of cars as they passed out on the street, but no one was near enough to help. Not even an alley cat watched his beating. Still gasping for breath, Laurie squinted up through already swollen eyes at a bent bulbous nose, now only inches from his face.

"Get on yer feet."

Monstrous hands grabbed Laurie by the lapels again, pulling him even closer until his eyes could no longer focus on the squashed snout.

The giant growled, "You look like you can afford to pay." He released Laurie, sending him sprawling on the pavement. Laurie blinked up at the beefy face as the man spit out his demands. "Toby wants his siller. I'll gie ye a break the now. You dinnae want tae make me do this again."

A wave of panic hit Laurie. "Rab. If you hurt him—"

"The old man's no been touched this time. Toby makes a point to ken who he's dealing with, aye?"

Laurie lunged to his feet, throwing all his weight into a punch aimed at the man's jaw. His foe threw up an arm to block, and Laurie's fist felt like it hit solid rock. With one punishing roundhouse blow, Toby's man sent Laurie back onto the cobblestones.

Laurie wiped a sleeve across his eyes. Blood and dirt smeared the white fabric. "Now look what you've done. This jacket's worth more than you."

A heavy foot kicked him hard in the side, punctuating the disgust in the man's gravelly voice. "Tomorrow, mind, and ye better pay what you owe. Dinnae make me get rough."

Laurie almost laughed at the trite gangster imitation. His chuckle turned into a spasm of wheezing.

"Here, what's this?" A little man in shirt sleeves and apron appeared with a bucket of kitchen scraps. As the alley filled with light, Laurie's assailant disappeared into the shadows.

The little man dropped his pail, calling over his shoulder for help. Powerful arms supported Laurie as he sat him up. "Are you all right, mate?"

Laurie squinted up at the work-worn face. He patted the little man on the arm. "No worries. You should see the other guy."

Chapter Two

Commerce Street
Edinburgh
March 1937

Alec's Little Chat with Father

Rain washed over Edinburgh, and the wind whipping up from the North Sea turned the early spring day icy. But, in the warm office, Alexander Frazer experienced a different sort of chill. Despite his twenty-six years, he felt like a chastised child as his father railed at him once again. The sign outside read *Thomas Frazer and Son, Solicitors*. They weren't partners or equals. He'd been summoned to his father's office for a little chat about the progress on the Ferguson Estate.

Why do I keep trying to please him? Alec knew the answer. He enjoyed the richly appointed office and prosperous clientele. He had standing in the legal community because of his father's firm. Over the years, he'd tried to be indifferent when his father's temper flared. Still, sometimes he wondered if it was worth all the criticism.

The old man's face was aflame as he leaned forward over his desk, spitting words like fiery arrows aimed at Alec. "Why would you let her come here? She should have stayed in Canada. Didn't you tell her we could handle the sale of the house and send her the money?"

Thomas Frazer's bulky frame swelled with rage. Though he fit the part of an opulent barrister, his suit from the finest tailor in Edinburgh, just now he looked ready to burst his suit's seams. *And for no good reason. I followed procedure: sent the paperwork regarding the Ferguson estate via courier and called to explain the situation. I can't force the heir to see things our way. And why is he so angry? I could just walk out of this office. But how would it look if I were sacked for incompetence by my own father? If I try to defend myself, this argument will never end.*

His face remained impassive as he directed his mind to wander to the ornate mirror hanging above his father's mahogany desk. Since he was a lad, he survived these tirades by distracting himself. He studied his own reflection, trying to counter all the negatives. *I'm well dressed, likable and people say I resemble David Niven, tall and thin.* He pushed a blond lock back into place. *Yes, the chap in the mirror has it all together.* Then he realized his father was still criticizing his competence. *Bloody hell, he does. I'm being read the riot act over a simple report.*

Something his father said caught his attention, and he made eye contact, a mistake. Alec tried to cover himself. "You have the file," he said. "We've done all we can. Miss MacDonald docks at Southampton tomorrow morning. We've arranged passage on the night train. She should arrive the day after tomorrow at eleven. I don't see what else we can do."

"Of course you don't." His father did not conceal his disappointment. "Which is why you will never be more than a junior partner in this firm."

The verbal blow took Alec's breath away. *That's the first time he's gone this far.* Alec clenched his teeth. *Someday,* he promised himself, *I will find a way out.*

Thomas continued, "Well, I haven't waited for you to do something right. I've got my man on top of things."

Alec waited for his father to elaborate. He wanted to ask, "What man?" but Thomas diverted his full attention to the documents on his desk. Alec's face flushed as he turned to leave, angry with himself that he hadn't said more in his own defense. *It's not my fault. If you wanted her to stay in Canada so badly, why the hell didn't you handle it?* He shook his head as he walked out of the room. *So what if she gets the house?* Looking back at the man one last time before he shut the door, his mouth twisted into a sardonic sneer. *So much for my 'little chat' with Father.*

Chapter Three

Off the Coast of England
Canadian Pacific Ocean Liner Empress of Australia
March 1937

Fiona's Dream

In the dream, she stood at the edge of the rubble, knowing her mother and father lay dead under the carnage. *It feels so real.* Grief overwhelmed her. Acrid smoke choked off a scream. She sat up, still coughing with panic, until the rocking of the ocean liner brought her into the present. Through sleepy eyes, she focused on the light from the passageway shining under her stateroom door. She must have slid to the floor while dreaming.

Her head in her hands, she tried to steady her heartbeat. Over the last three years, she'd had this same nightmare often. Every time she found herself tangled in bedding, as if by trying to escape her bed, she could somehow escape the dream. She struggled out of her blankets and stood to turn on the gaslight, surveying the mess she'd made in her sleep.

Her diary lay on the floor. Photos scattered across the small space. She bent to gather them but hesitated as she reached for a faded newsclip from *The Greenock Telegraph*. The paper was worn, the creases ready to tear from being folded and unfolded so many times. Her eyes took in the words automatically. Then she noticed the date.

It's only been three years, she thought.

"On Tuesday at 4 p.m., while workmen were away for their tea, a gas meter behind Drummond's Dispensary exploded, demolishing surrounding buildings. Lost in the blast were the Honorable Reverend and Mrs. James MacDonald. The Rectory and the Presbyterian Kirk built in 1789 were a complete loss.

"The Pastor and his wife are survived by their 19-year-old daughter, Fiona Ferguson MacDonald." The words blurred with unshed tears. Fiona's hands shook as she folded the clipping and slipped it into her diary. She stooped to pick up a picture of her with Aunt Tyna taken weeks earlier. Her heart had ached leaving Tyna. She was so grateful for all her aunt had done for her, but Canada would never be home.

The sky looked lighter through the porthole. She craved the fresh air of the open deck. Dressed in the clothes laid ready for the new day, she wrapped her MacDonald plaid around herself to keep away the chilly March morning. The passageway was empty as she made her way to the foredeck.

The doors to the outer deck were heavy. An icy blast of air threatened to rip the plaid from her grasp. Wrapping it tighter, she stepped onto the breezy deck, drawn to the greying darkness beyond the ship's railing. The waves made a crashing sound as they battered the ship, throwing their salt spray into the air. There was old Mrs. Abernathy, who'd adopted her since they'd met in the dining room on the first night. The older lady stood transfixed at the railing, watching the lightening sky. Mrs. Bee turned to give her a friendly smile. "Last evening, the captain announced we'd wake to see the shores of England."

Atlantic mist stung Fiona's cheeks as the sun peeped past the horizon to light up the clouds with streaks of grey, pink and purple. Its radiance skimming the waves, giving them luminescent white tops. But the cliffs stood waiting, dark shadows against the lightening sky.

They watched as the sun rose higher and the White Cliffs of Dover glowed with a golden brilliance. England stood in majesty against the restless sea. A tear ran down Fiona's cheek. Only three years ago, she said goodbye to these same shores to live with her aunt in Canada. *At twenty-two, I'm going home.*

Mrs. Bee pushed silver strands of hair out of her weathered face and whispered, "Now there's a sight to see." She added, "I couldn't sleep either." With a second glance, she asked, "You've had that nightmare again?"

Mrs. Bee seemed to take it as her personal duty to give motherly advice. This made her come off as being pushy. But she was just concerned about Fiona. And she was funny and easy to talk to.

"Aye, the dream still comes to me, and I can smell the smoke." Fiona's lip trembled, and she clamped it between her teeth, not wanting to cry.

"Well, never you mind." Mrs. Bee reached out to squeeze her hand. "Best to think about the future. You said your uncle left you a house. Where was that?"

"Edinburgh."

"Big responsibility that."

She didn't want to have this conversation again and said nothing.

But Mrs. Bee pressed her point. "You should sell the house and go back to your aunt." Mrs. Bee didn't understand why Fiona wanted to live alone in a big empty house, and Fiona wasn't sure she did either. *Except that I belong in Scotland.* She took a deep breath to settle her rising frustration. Her friend meant well. "You're a treasure, Mrs. Bee, but no, I've set my course."

"Well, my late husband was a Scot. You don't have to tell me how stubborn they can be."

Fiona rolled her eyes and scoffed. "I'm not stubborn." The thought came to her. *Maybe you're more stubborn than you think.*

Mrs. Bee's expression warmed, and she raised a finger in warning. "Don't you let those solicitors give you any trouble, eh? My late husband never trusted a lawyer a day in his life. Don't you either."

"I won't."

"That's a good lass, though, if you wanted to go back to your aunty …" She let the words hang in the air. "Your aunt will be lonely without you."

Fiona shook her head. "No, Tyna is never alone. She's a nurse. Works with the Indians. The First Nation people in the little town called Three Rivers love her." Her aunt lived with purpose, and it made her life full. *I wish I knew where I belong. The trouble is I don't know where to look.*

"You never met your mother's brother?"

"No. The lawyers said he died a month ago. I thought I was alone in the world. Why didn't Mum tell me she had a brother?" The wind blew Fiona's long black curls around her face. She pushed them out of her eyes.

Mrs. Bee smiled in reassurance. "I expect you'll learn more when you get there. Will you be all right? I've got to get back to my cabin and pack up a few things." She turned to leave but drew in a breath. "There's a man over there by the door, and I don't like his looks. Up to no good, I'll wager."

Fiona turned to see a tall man thirty feet from them. Strange that she hadn't heard him come on deck. He leaned against the wall near the passageway door in a black overcoat and muffler. The deck lamp shone on his face. A ragged scar ran across his large, hooked nose. Heavy dark brows cast ominous shadows, leaving his eye sockets with two black smudges. Fiona smiled at Mrs. Bee's protectiveness. The man wasn't bothering them. Then he said, "Morning, misses." His grin was toothy, and she had to admit he looked dubious, but she remembered her father always saying, "Ye canna judge a book by its cover."

Mrs. Bee humphed. "The cheek. Come with me, dearie."

Maybe she just needed to assert her independence, but Fiona gave the old dear a hug. "I'm fine, Mrs. Bee. I need to walk a bit."

She moved away down the deck toward the stern of the ship. This was the second time she'd crossed the Atlantic to find herself. A wry thought drifted through her mind. *How many more trips will it take me to find where I belong?*

Chapter Four

Saint Thomas Parish near Mittenwald
Bavaria, Germany
March 1937

The Children Must Leave

Father Hugo walked along the path leading to the convent. Bright sun sparkled off the snow. It'd been a cold March, but the promise of spring was in the air. A small crocus poked its purple head through the snow-covered ground next to the ancient stone walkway. His normal good nature demanded he enjoy even the smallest of the Lord's handiwork, but changes in Germany filled his heart with anxiety.

He shook his head and muttered to himself. "How can the Pope sanction what's happening? Doesn't he understand what Dachau is? That the Nazis arrest anyone protecting helpless Jewish children, even the sisters of St. Thomas. How can he look away?" Faces of the sisters who'd sacrificed their lives to save children flashed through his thoughts. His hand rested on the convent's garden gate. "Please Lord, don't let this evil stamp out the lives of these last four little ones. I looked everywhere. No family will take them in. Too much risk. Help me save them."

The aging priest entered the small garden at the back of the ancient stone building. Father Hugo felt a sense of trepidation at the sight of the convent's old arched doorway. It was time to face the unthinkable. For a second, he hesitated as he reached for the iron handle. He sighed, glancing up. A single cloud floated across the bright blue sky. "Lord, how can your world be so beautiful with so much evil present?"

The latch clicked, and the weathered door creaked open on its timeworn hinges. Sun framed him in the doorway as he waited for his eyes to adjust to the dimmer light inside.

Little Gretchen jumped up from her coloring. Light reflected off her golden curls as she raced across the room to hug him with her usual enthusiasm. "You're back. Papa Ugo, you're back!"

His heart constricted, but his expression was tender as he lifted her tiny four-year-old frame into his arms. "Gretchen, I've only been gone for a day."

He stroked her shiny blond curls and set her down. Gretchen skipped back to join her older brother. Deter dropped the book he'd been reading and jumped to his feet as if to stand at attention. Large brown eyes rose to study the priest. At six, Deter knew the seriousness of Hugo's mission.

"And have you been taking care of things for me?" The small head nodded, but the eyes remained locked on Hugo's face, searching for some sign of how things had gone. *Deter looks so Jewish with his dark hair and olive skin.* Hugo regretted the thought, but it was true that Deter bore the stamp of the Nazi stereotype for a Jew.

Sister Ana, the youngest of the Sisters of Saint Thomas, glided through the door to the kitchen with a tray of steaming soup bowls. "We're ready for lunch." She stopped to regard Hugo. His mouth tried to turn upward. The young nun hesitated and called over her shoulder, "Katrine, let's get baby Tony a bib."

Almost fifteen, Katrine was a Eurasian beauty. She walked into the room carrying six-month-old Tony. Hugo watched them with a broken heart. These last four children were special to him, and he'd failed them. So many children had come to Saint Thomas and only these last four left without a haven. He reached out to stroke Tony's dark curls, and the baby pushed off Katrine into his arms.

Father Hugo cuddled the healthy, chubby-cheeked baby. "I remember when I first saw your mamma." He glanced up at Ana. "She was no older than you, sister. Romani. When she slipped through the door, I felt a cold wind whip into chapel."

He stared past them, seeing it all again in his mind. "It was early Mass. She sat in the back. During communion, she was the last to come forward." He shook his head. "I remember how her tears fell down her cheeks as she accepted the sacrament."

Hugo touched one of Tony's chubby hands. "See what a big boy you are, but then you were a tiny bundle wrapped in your mamma's shawl. I reached out to bless the baby, and she drew back as if I meant to curse her child. I leaned closer and whispered, 'God calls us all, most especially the young ones.' She unwrapped the newborn from her shawl for me to see."

Hugo looked at Tony with such tenderness. "You stole my heart." Hugo reached out and made the sign of the cross on Tony's small forehead. "I anointed you with oil proclaiming the blessing. When I looked again into your mamma's eyes, I saw something. Resolve, maybe." Hugo knew he was rambling, but it eased his heart to remember the story.

"At the close of the service, I made my way back to her. I wanted to do something, baptize you or give her food. There you were, still wrapped in her shawl—a tiny bundle lying on the pew where she'd been sitting. No sign of your mamma."

Hugo shook his head again. What evil forces mothers to do such unthinkable things? "I baptized you Anthony Michael Thomas."

Tony grabbed the priest's hand and stuffed it in his sloppy mouth. Hugo chuckled. "Our boy's hungry."

Ana had been setting the bowls of soup out for the children. She looked up and said, "Father, you're just in time to say our blessing." Katrine took baby Tony.

"This time we'll let Katrine say it." Hugo slipped his hand over Sister Ana's arm, adding, "Let's take a walk to chapel." As he ushered her back down the path toward the village chapel, he thought of how he might tell her his news.

The sister turned to step in front of him. "No one could take them," she stated with finality in her voice.

"You're quite right." He opened his arms in frustration. "I've been to all the families I can think of. These children are a risk to any who take them." He was making excuses for his parishioners, but rightly so.

"Deter and Gretchen are Jews. Gretchen might blend in, but Deter will never look Aryan. A Eurasian girl and Gypsy baby are impossible to disguise." Hugo's voice trailed off.

"So many children have come to the Sisters of Saint Thomas, most of them children of people who spoke out against the new government policies. Nazis tolerate no dissent. My mountain families have opened hearts and homes to hide orphaned children. When they could take no more the nuns began smuggling children out of Germany. Some of them made it. Others? No one knows what happened to them. Dachau?"

He hurried Ana through the deserted chapel back to his small office. The time to face facts was upon them.

"There are new men in Mittenwald. They're visiting the mountain villages one at a time—Nazis. They claim to be registering families in a government census. I'd hoped the Reich would overlook our little hamlet."

He shook his head and sighed before dropping into his chair. "There are new laws. Stricter regulations to be enforced."

Anger bubbled up within him. He felt like hitting something.

Instead, he shut his eyes and blew out a long breath before continuing. "Bad news spreads. No one could chance taking any of the children."

He spread his hands in futility and watched the weight of his news engulf her. She sank into a chair, her dark brows knitting together with concern. He waited. *She is the last Sister of Saint Thomas. I should have been able to protect her.* Thoughts floated through his mind. *It would have been better for her if she were homely. Better to blend in.*

He was always a little startled by her beauty. Black curls escaped her wimple. Her skin was ivory and her eyes as blue as the mountain skies. *Young and beautiful, yes, but it's her heart you see, Lord. It is where her true beauty lies.* She sat grasping the arms of her chair. Her knuckles turned white with the strain, and he realized she was waiting for the rest.

"I spoke to Karl Beckmann. He's sure his brother Klaus would take you and the children, just until I can find a safe place for them." He sounded hopeful for the first time. "Karl will be your guide."

"Our guide?" Her voice sounded small, childlike. He knew she was fearful. The sisters lived a simple life of service and prayer. It was always hard for them to leave the safety of the church. She stood and asked, "When?"

He allowed himself pride in her courage. A hint of a smile touched his face. "We have no way of knowing how long it will take these men to show up on our doorstep. Our people, they are good people. But the Nazis have ways of learning things. One of them, a younger man—I think they called him Braun—is said to be quite zealous in performing his duties. They say he hates the church."

Father Hugo opened the antique wardrobe in the corner and pulled out five small satchels. "I borrowed some traveling things for you and the children."

He set them on the floor in front of Ana. "You will have to lay aside your habit for a time at least." Teary eyes implored him to take back his last words. "It would be dangerous to travel as a Sister of Saint Thomas. You know all too well how many of your sisters we've lost to Nazi persecution."

He reached out once again to pat her shoulder. To lose the vestments of her holy order would feel like stripping off armor before battle.

"We must move fast. I told Karl to be here at dawn."

Sister Ana drew in a ragged breath. She stood and gathered up their traveling bags. As she turned to leave, her hand still on the door, she whispered, "You're not coming." There was acceptance in her eyes, understanding.

He hoped she knew how much he wanted to come with her. If he left, it would get back to the Nazi men. No, it was best to stay and keep everything as normal as possible. Still, he wanted to encourage her. It was a lot to ask someone so young but there wasn't another way. Hugo said, "You can do this. Could be that our Lord brought you here for this reason. My duty is here but you won't be alone. God go with you, sister."

Chapter Five

Latimer Square
Edinburgh
March 1937

A Dark Night in Edinburgh

Laurie couldn't go back into the nightclub with blood all over his white dinner jacket and a face that looked like a punching bag, so he wrote a note on a napkin. "I've fallen on my face. I'm a bloody mess. Sorry sweetheart, but I'm in no condition to celebrate."

The irony of using a napkin note wasn't lost on him. For all his bravado with Toby's man, the incident had shaken him.

He was in a sour mood when he arrived at his house on Latimer Square. Luck was against him once more. His grandfather, Rab, was coming from the kitchen when Laurie came in from the front door. Rab stopped short, taking in Laurie's appearance. The old man's concern felt like a rebuke. Laurie didn't stop to think how backward his reaction was.

"Laurie, lad, what has happened? Are ye alright? Come ta the kitchen and have a seat. I'll find something to clean up yer cuts."

Laurie pushed aside his grandfather's concern. "It's nothing, only a misunderstanding." He started for the stairs, but Rab caught his arm.

"Come in and have a cup of tea. Ye canna go ta yer bed till yer cleaned up a bit."

A part of Laurie wanted to be taken care of—to talk to the old man the way he had as a boy—but Rab would never understand. His grandfather's moral compass pointed along the straight and narrow path. Still, he followed Rab into the kitchen.

Rab made tea and set a steaming cup in front of Laurie. There was comfort in the cup. It warmed Laurie's hands, and the steam opened his swollen nose. Rab soaked a bit of cloth in warm water and came around to dab off the cuts and bruising.

"Weren't you meeting yer lassie for a celebration?"

"I was, but someone met me first." Laurie clamped his mouth shut. He promised himself. *I will not get into this, Rab. You wouldn't understand.*

"It wouldn't be a big man with a nose like a prizefighter, would it?"

Laurie's mouth fell open. A faint smile touched Rab's lips but then disappeared.

"The man was here earlier this evening."

God, he was here? Laurie's mind pictured Rab taking the same beating. *I could have lost him.* "I'm sorry, Rab. Did he threaten you?"

"No, just lookin' for ye. But the man looks serious about his business. Ye'd best pay what ye owe."

Alarms were ringing in Laurie's head, and not from the beating. *It's impossible to keep anything from grandfather.* He tried to put nonchalance into his voice as he asked, "What makes you think I owe him money?"

Rab only looked affronted. "I wasna born yesterday. I was

young once and wanted to please yer grandmam. A lad can make some pretty bad choices for what seem like good reasons."

Laurie shook his head. Here he was again, the child, never measuring up. *I'm not in the mood for a talk about your God.* Instead, his voice dripped with sarcasm. "Well, I'm not you."

Rab blew out a puff of frustration. "No lad, and I dinna want that of ye. But it doesna take much ta puzzle out how you got yon dinner jacket." He was silent for a moment. "How much do you owe the man?"

Laurie felt like a child. "One hundred pounds."

Rab exploded. "A hundred pounds?" The old Highlander's anger could still burn when provoked. They stood there looking at each other, the heat of the moment showing on Rab's flushed face.

"You're going to tell me what a fool I am. I know, Rab." Laurie pointed to his face. "I've had enough lessons for one day."

Rab's eyes focused again on Laurie's bruised face. The old man seemed to shrink into himself. He turned with his head down and shuffled to the cupboard. "Did ye have any left after that jacket?

Laurie hated this conversation. He wanted to say, "Mind your own business. Keep your help. I don't need it." But if Toby sent his man round to Rab, the threat to his grandfather was real. His voice was quiet as he answered, "I still have fifty. I was going to use it to celebrate."

Rab was pulling something from the shelf. When he returned, he set two one-hundred-pound notes in front of Laurie.

"I was saving for yer graduation present." He pushed it to Laurie. "Meant to give it ta ye tomorrow. It's yers. And it seems ye need it now."

Laurie stared at the money—he couldn't look his grandfather in the face. He railed and wanted to say, "Keep your money and your judgment." But Toby's messenger said he had until tomor-

row. Instead, Laurie's hand swooped out and shoved the money in
his pocket.

    I'll take it for your sake, not for mine. He said, "Thank you, Rab."
But he stood and left the room without ever meeting his grandfather's eyes.

Chapter Six

Edinburgh

March 1937

Next Stop Edinburgh, Waverley Station

Fiona's new day dawned at sea but ended on the night train to Edinburgh. It wasn't easy falling asleep in a crowded train compartment, but she dozed off in the wee hours of the morning wedged into the corner seat, her cheek resting on the cool glass of the compartment window.

A shrill train whistle blasted three times. She jerked awake into a world of mid-morning sunlight and an empty compartment. She rubbed sleepy eyes and squinted in the bright light at the change in the scenery. Instead of small villages and open fields, they rolled past shops and ancient-looking tenements.

Lord, am I there? Excitement drew her from her sleepy state. *So, this is Edinburgh at last.* She feared the old train would shake apart before it came to a stop, but stop it would, and soon.

Fiona glanced around the compartment, wondering how she'd slept while so many travelers got off the train. Soon it would be her turn to leave. She gathered her coat and carrying case. "No, that's not right—" Panic clogging her throat. "Where's my handbag?" She spun around. Her eyes searched every corner. She sank to her knees to look under seats and still no purse. Nausea swept over her.

Through the windows to the passageway, Fiona saw the conductor pass her compartment, calling out, "Waverley Station. Next stop Edinburgh, Waverley Station."

She bolted through the door and into the corridor crowded with travelers returning from the dining car. She squeezed past them, trying to catch up with the conductor, almost bumping into a tall man in an overcoat.

"Sorry—" Her words cut off. The man from the boat with the scarred nose and bushy brows stood before her. Her mouth fell open. *Maybe Mrs. Bee was right about him.*

She was about to accuse him of following her when he slipped through a compartment door without as much as a glance. *Obviously, he's doing no such thing, you goose.* She caught sight of the conductor disappearing through the door at the end of the car. She pushed on and caught him as he entered the next car.

"Please, sir, I need your help."

The middle-aged conductor stopped, his tone quite businesslike. "What would be the matter, miss?"

She steadied her voice for fear she'd sound like a frightened child. "I fell asleep in my compartment and woke a minute ago to find my handbag missing."

He scowled. "Are you sure, miss? Mighten it be under your seat?"

Of course I checked under my seat. Steady on, she thought. *No point in biting the man's head off. He's only doing his job.* She took a deep breath and answered with the calm before the storm. "I'm sure. I've turned the compartment upside down."

He frowned. "Right. Which compartment is it?"

Fiona led him back to her seat. He looked everywhere she had and then turned to her, announcing, "It's not here."

Her storm was ready to break all over this poor man. "Yes, I told you that, but who could have taken it?"

He bumped his cap to the back of his balding head. "The thing is, I remember this compartment. It was a family, all off at Carlisle. Not the type to take a handbag. Perhaps the Missus thought it was her bag. A mistake like. If that's so, someone will return it, no doubt about it."

His greying mustache quirked up on one side, indicating a smile. "Now, miss, have a seat, and when we get to Waverley, you can speak to the stationmaster." And he was gone.

Fiona slumped back in her seat. *My handbag is gone. My wallet, passport and traveling money, all gone. What will I do? I don't even have cab fare.*

She'd spent the last three years with Aunt Tyna in Canada mourning the loss of her parents. She was back in Scotland, and it was like turning a page in her story. *I will not feel sorry for myself. I'm done with that.* Her da's voice came back to her with a clarity that calmed her storm. "There's my lass. You can sort this out. There's always a way. Just put your mind to it."

Fiona clenched her jaw and squeezed her eyes shut. A single tear spilled over her lower lashes, but she wiped it away. As an afterthought, she checked her coat pocket and found a crumpled piece of paper and her baggage claim ticket.

Through the compartment windows she watched the train roll into Edinburgh past the city gardens. High above the tracks, she could see the ancient walls of Edinburgh Castle. Her da said the castle perched on volcanic rock rising from the city below. Stately sixteenth-century buildings climbed up the hillside toward the fortress.

Train brakes squealed as they brought the old train to a stop below street level in a massive underground cavern. Fiona's pulse quickened from the moment she stepped off the train. *These were her people.* Their accents were a bittersweet reminder of her parents and the life she'd left behind three years ago.

Am I even the same person? I sound more Canadian than Scot.

After an hour of answering what seemed to be the same set of questions, the novelty wore off a bit. Fiona emerged from the stationmaster's office to find the platform deserted. She grabbed the door before it could close behind her. Even the office had emptied. A clerk emerged from a door marked "closet" with his coat in hand.

Fiona asked, "Where is everyone?"

The young man's expression registered surprise. "It's tea-time, miss."

Out of the country for a few years and already she'd forgotten the cadence of life in the British Isles. "Oh yes, of course. Can I leave my trunk and carrying case with you, till I find my uncle's solicitor? I expect he'll help me collect it."

"Certainly." He reached over the counter to take the small case. "You still have your baggage claim, do you not?" She nodded assent. "Aye, leave the case with me the now, and you can claim your luggage at your leisure." His hat and coat were already on as he disappeared through another door.

She turned to leave, and when the stationmaster's door closed behind her, she stood there alone and not at all ready to face the lawyer. It felt awkward without her handbag, so she shoved her hands in her coat pockets and tried to get her bearings. Emotions tossed about her thoughts like a sea in rough waters, wondering if Mrs. Bee was right. *Should I have stayed with Aunt Tyna? This was a poor start.* She had to calm herself before she faced the lawyer. Whenever she had to work out some problem or make an important decision, her da would take her for a walk. With her first steps came memories, reminding her that this wasn't her first time in Edinburgh. Da had taken them to the zoo and a night at the theater. There had been shopping trips with her mother.

But Mum rarely spoke of her past. It was as if her life began when she met Da, their lives so full the topic of relatives never came up. Oh, there had been letters from Aunt Tyna. Da's older sister had married a Canadian physician at the end of the Great War and emigrated to Quebec. But it always seemed, other than Aunt Tyna, that they were alone in the world. *Funny, Mum never said a word about having a brother living right here in the city.*

Fiona climbed the steps from the station onto Princes Street and wandered past shoppers. She was in awe at the dark spires of the Sir Walter Scott Monument. Four towers rose to meet at an ornate peak, and there in the center sat a statue of the author himself.

He looks as if he's thinking about what to write next. How many times did Da read one of his books to me? I loved Ivanhoe. They were full of the magic of history. Oh, she realized with a start, *Waverley was his first book. They must have named the station for him.*

Past the monument, she stopped to look up at Edinburgh Castle. It appeared to grow out of the hillside across the park. The castle dominated the city like a big stone lion watching over its cubs. *I remember thinking the castle was part of that mountainous rock. There isn't much change in color between the two.* The entire city was the rusty granite grey color of the castle.

Some might think Edinburgh is ugly, but I think it's beautiful—rugged and austere but handsome and strong, too. She sighed with pleasure. Da would say Edinburgh is like the people who love her.

Wind whipped around every corner. A fine spring day. Like any romantic, Fiona let the wind carry her through the streets.

Da's voice came with the breeze. "Walking is the best way to clear the mind." *Oh, Da, I wish you could tell me if I belong here or if I should have stayed in Canada.*

Her emotions settled as she crossed the Mound Bridge. She stopped to read a sign: "Old Town." This part of Edinburgh looked ancient. Tall stone buildings crammed together like ancient towers. Some stood erect, while others leaned forward to watch her walk by.

Cockburn Street wound up the hill and carried her to High Street. Fiona looked at the beautiful old church across the cobblestone lane. As she walked uphill, she could see Edinburgh was full of narrow passageways between buildings that led to shops begging to be explored. Later, she promised. *I'll make a point of getting to know all your hidden places.*

Without knowing why, her feet carried her up the old streets, past statues and shops with inviting storefronts until she found herself on the esplanade in front of Edinburgh Castle. Ramparts and battlements stood solid against the blue sky. Flags snapped as they danced with the gusty currents.

She didn't approach the guard at the castle gate but wandered about the wide parade ground until she stood at the edge of a small stone wall. The city stretched out below her and climbed up to challenge the fortress.

With a sense of awe, she realized, *This is going to be my home.* A peaceful expression spread across her face. Before, she'd never been sure she was on the right path. Leaving Scotland for Canada had been a misstep. She knew she didn't belong there. But this place welcomed her; she could feel it.

I know, Da. You'd say I'm being fanciful, but it feels right to be here. She turned away from the city view with resolve to find the offices of Thomas Frazer and Son.

Chapter Seven

High Street
Edinburgh
March 1937

The Solicitor

Fiona had written the address of where she was going and slipped it into her coat pocket. She was thankful for her mother's training. The brief note read: "Court of Justice, High Street. Office on the third floor." Only a few blocks back down the hill from the castle. The building looked impressive, a bastion of legal authority, old but still stately. A uniformed officer stood at the door. *I expect he's present to remind us that this is a courthouse.* She stopped to ask her way and followed his directions to a door with gold lettering. Thomas Frazer and Son.

As Fiona entered Frazer's law office, her inner peace dissolved. Butterflies danced in her stomach. A prim secretary asked her to have a seat while she left to check with Mr. Frazer. Ten minutes later, the secretary ushered Fiona into a large office. The thick oriental carpet underfoot deadened her steps, making the room quiet. Carved panels covered the walls. Large windows gave a commanding view of Edinburgh commerce, but between the buildings she caught sight of Sir Walter Scott's Monument. *At least I know where I am.*

Da's words floated to her from some childhood memory. "Oh, what a tangled web we weave when first we practice to deceive." *Odd, I should remember that bit. It's not even Scott.*

Bent over some papers, the man seated at the large desk didn't look up at first. *I expect this must be Solicitor Frazer.* Fiona cleared her throat, and his eyes rose to regard her from silver-rimmed glasses perched on his bulbous nose. His leather chair squeaked as he settled back, looking her over. She bit her lip.

No sense in asking what he's looking at since I'm the only other person in the room. The uncomfortable thought crossed her mind, *I slept on the train in what I'm wearing. All right, maybe I'm wrinkled.* She straightened her back and met his appraisal with a steady one of her own.

He addressed her with a dour expression. "I take it you are Miss Fiona Ferguson MacDonald?"

Without waiting for an answer, he pointed to a straight-backed chair. "Sit down," he commanded.

She had the odd compulsion to say no. With an inner shrug, Fiona capitulated for the sake of expedience and sat.

She didn't like Mr. Frazer. There was something about the man that put her off. He exuded an aura of superiority. She looked up, trying to distract herself.

She glanced at the large mirror above his desk. Its polished, carved wooden frame was beautiful. She studied the reflection of the room behind her while she waited. From her vantage point, she noticed the mirror reflected a bald spot on the back of his head. *Well, I'm not sorry one bit that this pompous old man is balding.* She pressed her lips together. *I've had a long day, and it's still just afternoon.*

She looked down again, trying to hide her annoyance as Frazer shuffled through papers. *What in the world is he searching for? I'll bet he has indigestion from being such a sour old man.*

"I beg your pardon, I'd like—" A rap on the office door cut her words off. Thomas Frazer's hand shot up to stop her.

"Enter," he responded. A tall, thin young man came into the room carrying a file. His welcoming expression brought warmth into the formal atmosphere. She couldn't help returning his smile as he approached her chair.

"Hullo, I don't believe we've met. I'm Alec Frazer. The son." He cocked his head. "And you are?"

His father's voice boomed across the desk. "This is Miss Fiona MacDonald."

She clamped her mouth shut in frustration.

"We've been expecting you, Miss MacDonald. I see the night train arrived late again. I trust you had a good crossing?" Alec offered his hand.

"Yes, thank you, I did." His fingers were as warm as his welcoming smile, though they were the only sources of warmth in the room. "I'm glad to be here and looking forward to my new home." A look passed between father and son.

The elder recovered with a discreet cough. "You can't mean you intend to live in your uncle's house?"

She stammered, "Why yes, I do. Why shouldn't I?" In the mirror, she could see Alec step back to lean on the bookcase behind her. He fidgeted, glancing through the file in his hand. Judging from his nervous behavior, something was wrong.

Thomas Frazer removed his glasses. The leather chair creaked again as he leaned forward. "The house hasn't been in good repair since your mother lived there as a child. When your grandparents died, I tried to talk Hugh into selling the place. But he wouldn't hear of it, and I'm afraid it's fallen into a state of neglect."

Mr. Frazer sounded sympathetic, almost sorry. "You understand your uncle lived in only a few rooms for twenty years? After his wife died in childbirth, Hugh never kept the rest of the house in repair. In short, it most likely needs to be refurbished. And unless you have funds to handle all this…" his sentence drifted off.

Cold crept over her, thinking how much she'd already lost. *Mum grew up here, and I'll not lose her childhood home.* Fiona bit her lip. It was almost too much to take in.

"Your uncle made many investments—not all of them were wise. I'm afraid there's little in the way of actual money to accompany the house." He added, "Of course, the house is free and clear. In fact, the only thing of real value is the house itself and, even then, only for historical considerations. Though, frankly, I'm not sure how much you could realize from a sale given its present condition."

His manner changed to conciliatory. "My advice to you, young lady, is to take the next boat back to Canada. Meantime, I'd be happy to put the house on the market, handle the sale, and send a draft to your Canadian bank. How does that sound?"

Fiona stiffened. *Why is he so eager to sell my house?* She took a deep breath. "Why would someone buy it if it's in such a dilapidated condition?"

"Well, I rather think someone with money might be interested. Built in 1740, you know, so it has some historical value. Preservation societies, that sort of thing."

He'd been looking away and finished with a not quite kindly expression. Though addressing her in a solicitous tone, there remained a hardness in his eyes. "We'd be happy to make all the arrangements."

Fiona started to speak, but Thomas held up his hand again. "It's no trouble at all."

There was something not quite right about this conversation, and his sudden attempt at friendliness clinched it. *If Da were here, he'd tell me to "Use the common sense God gave ye."* Her father lingered in her mind's eye, sturdy and strong. She matched Frazer's intense gaze with a stubbornness of her own, stood as tall as her five-foot-two frame would allow and squared her shoulders. "May I please have my deed?"

His features darkened, but she continued. "Thank you for your time, but I should like to see it for myself and make an assessment. Either way, it's not for sale. I intend to make Edinburgh my home."

Thomas Frazer's frown deepened, but he produced the document from the files on his desk. She held her hand out, and he gave her the deed to the house on Latimer Square. She paused for a second as the enormity of what she'd undertaken settled on her.

Either I've made the biggest mistake of my life, or I've walked through the door God opened. Fiona grinned at Alec Frazer as she turned to walk out of the office.

Chapter Eight

Edinburgh
March 1937

Remember the Key

Thomas growled at his son, "What are you standing around for? Wipe that smirk off your face and close the door behind you as you leave."

Alec sported a cheeky grin. "Not quite what you expected, aye Father? But you forgot to give her the key." He waited as Thomas tossed an old wrought-iron key across the desk. Then he slipped it into his jacket pocket and hurried out the office door.

Thomas didn't bother to look up as a narrow door next to the bookcase opened. A tall man wearing an overcoat and fedora slipped into the office. His bushy dark brows and scarred nose made him appear sinister. Thomas asked, "You heard?"

"Right little spitfire, isn't she? And our young lady didn't even mention this." He swung a lady's handbag into view. "Not that there was much to go missing. Not exactly plum, is she?"

Frazer's tone was incredulous. "Why in the world did you take her bag?"

"You said discover everything I could." The man shrugged. "I was lookin' through it to be thorough. She woke up before I could return it."

Thomas scowled and rubbed his chin, seeming to ignore his visitor. Finally, he said, "I think we've been wrong about Miss MacDonald." He paused, staring out the window. "See that her bag gets back to the stationmaster. I'll want your services for a bit more. For now, just watch her."

Thomas stared at his hireling, deep in thought. "If she knows anything, we'll find out soon enough." He punctuated his last words with a curt nod to end the conversation.

Chapter Nine

Bavaria, Germany
March 1937

Leaving Saint Thomas

Though spring was on the way, snow still covered the mountain village. The children chattered with excitement at the adventure of a trip. Father Hugo had given them a glorious description of the sights they would see as they traveled in Herr Beckmann's horse-drawn sleigh. He had also instilled in their minds the beginnings of a game. Sister Ana should be just plain Ana. She would still be a sister but only to Gretchen, Deter, and Tony. Katrine Wagner was harder to explain.

Katrine came up with a story. "I will be a hired companion," she announced, then added with a blush, "That's the way it always is in books."

Sister Ana shot Katrine a surprised look. But Father laughed and said, "I think our little China bud is about to blossom." Noticing her embarrassment, he added, "A fine idea, Katrine. Now we have our stories in place; we will begin our game with a prayer."

As they bowed their heads, he asked a blessing for each of them. When he placed his hand on the head of nearly fifteen-year-old Katrine, he asked for special care over this beautiful woman child.

Katrine Wagner could never hope to blend into the German mountain folk. The Wagners, her German adoptive parents, had returned with her from mission work in China. They'd rescued her as a newborn from a riverbank where she'd been left to die. Katrine's parentage was doubtful, with features not pure Chinese. She was a foreign devil in her own country but a gift from heaven to the aging couple.

The Wagners possessed a strong faith and deep love for each other, but their secret desire had always been a child. Katrine was their angel. Her spirit, like her parents, shone the brightest amid adversity. Nothing could have prepared them for the trouble waiting to greet them in their own homeland. They disappeared off the streets one cold autumn night in Hamburg. Their church made inquiries, but nothing came of it. As the church came into line with Reich doctrines, the Wagner's daughter became an embarrassment. How she made it to the door of Saint Thomas was a testament to the Christian souls still left in Germany.

Father Hugo's face grew sadder as he laid his hand on each child's head, asking perhaps the impossible. "Father, keep this precious life under your sovereign protection, and deliver them into a place of refuge."

As Hugo placed his palm on Sister Ana, he was at a loss for words. "Lord, the giver of life, wisdom and understanding, give this, your servant, all she will need to serve you." The rest of his prayer was more by rote than inspiration as his mind pondered all Ana would need to survive.

Within the walls of Saint Thomas, Ana had been a faithful servant. The rhythm of a cloistered life was a great comfort to many, and he could see her struggle as she prepared to leave. That much was clear in her expression and reddened eyes. Still, she was attempting to be lighthearted and cheerful for the children. He helped her settle them into Karl's sleigh and then asked the young farmer to wait while he spoke to Sister Ana.

Father Hugo sensed her discomfort at the borrowed clothing and wished there was some other way. "Let's step inside the convent for a moment. We need to talk."

Short, dark curls framed her pale face and made him think how much would be required of the young woman. They walked into the dining hall. She ran her hands along the old wooden table. A single tear fell onto the polished surface. Ana wiped it away with the edge of her heavy parka.

"You spent quite a bit of time polishing this table when you first came to us, I think."

"Yes ... yes, I did," she answered with a sad smile. "I'll miss Saint Thomas." She looked around, embracing each part of the room with her eyes.

"I can't say you'll be back soon. I don't know what the Lord's plans are for you and the children. But I know He will watch you with a father's eyes. As much as you loved your life here, we always have the security of carrying Him with us wherever we go."

He hoped to encourage her, but he could see she was near to tears. Hugo was at a loss. He searched for words and pushed on. "You are still a sister of Saint Thomas no matter how you're dressed or where you go. I know you will honor your vows with the heart of a servant."

She was looking down. Tears were falling on the floor at her feet. He stammered on, "These are difficult times for the true believer, but I think the Father placed you here for this very reason." He reached out and embraced her, feeling like a father to this young woman. "God is with you." His voice was husky, and he released her quickly.

Chapter Ten

Edinburgh
March 1937

The House on Latimer Square

Fiona was relieved when Alec offered her a ride to her new home. Her legs were a little shaky after standing up to Thomas Frazer. They left the solicitor's office, walking to a silver-grey Bentley parked at the curb. Alec held open the door and waited for her to slide in. The sun shone through the parting clouds and glinted off the shiny car. Fiona paused, her sense of hopefulness returning. She felt a bit like Daniel after facing the lions. "Your father's a formidable man." She smiled at Alec, then settled into his auto.

"I think you've surprised him." Alec's face was out of her vision as he shut the door, but he sounded pleased. When he slid into the driver's seat, his expression radiated friendship. "I don't like to see him get his way too often."

She studied him for a moment. He was nothing like his father. Alec was as cultured and impeccably dressed as any prominent lawyer might be. Not a blond lock out of place. His hands gripping the steering wheel were well manicured.

Fiona thought she could detect a chuckle when he asked, "Tell me, why did you insist on keeping the old place? My father has a point. It's in terrible condition."

He pulled the Bentley into traffic and glided past stylish metropolitan shoppers as if a reminder she was out of her element. She pulled her serviceable coat closer to her neck. *This isn't the world of a pastor's daughter. I can't remember a time when our needs weren't met, but it wasn't the vocation for someone with a taste for opulence.*

She thought back to her old friends in Greenock. *If they could see me now, they'd say I'd better guard my heart from the love of money. No worries. I don't have a ha'penny in my pocket.*

He waited for her answer, so she said, "I don't know, it feels right, like home."

"You shock me, Miss MacDonald. Have you lived in Edinburgh before?"

"No, never. We lived most of my childhood in Greenock. It's on the Clyde bank."

"Yes, a small town, right? I think there's a shipbuilder there."

Fiona nodded. They turned down the hill toward the city gardens. "I remember several trips here with my parents."

They turned onto Princes Street. She gasped and pointed, face flushed with pleasure. "There's Jenners department store." A vivid picture flashed through her mind. "Mum took me on a shopping trip for my sixteenth birthday. There was a spring dance at the Town Hall. We spent all morning looking for the right dress. All my friends were so impressed." *Where are all those girls? I've lost track of everyone from my past. Like Mum.* Her smile faded.

Alec leaned forward to catch her attention. "How long did you say you've been in Canada?"

"A little over three years. After I lost my parents, I went to live with my father's sister. She emigrated years ago and settled with her husband in Quebec."

"Mostly French there?"

"Yes, mostly." She wondered if loneliness showed on her face. "My aunt was wonderful, but it's so different there. She lives in the village of Three Rivers."

As if trying to draw her away from her memories, he said, "Did I mention we're neighbors?"

Fiona liked him for steering their conversation away from the past with the sudden off-topic comment.

"No. How? I mean, why would you live in a poor area?"

"I didn't say the neighborhood was poor, only the house. Our square is in New Town. We were one of the first homes built away from the oldest part of the city."

"New Town? I thought it was ancient."

"Age is relative when we're talking hundreds of years."

Confused, she asked, "How new is my house?"

"Oh, I think Father said a sea captain built it around 1740, but the rest of the houses in the area date from around 1775, built in the Georgian style."

He drove past stately buildings with different colored doors and slight variances to suggest they were residences, not businesses. Alec motioned to the buildings. "This was all farmer's fields when the captain built his house—guess he was a forward thinker. Soon after, people with money wanted out of the crowded old town and moved down here."

"Did you say my house is on Latimer's Square?"

"Named for the architect who built the other two houses. They came around 1765, and Latimer modeled them after the original house with a few fashionable changes on the interior."

Traffic was heavy. They waited for a minute before going around the statue of King George IV standing on a tall pedestal, watching their progress. Alec cleared his throat. "Father says your uncle was an eccentric. Did you know him well?"

"I've never met him."

It was his turn to register surprise. "Really?"

"I guess he didn't approve of his little sister's marriage or something. Mum never spoke of her brother." Feeling the need to defend her parents, she added, "He was wrong. They were happy. I mean, we were happy." Fiona lightened her tone. "My father pastored a congregation in Greenock. I suppose our lives revolved around his work."

The Bentley moved on through busy streets. Every corner of the city was full of history and times long past. Once again, the city reminded her of a weathered old Scotsman, rugged, grey but full of dignity.

Alec turned onto a broad cobblestone square. The auto seemed out of place as it bounced over old stones better suited to a horse and carriage. The square was bordered on three sides by identical four-story grey stone houses. Different from the Georgian houses they'd been passing, these were three separate homes. Instead of tall, narrow connected houses, they were wider and shorter but the same old stone as the rest of the city. Only the beautiful early spring color from the crimson buds on the hawthorn trees lining the square gave life to the houses.

She leaned forward. "Which house is it?"

"The one in the middle." Alec pointed to the house at the back of the square.

Although at first glance the houses appeared identical, the one in the center lacked vitality. The wood trim needed paint. The red front door was peeling. Stray shingles hung out of place on the roof. Ivy vines covered the exterior of the upper floors, and all the windows looked dark. Alec parked the auto and jumped out to open the door for her.

Fiona moved slowly, studying every detail in her view. As she lifted her head to take in the house on Latimer Square, the wind whipped her hair around her face, but she pushed back her black curls.

"It's so big," she whispered. Sensing the history of this old house, she lost track of her companion. The rest of the street—everything around her—faded away. It was just her and the house. She jumped when Alec pulled an old iron key from his overcoat pocket and held it up in front of her nose. "Your key," he announced.

Fiona shivered, realizing for the first time his nearness. Instead of handing it to her, he bounded up the stone steps toward the door. She shook her head, amused at his exuberance, and followed him. The key clanked in the lock. Alec pushed the old door open but didn't go in. Instead, he hung back, allowing her to enter first.

As she stepped into the entry hall, a breeze swept past her. Dry leaves swirled around her feet. A dusty white haze floated through the room. Even though it was a crisp spring day, inside it smelt sweet and old.

"Look, I'm afraid you got off on the wrong foot with father, but you'll see how unsuitable it is. Miss MacDonald, we could have handled it all by mail."

His voice sounded a long way off. All her attention focused on the house. The warm inside air reached out to embrace her like a hug. Fiona arched a single black brow and walked on into her house.

Chapter Eleven

Latimer Square
Edinburgh
March 1937

Welcome Home

Fiona took two tentative steps into the dark entry hall. A shadow behind her seemed to steal the remaining light. She turned around in time to see the door swing shut on Alec. His hand was out to catch it, but she caught it first and pulled it open.

"Sorry,"

He emitted a nervous titter. "At least you know the door hinges work. Funny that." He edged into the room, eyeing the large door, but it showed no signs of moving again. Heavy, dark draperies robed tall windows on either side of the front door. She pulled one curtain aside, releasing an avalanche of dust motes to dance across the flagstone floor in little grey balls. Alec stepped next to Fiona into the rectangle entry hall. Rough stone walls and irregular stairs disappeared into the shadows above them. He wrinkled his nose. "It's worse than I imagined."

He waved his hand to clear the air. "This must be the oldest part of the house. It was popular at the time to make all the houses match—at least on the outside. Inside, they're all different. After seeing this room, I wonder if the interior of your house changed much over the years."

"*Your house.*" She let the words settle in. *He's right. This is my house.* The thought warmed her, and she savored the feeling of belonging here.

Alec was saying, "... dates to the time of Bonnie Prince Charlie. I'm afraid it looks like it, too."

She'd forgotten the antiquity of this land. *Only three years in Canada and so many things once commonplace are now awe-inspiring.*

Alec walked over to the staircase. "This room couldn't have changed much." She followed his gaze up the dark stone steps. He was saying, "With no banister, those stairs look dangerous. Like a castle keep."

He was right. The stairs twisted up to a landing with no handrail. *There is a strong masculinity about this room, as if it belonged to a stern master. Was my uncle stern like the sea captain who built the house? Is that what made Hugh Ferguson die a lonely old man? Why name me as an heir? Did he throw away the love of his only sister? I can't imagine my mum leaving her family. And when my parents died, why didn't he try to reach me? Why choose isolation?*

Fiona looked back at Alec. "Were my uncle's rooms on this floor?"

"I believe they are through the door in the archway toward the back of the house." Alec hesitated. "I have to get back to an appointment." He seemed to notice that his hat was still on. He pulled it off like a self-conscious schoolboy and said, "Are you sure you want to stay?"

Her smile was so broad her cheeks dimpled. "It just needs a little work."

He grinned at her with lopsided astonishment. She laughed for the first time in days. "I want to do this. It's lovely to have roots again."

Alec motioned in the door's direction. "I live in the house on the right. We're neighbors, you and I." He glanced down at his shoes before asking, "Would you let me come back at six and take you to dinner?"

Since her last meal had been on the night train from Southampton, she answered him with enthusiasm. "That would be wonderful."

He twirled the fedora in his hand. "I hate to leave you, but I've got to get back to the office. If I can do anything. I mean, if there's anything you need…"

"Oh, I'll be fine. I want to look around and sort of get my bearings." She paused. "There is one thing. Could you arrange for my trunk and carrying case to be picked up from the train station and sent here?" She handed him the baggage claim from her coat pocket.

"Of course."

"And there is one other thing." She hesitated again before plunging ahead. "Someone took my purse while I was sleeping on the night train. I've made all the reports with the stationmaster. Would you mind asking if there's any news?"

"Why, Miss MacDonald, you are a marvel. You mean you stood up to my father with not so much as a ha'penny in your pocket?" Alec plopped his hat down on his head, then pulled it off again in a mock bow. "My hat goes off to you."

He reached into his pocket and pressed a few shillings into her hand. She protested, but he winked as he retreated through the still open doorway, calling out over his shoulder, "For the gas meter."

Fiona appreciated his thoughtfulness as she reached out to close the door, expecting to feel alone and afraid. Instead, a companionable silence welcomed her. *This is my home.*

She crossed the large entry hall with the uneven old stone

beneath her feet. The dips and ridges would take some getting used to. Oak doors on either side of the room begged to be opened, and the stairway called for her to climb up and find what lay beyond the shadowy landing above her.

But first things first. She must find the gas meter so she'd have light by nightfall. At her home in Greenock, her parents fed shillings into a silver box. It metered out natural gas to the house for light, their gas stove and hot water. They never had the luxury of a furnace and she expected nothing would be different here, but with coal fires, their home was always bright and inviting. It seemed important to keep that sense of welcome alive in this big old house.

She wandered through the hall door, framed by an archway cut into the side of the stone staircase. It seemed likely to lead to the business end of the house. A cold darkness encompassed her as she passed under the stairs.

Fiona stopped. Her pulse quickened, but she remembered her da saying, "Dinna be afraid of cold dark places; it's the icy darkness of people ye should be wary of."

She stood a moment, trying to see further into the gloom. *You goose, this can't be more than a short corridor.* As she took a step forward, the door behind her closed, enfolding her in darkness. Forced to feel her way along the wall, she opened the first door and stood showered in blessed light. It was the convenience or bathroom, as the Canadians say. The room glowed from the afternoon sun through high uncovered windows above an ornate clawfoot tub. *All the comforts of home,* she thought with relief. *At least uncle updated this room since the seventeen hundreds.*

She could see that the hall ahead of her led to a large green door and pushed through it with a renewed sense of confidence. Once again, she plunged into darkness. But this time she grabbed the green door before it could swing closed behind her.

The light from the high windows in the water closet shone on this new room. It must have been a butler's pantry. Glass-covered cabinets full of china lined the walls with a marble counter-top and small sink for polishing silver.

A thrill of excitement filled her. *So many treasures to discover—and clean,* she reminded herself. *It's all so dusty. Had Uncle touched this china in years?*

She noticed two more doors to her right. Like a child, she wondered how long it would take the green door to swing shut. Sure she could make it, she dashed through the door at the end of the hall.

She paused as she entered the room she'd been hoping to find —the kitchen. Large paned windows filled the room with a golden glow. The floor was brick, and an oversized wooden table dominated the center of the room. Still, there was plenty of space to move around. This was another "welcome home" room.

Her eyes took in the fireplace in one corner and the large sinks along the wall. She sighed with relief at the wrought-iron gas stove. *I was half expecting to cook over a fire. At least the old man liked to have his tea the easy way.*

Fiona wandered around the room, opening cupboards and finding, to her surprise, everything was full. *Most of this must have spoiled long ago. Still, it was as if the cook shopped and then left it, never to return.*

I wonder if Uncle Hugh had someone taking care of him? She'd heard her uncle had been ill for some time, but how long had this kitchen waited to be useful? Any food not in tins was nasty looking, but everything else was promising. She signed with pleasure. *Soap and water and this will be livable.* She even found a big old teapot and a tin of tea. Best of all, a gas meter hung on the wall next to the back door. She deposited Alec's shillings and turned the handle until it clicked on. There would soon be a pot of tea to strengthen her for "a good look around" as Da liked to say.

Chapter Twelve

Latimer Square
Edinburgh
March 1937

The Gulf Between Rab and Laurie Widens

Rab MacKenzie was a bit like his favorite chair, showing signs of wear but with excellent lines and many years of use left. He sat by the window, his tall frame settled in the old leather chair. His bushy brows pulled together as he tried to concentrate on the newspaper in front of him.

The heavy oak library door creaked on its hinges as it swung open. Rab looked up as his grandson crossed the room to get a book from the shelf. He noted Laurie's black eye and swollen lip. Wincing at the cut on Laurie's forehead, Rab remembered his own wild days.

Must have given the boy a devil of a sore head. But then that was Laurie's problem—he was a bit of a sorehead. Always looking for his niche but never feeling like he belonged. Rab cleared his throat. "The Pope's picked a fight with Herr Hitler."

Laurie turned, seeming surprised that he wasn't alone in the room.

"Chamberlain's at it again too," Rab said, commenting on the headlines. "He'll do anything it takes to keep his hands clean—no matter who he has to sacrifice." The old man scowled.

"What's that, grandfather?" Laurie's tone sounded anything but interested. But Rab needed to connect with his grandson.

"The Pope's issued a decree criticizing the Nazis for violating the 1933 Reichskonkordat agreement. Even published it in German." The subject filled his Highland blood with passion. "He says what yon Chamberlain should have been sayin' about their Racial Laws."

A spot on his beakish nose turned red, a sure sign this old clansman was about to blow his bonnet. "We're makin' a pact wi the devil himself if ye ask me." Rab crumpled the paper, carried away with the intensity of his outrage at Chamberlain, but the face of his grandson stopped him cold.

Laurie's exasperated expression said it all. He never looked much farther than his own concerns. The thought pulled all the steam from the old man's kettle.

"Marguerite says the press doesn't give an accurate picture of how things really are," Laurie said. "Hitler's done a lot of good. He's put that country back on its feet after the last war. Economically, Germans are better off." His off-handed tone sounded like he was commenting on the merger of two companies.

Rab sighed and pulled his paper up to stare once more at the printed page. His features sagged. *How did I let Laurie down?*

The death of his own son, Laurie's father, had a profound impact on the sensitive thirteen-year-old. Rab's wife died that same year, so he came down out of his Highland home to live with his daughter-in-law and help her raise the boy. Just one year later, Laurie's mother died too, leaving Rab to tend to the task alone. *It was hard for the boy to accept the death of both parents and of his way of life. Maybe I should have moved us both back to Peterhead.* It was a fleeting thought. *No, the lad dinna need to lose his home too.*

Rab realized Laurie was speaking again and asked, "Marguerite? That's the lassie whose father is German?" He tried to keep disdain from his voice.

"Yes, but her mother was a Scot." Laurie sounded as pompous as the young lassie had on her first visit to their home.

Rab was about to say, "You lay down wi dogs and get up wi fleas," but he clamped his mouth shut to control his tongue. He could feel the breach with his grandson growing, and he blamed himself for being so outspoken.

"Lord, I need ye more and more," he whispered to himself.

"What's that?" Laurie's eyes rose from the book he'd opened.

To change the subject, Rab asked, "Did ye see the Frazer lad takin' a young lady into auld Hugh's?" He nodded toward the library window. "I think the niece has come ta claim the place. There may be a battle on this very street lang afore Hitler casts his eyes in our direction." Rab's features filled with devilment.

Laurie crossed the room and pulled at the lace curtains. The door to old Hugh's house stood ajar, and Alec's silver Bentley parked in front. Laurie shook his head as he turned to leave.

"I won't be home till late tonight," he said as he left the room.

And I would na need ta be told that when the actual news would be your presence at the dinner table. Rab tossed the newspaper to the floor.

Chapter Thirteen

Edinburgh
March 1937

All the Wrong People Have Money

Laurie shoved his hands in his jacket pockets and turned up his collar. He'd left his topcoat on the chair by the door, but he wasn't going back for it. He was out of sorts and embarrassed after Rab presented him with such a generous gift. *The only reason I'm taking your self-righteous money is to protect you, Grandfather,* but that thought stood on very thin ice.

Alec's silver Bentley sat in front of old Hugh's house. He and Alec had lived on Latimer Square all their lives, their homes handed down from one generation to another. *No wonder Toby's thug thought I had money.* But Alec and Laurie were far apart in status, both financially and socially. *If my da had lived, it might have been different.*

He turned his back on Latimer Square and walked toward Old Town. His gaze turned inward as he thought, *I'm grateful to Rab—I know all he's done to keep our house and put me through school. But I'm not like him.* He shook his head. *All the wrong people have money.*

At the stoplight on Princes Street, he took a moment to glance at the sky. *At least it isn't raining.* He walked up the North Bridge Road and wound his way through Old Town. He wanted to see Toby first and be clear of his debt. Afterwards, he hoped to have a chat with one of his professors. *The man is a gifted teacher. At least he recognized my worth.*

Toby was businesslike, eyeing Laurie's face but saying nothing about the beating. Instead, he took his money, plus a chunk of interest, with a sardonic expression and ended with an offer of help whenever Laurie needed him. Laurie said little. *It's one thing to make a stupid mistake once, but you won't catch me again dealing with the likes of Toby.*

Then he was out the door, walking at a brisk pace up South Bridge Road toward Old College. The streets of Old Town were a dirty grey. Buildings leaned with the decay of years rotting away their foundations. The wind pushed him along and then seemed to pull him back. *The story of my life. Try to push yourself forward, and someone always tries to pull you back.* As he neared the university buildings, he felt more at ease. *This is my place.* It leveled the playing field for him. Academic excellence could trump money and social position. He'd earned the respect of his mates, graduating at the top of his class a full year early.

The campus felt deserted with all the undergraduates still in class. He glanced at his watch. *Professor Finlay should be in his office.* There were a few things Laurie wanted to discuss with his mentor. He hurried through the main entrance, colliding with someone. Both young men stopped a little off balance.

"Laurie, you devil, just the man I wanted to see." Bernie grabbed his friend's hand and shook it vigorously, slowing as he took in Laurie's appearance. "Speak of the devil. What has he done to you?"

Laurie smiled and winced at the pain of stretching his split lips. He'd forgotten what a mess he still was. If anyone else had popped off with that smart remark, he might have seen red. But Bernie was a good fellow. Which was fitting, since his last name was Goodfellow.

Bernie was a year ahead when Laurie started at the University of Edinburgh. The older lad had befriended him. Unusual in a system that encouraged snobbery in the older students. Laurie had moved through his studies in record time until they were neck and neck in abilities, both young men graduating with full honors.

"Good God, man. How does someone with your brains get into so many stupid fights?" The smile never faltered even if the words were a reproof.

"A little misunderstanding about some money I owe." Laurie rubbed his chin.

"Well, you look awful. You won't be able to impress your girl with a face like a prizefighter." Bernie chuckled and slapped Laurie on the back. "Say, how is the lovely Marguerite? You live a charmed life. I've heard she's filthy rich. She's been here for over a year, and no other lad's been able to get over two words out of her. Unless you're an earl's son or something. Which you are not."

"Sometimes you're a real ass, Bernie. You're jealous, anyway." Laurie folded his arms, smiling at his friend. It was bizarre—Bernie could say anything and it didn't bother him.

"Och, well, you're right. After all, she is a looker, too." He seemed to ponder it, tapping his finger against his chin. Bernie had devilment in his eyes as he asked, "Come to think of it, what in the world could she see in you?"

They laughed together, but Bernie had a point. He continued in the same jocular manner. "If she comes to her senses, let me know. Maybe she'll be ready for a nice steady chap like me instead of a real troublemaker like you. I might give up being an engineer altogether. It'd save me a long apprenticeship."

"Have any news?" Laurie grabbed his friend's arm.

"Had word yesterday. I'm going to work for Scotts."

"Oh, Bernie, capital. Congratulations, you couldn't ask for a better firm." He clapped Bernie on the back and shook his hand again.

The tall redhead assumed the stance of a learned professor. "Have you any idea which of the many firms bidding for your services you will grace?"

A nagging guilt settled on Laurie. "Well, Marguerite's father has shown interest in me."

"You're jesting. Looks and a father in shipbuilding? You're not serious." Bernie's face was a picture of disbelief. "No wonder you're so sensitive about her. All jokes aside, you know any firm would be lucky to get you. You're a legend around here. Nobody finishes his studies so quickly and at the top as well. He has to be thanking his lucky stars she met you. Don't let anyone say different. The way she looks at you, I think she's crazy about you. And you love her too, right? Of course you do. Who wouldn't be in love with her? She's beautiful."

Bernie seemed not to notice Laurie's hesitation. The very question he'd been pushing away for weeks. His feelings toward Marguerite were so complicated. *If her father didn't hold the key to a door marked "success," it might be easier to figure out.*

The look of admiration on his friend's face was touching. Bernie continued, "Where will you be going? Not too far to have a pint with your poor old friend, I hope?"

"Marguerite's father is a partner in Von Keil and Associates."

Bernie's mouth drooped. "Tell me you're not considering going to Germany?" There was an edge to his words.

"I haven't given him my answer yet, but it's an offer I'm not sure I can turn down." Laurie's excitement grew as he explained. "I'd be starting at the top. Even if I stay for only a few years, it could be a feather in my cap. I could have a job with any firm. I'm sure I could put in a word for you. It'd be great to have you with me." But the expression on Bernie's face still registered disbelief.

"Not for me, old man. I'm Jewish."

"Not even funny, Bern." This was going too far. Laurie countered with, "Anyway, I'm sure the things they're printing these days are way out of line. From what Marguerite says, this Hitler fellow's done wonders for the economy."

For the first time in their friendship, Bernie didn't have a snappy comeback. He stood staring at Laurie. His countenance darkened. Shaking his head, he asked, "Don't you read the papers?"

"Marguerite says they exaggerate. Hitler's not so bad."

Bernie sounded incredulous. "Unless you're Jewish or you speak out against his laws. My God, man."

The clock tower chimed out the hour, and the passageway filled with students hurrying to their next class. Laurie was glad for the interruption. It was impossible to stay in the doorway, and the noise prevented any further conversation.

"I've got to catch Professor Finlay while he's in his office. I'll see you soon, and congratulations, great news." Laurie pretended to ignore Bernie's stunned expression. He moved past his friend into the throng of people.

Chapter Fourteen

Edinburgh
March 1937

What's Father Up To?

After spending time with Fiona, Alec's steps were a little lighter and he couldn't help smiling. She was honest, unpretentious, and enchanted by her new home. He liked her for getting the better of his father. Then there was her courage—*no money, no family, and still she knew what she wanted.*

Good God, she'd even had her purse and all her money stolen this morning, and she still entered that dilapidated old house as if it was a castle. He was still smiling when his father met him in the office lobby.

"What the devil took you so long?" Thomas Frazer's face was red with anger. Heat rose up Alec's neck. The old man stopped him with a keen stare, eyes narrowing. Thomas appeared to change his mind. The corner of his mouth quirked upward in a sly smile.

"She's attractive, isn't she?"

Alec's father could use any turn of events to exert control. *Not this time, you old fox.* He pushed past the old man with a shrug. The secretary they shared looked like she'd like to ask a question, but he ignored her, eager to get away from his father.

"I have a client due in a quarter of an hour. So, if you'll excuse me." Alec reached his office and pushed the door shut, closing the conversation.

As he fumbled through the files on his desk, Alec thought of Fiona's warm brown eyes. He paused and stroked his chin. *She looks nothing like her uncle, quite beautiful in a common sort of way.* But something disturbed his thoughts. He'd seen the figures. There was very little actual cash with the house. Although it was unencumbered, maintenance of the structure could be costly.

Every time I've asked Father about the house, he's cut me off. Must be something there he's interested in. Alec's eyes looked at the papers on his desk without seeing them. His thoughts rambled on. He remembered thinking it odd that his father hadn't ordered a full inventory of the estate. Common practice but the old man pushed it off as unnecessary. His office clock chimed, reminding Alec of his next appointment. Time to focus on work. But the questions troubled him. He needed answers.

On impulse, he buzzed his secretary. "Get me the number of Waverley's stationmaster." It would be nice to have some good news for her. He buzzed again. "Make dinner reservations for two at the North British Hotel for the main dining room for six-thirty this evening."

"Yes, sir. Is there anything else?"

"No, thank you. Ring me when my appointment arrives, please."

Alec's eyes drifted to the view from his window to the spires of Scott's Monument and a glimpse of the streets leading to New Town and Latimer Square. He spoke aloud. "Whatever the devil you're up to, Father, I'll find out." *The lovely Miss Fiona is not likely to give you any help, but she already likes me.* Alec leaned back in his chair, lacing his fingers behind his head. His thoughts drifted to possibilities.

Chapter Fifteen

Latimer Square
Edinburgh
March 1937

It Was Just Waiting for Me

Within an hour, Fiona had washed a cup and made the tea. The pantry produced a tin of sealed Dundee shortbread. It was enough to fortify her for exploration. Beyond the kitchen she found a mudroom and peeked out the kitchen door into a small walled garden. The remnants of an old wooden gate swung on its creaky hinges, allowing quick glimpses of a cobblestone courtyard and a long stable. Tall beech trees surrounded the back of the mews. She smiled at the view. *It's so private and peaceful.*

Next, she found what must have been the cook's bedroom located off the kitchen, but this room belonged to a man. Wool blankets covered an old black iron bed. No frills or lace in this room. A massive oak desk stood under a top window.

Uncle, she thought, *was this your room?* A closer inspection of the desk revealed ledgers and bills, all bearing the shaky hand of an old man. The man dotted all his i's and crossed his t's. She sighed as she realized she would have to sort through all this later. The desk was a puzzle of slots and odd-sized drawers, many of them locked.

"Uncle, you're such a mystery."

She searched for a key and found what she was looking for taped to the bottom of a drawer. The first one she unlocked held twenty pounds and a handful of sixpence coins. She wanted to cry, thankful for her uncle's provision. In the last locked drawer, she found an envelope with her name on it. She drew it out, hugging it close to her heart. "Why would you lock this away? Why didn't you send it to me?" She rubbed away the tears gathering in her eyes and opened the unsealed envelope. The letter was dated three years ago, just after her parents died. It bore the same squarish writing but without the shaking.

FIONA,

I'm not sure if my sister ever spoke of her brother. We parted with harsh words. I regret the things I said to her, but something held me back from apologizing. I guess I thought time would prove me right about your father, but it didn't. Then it was pride and thinking I'd get round to it, there was time, but I was wrong about that, too.

I loved Helen. Our parents died when I was a young man, and I became father and brother to her. She was a lovely girl. I couldn't have been prouder of her. Now I've lost her again.

THE LETTER BROKE OFF. She stared at it for a long moment, trying to understand the man who wrote it. *Uncle Hugh never finished it, but why?*

Was she trespassing into his room, full of his personal things? She folded the letter and slipped it back where she'd found it. *Another time I'll tackle this room but not now. Too restless to* stay put in one spot, she decided to explore the rest of the house.

Back in the kitchen, she found a narrow stairway up to the next floor and one down to the cellar. The light at the top of the stairs was far more appealing than going down to the dark cellar.

On the next floor, she entered a wide hallway. To her left, a tall window stood with curtains drawn aside, filling the passage with sunlight. She looked through the dusty panes to the walled garden below. It was an overgrown thorny tangle, but all along the grey stone walls the skeletons of climbing roses reached for the sun. She could see a few tiny new green shoots.

"Mum always loved roses," Fiona whispered. This window offered a better look at the stable. The cobblestone courtyard and the long stone stables were the same ancient grey. Doors stood open in four stalls. A faded green door and shuttered windows at one end and large double doors at the other gave it a well-planned appearance.

She was glad others before her had planned and cared for this old house. At present, there was a sadness in its state of decline.

She brightened. "That's why I feel welcome, isn't it? You need me, don't you?" She shook her head in dismay. "I have got to stop this habit of talking to myself," she said again aloud. But somehow, she knew she wasn't talking to herself. The house heard her.

Only the sounds of her breathing and her own footsteps accompanied her as she moved along the passageway.

Through the door on her right, she found yet another water closet and across the way, a darkened bedroom with sheet-covered furniture.

Fiona jumped with a start as a creaking drew her attention back to the kitchen stairs. The door at the top was swinging shut. She blushed, feeling foolish, and pushed it closed. The paneling on the door matched the surrounding wall. Once shut, it disappeared. How could there be no handle on this side of the door? Pushing on the place where a handle should have been, she released a spring, and the door popped open. Fiona gasped with delight at the novelty.

The rich wood paneling continued the full length of the hall. "I wonder how many secrets you have to share with me?" she said, running her hands along the dark cherry wood wall. Within a few feet, the pressure from her touch released another spring. Fiona backed up to let one more hidden door glide open. She shivered as a rush of cold air engulfed her. The chill was more than physical. Little hairs on the back of her neck stood on end.

She remembered something her mother once said while staying in a spooky old house in the highlands. "In ancient houses, there are often places with a bad feeling. I'm not sure why, it's the way things are. When I'm afraid, I remember who stands with me."

Maybe she was talking about this house.

A wonderful peace flowed through Fiona's body. She peered past the open door. The bright daylight shone from the floor above, lighting the narrow stairway.

She shook her head. "Not so frightening after all, but you'll have to wait a while. I'm not finished here." She pushed the hidden door, and it disappeared into the paneling, taking with it the cold.

Her mind was racing ahead. *Will I be able to take care of this big of a house? What will I do with you? There has to be a reason for me coming here, but what if I never find it? Could this be another mistake?*

She was flipping from one emotion to another. She stopped and looked back down the hall to her mother's room. "I'm here, and I'm not alone. This house needs me. Right?" No one answered, but she was a good deal calmer. To pull her mind from uncomfortable thoughts, she paid close attention to the details of the hall. Smells, colors, textures all distracted her and helped her remember—good and bad. This was hers. It could hold the key to unlocking her mother's past and open her own future.

A carved door recessed under an archway beckoned to her

from the end of the corridor. She turned the handle and found it unlocked. She tried to open it, but it seemed to be stuck. It took several attempts, but the sticky door gave way, sending her tumbling into the room.

Instead of darkness, she stood in the afternoon sunlight. Heavy rose-velvet draperies were drawn aside. The light drifted through the beautiful lace curtains. With no covers on this furniture, it looked as if the owner had stepped out yesterday.

Though muted by a layer of dust, the delicate rosebud pattern of the chintz coverlet on the canopy bed seemed to match the wallpaper. Thick rose carpeting cushioned every step as she walked around the large room.

The windows overlooked the square below, and she realized she'd come to the front of the house. In an alcove to her left, several chairs and a small table stood ready for afternoon tea. She turned back to the room, looking for some clue to its ownership.

A cushioned lounge chair sat by a carved mantel. Coal still filled the grate, and on the mantel there were three silver-framed photographs.

Through the dust, she could see a familiar-looking man and woman. In another, a girl of about eight sat on a white pony, and the last photograph was of a young man and the same girl, perhaps in her early teens. The teen looked at the young man with such adoration. He had all the arrogance of youth, but there was something protective in the way his arm encircled the girl.

With a start, Fiona realized the girl must be her mother. She picked up the frame and stared. *This must have been my Uncle Hugh when he was young. What did he write?* "I became father and brother to Helen."

Yes, I can see that. It must have been hard to lose their parents and have everything fall on him. So young. But there was pride in his expression. *Pride seems to have been your greatest enemy.* She set the frame back in its place.

The man and woman in the other photograph must be my grandparents.

Do they look familiar because I see Mum in their faces? No. Fiona looked from one photograph to another. A rush of tears filled her eyes. *It's like looking at pictures of myself, both past and future.* She hugged the photo of the girl on the pony to her. *Oh, Mum, I miss you.*

In that moment, she decided this room would become hers as it must have been her mother's before her. Each new memento confirmed her feelings. A Victorian doll sat in the center of the rosebud coverlet. Through a door next to the bed, she discovered a dressing room full of clothing that looked to be about Fiona's size.

Though styles had changed the feminine fabrics, the exquisite cut of the clothing reminded Fiona of her mother. Her eyes brightened at the racks of dainty shoes and boots. *Mum loved shoes.* Fiona stooped to touch a pair of riding boots. Thick mud still clung to the fine leather as if the owner had taken them off only this morning.

Oh, Mum, Uncle didn't touch a thing after you left here. It was like he wanted to hang on to your presence. It makes me feel like I have you near me.

Still holding the silver frame close to her, Fiona sat on the bed. As she looked around, the room blurred in her vision. *Three years ago, I thought I'd lost everything.* She took a ragged breath and whispered, "Mum, it's like you're here with me." *Guess I didn't lose everything after all. It was waiting here for me to find it.*

Chapter Sixteen

Bavaria, Germany
March 1937

And I Will Depend on You

Ana couldn't believe how beautiful everything looked as they rode through the mountains on Karl's sleigh. Moonlight reflected off snow-covered fields. She took it all in with a kind of reverence. The bells on the horse's harness played a soft melody with the swish of the sleigh runners through the snow.

Karl Beckmann was not talkative, so the children had drifted off to sleep long ago. Even Katrine had snuggled under her blankets with baby Tony nestled against her.

Ana appreciated the way Katrine had taken over the infant's care, more like a protective mother than an adolescent girl. Even in sleep, Katrine curled her body around the baby's pudgy form. When Tony stirred in his sleep, Katrine's hand reached out to stroke his little back.

Poor child, she's taken on so much responsibility for one so young. Ana frowned. *It's not fair.* At least for now, each little face—even

Katrine's—was at peace. She caught her breath at their innocence. *And they depend on me to keep them safe.*

Ana's eyes rose to the majesty of the heavens. The stars sparkled above her. *And I will depend on you, Lord, to show me how.*

Karl cleared his throat. His voice sounded raspy, strained. "Sister Ana?" he began.

"Just Ana, I think."

"Ja, you are right. It will be safer." He nodded his head toward the hill before them. "My brother and his wife have a little farm over the rise. I didn't have time to warn him or even ask him if it was right to bring you and the children."

He glanced at her. "I've been thinking all day about what the priest has told me. My brother is a good man. He would welcome you without question. His wife Ursel is…" He slowed, choosing his words more cautiously. "What I am trying to say is—my brother's wife is a lowlander from Baden-Baden. I'm not sure she understands mountain hospitality. They lost their first child last summer. Stillborn."

"Oh," was all Ana could think to say. She shot an "arrow-prayer" skyward. *Please Lord, let it be all right.*

He said no more for a minute. Ana wondered what he was getting at. The rules of conversation outside the convent were difficult to understand.

Herr Beckmann slowed as they crested the hill. Ana drew in her breath at the view of a mountain valley. "Why, it looks like a picture postcard," she whispered.

The farmhouse sat snuggled among a stand of evergreens. From the windows, a golden glow shone out over the snow. The mare quickened her pace, giving the bells on her harness quite a shaking.

When they were still a few hundred yards from the farm, the door of the house opened. A tall man stood framed by the lamp-light. Ana said a prayer of thanks. Their journey was over. Karl waved his arm in greeting. The man seemed to recognize his gesture. He called back over his shoulder to someone inside.

Herr Beckmann's mare broke into a canter. Ana grabbed the side of the sleigh and looked to see if the children were secure. Even with all the jolting, they were snug in their warm cocoon of blankets. They entered the yard in front of the house as Karl pulled the reins in a seesaw fashion, trying to slow the mare.

Ana leaned forward to touch his arm. "Perhaps we should wait while you talk to him."

He nodded. The little mare stopped, and Karl secured her reins. His brother was already laughing with delight at this surprise visit. His face registered a question as he noticed the sleigh-load of travelers. It lasted only a moment. His smile was still friendly, full of joy at this reunion. Karl jumped from his seat, and the two men embraced, clapping each other on the back.

Ana turned her attention to the figure of a woman who appeared in the doorway. She was tall, like Herr Beckmann's brother, but very thin. Her posture seemed stiff, and she stood aloof from the men. *What will we do if we're not welcome here?* Ana frowned, trying to think of other options. *The thing is, there are none.*

But Karl laughed at something his brother said. He waved for Ana to come inside. She let her breath out. *Looks like we are welcome after all.*

"Are we there yet?" Blankets muffled Katrine's sleepy voice.

"Indeed, we are. Can you help me get the children into the house?" She brushed a silky black strand of hair from Katrine's face. The girl pulled her hand free from the blankets to rub her sleepy eyes.

The children wiggled. Drowsy eyes blinked to focus. Baby Tony let out a wail. "I think Tony needs his nappy changed," Katrine said as she shifted his position. Gretchen and Deter sat up, looking around in bewilderment. Ana reached out, reassuring them with pats on their pale cheeks and nods of encouragement.

She stepped down from the sleigh and pulled the blankets off the children, jumping as something touched her arm. The woman she'd noticed at the door appeared at her side.

"Let me help." She had the sharp accent of a lowlander.

"Thank you. It's Frau Beckmann, isn't it?" Ana looked up into the woman's thin, angular face. Ursel Beckmann's nod was curt as she pulled back the final blanket from the sleepy children. She stopped and stood staring at them. Only little Tony missed the distasteful expression on the woman's harsh features.

Gretchen's face pinched into a fearful expression while Deter appeared hostile. Katrine wore the blank wall of protection on her beautiful face. Ana's heart broke at their understanding. *They already know this will not be a safe place after all.*

Frau Beckmann resumed helping Ana. Her movements were crisp and efficient as she hurried the children into the house. But there was little comfort in this. *It would have been better if she had yelled at us to leave.*

The children huddled together in front of a warm fire. Frau Beckmann brought them hard rolls and mugs of warm milk on a carved wooden tray which she slammed down on the table by the fire. The children jumped at the noise of clinking pottery.

Ana pretended not to notice Frau Beckmann's hostility, hoping the farmwife was only tired. But the woman's first reaction to Deter and Gretchen made that a remote possibility. Ana busied herself helping them shed their heavy coats, carrying on a steady discourse about the sights they'd seen along the way as she served them the snack. Little Gretchen wrinkled her nose, asking, "But, Ana, when will we get to Herr Beckmann's farm?"

Ana said, "Gretchen, you sleepyhead, we are here. This is the farm with the little kittens Herr Beckmann was telling you about."

Gretchen's eyes filled with tears, but Ana wiped them with her hand. "You are tired. Things will be better in the morning." She whispered, "We don't want Herr Beckmann to think we are ungrateful for the big adventure he has taken us on."

She reached out to hug Gretchen. All the while, she wondered what she should do next. The fact was they had little choice but to stay here, at least for the night.

Karl Beckmann and his brother approached. "Ana," he said, "this is my older brother Klaus."

The brothers looked so alike. It was heartwarming to see the same friendly expression on each face.

"I have told my brother everything Father Hugo told me. He would be happy to give shelter to you and the children." Ana looked over her shoulder at the door Ursel Beckmann had just closed behind her.

Karl reached out to touch her arm. "Ursel will be all right. Klaus says she has been strange since they lost the baby."

Ana was ashamed of judging the woman's behavior. To lose a child would be very hard. She realized if she failed to keep her little lambs safe, she would be devastated.

"You will come to no harm in my house." Klaus was matter-of-fact. He added, "I will have my wife make up beds for you in the loft. I hope you won't mind sleeping all together." Even though he shared his brother's awkwardness when he spoke to her, Ana was relieved by the genuine friendliness of Klaus Beckmann's handsome features. If only his wife felt the same.

"Thank you both for your help." For the first time, she realized she was so tired. "May the Lord Jesus Christ bless you for your kindness to us."

The men crossed themselves and smiled. They seemed relieved as well. They might feel awkward with a strange young woman, but they understood how to treat a holy sister. The lack of black habit had at least not changed that fact.

Chapter Seventeen

Saint Thomas

Bavaria

March 1937

A Dangerous Game of Wolf and Rabbit

The chapel was full for morning mass. Father Hugo hadn't slept well since Ana and the children left. His hand shook as he placed the sacrament in the mouth of old Frau Mitzel. He noticed the tears running down her plump cheeks. Current events disturbed so many older Germans.

He was about to stop and comfort her when a dark shadow fell across him. The priest looked up to see a young man blocking the light of the prayer candles. The man waited in line to receive communion, but there was something foreboding about his presence. It was as if he snuffed out the light of prayers from the sight of God.

The stranger waited for his turn to stand before Father Hugo. As the old priest bent to offer the sacrament, the outsider's boyish face struck him as angelic. His hair was very fair, almost white, but dark lashes framed his clear blue eyes. Father Hugo noticed the swastika armband. As Hugo placed the host on the man's tongue, he watched his youthful lips curl into a mocking smile. The transformation was disquieting.

The man stood for a long moment looking into the old priest's face. Cold blue eyes radiated superiority.

An inward voice reminded Hugo that even Satan was beautiful, an angel before his fall. Hugo intoned, "The body of our Lord Jesus Christ broken for you." But in his heart, he thought, *This one looks like a hunter, a wolf studying which way a rabbit might move before calculating his spring. Yes, this young man means to spring at me. I think I'd better be a clever rabbit.*

He attempted to steady his hands and modulate his voice as he finished with the Benediction. Silently he prayed the sacrament might impart to the man a touch from his heavenly Father.

After mass, the old priest stood at the door visiting with his flock while trying not to think of the young Nazi. With a booming voice, Frau Mitzel asked after the children and Sister Ana. Hugo's heart raced.

He lowered his voice in hopes she would follow his example. He asked her about the new baby her daughter had just delivered. Thankfully, the old woman warmed to the subject of her first grandchild.

As the line passed, Hugo thought he glimpsed the stranger leaving through a side door. The anxiety gripping his throat eased, and he offered a quick prayer of thanks. He even chuckled at the antics of the Krause twins as they battled each other around their mother's skirts.

Then he made his way through the empty church to take off his vestments. The door to his office stood ajar. Cigarette smoke curled out the entrance like a snake waiting to strike. The priest straightened his posture, squaring his shoulders, but his face kept its usual expression. *Every soul, even the Nazis, need brotherly love.*

"How may I help you, young man?" he said as he entered the

room. The man half sat on Father Hugo's desk, his leg draped over the corner. "Do you wish to make confession, my son?"

The youthful face jerked. His mouth tightened. Hugo felt the struggle within the Nazi to hold his emotions under control. He turned to put his vestments in the old wardrobe.

Intuition told the old priest this young man grew up in the church. He looked heavenward. *So, you are concerned for this one, yes, Lord? Well, if it's information about the children he's after, I'll need your wisdom.*

When Hugo turned back, the young man had relaxed.

"Father, you will have to do better than that," he said, his tone superior. "Haven't you heard? There is to be one church—the Reich church. You'll have a new boss. Soon you'll answer only to the Fuhrer, not the Pope. I suppose we'll put you out on the streets, looking for a new avocation. But you must be ready for retirement."

"Each one should use whatever gift he has received to serve others." Father Hugo warmed to the Lord's lead. "First Peter 4:10. How may I help you?" He sat behind his desk and signaled for his visitor to take a seat. "Your name, bitte?"

"Eric Braun." The man's words had a crisp, businesslike quality. "I am here to take a census. I will require your full cooperation." This was an announcement, not a request. "You will make available to me all church records regarding births, deaths, marriages, that sort of thing. I am interested in the small order of sisters at Saint Thomas and their work with orphans." He paused, letting his last words hang in the air.

"Give to Caesar what is Caesar's and to God what is God's," Hugo added. "Matthew 22:21. I will contact my bishop for permission to do as you ask."

Eric leaned forward and placed a document in front of the priest. "It seems your bishop understands the importance of pleasing the Fuhrer."

The old priest moved to the window for better light, then

fished in his pocket for his glasses. He'd heard about the pope's letter criticizing the Nazi government for anti-Catholic policies. But some German bishops, his in particular, were siding with Hitler.

Eric shifted in his seat with obvious impatience. After reading and rereading the letter, Father Hugo stooped to open a large drawer in his desk. He brought out an ancient-looking book. The edges of the pages were uneven, its leather binding cracked with age. Father Hugo handled the record of Saint Thomas with a kind of reverence.

"Passed from priest to priest over many years," he said. "You will find the names of every Catholic soul in this parish for the last three-hundred years recorded on those pages." He placed the book in front of the Nazi.

Eric sighed and for the first time looked a little daunted. He opened the leather book with a light touch, fingering through the pages carefully.

It seemed to Father Hugo that Herr Braun had forgotten for a moment to treat the things of the church with the required Nazi disdain.

He asked, "Your mother was Catholic?" Another unbidden insight from above.

The impact of his observation was immediate and unguarded. Eric's face contorted into a grimace. It took a minute, but the young man reined in his anger. The wolf returned. He closed the book with a slam, shoving it across the desk to the priest.

"You will make a record for me of all church activity over the last year. I will, of course, check it with the book to make sure it is accurate." Eric's tone remained speculative as he asked, "How many nuns and orphans are you harboring?"

"The Convent of Saint Thomas has been empty of both for some time." *A small exaggeration only Lord,* he thought, deciding his next confession was likely to be quite lengthy. "She has been dead a long time?" he asked with sympathy.

84

"Who?" Eric's annoyance with this wandering speech pattern was clear.

"Your mother," Hugo answered. Shaking his head, he added, "Blessed are those who mourn, for they will be comforted. Matthew 5:4."

The Nazi stood and clicked his heels, genuflecting his god. "Heil Hitler." His posture remained military as he waited for the priest to give the expected response.

Hugo smiled. "Yes, of course you do."

Chapter Eighteen

Edinburgh
March 1937

A Kind Word Turns Away Disdain

Fiona spent the afternoon giving her new bedroom a good turning out. *Mum always said to put bedrooms in order first so you have a place to collapse when you're done for the day.* She beat the drapes with a broom and dusted every surface in the room. She found bed linens folded in the hall closet. *No telling how long they've been here. At least only the top set of sheets seems dusty.* She pulled out a set near the middle. *If I shake them out, they should be fine. Let's see if they fit.* They did.

She was sweeping the bedroom when she heard a loud rapping on the front door. She scurried down the stairs and crossed the entry hall. Her image in a dusty old mirror brought her to an abrupt halt.

Och, what a sight. They'll think I'm a cleaning lady. Black curls escaped from the confines of her scarf. Her brown eyes appeared overlarge, and dark smudges stood out on her pale skin. The knock came again, and she shrugged off her appearance to pull open the heavy door.

Two deliverymen stood on her steps with her luggage. "Is the lady of the hoose in?"

"Aye, and you're looking at her." Fiona stifled a giggle, delighted with her hoose.

"We, ah," one man stammered, "we have trunks to deliver to a Miss Fiona MacDonald and this—" He held up her dainty kid-leather handbag with his pinkie finger.

"Oh, thank you. Thank you. I can't believe it. However—? I mean, who found it?" It was almost too much to hope for. She took her bag, hugging it to her, eyes closed for a moment in a silent prayer of thanks.

The men seemed embarrassed by her exuberance. "The stationmaster says ta tell you nothing appears to be taken. He only did a cursory inspection mind, but your passport and a wee wallet are still inside. We think someone took it by accident, but I dinna ken how it came back." He cleared his throat. "We have orders to see your luggage taken to your room."

She stood aside and motioned for them to come in. "It's upstairs," she said.

"You lead the way, miss." They picked up the trunk with her one suitcase and her carrying case piled on top and mounted the stairs behind her. When they'd left her things in the center of the cleaned bedroom, she fished into her purse to give them something for their trouble. The delivery man held up his large hand to stop her.

"Already seen to by Mr. Frazer." He pulled a small envelope from his jacket pocket and handed it to her. "From the gentleman." They nodded and touched the front of their caps. "Good day to you, miss." Fiona followed them to the front door. Only after she'd thanked them several more times and closed the door did she turn her attention to the note.

It was from Alec. He'd be by to pick her up at six sharp. She glanced at her watch. Only an hour to finish making up her room, get washed and ready.

WHEN THE DOOR knocker rapped again at six, Fiona was waiting with a hearty appetite and dressed in her favorite blue suit. It was very gratifying to see the obvious appreciation on Alec's handsome face. "Beautiful," he said with an appreciative grin.

"Why, thank you, and thank you too for taking care of my things. It's grand to have them here, and did you know they located my purse? All my money and papers are still there."

"I wasn't aware of that. Now you won't need me to rescue you." He affected disappointment.

Fiona blushed and, laughing, said, "You'll always top my list of knights in shining armor."

"Why, Miss MacDonald, I think you can fend off any unruly dragons. After all, you handled my father." They laughed.

"How about rescuing my stomach? I'm starving."

He offered his arm. During the drive to the North British Hotel, they joked and spoke about unimportant things. Fiona felt a friendship growing between them. Only her first day in Edinburgh, and she already had one friend, a handsome one at that.

The hotel dining room was much too formal, even for her best blue suit. Alec did not seem to notice and carried on a sparkling commentary of Edinburgh social life. By the time the meal was served, she was enjoying herself. During dessert, she toyed with the raspberries in her trifle pudding, her thoughts drawn to her extraordinary day.

"What's this? My wonderful personality losing its charm so soon? Why so serious?" He made a mock frown to copy her expression.

"You've been too kind to me," she said, rather more intensely than she'd intended. "I mean, I've only been here one day, and you've made me feel so welcome." Fiona smiled, but her eyes were bright with unshed tears. Just now, she was overwhelmed and tired.

Alec reached across the table and took her hand. "I'd like us to be friends."

She nodded, feeling silly, being so close to tears for no good reason except the kindness of this stranger. No, not a stranger. "Friends, yes, I'd like that very much."

"Well, well. If it isn't the golden boy." The low voice jolted them out of their mood. Alec rose to his feet and seemed to fix his features into a pleasant expression. Although Fiona was glad for the interruption, she noticed a wariness in Alec's eyes.

She turned to regard the speaker. A couple had paused a few feet behind her. The woman was exquisite, but it was the man with her that held her attention. As a fan of American films, she thought for a moment she was looking at the darkly handsome leading man Tyrone Power. Although this young man's hair was a deep auburn, his brown brows and handsome brooding features were so close to those of the actor they might have been brothers.

Alec hesitated, giving the young man a double take. Her attention was drawn to the stranger's bruised face. Alec asked, "Are you all right? Been in an accident?"

Tyrone Power rubbed his jaw and blushed. "Ah, only an accident coming down some steps. It's nothing." He looked sheepish.

A slender, silk-clad woman held his arm possessively. Her light-blond hair hung in heavy waves over her shoulders. She could be a movie star, the way she carried herself with an air of self-importance.

The young man shifted his attention to Fiona. He said with an air of nonchalance, "This must be our new neighbor?" His voice was deep and smooth, but Fiona decided she didn't like his tone. He seemed to mock her. The woman on his arm looked down her perfect nose.

"Laurie MacKenzie, this is Miss Fiona McDonald," said Alec,

adding as an aside to Fiona, "Laurie and his grandfather live in the house on the other side of the square. And this is Miss Marguerite Voss."

The woman inclined her head but remained silent. *Did she expect her to bow or something?* Instead, Fiona did as her da would have expected. She rose and extended her hand to the woman, smiling her warmest. "How do you do? It is so nice to meet you." She might have been a dead fish the way Marguerite took her hand for the barest moment.

Fiona turned to Laurie. "And Mr. MacKenzie, it is nice to meet my neighbors so soon." He took her hand and held it a fraction of a second too long. And when he spoke again, the blasé attitude was replaced with a respectful greeting. *Da always said it is best to turn away disdain with kindness instead of a harsh word.* Then she thought of her run-in with Alec's father. *Of course, there were always exceptions.*

Chapter Nineteen

Edinburgh
March 1937

Ghost Horses

"Ninety, ninety-one." The brush slid through her hair, but Fiona's mind replayed the ride home from dinner. *I can't believe Alec had to wake me up.* Heat flooded her cheeks. "Nighty-nine, one hundred."

She sighed and laid her mother's silver hairbrush aside. The memory of falling asleep on the ride home was hard to shake.

She smiled wistfully at the thought of Alec's handsome face. He was so understanding. He said, "You've had quite a day. Don't give it another thought. I understand." But she was still embarrassed.

Another face floated through her thoughts. Handsome too but not refined. Rugged, dark, brooding. *I'm not so sure about that one.* Narrowing her eyes, she speculated, "Rude, too."

She replayed meeting Mr. MacKenzie. The man's tone was sarcastic. "Wonderful, so my neighbors don't like each other, and

I sit right in the middle. What have I stepped into?" At least Alec was polite.

"Looks like I'm not breaking the habit of talking to myself." She pulled down the covers. "The other one, handsome, yes, but looks like someone with a lot of rough edges. I don't believe for a minute he fell on his face, looks more like someone's fist fell on it —more than once.

"And the woman with him. She was on her high horse as Da would say." She tried to settle her thoughts, yet one last question floated to the surface. "I wonder why Alec doesn't like Mr. MacKenzie?"

Fiona turned out the gaslight and finished braiding her thick black hair in the dark. She was tired beyond belief. She climbed into her mother's big bed. Her body fit perfectly into a depression in the mattress. "Good night, Mamma," she whispered, sleep already slurring her words. A bittersweet peace filled the dark bedroom.

SOMETHING like an electric shock ran through her body. Fiona bolted up out of bed. Only a moment could have passed since she'd laid her head on the pillow. She fumbled in the pitch-black room for the match and candle on the nightstand. She was shaking when the match flared to life.

Her little travel clock read two, which meant she'd been asleep for hours. The house was so dark and silent, yet she'd been startled into full wakefulness. *What woke me? I feel like someone shook me, but the room's empty.* She touched her cheek. No tears and no memory of her usual nightmare. Yet her heart beat with some unknown fear. Breathless, she listened for… for what?

A faint sound came from the square. She drew aside her front curtains and peered into the darkness. The sound of horses and a carriage bumping along the cobblestone street grew louder.

She rubbed her eyes to look again. Harnesses jingled and shod hoofs clattered on the roadway below. Wood clanked and iron wheels rumbled along. But the square was deserted. The sounds were so clear, but only the rain touched the surface of those old stones. A stiff gust of wind pushed leaves, not horses, along the roadway.

What had seemed to come from the center of the square drew nearer to her window and then to the side of her house. She could hear the beasts snort and quicken their pace like horses nearing warm stables.

Fiona tripped over furniture as she followed the sound. It was passing under her little sitting room. She realized this part of her room must be built over the archway leading to the rear of the house. The phantom carriage was bent on entering her own back stable.

"I must be sleeping still." She looked back at the bed, half expecting to see her own head resting on the pillow. But the covers were pulled back, and she was indeed standing in the chilly night looking into the darkness for a coach and pair of horses. She heard it move to the back of the house.

She looked toward her bedroom door. It was just a dark, empty house—her own house—and she was a big girl. *Da always said fear was not of God. What would Da have to say about this?* Her feet seemed to be rooted in place. Still, she wondered if she looked down upon her stables, would she see a phantom coach? The desire to investigate was overpowering her fear.

Here in her mother's room, she wondered if Mamma, too, had been someone who needed to meet every challenge head on. That musing gave Fiona the last bit of courage she needed to spin around and head across the bedroom, stopping only to pick up the candle before she swung open the heavy door.

The long, dark hall stretched out before her. Weak moonlight shone through the window at the far end, leaving most of the hall in total darkness.

A breeze from the front staircase made her candle flicker and almost die. Fiona ran one hand along the paneling and used that to guide her steps down the hallway. Her candle wavered again in the cross draft and then flared, sending her shadow to dance along the wall. She imagined she must look like a ghostly apparition floating in a circle of light.

She told herself she was being ridiculous—until the candlelight flickered for an instant and died. It was like someone puffed it out. She paused in the darkness. *Old houses are drafty*, she assured herself. There was a damp coldness and the smell of the sea. She took a deep breath to steady herself. She remembered the door to the attic, sure she must be standing across from it. *Don't be a goose. All houses have drafts and odd smells.*

At a quicker pace, she moved toward the window at the end of the hall. Clouds parted, bathing the walled garden and cobblestone courtyard beyond in soft moonlight. Stall doors stood open like dark eyes on an enormous face. The sounds were gone. No horses stomped demanding their feed. No drivers rushed to unharness a team. Only an empty, long-deserted stable. She was a foolish bairn, even more so when she hesitated to walk back to her bedroom.

Her father said many a time, "Remember who it is who walks wi ye, lass."

With one hand touching the wall to guide her steps, Fiona walked at a slow pace back to her room. If the old house had ears, it would have heard the words to *A Mighty Fortress is our God* sung in a sweet soprano voice, all four verses. By the time she reached her room, the last words: "God's truth abideth still: His kingdom is forever, amen," were sung with surprising force and conviction.

The horses were silent.

Chapter Twenty

Bavaria, Germany

March 1937

One Last Night in the Trenches

Father Hugo wasn't surprised when the soldiers came to escort him to an "interview" with Herr Braun. After overhearing a conversation, the village innkeeper sent him a warning. The note read, "Officials looking for Sisters of Saint Thomas accompanying children of subversives. Expect questioning soon." Hugo wondered how much the Nazi had discovered. They came for him and deposited him in the jail in the beautiful mountain village of Mittenwald. The jail was old and not so picturesque.

That was yesterday. Today they left him in what must have been an office for some minor government official. It was small, furnished only with a battered desk and two chairs. A grey sky was visible through a single small window high on the wall behind the desk. Father Hugo sat alone in one of the straight chairs, trying not to feel uncomfortable. His bones ached after a night in a crowded cell with no place to stretch out and sleep. For all that, it was a good night. A useful night. He'd always wanted to be in the trenches doing God's work, bringing whatever comfort the Lord could impart through this old servant.

His cell held Jews and politicals, those Germans brave enough to disagree with Nazi politics. But he heard the confession of three good Catholic souls. He anointed another with the holy oil kept in the pocket of his cassock and prayed for healing of what must be pneumonia. A far greater affliction among the men was the blackness of despair. He'd prayed for this as well.

He spoke with another man, not a Catholic, still a true believer. This man, Joseph, had been hiding a family of Jews in his cow barn. His wife and small daughter were in some prison, perhaps even this very one. They prayed together for God's protection for his small family and for the fate of the family in the cow barn and even the cows.

He felt like a farmer in the midst of his flock, not cows but God's own sheep. The work was most satisfying when he could see the need. They prayed, too, for the young Nazi, Eric Braun, so bent on finding four small children and one young nun. Father Hugo was sure Herr Braun must have learned of their existence by now. Hugo asked for forgiveness for the person who told Herr Braun. *Lord, even here in this remote part of Germany, even here?* He shook his head. *How could such a man as Hitler come to power? Why does he hate even the smallest children for their heritage? I don't understand.*

A wave of panic rolled over him as he contemplated how he might warn Sister Ana to leave Bavaria as soon as possible. He was certain of one thing—Eric Braun hated the church. The man was a wolf with the scent of his quarry. If the young nun wasn't clever, she and the children would be run to ground.

The door opened, and the young man with the face of a choirboy entered the room. Father Hugo prayed for strength to be silent.

Chapter Twenty-One

Edinburgh
March 1937

Legend of the War Chest

Fiona pulled the front door closed and dropped the large iron key into her handbag. A stiff breeze tugged at her curls, pulling them out from under her scarf. She stood for just a moment and looked around. Three old stone houses lined a seventy-five-foot-wide square like three old men. Each one a brother to the other, mostly identical, but each house had a character of its own.

Da would say she was being fanciful. Still, the houses on Latimer Square were like dignified old men. After last night, she wasn't sure how she felt about hers. The door to the house on her left opened, and an elderly man stepped out. Fiona smiled. The old man looked something like the house he stepped out of—tall and granite-like—still straight and strong but very craggy. He stood for a moment and then plopped his cap on his salt-and-pepper hair.

He turned from his door to look up at her. Fiona realized she was staring at him, smiling to herself. The man smiled back and waved in greeting. By the time she came down her steps, he was hastening to meet her, his face lit with welcome. The transformation was amazing. He looked twenty years younger.

Nothing could match the tenderness in his brilliant blue eyes. "Good day to ye," he said with the brogue of a true Highlander. "Robert MacKenzie, pleased to meet the niece of my guid friend. You would be Helen's wee barren, and don't ye look enough like her to be herself standing here twenty-five years ago."

"You knew my mother?" Fiona felt stunned. So much about her mother's past was unknown to her. She surprised herself by blurting out, "Mr. MacKenzie, was she happy here?"

"You'll be wanting to do a spot of shopping this morning. And I'm headed that way myself."

She wondered if he always read people. The old gentleman just smiled and said, "My friends call me Rab. Walk wi me, and I'll tell you what I remember of Helen." He held out his arm, and she accepted without hesitation. They fell into step together toward the shops near Princes Street.

"My son, Willy, married Jean Sutherland, who grew up in our hoose. She were older than your mam, but they were still friends. Jean often spoke of her after the shock of Helen leaving home to marry. That were quite a row. Yer Uncle was very against it. You could hear him yelling through those old stone walls. I think it hurt his pride more than anything when she left. Before then, I only ever saw your mam to say a word or two in greeting when I visited my son and his new wife. Helen always gave me a pleasant smile. You're the spitting image of your mam."

She could feel her cheeks flush with pleasure. Rab set a steady pace as they walked toward the shops.

"I think from what our Jean said, she'd had a happy childhood except for losing both her parents in an accident. It was hard on Hugh, taking on the responsibilities of his father at only twenty.

Aye, but he doted on Helen." He said again, "You are very like her." His smile grew tender, bringing her near to tears. "Your father was a Presbyterian minister, aye?"

She nodded. "You know so much about me already. I feel like we've been friends for years."

"Well, in a way, we have. Your uncle had his sources, and he kept track of his little sister. He was a stubborn man."

"Stubborn? You mean because he didn't reconcile with his sister?"

"Aye, but no just that. His wife softened him a bit, but if he got a bee in his bonnet, he could be determined."

"Was he married long?"

"No long, poor wee thing. She died in childbirth an' took the bairn with her."

He stopped and turned to look at her. "Ye ken how Hugh died? Well, they say he had a heart complaint, but it was no so much medical as it was emotional. After his wife died, he grew into a bitter, lonely man and stayed that way for years.

"We became friends after your mam's death. I heard about it from his housekeeper and went to visit him. I think it was the first time he'd spoken to anyone about his life in years." Rab shook his head. "Locked in grief and remorse, he was. It made him old before his time. He wasn't an old man, ye ken, but he lived like one." They walked on in silence for a few minutes.

Her life had become a puzzle with lots of missing pieces. There was still a big hole where her family history should have been. "Could I meet your daughter-in-law?"

"I wish you could, lass. She's been gone some years. There's only me and my grandson Laurie." His smile faded a bit. "My son died of influenza. Lost my wife Daisy of the same epidemic, so I came doon frae Peterhead to help Laurie's mam raise our laddie. He was only thirteen and a handful, I can tell ye. His mam died only a year later. It were that hard on the boy."

"Oh, I met a Lawrence MacKenzie last night."

"That would be himself."

"He must take after his mother. He doesn't look a thing like you," she said.

"Aye, he looks like his mam, God rest her soul, but I'm afeard he takes after me as well." She must have looked doubtful, because he laughed and added, "I was much the same as Laurie as a young man. I wanted everything, and I didn't enjoy waiting." His eyes had a far-off look. "Then the Lord got his hands on me. Put me through the fire. But it was what I needed." She wanted to ask more but decided not to pry.

His mood lightened again. "And how did you sleep your first night in your new home?"

A simple enough question and asked with a casual air. But she wasn't sure how to answer. The blood drained from her face.

"Ah, well, you've heard the horses then." A simple statement, but it tore down all the excuses she'd been giving herself for what had happened in the night.

"Have you?"

"Och, nay, lass. But I've heard of them often enough. Yer uncle spoke of his night visitors."

"Can you tell me anything about the horses, and there was a carriage as well? I'm sure of it."

Rab told her what Uncle Hugh said about his night visitors. He had heard the horses many times over the years. He believed they came during times of change. She shivered as Rab described her own experience.

"It didna trouble yer uncle. And rightly so. Some things are unexplainable, and we must accept that they are. He told me most of the oddities about the hoose are related to the time of the 'Black Captain,' a distant ancestor of yers. He lived during the time of the Bonnie Prince. It were the captain who built the hoose."

Fiona looked around. She didn't care if they ever made it to the shops. This old gentleman was a treasure. She slowed her steps and listened with interest as Rab wove his story.

"The captain was a rogue, but a fierce Jacobite, ye ken, a supporter of the king James Stuart across the water. Ye see, James was the rightful heir to both the Scottish and the English throne, but he were cheated out of it because he was Catholic and refused to become a Protestant."

Fiona chimed in, "Oh, I remember this from school. They called him 'The Old Pretender' and exiled him to France or Italy."

"Aye, that would be him, and he attempted to reclaim his throne. His followers were called Jacobites, ye see. And yer Captain was a—"

"—a Jacobite." She enjoyed this bit of history.

"Well, when James' son Charles Edward reclaimed his father's throne, the Black Captain amassed quite a treasure by smuggling. It was common enough." He winked at her. "Still is, to some extent. Yon captain gave the treasure box to the prince."

Rab shook his head. "But Charlie disappointed many a Highlander. He did well at first but failed to listen to his best advisers. At the last battle of Culloden, his men were starving. Still, Charlie never used the treasure to feed or outfit them. Thousands died that day and thousands more when the English took their revenge on the common people of Scotland.

"After Culloden, the captain wanted his treasure box back. Said he'd been cheated when the prince slipped away to save his own hide, leaving the Jacobite clans to pay for his poor leadership.

"So the rumor was the Black Captain chased the prince doon and took back his box. Yer captain said the money wasna meant for selfish desires but was gathered to help the people in need."

"What happened to the treasure?"

"There's the rub. No one knows but the captain, and the Lord, of course. Well, here we are. Not so far to the shops, is it?"

With a start, Fiona realized she had no idea how they'd arrived in the busy shopping area.

Chapter Twenty-Two

Bavaria, Germany

March 1937

Bad News Travels by Sleigh

Bone weary from yesterday's long journey, Ana struggled to stay asleep. The blankets cocooned her in warmth like when she was a little girl snuggled into her small bed in Grand-mere's cottage. For a while, she floated on the delights of being loved and cared for. Other memories filled her mind. Grand-mere's words came without warning.

"Mon chère, the past is not a place you can stay. Reality has a way of pulling even the unwilling along."

Ana inhaled the smell of frying sausage. She squinted at the early morning light and looked over at her children in time to see the baby reach for a lock of Katrine's hair. It was a tender scene. However, it was quickly followed by the fearful thoughts that had plagued her every waking moment since Father Hugo had put these children in her care. When she was a girl, Grand-mere told her to say her rosary when she was afraid. Ana's hand felt for her rosary. To remember Jesus was to pray. Just as quickly, the "what if" rushed through her mind, drowning out her Hail Marys.

Katrine's hand pushed at the hair in her face, and baby Tony squealed in delight. He never noticed Katrine looked different from everyone else. He had claimed her as his own.

"Lord, protect their hearts from loss." Ana turned to see Gretchen curled into a ball with her thumb in her mouth. Deter slept with his arm protectively encircling his little sister. Ana frowned. How quickly he was losing his childhood. The responsibility of caring for little Gretchen was something Deter felt even in his sleep. Ana rolled her blankets to the foot of her mat and scooped up the baby. "And my little gypsy boy, your nappy needs changing," she whispered against his cheek.

Katrine rubbed sleep from her eyes and smiled at Sister Ana. "Do you want me to do it?"

"No, I'll take care of this imp." She tickled his fat chin, and Tony giggled and pushed at her hand. "You take your time and wake up."

Gretchen and Deter blinked at their surroundings.

"We are in the home of Herr Beckmann," Ana reminded them.

Gretchen sniffed the air. "Something smells good." At least Gretchen could still find delight in life.

Frau Beckmann's sharp call from the foot of the stairs stole their morning peace. "Breakfast will be ready in five minutes. See that you are."

As the days passed, the children loved helping Herr Beckmann with chores in the cow barn. They learned the names of each cow and spoke to them as beloved pets. It was wonderful how a safe bed, good food, and love could right the world. Their laughter was pure joy to Ana. Herr Beckmann seemed to delight in their antics. He let them help feed and even milk the cows. He laughed with them when a young kitten wandered under the belly of Gerty, a gentle black cow. The kitten danced on wobbly hind legs to reach Gerty's udder. Herr Beckmann squirted a stream of milk, knocking the little fur ball over. She lay in the straw, happily licking up the warm milk as she cleaned herself.

Gretchen had secretly named one cantankerous old cow Frau Beckmann. It was hard to scold her. Sister Ana agreed the ill-tempered old cow was a lot like Frau Beckmann but said, "God sees us all as His children. It would hurt His heart to hear you say such a mean thing."

Gretchen's large brown eyes grew teary, and her lip trembled. Instantly, Ana wished she hadn't said a word. She scooped Gretchen up in her arms and hugged her, whispering, "We will ask God to make each Frau Beckmann happier."

It was true Ursel Beckmann grew more sullen by the day. Stony silence was a wall she kept around her. Herr Beckmann said again, by way of an apology for his wife's lack of hospitality, she hadn't been the same since she had lost the baby. But the way Ursel looked at Ana and the children made Ana feel there was something more to the woman's attitude. Ana tried to feel pity for the farmwife and attempted to be friendly and helpful. It only made things more difficult. So she prayed the danger would pass, and they could return to their home at Saint Thomas.

This evening they were all helping feed and milk the cows. The children grew bolder in their play around Herr Beckmann. He encouraged them despite his wife's disapproval. As Ana milked Gerty, she leaned her cheek on the belly of the warm cow and prayed, "Holy Father, please give this gentle man children of his own."

The milking was almost done, and the children were playing with the kittens on the straw-covered floor of the milking barn. Herr Beckmann forked a load of fresh hay from the loft, covering Gretchen and Deter in sweet smelling hay. They squealed in delight and wiggled deeper into the pile. Katrine laughed openly and dove in with the baby still in her arms.

Ana picked up her bucket of fresh milk and emptied it into the milk can, but as she turned to watch their antics, a shower of hay engulfed her. Little heads popped up with round watchful eyes, waiting to see what she would do. Herr Beckmann looked down with the same worried expression. "Sorry, Ana. I didn't see you standing there." He scurried down the ladder and began brushing the straw from her shoulders.

"Oh, that's all right, Herr Beckmann." She turned quickly to scoop up a handful of hay and toss it at the farmer. "The Sisters of Saint Thomas believe in sharing all blessings." Laughing with surprise, Herr Beckmann tossed a handful at Katrine, who threw hands above her head, scattering hay into the air. And the free-for-all was on.

Baby Tony waved his arms wildly, giggling so hard every few seconds he hiccupped. Katrine, for once distracted from her tiny charge, dove through the hay to tickle Deter. When Gretchen rolled into Ana, knocking her over, Herr Beckmann reached down to offer her a hand up. As he stepped forward to brace himself, his feet touched tiny baby toes. A quick step to the side to avoid Tony sent Herr Beckmann tumbling into the pile of hay. They were a jumbled mess of arms and legs when Frau Beckmann suddenly opened the barn door.

"What's wrong, I could hear screaming from the—" Her sentence cut short. She stood for a second staring in disbelief. Ursel drew in her breath, then clamped her mouth shut. It was as if she had sucked in all the happiness and laughter with her breath. Baby Tony took one look at her angry face and wailed.

"Wait, we were only playing..." Klaus Beckmann called after his wife, but she turned on her heel, slamming the door behind her as she left. He turned to Ana with obvious confusion.

"I think you'd better go after her, Herr Beckmann. We will clean up here." The farmer nodded and left without a word. "Come, children, let's clean this up. Katrine, hand me baby Tony," Ana instructed. If laughing was good for the soul, as her Grand-mere had always said, why did they all look so miserable? Katrine handed her the baby, and Ana cuddled him close, patting his back until he settled down. Then she, too, helped restore order to the cow barn.

They shuffled back into the house with downcast eyes. Gretchen said, "We cleaned up our mess, Herr Beckmann."

"Danke, Gretchen." But Klaus still looked miserable. His wife was still angry. She seemed bent on believing the worst of them. They ate dinner in silence. The children looked nervous and afraid. Ana prayed they could return to Saint Thomas soon. She watched for the sleigh and fat little pony to come jogging over the rise above the farm. Her heart longed for the familiar walls of her home, the peaceful hours spent in prayer. If the children needed the safety of routine, she needed it even more.

Ana hurried the children through their evening regimen and spent the quiet time before bed telling them happy stories. They seemed less worried as they drifted off to sleep.

Over the next two days, a tension built between Herr Beckmann and his wife. One afternoon a few days later, the frau returned from the village in a nervous mood. It wasn't so much that she flitted around the house. It was the way her eyes darted from child to child, especially to the baby, that troubled Ana.

Klaus had been busy all day. One of his cows, the one with the chocolate eyes, groaned and bellowed with labor pains. It was the cow's first baby, and she was nervous. Herr Beckmann wanted a quiet barn, but he promised Gretchen they could visit the baby when it was safely in this world. Gretchen drew pictures of baby cows. She and Deter wrote a list of names they should consider. When the farmwife came home, the children looked toward the barn with longing. It had been their refuge.

Frau Beckmann made them hot chocolate. It was a miracle. Only Ana noticed the expectant way she stared out the window. Then it came. At last, the sleigh was here to take them back to the safety of Saint Thomas. Gretchen squealed with delight.

Klaus came out of the barn to greet his brother. The children watched with little noses pushed against the glass. Something was wrong. It was plain this was not a joyful reunion.

Ana looked up at Frau Beckmann. She too watched. Curiously, no one ventured out the door. Bad news was a language everyone understood. Time enough to find out what it was when the men came in. The brothers disappeared into the barn, and the children returned to their hot chocolate. It was a full hour before the men came in the cabin door. Bits of straw and the unpleasant aroma of cow manure came in with them.

Klaus spoke to the children with a forced joyfulness. "The baby is here. You can go see her if you are very quiet and stay well back." He turned to Katrine. "Will you take them out to the barn? I need to talk with Ana."

Katrine looked at Klaus with serious eyes, nodding. If Katrine understood something was wrong, the children were unaware. Deter and Gretchen scrambled into their coats and chattered about girl names. Tony clapped his hands and giggled at their excitement. Within minutes, they were out the door and across the barnyard.

Ana turned her attention to the scene before her. Frau Beckmann was pale and silent. Ana stepped forward to welcome Karl Beckmann.

"It's so good to—"

"Father Hugo is dead." His words were sharp, cutting off anything Ana might have said. "They arrested him four or five days ago. No one knew until he didn't show up for morning mass. We looked for him and found them in his vestry."

"Found who?" Ana willed her voice to be strong.

"Two men. Gestapo. They had torn the room apart, papers everywhere." Karl ran his hands through his hair.

Ana could see his distress. But she felt empty, numb. She needed to know the entire story and waited in silence for him to collect his thoughts.

"They started questioning us. Who were we? Did Father Hugo

preach against Reich doctrines? They took him for questioning. The men asked us about you, sister, and the children. How could they know? But they do know about all of you. Your names, descriptions"—he stepped forward—"but not where you are. They would have arrested me right away. When they left, they put up a notice on the church door. It said Father Hugo had died of natural causes, and the church was being confiscated by the order of The Gestapo Headquarters, signed by an Eric Braun. I went back to my farm until I was sure no one was watching me."

Ursel sharply drew in her breath. "I told you not to take them in. Not to get involved. You wouldn't listen to me. What you've done is treason. They could arrest us. Mein Gott, we could lose everything. For what?"

Klaus gave Ana an embarrassed glance. "Shut up, Ursel. We have to think about what to do."

"What to do? Listen to you. All you think about is this woman and her brats. As if they belonged to you. They are trying to take everything. Can't you see? The way the Jew girl climbs on your lap for a story. The boy. Do you see the way he looks at me? He might murder us in our sleep."

Klaus looked at the ceiling as if asking God to calm his temper. But his face had become a dark red. "They are children, just children. Why do you hate them?" His anguish was visible.

"They are Jews, Gypsies, Untermenschen and whores." She spat the words at Ana.

Klaus slapped Ursel with such force she staggered backwards. Her hand covered the redness already showing on her cheek. It happened without warning. This kind, gentle man stared down at his own hand as if it had acted without permission. He moved again toward Ursel with compassion and comfort in his eyes.

Her face twisted in a mask of rage. "You'll regret that."

"I'm sorry. I know you don't mean what you're saying. It was so unthinkable."

"It was unthinkable you put us in such danger. I had to do

something." She glanced again at the window as sleigh bells broke the silence.

"Ursel, what did you do?" He considered her for a long moment before going through the door as the sleigh pulled to a stop. A friendly greeting floated in the cold air. Ana let out her breath. A neighbor? The door swung closed. Karl, Ursel and Ana stood there waiting for Klaus to return. He was back within a few minutes, his face again a deep shade of red. He spoke to his brother. "We have no time to lose. She complained about our guests to everyone in the village. I'm so sorry, Sister Ana. I didn't know she would betray you."

"Betray... Did you say betray?" Ursel said. "You've been betraying me with this whore for days. But I'll let officials know I had nothing to do with this. It was all you and your brother."

Ursel flinched as his hand shot out once more, but this time he pointed his finger in her face. It shook with the power of restraint. "Ursel, you fool. You've doomed us all. If I'm taken, you will be too. Haven't you heard of Reich policy regarding enemies of the government? They consider their whole family guilty."

Klaus turned back to Ana. "This Eric Braun is in the village. My friend came to warn me. He's visiting many of our neighbors and asking questions." He turned to glare at Ursel once more. "It seems there is a rumor about a woman and a group of children begging shelter near our village." Ursel shrank. "My wife's been complaining to our village grocer about all the food we need to feed unwelcome guests. Our grocer is a known town gossip." Klaus narrowed his eyes at his wife. "And everything you said will get back to Herr Braun. You can be sure of that. We need to move quickly."

Ana found her voice at last. "Saint Mary's Convent is in Kempten. I know the Mother Superior there. She'll give us shelter."

The chatter from the children announced their return from the barn. Ana hardly had time to collect herself as they tumbled through the door. She welcomed them and waited through their chatter about the new baby cow. "I've a big surprise for you. We're going on another adventure today."

"Where are we going?" Deter looked suspicious. Gretchen whined. "Will there be baby cows and kittens there too?"

"Katrine." Ana touched her arm and implored her with a look not to ask questions. "Can you take the children to the loft to pack their things and put on warmer clothing for traveling?"

Klaus made coffee. Ursel had not recovered her previous bravado. She started preparing dinner as if everything were back to normal. Ana wondered if Ursel was frightened or if she was glad to be rid of them all.

They decided Karl must return home without delay. Ursel protested when Klaus volunteered to take the children to Kempten.

"Can't Karl take them? Why do you have to go?"

A glare from her husband cut off her words of protest. He spat out, "I don't know who you are, Ursel. I need time to think. I will take them."

Within an hour, the children ate a quick meal and bundled into Klaus' family sleigh. He had two fine draft horses to pull for him, which especially pleased Gretchen. She announced Berta and Francs were her friends. Leaving without a word to his wife, Herr Beckmann drove the sleigh over the rise above his farm.

In the gathering darkness, they saw headlights from a lone car making its way up the road from the valley. Ana was sure Klaus had seen this as well, but he didn't turn back for his bride.

Chapter Twenty-Three

Edinburgh
March 1937

I'll Never Desert You

Fiona turned as she surveyed her uncle's bedroom. A thought struck her. *Uncle Hugh wouldn't have given it to me if he wanted it sold. He wanted me here.* A smile spread across her face.

She spoke to the ceiling and walls. "I'll sell every scrap of furnishings before I sell this house. I'll never desert you." The house didn't answer back, but after the ghost horses, she wouldn't be surprised if it had.

As she strolled through her house, Fiona embraced ownership. *I love the sound of that—my house.* She polished the dusty ornate gilt mirror in the entry hall, wondering if it was old enough to be an antique and valuable or just old.

Two oak double doors stood closed on either side of the hall. *I want to open all the doors and look in every room.* Her first venture was the double doors on her left. She flung them open to enter a Victorian drawing room. Gold-fringed swags pulled the heavy burgundy drapes back. Beautifully carved panels framed the bowed-out front window on each side. Fiona reached out to pull what appeared to be a handle in the woodwork. The panel slid to cover half the front window. Intrigued, she found a similar handle on the other side, pulling it along until the entire front window disappeared behind the paneling, plunging the room into darkness. When opened they stood to the side, looking for all the world like part of the wall.

Fiona decided this must be a sitting room. A burgundy oriental rug covered the wood plank floors. The walls were a pale gold with white crown molding and a white carved fireplace. Dark cherry furniture crowded the room. The thought struck her. *I should make a list of items I could sell. When I do, I can draw from here without detracting from its charm.* Dust covered everything. *I'll have to make the list as I clean. That way, I'll see each piece dusted off. It should give me a better idea about their value.*

Back in the entry, Fiona opened the other set of doors and peered into the dark room. *That's all right. Now I know your secret.* With enough light from the hall beyond, she found the panels covering the windows. Fiona pulled the wood shutters aside and turned to see her library.

"Oh," she gasped, "this is a beautiful room." Books filled the shelves of three walls, crowding close to the fireplace. She picked up the silver-framed photograph of a lovely young woman from the mantel. *It's not Mum. It must be at least twenty years ago from her dress. I wonder if this was Uncle's wife. It must have been devastating to lose her and the wee bairn.* She set the photograph back in its place.

This room looked used. It wasn't as dusty as the sitting room. *Did you spend time here reading and sometimes looking at her?* The room was a peaceful light blue with comfortable chairs and two settees.

Fiona sighed. Her thoughts turned melancholy as she wandered down the hall under the stairs, past a bathroom, and into a butler's pantry. She wondered about the china and silver she'd noticed on her first day. *Some of this must have value.* Fiona picked up a plate and wiped off a layer of dust. A blue Chinese design covered the white plate, with blue roses along the edge. "So pretty." *Mum must have eaten off these.* Fiona straightened her back and reined in her emotions. *Of course she had. And she sat in all the chairs and read the books, but that doesn't change the fact I need to sell enough to keep the house until I can find work.* The enormity of finding work to support this big old house wasn't lost on her. What balanced her from falling into despair was a sense that she belonged here. In this house. It gave her hope everything would somehow work out.

From the pantry, she pushed open a large door and found the formal dining room. It was pale gold and linked to the sitting room by yet another set of double doors which slid to the side. The rooms were alike, right down to a second fireplace. The painting of a young woman hung on the wall above the mantel. It was quite good. *So, you weren't always poor, were you, Uncle? Perhaps that's what made it so hard later.*

She turned back to the kitchen. It was fast becoming one of her favorite places with its large wooden table in the center where she ate and did her planning. The black cast-iron gas stove worked like a gem. But it was the enormous fireplace against one wall that made it so homey. Fiona walked over and touched the swing-out rack for roasting. *I'd like to try roasting over a flame if I ever have money to buy something big enough.* She frowned. *Or have someone to roast it for.*

The kitchen was the hub of the house. From here she could go back to her uncle's bedroom or take the stairs down to the cellar or up to the next floor. She stood for a moment looking up the narrow servants' staircase. Five bedrooms and a bathroom up there. Fiona opened the cellar door and looked down the dark stairs, shaking her head. Not yet. *I'll look down there later.*

Instead, she walked past a small mudroom and out the back door into the kitchen garden. *The house is so big, and that's only the first floor.* Her excitement dimmed. *It's overwhelming.* Ideas of what she might do with this big old house came to mind, but nothing seemed plausible.

When Mum had a decision to make, she always cleaned something. I expect I'll have plenty of time to think.

It took her half the week to clean the first floor, the longest time spent in her Uncle Hugh's bedroom. It was crowded with furniture. Fiona pulled out her list, writing down all the pieces she could sell, but she excluded the old desk from the list. It dominated the room. Instead of treasures, the desk was full of receipts for expenses—discouraging but making her list even more important.

She made a pile of receipts for the house, coal and other necessaries. She'd have to start her own ledger, and these would help her understand her new expenses.

Then she pulled all his personal receipts into another pile. It told her Uncle Hugh spent little on his own needs and not very much on the house. She looked up as a thought dawned on her. *You were poor as a church mouse, and you stayed here.*

She heard the words of Thomas Frazer: "Your uncle made some investments, not all of them wise." *No wonder you didn't send for me. You thought you had nothing to offer.*

"But that's not true, Uncle. We were family. That's more than enough for me." *How long were you like this? Was it embarrassment or pride that made you feel you couldn't reach out to your own sister?* Fiona spoke out loud. "Mum wouldn't have cared, either." *I'm sure of it. It's just who she was.*

Her mind went back to meeting the lawyer. Could be the old sourpuss didn't want another poor neighbor. Then she thought of Rab MacKenzie. *Well, money isn't everything, is it?* Her inner voice whispered back, *You still need it to keep this place.*

Fiona cleaned the house from early morning until she climbed exhausted into her bed every night. Her list was growing, and she was feeling more hopeful.

On the second floor, her bedroom and the bathroom were

already clean, but she hadn't touched the other four bedrooms. She scrubbed her way up the main staircase and worked her way to the back of the house. On the other side of the landing from hers was a large, beautiful room. The walls were a mint green with drapes and bedding in a deep royal blue. She ran her hand down the wood on the poster-bed. Even with all the dust, you could see the rich, dark cherry wood underneath. *Whose room were you? My grandparents?* With every room she cleaned, Fiona thought about who might have lived there.

As she passed the attic door, cold air brushed her skin, sending a shiver down her spine. She put out her hand to feel a slight breeze. "Hmm, an open window?"

She pulled the door open and peered up the narrow stairway. Worn stairs led to a big room filled with boxes and old furniture. Fiona could see her own footprints on the dusty, wood-plank floors. *No one's been up here in a very long time.*

She stood in the bright light coming from windows lining one wall of the room. Ivy grew through two broken windowpanes and up the wall. *There's my spooky draft. Must have been like that for quite a while.*

Her eyes traced the green vines up the old stone wall. It gave her an odd sense of decay and abandonment. Along the far wall, several doors stood ajar. She entered one to find only the basics—an old wooden bed frame, a chest and little else. *Must have been used as servants quarters.* From the view from the window, she realized she must be over her own bedroom.

She turned back to the main room with a sigh. *What a mess to clean.* She felt goosebumps on her bare arms. *Those broken windowpanes will need to be repaired and soon.*

A glint of gold caught her eye. The edge of a large, ornate picture frame wedged between several other wooden frames.

"Hello, you look promising." When liberated from its hiding place, the old painting was at least three feet by four. The top edge of the frame looked as if someone had wiped it clean, which seemed unlikely. The rest of the paintings were covered in a grey shroud of dust and cobwebs. Without thinking about why, she worked to free the painting from the surrounding frames. It seemed important to get the old painting out of the attic. Using her dust rags to protect the bottom edge of the frame, she pulled it back down the stairs. On the hallway floor, she leaned the picture against the wall, wiping the frame and canvas until the painting was visible.

Her pulse quickened as an image of a man stared back at her. *Must be ancient. His clothing and hair… yes, this is an old painting.* There was something about him. *He's so interesting. No, what he's interested in is more the point. He's intense. Alive.*

Hair tied back at the nape of his neck. Like hers, it was long, curly, and very black. He looked well-built and muscled. Intelligent eyes looked back at her, so full of life. Not kind but not snobbish either. He was a handsome man, with a long nose and a firm chin. No expensive dress here. *If you're having such a fine painting done, why dress like a buccaneer?* The thought struck her with an invisible blow. *This is the Black Captain.*

Chapter Twenty-Four

Kempten, Germany
March 1937

Saved by a Fallen Angel

The ride from the mountain farm to Kempten had been long and silent. At first, the silence was full of anger. Klaus looked like a granite statue, his mouth set in a grim expression. Ana tried several times to talk with him about Ursel, but her words seemed to hang in the cold air. She concluded he needed to work out things on his own. Later, she noticed his eyebrows pulled together in concern. He asked his horses for more speed.

Even in mid-March, the roads were covered with snow, and the little sleigh traveled easily. Traffic was light. A mile or two from the convent, a long caravan of canvas-covered box trucks sped past. Military vehicles. The last truck swerved to maneuver around them. Its back curtain blew to the side. Men with guns filled the covered area.

Klaus looked at Ana. "I didn't know it was like this down here." His eyes drifted back to the hills they'd come from. It wasn't difficult to guess Klaus wanted to get back to his wife. On their little farm, they were far removed from modern Germany. Ana felt it, too. *So this is what we rescued the children from. This is what Father Hugo gave his life to protect them from.* She'd heard about what was happening, but knowing and seeing for yourself were two different things. This was real. Threatening.

In Kempten, soldiers walked the streets with rifles slung over their shoulders. The sleigh passed people being stopped by black-uniformed men. Ana looked at the children. Their eyes were round with terror.

The Church of Saint Mary's was just ahead. "Go around to the back," she instructed Klaus. When they came to the large iron gates of the convent, Ana turned to the children once more. "Remember the game. I am your Aunt Ana, and we are traveling on vacation. If we play the game well, we will be safe." She turned to Katrine. "You are?"

"I am your helper hired to care for the children," Katrine answered with a steady voice.

"The one who always meets the handsome gentleman in those novels you've been reading." Katrine laughed a little, and the children seemed to take up the game.

"I know the Mother Superior. She's a kind woman and will give us shelter." Ana touched the farmer's muscular arm. "You shouldn't wait for us. We will be safe within these walls. And I think you need to get back as soon as you can." His face was relieved, but he hesitated still.

"Please help me get the children out of the sleigh," Ana added, asking, "What will you do?"

"I don't know, but I shouldn't have left her." The anguish on his face broke Ana's heart. "I don't think she thought things through. She's been a good wife."

Klaus secured the horses and gently lifted Gretchen out of her seat. Deter jumped down beside her. Ana scooped up baby Tony as Klaus gave Katrine a hand down. He looked at each of the children for a long minute. Little Gretchen reached for a hug. Klaus gave her a bear hug, and she giggled, but when he set her down, tears filled his eyes.

"Go with God," he said, and he was on his way.

Panic closed Ana's throat. She wanted to call Klaus back. Instead, she took a deep breath and surveyed her little tribe. Bundled in the sleigh, they'd looked like a mountain family come down to do shopping. The children were so covered from head to toe in coats, scarves and hats, you couldn't tell they weren't pure Aryan children. She nodded her approval and whispered, "We go with God." She pulled the old bell rope next to the gate and gave each child a quick straightening as she waited.

The sound of boots on cobblestones drew her attention. A soldier was approaching the gate from inside the grounds. "Remember the game." Ana steadied her emotions and tried to breathe easy. When the man challenged her, she explained she was looking for the Sisters of Saint Mary's Convent. She searched the soldier's boyish face. His eyes weren't hard even though his voice was abrupt.

"The convent is now the property of the Reich." He leaned forward to look more closely at Ana. "You have business with the commander or someone inside?" He seemed concerned.

"No, no. Only, I once attended this school and wanted my sister's children to see it."

"No one may enter unless they are on official business. You are perhaps visiting someone in town?"

Thankfully, baby Tony fussed. "Sorry to bother you," Ana said. "It seems we need to get the baby back for his dinner. Come along, children. We must hurry home."

She called a thank you over her shoulder and marched off at a brisk pace. She could feel eyes on her back, but no one called out for them to stop. It was not until she rounded the corner that Ana cast a glance behind them. No one had followed. Her relief only lasted a moment.

Where do I take them now? God, do you see us? We need your help, or we will perish. This evil will scoop your little ones up.

There were so many men in uniform. She tried to walk with purpose, look like she was going somewhere. Ahead of them, the soldiers were stopping everyone to check their papers. A man in a black uniform pushed a woman to the ground and held her down with one foot. No one made eye contact. Hands went into coats and documents were produced. It began to rain, and heads tucked into scarves, faces turned down.

Surely, God has sent the rain. To her right, a small alley opened up between the buildings. Ana led the children down to the back wall. They huddled under an awning next to some rubbish cans. Water dripped from Ana's wet hair onto little Gretchen's head. The baby whimpered. A door opened on the brick wall next to them.

There wasn't even time to pray. A woman stepped into the alley with a bag of papers in her hand. She was tall with golden blond hair. Her features were aristocratic. Even in the pale light, she had a flawless complexion with bright red lips. She stopped short of the cans when the baby whimpered. She stood there staring into Ana's eyes and then studied each of the children. *Should we run? Make up some kind of story about what we are doing hiding next to her trash cans?*

The woman moved toward them, reaching out her hand to little Gretchen. Deter held Gretchen's arm back.

"Come with me," she commanded. She smiled down at Gretchen and scooped the child into her arms, disappearing back through the doorway.

They followed her down a dark hallway and emerged into a warm, well-lit kitchen. A bulky woman stood with her back to them, scrubbing pots at the kitchen sink. Her rolled-up sleeves revealed muscular arms. She might have been a man except for the dark braids and her beautiful soprano voice. She sang a sweet hymn.

"I wish I could sing like that," Gretchen said. Her own sweet voice was full of admiration.

The woman at the sink dropped her pan. Bubbles splashed into the air as she turned toward them. She stood looking at the children and locked eyes with their rescuer. By some pre-arranged plan, she moved with remarkable speed to open a door. They descended some stairs into a cellar crowded with wine bottles and old cases. The door closed soundlessly behind them.

There was music again upstairs but not the beautiful hymn. A radio played traditional Bavarian music. It was loud but not unpleasant. No one spoke. They stood there in the dark, waiting. The tall woman set Gretchen down and reached to the back of an old wardrobe. They heard, more than saw, a door open. A match flared, revealing a small room. Their hostess lit a lantern and stepped into the wardrobe, beckoning them to follow.

"My name is Madam Leona, and this is my house. Let's get the children settled, and then you can tell me your story."

Chapter Twenty-Five

Edinburgh
March 1937

Tea with Rab

Fiona pulled the tray of scones from the oven. The smell of baking filled her kitchen. They would make a fine afternoon tea. It'd been over two weeks since she'd arrived at Latimer Square, and she'd spent most of that time trying to put her house in order. Earlier, she asked Rab if he'd come for a wee visit. On cue, the heavy door knocker announced his arrival. *It's wonderful to find a friend to visit with.*

They sat at the kitchen table. Rab was full of stories about her uncle, and she feasted on every word. When he stopped to have another scone, Fiona said, "I have a surprise for you. I've been so excited since I found this on the top floor. I pulled it all the way down here to show you." She stood to lift a covering off the painting and waited for Rab's reaction.

He rose and came closer to examine the portrait. "That be the captain. Found him in the attic, did ye?"

"A few days ago, I found this in a pile of old frames on the top floor. They were all covered in dust, but this one looked like someone had just polished the edge of the frame."

Rab stroked his chin and said, "A fine old painting. I'm sure it would fetch a good price if you've a mind to sell it."

There was something about the captain that drew her. She felt connected to him. She said, "Oh no, I couldn't sell him. He's family, and there's something about him. I know it sounds silly, but every time I passed those stairs to the attic, I was drawn and a little afraid at the same time."

She blushed, feeling very foolish as she poured more tea in their cups. "He looks so lifelike. I know what my da would say, but do you believe in ghosts?"

Rab considered her words. "Well, I'm not so sure, but we live in an old country, and some places feel so full of history. Sometimes I can hear the claymores clash, and clan battle cries seem to vibrate in the surrounding air." Rab was a Highlander. His eyes burned with the love of his land.

He settled himself in his chair, turning his clear blue eyes on Fiona. "What I believe is the Lord has a purpose for you and this hoose."

She smiled at the portrait. *I'm glad I found the captain, but if I'm supposed to be here, maybe he found me.* She took another sip of tea. There was the rub, as Da would say. *What is my purpose?* The thought lingered until Rab cleared his throat.

"Do you know how you'll keep the hoose?"

"I've made a list of everything salable—at least things I can part with. If I can find a buyer, I'll have enough to keep me going for a while. Would you take a look and tell me what you think?" She slid a piece of paper across the table.

"Aye, sure." Rab pulled out a pair of ancient spectacles, scanning the list. A smile pulled at the corners of his mouth. He slapped the paper with the back of his hand. "I know just the chap who would jump at the chance to buy some of the older pieces."

Fiona laughed with relief.

"Neville Smythe, he's English but a nice bloke all the same. Runs an antique shop in Old Town. His customers are all in money. He'll snap these up. I can have him call round for a visit. Give you an estimate."

She reached across the table to touch his arm. "Thank you so much. Can I ask for one more thing? Will you come with him? It would mean a lot to me."

"It would be my honor."

Chapter Twenty-Six

Latimer Square
Edinburgh
March 1937

Ready for a Fight

Laurie patted the formal contract in his breast pocket. Marguerite's father had made him a generous proposal which he'd signed without hesitation.

He stepped out Herr Voss's front door. Even with the bright sun, the wind was sharp. The afternoon air had a bite. He took the stairs to the street and set course for home. A stiff breeze threatened to pull his fedora off, so he jammed it low over his brow and turned up his collar. His frown deepened. *Why the hell am I uneasy?* But there was still one hurdle to climb over. *Rab's going to blow his bonnet.*

He set a brisk pace toward Latimer Square. *One thing is certain; Rab won't take this well.* The thought annoyed him. *Herr Voss thinks better of me than my grandfather. Voss values excellent engineers. I'll be starting in a top position with top money. Rab will change his mind when I send him my fat pay packet. Don't guess he will say I should have worked my way up from the bottom.*

Laurie shook his head. He knew the money wouldn't sway his grandfather. "Money from the devil himself." Rab's very words the last time they'd talked about the possibility of a job in Germany. By the time Laurie reached Latimer Square, he was ready for a good fight. Eager to get it over with, he took the front stairs two at a time. The door opened into a silent house. He called out, but the old man didn't answer.

It was only after a quick search he found the note his grandfather left on the kitchen table. "I've gone for tea with Fiona."

I don't know what she sees in Rab. If she's some kind of gold digger... The thought trailed off, stuck in his jumbled emotions. *Haven't I done the same thing, taking a job from my girl's father?* He shook it away. *Well, this Fiona can afford to keep her old place even less than we can afford this one. At least our fortunes are about to change. If only Rab could see the possibilities.*

Laurie wanted to tell Rab and be done with this waiting. He stormed into the study and peered out the front window. *How long could afternoon tea last?*

He plopped down in Rab's favorite chair. *Rab's likely to repeat all the things he's hearing about Germany. But it's all propaganda, gossip and politics. The world is jealous of all Herr Hitler's been able to accomplish. In a few months' time, I'll be able tell Rab how wrong he was.*

When the study door opened, it took Laurie by surprise. Rab had a relaxed, cheerful expression on his face.

"Home early. You'll get overheated sitting there in yer overcoat. I've had my tea with yon Fiona, but I can rustle you up something if you've time."

Words failed to come as planned. Laurie stood and pulled the job offer from his pocket. He handed it to the old man. Rab's smile faded as he read. "So soon?" His eyes were bright when he looked up at his grandson. "Yer mind's made up?"

Laurie gave a curt nod. His grandfather handed the document

back. But instead of the argument Laurie had expected, the older man put his hand on Laurie's shoulder. Rab locked eyes with his grandson. His feelings were all there on his face. They were easy enough to read. They spoke volumes of disappointment, but there was love there, too. "I'll gee ye some tea then." Rab headed to the kitchen.

Laurie watched his grand-da walk away. *I'll never understand Rab.* He scrubbed his hands over his face as frustration washed over him. *I need a stiff drink.* Instead, Laurie stepped outside, pausing on the steps to light his cigarette. A movement at the end of the square caught his eye. There she was, pulling up weeds in the small front garden. It would take a lot more than a tidy garden to bring the old house back to life.

The wind died, and the sun shone warm again on his back. Not sure why, he strolled toward her. She looked up. Her smile started with her full mouth and sparkled from her warm brown eyes. Light glinted off her black hair. Curls escaped her long braid, falling about her face. Laurie found it hard to breathe. She was beautiful.

She rose and brushed her hand on her skirt, extending it in greeting. "You probably don't remember me. I'm Fiona MacDonald. Alec introduced us a few weeks ago."

He colored with embarrassment at the memory of Marguerite's comments about Alec's choice of a country girl for a dinner partner. Marguerite was stunning, sophisticated, but the young woman before him had an innocent beauty.

"You know, you should take Alec's father up on his offer to sell the place for you." It was out before he had time to think. But she extended her hand in greeting. When he reached out, he received a firm handshake. While her expression was still friendly, Laurie read determination and strength in her steady gaze.

"I can't give it up," she said. "It's all I have of my family on this side of the world."

He understood. Looking back over his shoulder at his home,

he nodded. It was all he had left of his parents. *Maybe that's why Rab never suggested they get into a smaller place.*

"I know what you mean about the house and family. Rab's all I have left of my family."

When he looked back at Fiona, he realized he still had her hand. It felt good in his. He let go. Heat crept into his cheeks. He shuffled his feet, wondering if he should walk away. "Say, I think I owe you an apology for the other night. I'm afraid I wasn't friendly."

"That's all right. I must have looked like a country girl to your friend. She was beautiful."

His embarrassment grew. "It's nice of you to spend time with my grandfather." *Not sure why I said that but guess it's true.* "I'm guilty of neglecting him." *That's true too.* "He likes you."

"I value his friendship. We get along well."

Guess you would. "We've been at odds." Laurie scratched the back of his neck.

Her quiet, steady gaze made her so easy to talk to. Or maybe it was the fact that he wasn't ready to walk away. Laurie sat on her steps and started a conversation. He told her things he would never share with a stranger. He told her about his struggle with his grandfather. "I wish we were more alike."

She stifled a laugh. "He was just saying how like him you are."

Astonished Rab would make such a claim, Laurie said, "Not in a million years."

She cocked her head to the side, squinting a bit as she regarded him. "My da always said we get the most annoyed with people who remind us of ourselves."

"Your father sounds like a philosopher." He didn't want to contemplate her insight.

"Close, he was a pastor."

Laurie almost rolled his eyes. *Another do-gooder. Now I know why grandfather likes her. Wonder if he told her to pray for his wayward grandson.*

Fiona was saying, "Your grandfather is so proud of your success at university. He says you have spirit and courage and aren't afraid of hard work."

Astonished, Laurie said, "No, he didn't say that."

She laughed. "Why, Mr. MacKenzie, you question the word of a pastor's daughter?" She had dimples and even with her black hair, her skin was pale, freckled over her nose.

He cleared his throat, realizing he wasn't responding to her jest, but his tone was serious when he said, "You're different from what I expected."

"Different bad or different good?" She was squinting with the sun in her eyes, so he shifted his position to cast a shadow over her face.

"I'm not sure yet, just different." He watched for her reaction, but she didn't seem perturbed with his frankness. She dusted her skirt off and came to sit with him. They talked about everything. She told him about her parents' deaths and her three years in Canada. How she didn't fit in.

Laurie answered with his struggle to fit in after his parents died. "I guess school became my niche, but I always felt I had to prove I was as good as anyone else. Guess I was pretty angry about losing both of them." He realized she'd suffered a similar loss. "Sorry, that was insensitive."

"It's all right. I was angry too, yelled at God. Not so much now. I feel like I've been given back something. My mother grew up here. I'm sleeping in her room; some of her clothes are next to mine in the closet. It's like having her with me." A look of such loss and love passed over her face as she added, "At least a little."

"I can see why you want to keep the place. I can tell you it's hard without a good income." His eyes strayed to Alec's house. She followed his gaze.

"Well, money isn't everything."

He shook his head. "You sound like Rab." But he couldn't help smiling at her misguided innocence. "It sure makes everything easier."

Laurie told her how much he wanted to get ahead. He was tired of only scraping by on his small inheritance. He told her about the job he was taking in Germany. She didn't judge. She listened. Those soft brown eyes seemed to see into his heart. They spent a good hour there before Fiona shivered, and he realized he was keeping her outside. Laurie looked at the sky. Grey clouds were rolling in. The wind had picked up again. Rab's tea would be stone cold by now.

"I'm keeping you sitting out here in the cold."

"No, not at all. I feel like we've taken time to get to know each other. Friends?"

Laurie nodded. "I rarely tell strangers about my life...so yes, friends. You should get in out of the cold." She bent to pick up the forgotten bucket of weeds. He reached down to pick it up first.

She laughed. "That's pretty empty. I think I can handle it."

"Hope we can talk again soon, friend."

"I'd like that, friend."

Chapter Twenty-Seven

Kempten, Germany
March 1937

Angels Come with Cookies

Madam Leona held the lantern high, casting light into a hidden room. She motioned again for Ana and the children to follow. Ana looked around the small room as they crowded into the center. No window, a little table with several old chairs, a sink and a commode behind a curtain. Bunks lined two walls. Something else—she couldn't hear the music. She realized, "This is a room made for hiding people."

The tall woman encouraged Ana. "Quite right. You will all be safe here." Madam Leona set the lantern on the table and turned to leave. "I'll be back soon."

Ana felt the tension drain from her body. "God has sent us an angel to keep us safe. Let's thank him." They reached out to take each other's hands and closed their eyes. "Thank you, Father, for how well you take care of your children."

"Do you think our angel has food for us?"

Gretchen always thought of her stomach. Just now, Ana agreed.

"Let's hope she brings us bread and soup."

"Cookies would be good, too."

Ana laughed. "Yes, thank you, Father, for cookies." Ana crossed herself as she closed the prayer. With a sigh, she turned to the children and said, "Let's get out of our coats and get settled." Baby Tony had fallen asleep. They laid him on a bottom bunk.

The wardrobe door opened, and the large cook came in with a pot and some bowls. The room filled with a wonderful aroma. She set the pot of chicken soup on the table and put a finger to her lips. She left again but only for a moment. When she returned, her arms were full of bread. Still, she balanced a pitcher of milk on her hip. The children were all smiles. One more trip through the magic door and back again with cookies and a bottle of warm milk for the baby.

Closing the door, she said, "It's safe to talk. When the door is open, your voices might carry, but with the door closed, even the baby's cry won't reach upstairs."

Ana clapped her hands together. "You're just what we prayed for."

"Well, I've never been told that." The cook chuckled. "My name is Dorcus."

Everything about this woman reminded Ana of her own grand-mere. It was almost too much to bear. Relief flooded her eyes, and her reply caught in her throat. "I'm Ana, and the children are Katrine, Deter and Gretchen, and baby Tony."

"Are you an angel, too?" Gretchen asked. "You sing like one."

Dorcus bent and spoke at Gretchen's level. Her voice was warm with delight. "No, dear, but God whispered in my ear that little girls need cookies with their bread and soup."

Gretchen looked up at Deter. "I told you God listens to me."

Ana laughed and said, "I think you are an angel."

An hour later, even baby Tony was fed and changed and put

back to sleep. Dorcus left and returned with a pot of tea and two cups.

"I thought you might have a lot of questions and we could chat over a cup of tea. Madam Leona had an unexpected visitor. It will be safer if she waits until morning before she returns."

"You've done this kind of thing before?" Ana gestured to the surrounding room.

"Before I answer, I need to hear your story. For one thing, your hair is very short. Can you tell me why?" Her question was very serious.

Ana hesitated, weighing her risks. *If they meant to do harm, they wouldn't have taken us in.* She said, "I am a Franciscan sister. I was serving at Saint Thomas, a small parish near Mittenwald. We were taking in children and trying to place them with parishioners. These children were harder to place.

"Katrine is the adopted daughter of missionaries in China. Nazis took her parents for questioning. They never returned.

"Gretchen and Deter—"

"They are Jews," Dorcus said. "I'm afraid there is no mistaking that." If her words were a judgment, her face and voice remained kind.

"Yes. Deter is very protective, but God gave Gretchen a trusting heart." Ana's eyes caressed the sleeping children.

"The baby?"

"He is Romani. Left in a pew and found after Mass." There was sadness in Ana's voice. At first, her words were guarded, but as she looked into the older woman's eyes, she saw her pain reflected. Every detail of their journey poured out of her heart. And something more. Grief for Father Hugo. For Herr Beckmann and his wife. Fear of failing the children. Failing God. And, though she knew the risk of being put out on the streets again, she shared her certainty that someone was hunting them.

Dorcus leaned in to touch Ana's arm. "You are saying you think an SS officer is following you?"

Ana nodded, tears flooding her eyes. She put her hand up to wipe them away. "I haven't told the children. We got word while we were staying with the farmer. They said Father Hugo was— that is—he died of natural causes during interrogation. I don't think that's true, unless they pushed him so hard his heart couldn't handle it. They were questioning him about a rumor he was hiding children.

"Why would they care about us? We are insignificant." She paused, shaking her head. "They are only children." She turned to look at the sleeping forms. "They're so beautiful, especially when they're sleeping." She lingered on them for a moment, drinking in their sweetness, but her body began trembling.

Dorcus reached across the table, taking Ana's hand and pulling her into a warm embrace. It had been a long time since she'd felt the comfort this woman gave her. For the first time in weeks, she let the emotions come unguarded. As they came to the surface, she gave them to this stranger.

Ana loved the children. They felt like her own. The need to protect them went far beyond a sense of duty. She cried, surrendering her burdens to this kindly woman, if only for a minute.

When she pulled back, Dorcus handed her a hankie. Tears clouded the older woman's eyes as well. Her voice was husky with emotion.

"There are things you should know." She cleared her throat and continued. "You are right about this room. Madam and the ladies have been using it to help smuggle out people since the stormtroopers came to town. We have helped twenty souls to safety," she added with pride. "We can do this for you and the children. It will take time and planning, but we will do our best for you. You must do your best for us."

Ana nodded, but Dorcus looked her in the eye and said, "This is a house of pleasure."

When Ana didn't react, Dorcus pressed her meaning. "It is an expensive brothel. You know the meaning?"

Ana drew in a sharp breath, heat climbing up her cheeks, but she understood.

"We entertain officers, so the children will stay downstairs in the afternoons after three. We have early callers, so even when the children come upstairs, they must keep to the kitchen. This is most important. You must understand. God uses who he chooses, but these women are my family. Any mistake could cost all of us our lives."

Chapter Twenty-Eight

Latimer Square

Edinburgh

April 1937

A Plan to Keep the House

A week ago, Laurie was irritated that his grandfather was spending so much time with their new neighbor. Today Laurie was helping her repair the back door while listening to her plans to sell furniture and the family china in an effort to hold on to this broken-down old house. *Impractical, doomed to fail. But here I am helping her repair it. I want her to stay in the house. I feel like she belongs here. Odd, I don't remember when I changed my mind.*

"If I tell you something, promise not to laugh?" Fiona's expression was so serious.

Laurie inclined his head in an effort to keep from smiling.

"My father would say, 'Look for God in everything, good and bad.' I'm here in this old house for a reason. It's scary, and there have been things I can't explain." She stopped and bit her lip. "Well, let's say this house has its own personality."

He smiled too, but it faded with the thought, *If grandfather said something like that, I'd put it off to the ramblings of an old Highlander full of superstition. No, I'd be angry with him.*

"Is there a problem?" Fiona asked.

Laurie realized he was scowling. *Grandfather used to say my thoughts were written on my face. I'll have to work on that.*

"No, I'm finishing up." He opened and closed the door several times. "I think that should do it."

"Thank you." Fiona beamed. "Do you have time for a cup of tea? My biscuits are out of the oven."

"I was hoping you'd ask. I've been smelling them for the last quarter of an hour. Rab says you've quite a bit to sell." Laurie washed up in the big kitchen sink. She handed him a towel. "Our kitchen is much the same as this. It was always my favorite room."

"I know what you mean." Fiona hesitated. "Would you like to see my treasures? I've pulled everything into the sitting room. Your grandfather is bringing his friend by on Friday."

Laurie finished with the towel and was rolling down his shirt-sleeves as he followed her to the front of the house. She opened the double doors to the sitting room and stepped back.

"Sensational." He looked around the room. "You have some bonnie things here." Laurie wandered around, studying what appeared to be family heirlooms.

"Rab's going to help value my things."

He caught the slight change in her—a momentary frown and new lines between her brows. *Must be hard letting go of family history before she's settled.* Laurie picked up a dirk. He unsheathed the knife and examined the blade. "This has beautiful engraving. Is it old?"

She shrugged. "I don't know." She looked around the room and turned back when Laurie said, "Say, what's this?"

He pulled a gilt frame from behind the settee. "This should bring a good price."

Her expression clouded. "I've changed my mind. I was going

to sell him." Her eyes locked on those of the man in the portrait. "But no, he stays. He belongs here."

Laurie couldn't help smiling at how serious she was. "He's a relative? He doesn't look a thing like you. Of course, it could be the mustache."

She chuckled. "Well, thank you. But there is something about him. He looks so real. I look at him, and I see..." She hesitated.

"Go on. What do you see?" Laurie asked.

"His—his eyes hold me. Like he knows who I am. There is a hardness in them but a fairness, too." She exhaled. "I'm not crazy. I like him."

A blush settled over her face, and her innocence touched his heart.

She went on saying, "He was quite infamous from what Rab tells me. They called him the Black Captain. I've been looking through the books, and I found an old ship's log." She picked up a large, leather-bound book. Its pages were rough cut.

Laurie took it from her and opened it. Its formal script was handwritten with a quill pen and was signed by Captain George William Ferguson. "This is his book?" He gestured to the painting.

"See the little placard at the bottom of the painting?"

He examined the frame and found a small sign. "Right. Captain George William Ferguson. Well, that's something. You should think again about keeping this. It looks to be museum quality, and with the captain's log, it will fetch a good price."

She was already shaking her head. "I can't. Could you help me get him back upstairs?"

"Aye, sure," he said as he hefted the large painting. Fiona led the way up to her room. She'd already cleared a spot on the mantel. "I want him just there."

Laurie settled him in place and stepped back. "It's a trick of the artist, but the captain has an odd way of looking right at you. Are you sure you want him in here?"

"Laurie, you're beginning to sound like me." He tried to look affronted at her comment but couldn't keep a straight face.

There was laughter in her voice. "Yes, it's where he belongs. Then I won't feel so alone in this big house. I can see the captain watching over me." Her dimples deepened at his expression.

It was nearing the dinner hour when Laurie slipped on his jacket. He had an urge to ask her out for the evening. But he remembered he was meeting Marguerite at the club at seven. He was sure she wouldn't understand. He wanted to befriend Fiona. *Is that all I want?*

"If you need any doors fixed or sea captains put in their place, I'm your man." He sounded like a schoolboy asking for attention. It was his turn to blush. She seemed not to notice and handed him his hat.

"Thank you for all your help this afternoon." Her face was alight with warmth. "I've enjoyed your company." She cocked her head to the side. "You know, Rab's right. You two are alike."

His back was already to her as he jogged down her front steps. If she'd seen his face, she would have read his thoughts. Her words left a sour taste in what had been a sweet afternoon. He frowned. *But she doesn't know me, does she? I could never be like Rab.* He realized how dark the afternoon had become.

Chapter Twenty-Nine

Latimer Square
Edinburgh
April 1937

Alec's Watching

Alec fumed. Over the last two weeks, he'd reviewed the Ferguson estate file several times, even looked at the public records on the house itself, but he'd failed to uncover anything showing some secret value. *Father's been in a devil of a temper since Miss MacDonald's visit.* Alec was convinced something was afoot with that house, and he hated it when his father hid things from him. *He doesn't trust me with the entire picture. Why would anyone want Fiona's dilapidated old house?* Nothing at the office pointed to a plausible reason. He stood in his father's office at home.

The old man often worked from home but not today. Large, lace-covered windows faced the square, so he'd have plenty of warning should Father return. For safety's sake, he glanced out at them every few minutes. He was careful to replace every file, every scrap of paper where he'd found it. There didn't seem to be anything at home pointing to the Ferguson estate.

A movement drew his attention. He watched MacKenzie coming from Fiona's house. Alec smiled at the frown on Laurie's face. *Looks as though our girl sent him packing.* "But what the bloody hell was he doing up there?" he whispered to himself. Alec shook his head. "I think I've spent too much time away from our Fiona. Can't have MacKenzie stepping in."

The house itself disturbed him. Although he'd already been inside several times, it gave him an uneasy feeling. It was distasteful to think of old Mr. Ferguson's body lying dead in his bed for three days. *The place is a mess, every nook and cranny stuffed with worthless clutter.*

Then there was Fiona. *She's lovely to look at but not my sort, never attended university. All she'll ever be is a shopgirl.* Alec paced back to the desk. *Unless she discovers what's so special about her house. Why the bloody hell is she so keen on keeping the place?* He glanced up the street to her house. It should be easy enough to find out. *She likes me. After all, I came to her rescue. What did she call me?* A smug smile touched his handsome features. *Her knight in shining armor.* It would bear looking into. Alec decided he would pay the young lady a visit and find out just what she'd been up to.

<h1 style="text-align:center">Chapter Thirty</h1>

Edinburgh
April 1937

I'll Never Be a Lap Dog

Laurie was still frowning when he came through his front door. *Where does Fiona get the idea that I'm like Rab?* Without thinking first, he marched to the kitchen. *Why would he put that ridiculous notion in her head?*

Rab stood at the stove, stirring a pot of soup. "Oh, laddie, aren't you having your dinner with the Voss lassie?" A smile quirked at the corners of Rab's mouth. "Did ye manage Fiona's door all right?"

Laurie had the definite feeling his grandfather was trying to set him up. *Not on your life, you old fox. I'm headed for Germany, no matter who you throw at me.* He stopped himself. There were things he wanted to know, and blowing up at Rab wouldn't help him with the answers.

"Her door is sorted, and I'm headed upstairs to get ready for my date with Marguerite." He paused before asking, "Fiona said something about unexplained things happening at the house. What's she talking about?"

"Well, it's something that old Hugh used to talk about, so I wasna surprised when she told me." Laurie wanted to say get on with it, but that would only make this take longer, and he had to hurry. "Some nights Hugh would hear horses pulling a carriage. They'd enter the square and go round the back to the stables. He was reading in the library, but when he looked out ta the square" —Rab shrugged his shoulders—"nothing was there. Only the sounds of hooves on the old stones and carriage wheels and the creak of leather. Hugh thought the horses came only when something was about to change."

"Poor girl, must have been frightened to death."

"Nay then, that lassie is stronger than she looks."

"But, Rab, why would she want to stay after an experience like that?"

"And when ye love something, ye might be willing ta take the good with the bad?" Rab cut some bread and pointed with his knife toward Fiona's house. "That lass has mettle. She'll do fine."

Laurie pictured Fiona's face all lit up while she showed him the things she'd collected for sale. "Do you think she has a chance of keeping that old place?" *Rab may like the girl, but he's practical, honest.*

"I wouldna say she had much chance at all, but now that I ken her—" He paused and gave Laurie a steady look. "Aye, I do. Mind it willna be easy, but aye, she has the heart to make it happen."

Laurie let out his breath and smiled. "You might be right."

Rab poured a bowl of soup and brought it over to the table. "I thought yon Voss lassie doesna like to wait."

"Oh." Laurie glanced at his watch. "Right, I'll see you later."

It was a rush to get ready for his dinner date. As he sat in the back of the cab watching the city speed by, Laurie mused, *I actually had a conversation with Rab. It's the first time we've been on the same side for more years than I care to think about. And I forgot to ask him why he thinks we're alike.*

Laurie hurried up the steps to Marguerite's front door. He was late and knew she wouldn't like it. She answered his knock herself. His girl was stunning. Her hair was silky golden blonde. Her dress followed her curves. "Beautiful," and Marguerite smiled for a minute at his honest admiration before her lower lip edged into a pout. "You are so late. We will miss our reservation."

"No, we'll be fashionably late," he said with as much charm as he could muster. She didn't answer but shoved her fur coat into his hands. As he helped her into the mink, he noticed how soft and luxurious the fur felt. Her perfume was intoxicating. The lights played off her pale gold curls, daring him to run his hands through them. *If this is the life I've chosen, it isn't so bad. Beautiful woman, prestigious job, powerful friends. I can live with that.*

"You will have to be punctual in Germany. We Germans put great store in proper etiquette. You cannot just turn on the charm. I am so glad my father was not home to see how little you…"

Her words doused his machismo with cold water. *If she thinks I'll turn into her father's lap dog, she doesn't know me. Come to think of it, that's one way Rab and I are alike. Can't see him browbeaten to please an employer. So maybe he's right about us.* Laurie stopped listening. *She's beautiful, but is she worth it?*

Chapter Thirty-One

Kempten, Germany
April 1937

A Chance Meeting

Ana blushed, speaking her thoughts aloud. "If Sister Mary Clare could see me now." She remembered the stern mistress of the novices. The older nun always looked like she was sucking on lemons.

Ana covered her short black hair with a blue scarf, but she wore a beautiful wool skirt and matching blue sweater. Even her jacket had a fur collar. She swung her shopping basket as she walked to the market. It might be a sin, but she enjoyed feeling pretty.

Over the last week, she and the little ones had grown to love the ladies of Madam Leona's. They played with the children, teased Deter into blushing and fussed over Katrine. They hugged Gretchen and fed her cookies, and baby Tony had bounced on every knee and captured every heart.

Oh, there were moments when she'd been terrified. Especially when the upstairs was full of noisy visitors. But she read stories to the children and pretended all was well. After a while, her children looked forward to their nightly story time, and Ana forgot the awful truth that death itself was upstairs.

She was settling into her role as downstairs maid. Ana ran errands for Dorcus and helped with the cooking and cleaning. Madam Leona said, "You must play a role like you are a heroine in a story. But remember, never step out of character." Ana was learning to do this, and it was becoming easier.

Ana thought, *It's good Mary Clare can't see me. She would give me one of her disapproving looks.* Then she bit her lip. Mary Clare had disappeared smuggling children to safety. Ana shuddered. She whispered, "Father, I hope Sister Mary Clare is somewhere safe even if she's scowling."

Hitler Youth, boys of about fifteen or sixteen, were swaggering across the street. They held up traffic because they could. One boy turned to regard her as she passed and said, "Hey there, beautiful, where are you going in such a hurry?"

Ana's smile faded. Her eyes lowered, and she quickened her pace. Her heartbeat sped up as she remembered, *Evil is all around me, even in the mouth of a boy.*

Her head was down as she pushed through the crowd. She didn't see the gentleman step into her path until she charged straight into his chest.

"Oh, pardon me, I wasn't looking where I was going. I am so sorry." She looked up into the face of a tall young man. He was very handsome. When he smiled down at her, his face had a child-like innocence.

"Quite all right, Fraulein. I didn't see you, either." He took her hand and kissed it. Something unexpected. "Eric Braun. And your name, bitte?"

Alarms went off in Ana's head. It was a name she'd heard before. *The SS officer chasing us? Could this be the same Eric Braun who caused Father Hugo's death?* Her throat nearly choked off her words, but she answered with surprising calm. "Ana."

"Just Ana?" His manner was charming. She pulled her hand back and copied the haughty attitude of Berdine, one of the ladies upstairs.

"Good day, Herr Braun." She moved past him with an upturned chin, hoping the man didn't notice her shaking hands. She wanted to go back to the house, but she knew it was important to act as if nothing of significance had happened. *Do not turn to see if he watches.* The urge to look over her shoulder was overpowering. *I feel his eyes on my back. Oh, Father, help.*

She thought of her grandmother. As a child, Ana feared passing Herr Durchmeyer's barking dog. Her grand-mere said, "Ana, keep your eyes straight ahead. Do not give the animal your attention. Keep walking. Do not run and do not show fear. You must be the one in control." Only she was about to lose control.

A grandmother ahead of her spilled the contents of her shopping bag. Ana rushed to help the woman. As she picked up apples and carrots, she managed a quick glance down the street. Relief washed over her. Eric Braun was nowhere to be seen.

HERR BRAUN SAT at a window table in the pastry shop. He sipped strong coffee and regarded the young woman shopping. There was something about her he found interesting. He watched her help an old woman pick up a spilled basket. Such a good girl. So innocent and beautiful. Ana finished her shopping and walked away from the market.

On impulse, Eric followed at a discreet distance. *Next time we meet it should look accidental.* The girl turned down the alley next to the brothel. Eric raised an eyebrow. Maybe not so innocent. The wolf leered. *I think Ana and I will be good friends.*

Chapter Thirty-Two

Kempten, Germany
April 1937

You Will Tell Me What to Do Next

The door slammed behind Ana, but fear followed her in. She stood there shaking. Cook hustled from the kitchen. "What's wrong?"

It started with a few tears rolling down her cheeks, but soon Ana was crying hard. She stifled sobs, trying to explain. Her words came like hiccups. "I saw him." She couldn't breathe. "My God, I spoke to him. What will we do?" She gulped for air. "He's—he's followed us. Oh, dear Lord, the children. I have to get them out of here."

Big, strong arms pulled her into a hug. "You come with me. We'll get some hot cocoa and sort this out." Dorcus guided her like a child to the kitchen table. Within a few minutes, she sat in the bright, cheery kitchen with a steamy cup of cocoa in her hands.

Ana began again with a deep breath to steady herself. "I was on my way to market, and some silly boys were trying to talk to me. So I hurried past them. I didn't see him." She shook her head. "Then he was there, and I ran right into him."

Ana slowed her breathing, trying to remember the details. "He's handsome, you know? His face is so innocent. Such eyes. Sky blue. Then he introduced himself. The name, Eric Braun. It is the name of the man looking for me and the children. My God, Father Hugo died while this man was questioning him."

She stopped as she realized the implications of his presence. "Herr Beckmann. Oh." She wiped new tears from her eyes. "But I thought of our own Berdine. You know how she talks when she wants to put someone in their place? I was Berdine, and I said, 'Good Day' and walked on with my chin up."

Dorcus smiled. "At least Berdine's airs have done some good." She patted Ana's shoulder. "He might not be the same man. You said he was innocent-looking? He might have the same name."

In her heart she was sure it was the SS hunter, but Dorcus had thrown her a lifeline, and Ana caught hold of the hope. *Dorcus could be right. Could it be someone who lives nearby?*

"We'll talk to Leona," Dorcus continued. "She knows every-one. She'll find out who he is. In the meantime, you can't let the children see how frightened you are. Yes?"

Ana nodded, trying to get a grip on her emotions. "You're right," she agreed.

Dorcus cut a sizable piece of streusel and set it in front of Ana. "This will help. You eat something and drink your chocolate. The children are with Lilly, so we have time. I'll go find Leona. We'll decide what's to be done. Yes?"

"Yes." Ana's voice and her feelings were quiet. She prayed. *Holy Father, please tell us what to do next.*

Chapter Thirty-Three

Kempten, Germany
April 1937

Lessons from the Ladies

By the afternoon, Ana had settled down. It helped when Madam Leona promised to make discrete inquiries about Herr Braun.

"Since the Nazis confiscated the convent for their new headquarters, everyone in the region reports to Commandant Ackermann. Many SS officers visit us. Besides, Ana, you said Herr Braun has never seen Sister Ana."

"There could have been photos with my old identity papers, but Father Hugo said he destroyed all our records. So I don't think he knows much about us." She thought of Ursel Beckmann. "Still, who knows what he might discover?" She wiped away a stray tear. "We should leave. We're putting you in danger."

"As soon as we're able, we will get you and the children to safety." Madam put her hand over Ana's. "In the meantime, we'll stay the course." She smiled and handed Ana a dry hanky.

Berdine gave her a lesson on repelling unwanted advances. Dorcus made her more strudel, which she said was sure to calm her nerves. And Madam Leona spent an hour going over her new life story. "Just in case." The madam patted her hand. "I'll push my friends in the underground for a safe route out of Germany for you and the children." Her smile was full of reassurance.

Two days later, Herr Braun visited Madam Leona's for the first time. Leona welcomed him into the parlor and offered strong coffee and a pastry while she discussed his preferences and the charge for services.

"I think you have a young lady in your employ who would suit me well. Her name is Ana," he said.

Madam relaxed in her chair. "You are quite right. And she is free. If you will excuse me for a moment, I will send for her." Eric's face lit up. The madam noted how angelic he looked. A shiver moved up her spine. *Often the nice-looking men are monsters underneath. I will need to keep an ear out for Anne. This one could give her trouble.*

She returned in less than five minutes with a buxom blond sporting a seductive expression. Her Lady Anne was popular among the officers and sure to please anyone. As she entered, she found Eric sipping coffee and staring out the window. "Here we are, Herr Braun. May I present Anne?"

As he turned to face them, his mouth hardened. "Perhaps you have another girl with the same name?" His tone was still pleasant.

"I am the only Anne here, Herr Braun. I am sure if you heard about Anne or Anna, it was most definitely me they were talking about." Of course, Anne knew he was not expecting her, but her ability to handle the situation was impressive.

Eric hesitated only a moment, then described the Ana he'd met at the market.

"Herr Braun, none of my girls go to market as part of their duties." Madam's voice carried a hint of incredulity.

"But I saw her go in through the kitchen door." He stopped, realizing they'd know he'd followed her.

"Oh, that Ana is our downstairs maid." The madam allowed amusement to creep into her voice. "A country girl who helps in the kitchen. She's an innocent young thing and not available to entertain gentlemen. But our Anne"—she swept her hand toward her lady, who was still smiling—"would be happy to spend time with you."

Again, she saw hesitation. Eric set his coffee down and bowed. Without saying another word, he walked out of the house. They stood in stunned silence. Lady Anne shook her head. Leona had to agree. This was not the reaction they expected. Still, the madam was sure they hadn't seen the last of Herr Braun.

Chapter Thirty-Four

Kempten, Germany
April 1937

The Wolf

Eric's fist hit the wall with enough force to punch through the plaster. *Those whores were talking to me like I was a boy. They're laughing at me for thinking their maid was a prostitute.* He'd held his anger, maintained his neutral face, until he was back in his hotel room. Frustration exploded from him in a growl. The wall was just in his path. He spun around; his forearm swept across his dresser, sending a picture and bowl smashing to the floor. "God damn them," he spat. "Stupid bitch whores."

He glimpsed his face in the mirror, flushed, contorted. The mask was gone. Shaky fingers smoothed his hair. He hissed, "She will pay. I'll make her pay..."

An image of the madam flooded his thoughts. *Made me feel like a Dummkopf. Who the hell does she think she is? It's laughable.* He looked at himself again and tilted his head upward, imitating the madam's superior airs. "Anne's a high-class whore." *As if I'd find her Anne attractive.*

"She said the Ana in the market was an innocent? There isn't an innocent woman alive. They always want something."

A smile worked its way to the man in the mirror, then clouded with the thought, *Why do I even care?* Eric shook his head, imagining what Ana would be like to hold in his arms.

I should have known she wasn't a whore. The woman was right. You could see her lack of experience with men. But she's still no different from other women. She wants something, and I can use that to get close to her. The approach may be a bit more challenging.

He closed his eyes. *Think. There's always a way to get what you want.* Eric felt his inner wolf come to life again. *It's only a game, after all. I'm the wolf, and they're all sheep, red meat in my claws.*

His mind raced ahead. *I should trust my instincts. There's a reason I'm drawn to Ana, young and innocent as she is.* His thoughts shifted to the young nun. *Now there's a paragon of holiness. She's been able to stay out of my reach for far too long. Someone's always helping her.* He snapped his fingers. *Yes, good people like our Ana. I should be looking for people likely to help a poor holy sister and her orphaned Kinder.*

He sank back onto his bed, his rage cooled, and a plan began. *They are all sheep following outdated rules. Stupid people. I could join the flock.* His smile broadened. *Tomorrow is Sunday. Maybe I'll seek the Lord's help too.*

ERIC ROSE EARLY and dressed with his usual care. His uniform had a tendency to make people afraid. This worked to his advantage, but as he regarded himself in the mirror, he realized the wolf needed a new look. *On Monday, I'll find other clothing.*

After breakfast, he strolled through the town, edging out of the business area. He turned down a side street bordered by a small park. A large stone Lutheran church occupied the opposite corner lot. This denomination was neutral to the new state doctrines, but there were some notable exceptions.

Eric took a seat on a park bench, giving him a chance to observe the people filing in for morning service. Families. He noticed the men looked at him with wary glances. The women kept their eyes down. They all wore the same sort of drab-looking suit or even white shirts with black ties and black pants.

After walking past the Catholic church and one very small Methodist church, Eric knew what he would need to pass himself off as a sheep.

Monday, he visited a local store and purchased clothing to match his new persona. He stood looking in his hotel mirror at the full effect of the new Eric. He raised one brow. *This might be the best way to approach Ana.* He spoke to the drab-looking man in the mirror again. "You're still not right."

He tried to affect a sincere expression. It wasn't a mask he used often. His features slid into a sneer. Yes, the wolf was always there under the surface. It would need to be fed at some point. *In the meantime, I'll play the game.* He was powerful again.

Chapter Thirty-Five

Edinburgh
April 1937

Selling Treasures

Laurie came down to breakfast in his robe and slippers. He found Rab standing in the kitchen, finishing the last of his tea. Rab set the cup in the sink and picked up a jacket. Laurie said, "You're up early." He glanced at his wristwatch. "Plans for the day, then?"

Rab had one arm in a jacket sleeve as he answered, "Och, Laurie laddie, do you no remember? I told ye aboot taking Neville Smythe up ta see Fiona's things."

Right, that's Rab's friend, the antiques dealer. Laurie hadn't remembered when it was happening.

"That's today? When?" He knew she was pinning all her hopes on the sale. As Rab turned to leave, Laurie added, "I think I'd like to come along."

Rab pulled up mid-stride and cocked his head as he turned back to Laurie. "I'm ta meet Neville at his office at 8:30, but we'll be back at the hoose by nine o'clock." For a moment, one eyebrow rose. "Now, why would you be wantin' to be there?"

Laurie ignored the hint of amusement on Rab's face. "I want to make sure everything goes well for her." A weak excuse. "She's a nice lass, and I'd like to leave for Germany knowing you had a friend next door." *And if I said I want to spend time in her company?* He pushed away the thought. He already had a girl.

Rab's grin broadened, but he held his peace. Laurie fumed. *Don't get the wrong idea, old man. I'm not interested in any local lass. We're friends. I've made my choice. No matter what you think, that's that.*

He sighed as his emotions shifted. He wanted to say something, but it would only feed the fuel for another fight. *Fiona's the reason things are better between us.* He made a quick decision. Instead, he said, "I'll meet you at the house at nine."

When the Edinburgh Antiques van entered Latimer Square, Laurie was out the door and waiting at Fiona's steps by the time it parked.

He nodded to Smythe and rapped on Fiona's massive front door. A smiling Alec Frazer opened it. "Right, they're here, Fiona," Alec called over his shoulder.

Laurie rocked back on his heels, recoiling from Alec's presence. *What the bloody hell is he doing here?*

Alec stepped aside, beckoning them in. They nodded to each other in silent greeting, as Neville, Rab and Laurie filed into the entry hall. *Alec looks so smug. If he's interested in Fiona...* Anger bubbled up in Laurie, but it was Neville who spoke first.

"I'm a bit surprised to see you here, Mr. Frazer."

And he's not the only one.

"Did Miss MacDonald hire a solicitor for this meeting?" Neville sounded insulted.

"No, nothing of the sort. Our cook made a batch of his wonderful tea cakes, and I brought a plate of them for Miss, ah..." he at glanced at Laurie. "Fiona."

"Well, all right then." Neville stepped forward as a flushed

Fiona hurried to greet them. "I'm happy to meet you, Miss MacDonald."

"Fiona will do, sir." She took his hand and glanced around at the group. Laurie realized she must be wondering how her appointment had grown into such a gathering. "Please come in, all of you." Of course, they were already in, so to speak. She seemed to realize her blunder with an endearing blush. "Well, thanks to Alec's cook, I can offer you tea and cakes."

Neville held his hand up. "It would be nice but business first, if you don't mind?"

She recovered herself and turned to open the double doors to the sitting room. Neville's face was alight with anticipation as he moved past her to examine her collection.

"You have some beautiful pieces here," he said, running his hand over a polished library table. She gave him the list of the items she was offering for sale.

Rab stood to the side but winked at Fiona, saying, "And didn't I say the same ta ye, Neville?"

"That you did, Rab. I should hire you to help with the business." The two men chuckled.

Laurie moved to stand next to her, watching from the sitting-room door. Alec followed Mr. Smythe like a puppy on its mother's heels, taking special interest wherever Neville did. His eyes inspected every item. *I know for a fact Alec's not interested in antiques, so what is he up to now?*

Fiona interrupted his thoughts. "Is something wrong, Laurie?" she whispered. "You look so fierce." She gave him a playful nudge.

It was his turn to color with embarrassment. "Not at all. I'm concerned whether you will get what you need. I know how important this is and want to help ... um, if it's all right?" Her eyes never left his face, and what promised to become a smile blossomed, dimpling her rosy cheeks. He smiled back. But he wondered, *Is she smiling because she knows I'm making excuses, or is she happy to see me?*

Neville cleared his throat, and they both looked at him. "I'm checking the list, and you seem to be missing a few pieces. A portrait of Captain George William Ferguson and his ship's log?"

Laurie blurted out, "Oh, it's in her bedroom." All eyes turned to him. He added, "I mean to say, I took it up for her a few days ago."

"I'm keeping those," Fiona added.

"If it's the captain I'm thinking of, I wonder if you'd mind showing it to me. I'm a history buff, especially the history of Edinburgh." He turned to Rab. "Why didn't you tell me about the captain's painting?"

Rab only shrugged. "Our Fiona's keeping the painting."

Neville looked so anxious. "I'd love to see it." He held his hands together as if praying. Fiona agreed, and all four men followed her up to her bedroom.

She held the door open, and Alec, Rab, Neville and Laurie shuffled in. Laurie looked around. *It feels like her—warm, inviting.* Sunlight lit the walls with a pink glow.

"What a lovely room." Neville sighed in appreciation.

"Thank you." Her voice caught. "It was my mother's room when she was a girl. It makes me feel like I belong here."

But Neville was already crossing to the painting on the mantel. He stood for quite a while, examining the details.

"I'm familiar with this artist. A Dutch painter. He's dated it here under his signature—1742. Captain Ferguson is indeed a commanding presence." He pulled his gaze back to Fiona. "You have the ship's log as well?"

Fiona nodded and lifted the old book from her bedside table. For the first time Laurie noticed a bookmark. *She must have been reading it.*

Neville took the book from her as if she'd handed him the Bible. He set it on her tea table and scrutinized it, stopping to read something which seemed to give him great pleasure. He stepped back to examine the painting. Neville turned to Rab.

"Do you know who this is?"

"Aye, Neville, that I do."

"Why didn't you tell me?" Without waiting for an answer, Neville turned to Fiona. "Young lady, you have something of great value here. Did Rab tell you about the Black Captain?" She nodded. "He is the key to finding his treasure box. They say it's somewhere in the house."

Alec broke in. "Wait, are you saying there is an undiscovered treasure in this house?" He had an eagerness in his eyes. Laurie wondered how he could believe all this nonsense.

Fiona said with conviction, "My treasure is the house."

Laurie wanted to throw a bit of water on the fire that lit Alec's eyes. "If there was treasure here, wouldn't her uncle or someone else have found it years ago?"

"Mind you, many have looked for it." Neville nodded as he went on. "The tale says the Black Captain's ghost will keep it hidden until the time is right." He looked at the incredulous expression on Laurie's face and held a finger up. "According to the story, he held it for the rightful king of Scotland. But in later years, he became less and less convinced there would be a king strong enough to take his country back from the English.

"A friend of his wrote in her memoirs that Captain Ferguson reconsidered. He believed the box was meant for someone special. Many people have searched for it, but no one ever found it. Some say Captain Ferguson made up the story himself. Eventually interest died out.

"Nothing more was said about the Black Captain's treasure. Until now, of course." Neville turned to Fiona. "Thank you. It's been a pure pleasure to see the captain face to face and to look at his very words." He flushed with exuberance.

"You're welcome," she said. "Shall we have tea, and you can finish looking at my things?" They all made sounds of agreement.

Rab and Neville chatted as Fiona led the way back down to the sitting room. Laurie watched as Alec lingered in the room, looking from the book to the painting with a speculative expression.

"You don't believe all that, do you, Alec?" Laurie asked.

"No, not for a minute." Alec left the room. Laurie glanced at the captain, who seemed to stare back at him with a fierce intensity. Before Laurie closed the door, he said, "Well, see what you've started."

In the end, Neville made a generous offer. Not enough to keep the house forever, but enough to buy the time Fiona needed to sort things out. She glowed with relief, and Laurie realized he was relieved as well. He couldn't take his eyes off her dimples. *What the hell am I doing going to Germany?*

Chapter Thirty-Six

Kempten, Germany
April 1937

Your Oma Would Be Proud

Only this morning, Eric had a phone conversation with his friend. He didn't talk about private things with many people, but he and Michael had been friends for a long time. They were choir boys together, then later both were in the Hitler Youth. The priest's death had bothered him, yes, but what bothered him even more was his inability to find out anything about the nun and the missing children from Saint Thomas.

Michael said, "Eric, you have to be careful."

He retorted, "How much can they matter?"

"They don't, but your failure does."

Eric was silent. Michael said, "Don't worry. I've been telling my captain here in Hamburg what a dedicated officer you are. I'm hoping to have good news for you soon."

Eric felt encouraged. "Thanks, Michael."

"No worries. It'll be like old times, the two of us working together."

ERIC TRIED to keep Michael's conversation in mind as he stood in his superior's office. Commander Ackermann sounded like a schoolmaster giving a lesson.

"Unfortunate that the old priest died." He gave Eric a sharp glance. "You were perhaps too vigorous in your questioning?"

Eric stood at attention, his face impassive. He didn't like this fat little man. "It was his heart. I think it failed." He added as an afterthought, "He was old."

Ackermann's voice sounded patient, but Eric could see the redness creep up around the man's collar. "Most regrettable. The church is asking questions. The Vatican sent a letter asking what has become of the children and"—the commander looked at the paper on his desk—"the Holy Sisters of Saint Thomas." He hit the letter with the back of his hand. "But we can't say, can we, Herr Braun?"

"There could only have been four children left from what I've been able to discover and one nun." Eric let frustration creep into his tone. "What does it matter? They're unimportant."

Ackermann exploded; he was on his feet and around the desk. "I gave you an assignment!" Spittle sprayed Eric's face. "How hard can it be to find one nun and four children?" The commander's face grew redder with every word. He moved closer.

Eric had learned a trick long ago in Catholic school. When the nuns scolded him, he'd imagine how ridiculous they'd be with no clothes on. *It is gratifying this fat little pig of a man has to stand on his pudgy toes to make eye contact with me.*

The commander took a breath and spat out more rebuke. "How do you think it makes us appear? A woman has sneaked inhuman little brats right under our noses." His finger pointed to the ceiling. "And now we have to say we don't know where they are. Herr Braun, you don't appreciate how that makes me look."

Well, actually, I do—incompetent. I wouldn't mind that at all if it didn't make me look incompetent, too.

But Ackermann echoed his thoughts. "If this makes me look bad, I will pass the nasty stain on to your record as well." A pudgy finger stabbed Eric in the chest.

Eric interrupted the commander's tirade. "I was quite thorough in my investigation. I followed every lead, went through all church records, even followed a rumor to a farm near Garmisch-Partenkirchen." His voice remained calm. "Turned out to be some farmer who ran off with another woman." Eric spread his hands. "Before the priest died, I could learn very little."

Ackermann's face sagged. His anger spent, the commander returned to his chair. "Get out."

He blew his piggy nose, not even noticing Eric's snappy, "Heil Hitler."

Eric closed the door to the inner office, wondering what it would feel like to put his hands around the fat little pig's neck. It took him a minute to compose himself. He straightened his jacket and used his handkerchief to wipe the spittle from his face, catching his reflection in a window.

His wolf still projected an air of superiority. It was, after all, acceptable to appear to be bored, and sometimes it served his purpose to appear innocent. He thought of it as wearing a mask to cover his true thoughts.

Eric moved into the hall, elbowing his way through the crowd. He stared straight ahead—all his attention had turned inward as he wondered, *Why are they so important? And who would dare to help them? Putting their lives in danger for nobodies?* He shook his head. *Fear and intimidation can only get me so far. I need to come at this from another direction.* His thoughts wandered back to the young woman he'd seen in the market. *What kind of man would she confide in?*

He slowed his pace and schooled his features. With a sweet

smile and doe-like eyes, he stopped the cleaning lady as she struggled with her mop and pail. "Oma, grandmother, let me help you carry all that."

She didn't pull back in fear but smiled into his face. "Why thank you, son. I'm taking it to the small washroom." She pointed to the door twenty feet away.

"I will carry it. You must be tired." He patted her shoulder.

When they arrived at the door, she reached out her dirty hand and touched his cheek. "Your oma would be so proud of you." *Hmm, she didn't see the uniform. She's not even afraid of me. All she sees is the mask of kindness.*

As he turned to leave, Eric pulled out his hankie again to wipe his cheek. A plan formed in his mind. The wolf reveled as the thrill of the hunt returned. *I'm not letting one scrawny nun and four dirty children muck up my record. I will find you, and when I do, you will pay for this humiliation.*

Chapter Thirty-Seven

House on Latimer Square
Edinburgh
April 1937

The Letter

Laurie watched Alec linger near Fiona, chatting while the last of Fiona's things loaded into Neville's box truck. *Something's afoot with Alec.* Once again, Laurie felt pulled in two directions. He didn't like leaving Fiona with Alec still there, but Marguerite was leaving for Germany, and he had to see her off at the boat.

At his touch on her arm, Fiona turned, glowing with relief. Laurie couldn't breathe. He just stood looking into her warm eyes. "I have to leave." He hesitated, thinking of some way to prolong her attention. "I'm seeing Marguerite off. She's leaving for Germany." He wanted to say something else.

Her smile faded a little, but she took his hand. "Thank you for being here. For your help."

His eyes lingered on her full lips. The urge to kiss her was overwhelming. Instead, he nodded and turned to leave. By the time he reached his front door, his temper was flaring at himself, at Alec, and at Fiona.

"Why does she make me forget what's important? I'm not some lad gone girl crazy." He slammed his front door behind him, stomped up the steps, and slammed his bedroom door. "I have plans." He was peeling off his shirt. "This is my big chance." He tugged a clean shirt off a hanger and stuffed his arm into the sleeve.

"You'd like that, wouldn't you, Rab? Forget about Germany, settle down with Fiona, if she'd even have me."

This is crazy. In a month, Alec will have a clear field. I'll be in Germany. From his window, he watched the van still sitting there, and Alec was talking with Fiona. His frown deepened.

Where the bloody hell was Rab? He shouldn't let Alec worm his way into her life. He stalked to the mirror, growling at his reflection, noticing that he'd mismatched his buttons. While he refastened his shirt, he thought, *What the bloody hell is Alec is playing at? He wouldn't be interested in Fiona unless it benefited him in some way. God, I'd hate it if she got hurt.* Right now, he needed to make Marguerite's sailing and try to stifle his growing aversion to the gorgeous blonde.

Marguerite is beautiful. Everything about her is intoxicating. His thoughts flitted to feeling like he couldn't breathe when Fiona smiled at him. *She's not even my type. A minister's daughter, another do-gooder like Rab. But she is also honest, kind, and she cares about what I'm saying and about other people.* He paused, staring at the mirror but seeing Fiona's face. *She has this inner light. She glows when she's excited.* He focused once again on his sour reflection. *I need answers. What have I worked for all this time if not to take Voss up on his offer and his daughter?*

Laurie looked at his watch. He should be at the docks in plenty of time. He hustled down the stairs and pulled the front door open.

Bernie stood before him, his hand raised to knock. "I'm glad I caught you home." Laurie wanted to tell him to bugger off, but Bernie looked anything but happy.

Instead, Laurie stepped back and said, "I thought you'd be on your way to Greenock and that new job by now." Bernie looked like he'd been gut punched. "What's happened?"

"Are you still set on the job in Germany?" Bernie pushed past him into the foyer.

Laurie turned to his friend. "I've been struggling with my doubts, but it's still a grand opportunity. Why? Want to come with me?"

Bernie snapped, "Hardly. They'd never have me." His jaw clenched. "Look, I know what you think about all the news coming from Germany, but it just got very personal." He held out a rumpled letter. "Read this. It won't take long."

Laurie gave him a hard stare, expecting more, but Bernie's lips pressed into a thin line. He looked down at the letter now in his hand and unfolded the pages.

Bernie muttered, "It came from neighbors and good friends of my aunt and uncle. I'm just thankful they wrote in English. Otherwise, I might not have read it."

"God, Bernie, you have family in Germany? Sorry for all the comments."

"Read the damn letter."

Laurie read.

We've been neighbors and friends with Max and Rachel for many years. Rachel often spoke about her sister and family in Scotland. Two months ago, Max asked us to get their children out of Germany if anything happened to him or Rachel. Just being asked to do this was dangerous, but he knew we would do anything we could. We've always loved Deter and Gretchen as if they were our own.

Thank God, those young ones were on an outing with their nanny when the Gestapo came without warning. Men in black uniforms kicked at Rachel's door. They dragged her and Max out of the house. We never saw them again. We waited to see if the children would come back with their nanny, Marta, but they didn't return.

A week ago, a new family moved into their home. We tried to ask them a few simple questions, but they wouldn't tell us anything. From what we could tell, all Max and Rachel's things were still in the house. But they didn't take the children, because the next day two men came to our door. They asked if we knew anything about the Jew children. We said no, but they didn't believe us. They hit my husband and turned our house inside out searching. They want Deter and Gretchen. Why would they try so hard to find two small children?

We're afraid. When we were young, things like this only happened to criminals. Now evil officials do things like this to good people all the time. I fear your family is gone forever, and we could do nothing to help them. Not even the children. Deter is only six, and Gretchen is four. God help them. I pray every day for them. It's all I can do, that and write this letter.

But I hold this hope: They are still asking questions, so I think the young woman Marta hid those little ones. I remember she was from a village in Bavaria. I hope one day Deter and Gretchen will make it to safety. But there's nowhere safe in Germany. We are so sorry for your loss.

"The letter was sent to a family in Holland. See the note at the end?" Bernie pointed to a postscript. "She says so little information is getting out of Germany. Those friends tucked it in the pocket of a birthday gift with instructions to send it on to us."

Laurie looked up. "Ah, Bernie, I'm so sorry. Maybe you're right. This idea about going to Germany is getting less appealing all the time."

Bernie grabbed his arm. "You've got to go."

Laurie shook his head. "You can't be serious." He pulled away from his friend. "I'm sorry for your family, but how am I going to find two small children in the middle of Germany? I'm going to Hamburg. It's nowhere near Bavaria."

Bernie's face was inches from Laurie. "If Germany is your big chance?" Bernie spat the words out through gritted teeth. "You're our only chance. Said it yourself, starting at the top, they trust you. We're Jews. They'd arrest us the minute we stepped off the boat." Bernie seemed to deflate. "They're only children." Silence filled the space between them. Bernie's voice came in a whispered plea. "How can you not try?" The question hung in the air.

Laurie tried to think. "Did you contact the British Consulate in Germany? They'd help you, wouldn't they?"

Bernie was shaking his head. "We've already tried. Seems they're overwhelmed with requests like ours. They will get to our report when time permits." Curly red hair slipped over Bernie's brow.

"Don't you have other family in Germany who could help?"

Bernie scrubbed a hand over his face. "No one. They all left years ago. We were trying to get papers so my mum's sister and family could emigrate." He took a ragged breath. "That may have called attention to them. Mum cries all the time. You're the only person I know even traveling to Germany." Bernie reached into his pocket and handed Laurie a picture of two sweet-faced children.

Laurie looked from those innocent bairns in the photo to Bernie's bloodshot eyes. He recognized desperation. He wanted to say no, wanted to say he wasn't some goddamn detective, but this kind of suffering made his doubts seem small, unimportant. *Is this the answer I've been searching for—a sign that Marguerite is the right direction to take?*

Marguerite. Lord, I'll be late. Laurie inhaled. "I don't know how, but I'll see what I can find out." Laurie tried to hand back the letter and photograph, but Bernie shook his head.

"It might help you. Keep it." Relief washed over his face. "You have no idea how happy that makes me. My mother is heartsick over losing her only sister and not being able to help the children." He seized Laurie's hand, shaking it with vigor.

"I'm not making any promises, but I'll try."

Chapter Thirty-Eight

House on Latimer Square
Edinburgh
April 1937

Rab Talks about the Captain

As everyone was getting ready to leave, Alec took Fiona's hand and gave it a warm squeeze. "I hope we can become good friends. If you need anything at all, you can always call on me."

Fiona stood in front of her house watching Alec walk away. He passed Rab without saying a word of acknowledgement. *Funny that. Rab's so friendly, but when he looks at Alec, he seems on edge, wary.*

She couldn't help but wonder about the friction between Alec and Laurie. *They're friendly enough, but I'm sure they're not friends. Laurie doesn't hide his feelings well.* She smiled. *I like that about him. Alec is harder to read.* Fiona shook her head. "He's been that nice to me, but...?" A flash of him following Neville around looking at her things came to mind. His face was so intent. She shrugged. *It could be the barrister in him. He's been kindness itself.*

In fact, this morning was an answer to a prayer. Neville bought everything she was selling and called for two of his men to help with loading. Movement in the van caught her eye. They were getting ready to leave, but Neville turned back to shake Fiona's hand.

"Thank you for your business. It was a true pleasure meeting you and seeing this fine old house. If ever you change your mind about the captain's painting and his log, be sure and come to see me first. I'll make you a fair offer, and I'd love to have them."

"Thank you, but I couldn't part with them. I can't explain it. They belong to the house."

Neville looked at her with a thoughtful expression. "I understand. Well, good day to you."

Fiona reached for Rab's arm before he could climb into the van. "I wonder if you can give me some advice?"

Rab nodded once and called out to Neville, "Will your lads help ye unload?"

"That they will. Thank you, Rab. We'll talk soon."

As Rab waved goodbye to his friend, Fiona said, "I can make us another cup of tea, if you have a wee bit of time to spare for a chat?"

Rab's grin broadened. "Smashing idea. Don't suppose there are any cakes left?"

After the kettle was on the stove, and they settled at the kitchen table, Fiona asked which bank she should put her money in.

"Aye, well, it's the Bank of Scotland for me. If it suits ye, I can take ye doone and introduce ye to the manager. He's a guid friend of mine."

Fiona's eyes twinkled. "Do you know everyone?"

"Not hardly, lass, but when you get to my age, you're not living well if you have nay friends."

"Thank you. That would suit me fine. Thanks too for being my friend." Her expression sobered. "Hope you don't think I'm foolish not to accept Neville's offer for the captain and his log. I've been reading the log." She gathered her thoughts. "Well, it's more like a diary. I have to tell someone all about it, and you might be the only person who wouldn't think I was daft."

Rab radiated warmth. "I'm a Highlander, born and bred. We ken the world isn't all it seems. There are things the good Lord has seen fit not to explain, and I can trust it all makes sense to him even when I don't understand."

Fiona's shoulders relaxed, and she let out a sigh of relief. "That helps me." The kettle began whistling, and she poured them both a cup of tea and set out the rest of the cakes. "I like the captain. Reading his log with his picture on my mantel helps me feel like he's telling me his story."

"Your Uncle Hugh read everything he could get his hands on about the time and, in particular, about the captain. Did ye ken the actual Black Captain was John Ferguson?

Fiona interrupted. "The name on the log is George Ferguson."

"Och aye, John Ferguson is yer captain's older brother," Rab continued. "The older brother hated Highlanders as much as your captain loved them. I like to think of him as 'English John' because he hunted Charlie for the English. The man had a black temper and spared no life when chasing Jacobites—that's why folks called him the Black Captain. He burned many Highland estates. But that's another story.

"Our captain was his younger brother, and they were mortal enemies. Hugh and I often talked about it, so I know a thing or two. Your captain, George Ferguson, was reputed for outrunning English ships." Rab chuckled. "I'm sure that was a sore point with his famous brother.

"The English were no on good terms with the French. They put an embargo on all French imports. Captain George Ferguson ran French goods through Rotterdam and brought them up the coast into Arbroath and Montrose. The English suspected your captain of smuggling but never caught him. Then, too, George made friends with some powerful people who were more than happy to get French claret for their cellars, amongst other things.

"So, your captain became rich despite his brother. He built this house and paid his men well. And no one ever questioned his business dealings."

Fiona added, "He talks about some of that in the log. He mentioned his first mate, a Tamash. He seemed more of a friend than a crew member. Well, not even that. When in port, Tamash stayed in this house and served the captain."

Rab interrupted. "I expect he'd be a clan member, and that would speak of a deeper loyalty than just a crewman or a servant."

"Tamash was a firm believer in Christ. He didn't judge the captain, but Tamash had a tempering influence on him."

"Aye, well, do you know why they called George the Black Captain too?" Rab stirred his tea. "Mind, part of that was to taunt him about his brother, but he got the name for a similar reason." Rab was eating his cake and looked up at her with a twinkle in his eye.

"Was it because of his coloring? Dark eyes, dark hair like mine."

"No, lass, your George was called the Black Captain because of his temper, though not so black as his brother John's. George was a fair man. He treated his business dealings with honor, even with the English. But he wasn't a man you'd want to cross, not if you wanted to go on living."

"Can you tell me about the captain? I want to know everything."

Rab said nothing for a minute. He looked up at her with such intensity. "I don't think so. I have a hunch I'd cheat you out of hearing the captain's story from his own hand. But I'll be glad to fill you in with any details I can recall. You may jog my memory as you go along. One thing, aye? I saw your uncle eaten up with the need to find the captain's treasure. It became an obsession. That's why he asked me to put the painting and log in the attic. Mind, I'm not implying any evil possession, but the love of money makes no one the happier or the wiser."

Rab was quiet again, and Fiona sipped her tea and thought about what he'd said.

Chapter Thirty-Nine

House on Latimer Square
Edinburgh
April 1937

So, the Black Captain was a Smuggler

Fiona felt at peace as she climbed the stairs to go to bed. The sale would provide for this house for quite a while. "Of course, I'll need to find work and discover why I'm here." She spoke to the walls in her dressing room. "I have no idea why I own you, but I'm sure I'll figure out our purpose." Da was a practical man, not given to superstition. But he believed everything happens for a reason.

Her dimples were showing as she wondered what Da would say if he knew she talked to the house. Since the captain's painting had been moved to her bedroom mantel, she had the odd sense of him watching her. *Wonder what Da would say if he knew I changed in my dressing room?*

She padded across the floor and climbed into bed with her flannel nightie and warm woolen socks. Feeling a little foolish, she said to the captain, "Nothing wrong with a little modesty." He smiled back at her.

Instead of turning down the gaslight, she picked up the captain's log. It was the size of a rough-cut encyclopedia, and she'd only read the first few pages of it. She traced her hand over the ornate penmanship. *Not light reading but so worth the time.*

MAY 25 in the year of our Lord 1745

Leith

I picked up a cache of French wine from my contacts in Amsterdam. I've got my lads putting Portuguese labels over French ones. If we get boarded, we'll look like an honest merchant trader.

Soon enough, we'll be at war. The Highlands are holding their breath for the prince to come home. I, too, have given my pledge to Charles Stewart.

Some say the French will send reinforcements, but we canna depend on them. I've heard a rumor the Spaniards promised Prince Charles gold. This is our war, and if we believe in freedom, we've got to stand behind it with all we have. I am gathering a war chest to help with the effort. I like the idea of selling French wine to English gentlemen and using their own gelt to free Scotland.

Fiona looked up at the captain. "So, you are a smuggler." He seemed to answer her with a twinkle in his eyes. She imagined one dark brow arched as if to say, "What did you expect?" And she read on.

My new ship is bonnie, even if she's a close cousin to my brother's cruiser, the Turace. I've named her the Tearloch, the Instigator. She's fast and at a distance could be mistaken for my brother's ship. This trip I've made some additional changes to her riggings. Tamash worked out a clever way to change her name to the Turace on short notice if needed. I've no worries. She will fool even a ship of the line. Without too close a scrutiny, we should slip past their patrols.

I visited the tailor this morning to collect my new clothes, an identical match to my brother John's uniform. I'm well pleased with the outcome. If I will have them think I'm John, I canna dress like Geordie.

Even as lads, we were much alike, though I was the better looking of the two of us. It wouldn't do for two Black Captains to show up at the same time. The rub is knowing where John is sailing.

My meeting with Charles Stewart went well. I don't like the man—well, he's little more than a lad—but he will have some good advisers to help him. Lord George Murray for one. The prince charged me with calling out the Keiths, the Farquharsons, the Gordons and as far north as the Sutherlands, Gunns, Sinclairs and Mackay.

I'll be sailing to Arbroath first to deliver my goods. I plan on staying long enough for a good meal and to catch up on the news. Then, too, there's Mairi. I respect Tamash's concern for his sister. A feast for the eyes. She's a bonnie lass. I love to spend time with her, but I can be a gentleman when necessary, though Tamash may have his doubts.

Fiona closed the log and set it on the chest next to her bed. *So, you're sweet on Mairi?* She turned down the gas lamp but not all the way out. In the flickering light, she looked up at her Black Captain. He reminded her of Laurie in a way she couldn't put her finger on. Just something in the eyes, maybe. Her own eyes grew heavy, and she slipped off to a deep sleep, her dreams full of handsome Highlanders who looked like her new neighbor.

Chapter Forty

Edinburgh
April 1937

Two Wee Bairns

Laurie pushed through the crowd, his eyes searching the passengers standing at the railing. At least he hadn't missed his chance to say goodbye to Marguerite. *Thank God, the cabbie was quick. There she is.* He waved and called out, "Marguerite." Her face lit up with recognition.

Within minutes, Marguerite was down the boarding ramp and in his arms. Her kiss lingered, full of promise. As she pulled back, she smiled. "There, that should keep you until you finish up whatever keeps you in Scotland and come to Germany."

In the past, there was a kind of electricity between them. Laurie heard himself say, "You know it, baby." But he still had Bernie's letter in his pocket. The letter crinkled as her body pressed against him.

"Laurie, you need to get this habit of being late under control.

It isn't done." She smoothed his coat collar back. Her blue eyes twinkled as she said, "I've lots of plans for us."

He chuckled. "You do remember I'll be working for your father, right?"

"You won't always be at work. Then you're all mine."

The warning blast sounded, calling her back aboard. He kissed her one last time, searching for the thrill that always came when he held her in his arms. Her father called to her from the railing. She squeezed his hand before hurrying back up the ramp.

Relief washed over him as he stood on the dock watching her sail away. *I've been crazy about Marguerite, excited about the job. Sure of everything. Even Rab's constant jabs about German politics didn't sway me.* Laurie shoved his hands in his pockets as he walked uphill from Leith to Edinburgh. There it was again—Bernie's letter. *So, could Rab be right about Germany?*

People and traffic moved around him, but Laurie had to think, and walking home seemed the best way to clear his mind. *If that's possible. Only a week ago, I was positive that my course was set. My future seemed so clear.*

The haar, a mist that rolls in from the North Sea, lingered overhead. The cobblestone streets glistened in the lamplight. He remembered how he used to love Edinburgh. There was peace in the stones of this old city. You could almost hear the echo of all the years.

As he reached his street, Laurie looked up at the house at the end of the square, searching for lights or any sign Fiona was still up. Nothing. With a rueful shake of his head, he turned to his front door. It was good to be home. He peeled off his trench coat, giving it a good shake. Most of the Highland mist slid off. Another thing he'd miss in Germany. *Only in Scotland is a mist so light it won't penetrate your coat.*

Rab was sitting before a crackling fire in the study. Laurie came in and sat in one of the easy chairs, rubbing his hands together for warmth. He stared into the flickering flames. His grandfather looked up from the book he'd been reading and slipped off his glasses. Laurie could feel Rab watching him. "Are ye aright, laddie?" Rab asked.

"No, Grandda, I'm anything but all right." Laurie raked a hand through his hair. "I'm lost..." he said, letting his answer trail off.

"If ye need an ear, I'm yer man." Rab was so sincere in his offer, Laurie's heart broke. He felt like a boy again with his grandda. Before his parents died, Laurie would go to Rab with all his troubles. Rab said little, but he listened, and there was never a worry that he'd get scolded or punished. He knew Rab was always on his side. *When did it change?*

When he found his voice, the words came pouring out. Rab listened and waited. No criticism, no judgment. Love shone through his eyes. Laurie talked about his changing feelings for Marguerite, cheapened with the realization he'd been using her to get ahead. "I have to admit, I wanted to show my mates. She was so beautiful, but she wouldn't give any of them the time of day. I guess I'd beat them out." All pretense gone, Laurie spoke with candor about the money and prestige he'd gain by taking her father's offer of a job. "Without this job, I'll be like all the rest, putting in my time at a shipyard as an apprentice." *Would that be so bad?*

He didn't say it, but Laurie was sure Rab must be thinking the same thing, but when he looked, there was no sign of gloating or I told you so. Laurie took a deep breath and pushed on. "Then I met Fiona." He shook his head. "I didn't like her at first. You were always talking about her, and it put me off."

He stared into the flames, picturing her face. "She has the most beautiful dimpled smile. Her eyes twinkle. I can't help being attracted to her, but it's not only that. I want to protect her as well." He talked about Alec's interest in her. "Alec's not right for her. I think he's up to something, but I can't imagine what it might be." Laurie stood and paced. Restless hands kneaded the back of the easy chair. He plopped down again.

They didn't talk for a while. Rab seemed content to wait. Laurie's voice cracked as he told his grandfather about Bernie's visit that afternoon, explaining about the missing children. "I was thinking about giving up this job and Marguerite before Bernie's visit, that letter. You should have seen his face. He's desperate, and I don't blame him. They're just two wee bairns."

He handed the letter and photograph of the children to Rab, who slipped his glasses back on. Rab studied the picture with a tender look on his weathered old face. He looked up when Laurie blurted out, "Hell, chances are slim I'd even find them. Two children in one enormous country. I have no idea how to look for them. If it's as bad as you've been telling me, they may already be dead. What could I do anyway?" he asked with hands spread open. He leaned down with his elbows on his knees. When he looked up into Rab's face, tears clouded his vision. "They're two small children. How can I say no?" His head dropped into his hands, and he sat in silence.

Rab waited and said, "So yer course is still set. It's just yer reasons have changed." For the first time in years, Rab looked at him with pride.

Laurie nodded. Something had shifted. The guilt was gone. He knew what he would do. Rab rose and crossed to the sideboard. He poured them both a wee dram of whiskey, handing Laurie his drink. Laurie looked at the amber liquid, thinking out loud. "How can I get them out if I find them?"

Rab took a sip of the Taliskers and grinned. "Well, that's something I can help ye with. Ye ken I still have the lads working my fishing boat out of Peterhead? I think she could be useful. You'll need to get Bernie working with the authorities on proper paper and such. Have they made a formal inquiry about them yet?"

"Bernie said they tried and were told the family moved with no address for their new location. Lies. You sound so sure I'll find them. I don't know where to start."

"You'll have help. I'm certain of that. I can tell when God's got

His nose in something. You'll have help." Rab winked. "If all else fails, ye have a few smugglers in yer family line. Maybe not so far back as ye think."

Laurie grinned as he lifted his drink in salute. "To smugglers."

Rab lifted his, adding, "To smugglers, rascals and rogues, and whoever else the Guid Laird has use for." They chuckled and finished their whiskey.

Chapter Forty-One

Latimer Square
Edinburgh
May 1937

An Unexpected Turn of Events

Alec glanced at his pocket watch. *Good, it's only nine.* He'd gone back to his bedroom twice for things he'd forgotten. *Should still be at the office in time for my appointment.* He was about to come downstairs when the doors to the study opened. *Bugger, the old man's usually gone by this time.* Alec stepped back into the shadows at the top of the stairs. A familiar-looking man in an overcoat stepped into the foyer below and said, "Right, sir. Oh, and did you want the key back? Going to be tricky with the young miss at home."

His father moved into view. "I'm afraid you're right. I'll take it for now, but keep digging into the matter. We may get lucky." Positive words from someone who looked so sour.

The stranger added, "Not so sure there's anything to discover. One thing's for certain. If there is a war box, she doesn't know where it is any more than we do." The man slipped his fedora on his head and nodded to Mr. Frazer as he turned to leave.

Frazer made a humphing noise and returned to the study. Neither man noticed Alec.

Alec felt a surge of excitement. *I knew it. There had to be some reason the old man wanted Fiona's house. If Father's interested in the war chest, it's because he's convinced it exists, and that's good enough for me. I just need to find it before Father does.* Alec waited a moment more, wondering where he'd seen the man before. Then he snapped his fingers. *In the office the day Fiona came to collect the key to her uncle's house. Well, well, it appears there's more than one key.* Alec continued down the stairway into the entry hall. He rapped once on his father's study door and poked his head in. Mr. Frazer was slipping something into the top left desk drawer.

"Father, I'm off to the office. Anything I can take care of for you?"

"See to your own business if you please." The old man was as unpleasant as ever, but Alec had gained some valuable information. So he smiled back at his father and wished him a good day.

Pausing at his front steps, he cast a look up the square to Fiona's house. He was sure he could use this turn of events to ensure his future prosperity.

Chapter Forty-Two

Princess Street
Edinburgh
May 1937

My Love is Like a Red, Red Rose

Fiona carried the captain's log to the breakfast table. The compulsion to keep reading was almost overpowering. Even while she made her tea and porridge, she found herself glancing over at the log. She brought her breakfast to the large kitchen table and began reading again.

June 1 in the year of our Lord 1745.

Second Day at Sea off the Coast of England, bound for Amsterdam.

We put to sea after a close call in Arbroath. Seems yon tariff official, a Scot by the name of Allen Sutherland, requested more of the king's troops to help him catch merchant ships trying to avoid the high taxes. They call us smugglers and would hang us for trying to make a decent living. I canna see how a man can turn against his own people.

But then there's my brother John. He hates Highlanders, and it's driven him to sell his soul to King George. It cuts me to see this. As lads, we were mates. Now I canna bear the sight of him, nor he of me.

We had anchored as far out as we dare, and I had the lads row me in at night. Tamash's father runs a public house, and he's always a guid source of information.

To be honest, finding a way around the English was not my only purpose. I wanted to see Mairi again. I canna get her from my mind since our last visit. She's beautiful but fierce in her love for God. I dinna ken such devotion to a God who wants nothing to do with us humans. Even if I offered marriage, I'm not sure I could have her. She'll no want a rogue such as me.

Then again, I saw her face light up when I came wi Tamash to her door. She gave me such a smile and called me Wee Geordie. It was grand. I'm in dangerous waters and should keep my mind on the task Charlie trusted me with.

Fiona looked up. "I shall have to stop calling you the Black Captain. After all, you like to be called Wee Geordie." Her eyes were soft with the growing admiration for this man, and she imagined him smiling back.

She closed the book and made quick work of finishing her meal. The mantel clock in the library chimed the quarter hour. *I've stayed too long with my book. I'll need to hurry.* This morning, Rab had agreed to introduce her to his friend at the Bank of Scotland.

She was ready and waiting when Rab knocked on her door. "Och, lassie, yer a rare woman to be so punctual." Rab's thumb pointed behind him. "I picked up a stray to come wi us."

She looked past Rab to see Laurie. Heat rose in her cheeks.

"I'd like to come along if you don't mind?"

Laurie sounded so tentative. If she didn't answer, it was because she couldn't stop smiling. *Of course I don't mind. I love the idea.* She nodded her head and joined them on the front steps.

They walked into town together in comfortable conversation. Fiona was introduced to Mr. Hamish Morrison of the Bank of

Scotland and treated like a grand lady. She deposited her check from Neville and planned for the money that came with the house and her money from the bank in Quebec to be transferred to her new account. She would have enough money to pay taxes and keep a roof over her head until she found work—or whatever God had planned for her. They celebrated her fortune with steak pies at a small pub off Princess Street. Over lunch, Laurie told her about his next adventure.

He started, "See, it's like this. I've known it was wrong between Marguerite and me for some months now." He shot Rab a sharp glance, but Rab was looking down. "Rab tried to tell me, but I wouldn't listen." Rab glanced up at Laurie with such an expression of love and relief. Laurie smiled at his grandfather but went on. "I told myself I was one lucky guy—beautiful girl, great job. I could make our lives a lot easier."

Rab interrupted him. "We dinna need the money, laddie. Haven't we always managed?"

"I know, Rab. I've seen how you stretched our money to provide for me at school and keep our house, but I wanted things to be easier for you." Laurie paused and said, "What I really wanted was for things to be easy for me. I didn't let myself think I might use Marguerite. I convinced myself I loved her."

"Laurie, you don't have to tell me all this."

"I want you to know who I am, all I've done."

He wants me to know about his failures? Her pulse sped up. *Does that mean he cares for me, or am I reading something into this?*

Laurie played with his fork like a child admitting something distasteful. "When I started thinking about calling it off, Marguerite's father offered me a grand opportunity at a great shipyard in Germany. I guess I lied to myself after that. I thought of the years I'd be saving on an apprentice program at Scotts Shipbuilding." He looked embarrassed. "I wanted to skip all the steps my classmates were taking, shoot straight ways to the top. But yesterday I was ready to give it all up."

Fiona hadn't realized how tense her muscles were. The tightness in her neck eased, and she sighed. "I'm glad you're not going to Germany." A blush spread across her cheeks. *Oh Laurie, I want you to stay.* It was as if he could read her mind, and he answered her thoughts with a warm smile. Something passed between them. The silence that followed was charged with emotion.

Until Rab said, "Oh, but he is going." He broke into a broad grin at her astonishment. "Och, lass, now he must go. For those children." She sat back in her chair with her mouth still open. "Aye, well, ye understand they are not his children."

Laurie said, "Rab, let me tell her. You're only making matters worse." The telling of the tale of Bernie's two young cousins lasted until it was time for dessert. Laurie pulled out the little photograph of the two wee bairns and passed it over to Fiona.

She picked it up and studied the two little faces. She felt the prick of tears in her eyes as she whispered, "Och, poor wee ones." When she looked up at Laurie, her dark eyes glistened with sympathy. "You're saying the German government took their parents, and the children are in hiding? But how will you find them? Won't this be dangerous for you as well?"

Laurie seemed touched by her concern. "It can't be helped. At the very least, I need to find out what happened to them. And hopefully get them out."

Rab winked. "And that be the reason we're telling you. According to Bernie, the family has exhausted all legal channels. To say the Germans hate Jews is a colossal understatement. They're killing them. That's what we're hearing. And our government isn't any help. Yon English politician Prime Minister Chamberlain is making friends with the Nazi government. From what we hear, Chamberlain isn't doing anything to rock the boat. 'Peace in our time,' he says, but at what cost? At the cost of wee bairns?"

Fiona asked, "What can I do to help?"

Laurie stared into her eyes with such intensity. "We, that is I, wanted you to know what was happening." Warmth spread through her body. "I didn't want to leave with you thinking I was set to build ships for the Germans. I mean, I just felt it was important you know." There was such depth in his dark blue eyes. Speechless, Fiona reached out to squeeze his hand.

Rab said, "For the now, just pray for them. There may be more later, but..." He spread his hands.

After lunch, they did some shopping in the open-air markets. Rab found another old friend and left them to have a chat. Laurie and Fiona wandered through the stalls looking at everything from produce to old books. She held up an old copy of poems by Robert Burns. Laurie took it from her hand.

"You like poetry?" he asked. "This is a fine old book. I have a book of Burns' poetry, but it's newer."

"You never cease to surprise me, Mr. MacKenzie."

Laurie paged through, showing her the old prints. "The rough-cut paper is a hint at its age." He found the copyright date. "1912, hmm, there's a book worth saving." He smiled with genuine delight. His eyes held hers.

She couldn't look away. Those sea-blue eyes held such promise. "You aren't leading a girl on are you, Mr. MacKenzie?" Silence stretched on.

"I can prove my sincerity." Laurie handed her the book open to the poem "My Luve is Like a Red, Red Rose." He smiled again, his eyes soft like the glassy surface of a quiet bay. His voice was deep and smooth.

"O my luve is like a red, red rose,

That's newly sprung in June:

O my love is like a melody

That's sweetly played in tune."

His voice was so soft, she had to concentrate to listen over the noise of the market.

"As fair art thou, my bonnie lass,

So deep in luve am I;

And I will luve you still, my dear,

Till a' the seas gang dry.
Till a' the seas gang dry, my dear,
And the rocks melt wi the sun;
And I will luve thee still my dear,
While the sands o' life shall run.
And fare thee weel, my only luve!
And fare thee weel a while!
And I will come again, my luve,
Tho' it were ten thousand mile."

He spoke the words as if meant for her alone. He finished, and she closed the book, saying, "That was wonderful."

A woman bumped into her, reaching past Fiona for another book and the spell broke, the crowded market reminding her they weren't alone.

"Well, there's a lot you don't know about me ... yet." He turned to the vendor and purchased the book.

Rab waved to them across the square, and they walked over to join him. Rab said, "I've been talkin' to Jock. I haven't seen him in years."

The fine day was waning when they started back toward Latimer Square. It had been a wonderful afternoon. They laughed and talked, enjoying the companionship. As they walked toward home, Fiona felt a twinge of sadness. Not wanting her perfect day to end, she looked back across Princess Street Gardens and the Castle. "Thank you both for this afternoon. I've had such a good time."

"Och, lassie, if not for ye, my grandson and I would still be at odds."

Laurie reached out and took her hand. "Rab's right. You've changed things more than you realize. Not just for Rab and me."

No one said anything. They stood with the wind whipping round them. Not sure why she needed to lighten the moment, she said, "You remind me of the captain." Laurie's reaction was comical.

He put a hand on his chest in mock offense. "Me? Whatever gives you that idea? Except for our roguish good looks, we're nothing alike."

Rab adopted a thoughtful stance. "Aye, I can see it now. Our Laurie has the look of a smuggler."

She teased, "Not that so much, although you are a bit of a rogue, as he was. It's something in your eyes." She withdrew her hand from his to push her curls off her face. "You both have such kind eyes." But her eyes lingered on his full lips before she turned to walk onward.

Soon they were at Latimer Square. Rab said his goodbyes, claiming tired feet, and went home. But Laurie seemed reluctant to let her go. She was as reluctant for him to leave. He walked her to the door and waited while she unlocked it. When she turned around to say goodbye, he took her hand again.

"I had a wonderful day." His confident persona was gone. "You must think I'm rotten for leading Marguerite on while I find those children." He scrubbed his other hand through his hair. "I feel rotten. She doesn't deserve this. Honestly, I can't think of any other way to look for those bairns but to keep up the pretense that everything's the same between us." He was so serious. "I don't want you to think—I don't know—that I'm a terrible person."

Fiona shook her head in protest. "There doesn't seem to be any other course for you to take." Embarrassed by her own forcefulness, she said, "Well, anyway, I had a wonderful day, too. In a month, you'll be gone. I hope I'll see you before you leave."

He leaned forward and gave her a gentle kiss on the forehead, saying, "Every minute you can give me." He left her standing there wondering what would come of this perfect afternoon.

Chapter Forty-Three

Kempten, Germany
May 1937

The Wolf Goes Hunting

It was only the second time Eric had worn his dark suit. He was still perfecting the art of ordinary. *Look down, don't make eye contact with anyone in uniform. Smile and nod at the other sheep as I pass them on the street. Oh, and take off the fedora when entering a church.* It was both exhilarating and uneventful. He savored his disguise each time a fellow officer passed him without recognition. He commended himself on his excellent acting skills. It was also boring, because these people were living mundane lives. So far, there had been little to spike his interest.

He'd discovered only one secret worth chasing. *The commandant was meeting with a pretty young woman.* He had every intention of exploiting this indiscretion if the opportunity arose. "So, I'm incompetent?" he whispered under his breath. "You stupid little man. I know who your wife is, and I wonder how she'd take this news."

It was market day again. Eric strolled through the stalls, appearing to be interested in everything but not really looking at anything. Until he spotted his Ana. She was buying produce a few feet away from him. She completed her purchase and was struggling with her shopping bags when he approached her.

"Fraulein Ana." He took his hat off and tried to appear sheepish. "I'd like to apologize to you if you have a minute." As she turned to him, he thought he'd never seen eyes so blue. He heard a quick intake of breath. *So she does remember me, even in my ordinary costume.*

Ana hesitated a moment, looking down and then up again. "I'm sorry. You must have mistaken me for someone else. We've never met before." She lifted her bags and turned to walk away.

Good try, he thought. *You're too honest to make an effective liar.* Still, it was all he could do not to grab her arm and spin her around to face him. Instead, he fell in step beside her. "My name is Eric. You might not recognize me out of uniform."

His inner voice argued back. *Why make it easy on her? Call her on her lie. But an ordinary fellow wouldn't challenge her, would he? And that's the point. My wolf will just have to stay caged until I ... what? Learn about being a sheep?* He looked down at this innocent young woman. *Until I seduce her? Is that what I want?* Eric shook off his question. He wasn't sure what he was doing. *Perhaps I'm only amusing myself.*

Ana stopped for a moment, her eyes still down. With his hat in his hand, Eric said, "I'd really like it if we could talk for a few minutes. Let me buy you a coffee." He bent to look into her downcast face. "I am a nice person when you get to know me." *What's one more lie?* "Just an ordinary man."

She looked up with hesitation. "My employer is expecting me back with the shopping."

He reached out and took her shopping bags. "A minute, bitte. Please, it would mean so much to me." She waited only a split second longer before nodding. He looked around and found luck was with him. He spotted a cafe down the street. They walked in silence, and when they entered the cafe, he asked for a seat by the front window so he'd be able to observe her when she left.

She was afraid. He sensed it. He wanted to put her at ease. Eric's mind raced ahead, looking for some way to reach her. "It's not always pleasant, my line of work. I am alone most of the time." The waiter came back for their order. Eric looked up with irritation. He quickly covered his irritation with his pleasant mask, sliding back into his role, and he asked for two coffees and two apple streusels. *Not that I would be eating anything in this dump.* Looking back at Ana, he smiled. "I was raised in the church, you know. My mother was a good Catholic." Surprise registered on her sweet face. There was his hook. "I sang in the choir." She still said nothing. "And you?"

She looked out the window as if deciding something. Turning back to him, she said, "I, too, was raised in the church."

"See, we have something in common already. Is your family from around here?" Again, the meddling waiter interrupted them by serving the coffee and pastry.

"Where are you from?" she asked.

A start at least. Without stopping to think about it, he decided to be as honest as possible. "I am from Strasbourg. Have you been there?"

She shook her head, stammering, "No, I don't get out much. Do your parents still live there?"

"My mother is dead." His own voice sounded flat and foreign to him. "She died when I was thirteen. Bad pregnancy—it was her life or the child's. You know the church's teaching about abortion. In the end, neither of them survived. My father drank after that. He blamed the church." He shook his head with a rueful chuckle and leaned forward. "I rarely tell people that."

Drawn by those striking blue eyes, Eric wondered, *If eyes could talk, would hers tell me she felt sorry for my loss? She is sympathetic, and it doesn't make me angry. How odd.* "What about you? Tell me about your life."

"It's simple. Work and sleep. Please, I really must get back to work."

"A little longer. Here, you haven't even touched your coffee." Eric took a bite of the streusel. He smiled with his mouth full. "It's quite good." She picked up her fork.

"I'm not used to talking with men." She took a bite of her pastry and smiled, too. "You're right. It is very good." They chatted for a few minutes before she said again. "The people I work for are waiting on these vegetables for a soup. I must go."

Not now. We are making progress. We shared ordinary conversation. She sees me as a man, not a uniform. It was his turn to hesitate. *I will let you go to make it all the easier to catch you next time.*

He stood and went around to pull out her chair. "It was good to have someone to talk to. Thank you for your time." It made him feel good to see her face radiate kindness. "I will watch for you again on market day. Perhaps we could talk some more?"

This time, her smile was relaxed and friendly before she turned to leave. Eric sat and watched her go from his window seat. She didn't look back as he'd hoped, but that would come in time. He was sure of it. *Today was only the start.*

Chapter Forty-Four

Downstairs Brothel
Kempten, Germany
May 1937

A Dangerous Time for a Woman Child

Ana struggled with the laundry basket as she came down the cellar stairs. She didn't mind the work; it made her feel useful to help with the chores. She turned to go back upstairs for the hot water. The murmur of female voices caught her attention. The ladies upstairs spent as much time as they could down here with the children. The constant attention was a pleasant distraction. It kept her little ones from becoming too restless.

The secret door stood open, and she peeked in to see what they were doing. Deter and Gretchen sprawled on the floor drawing pictures. Crayons and papers spread out all around them. As she entered the room, she saw Katrine with Berdine and Sophie. Katrine's hair was piled high on her head, her innocent face transformed with make-up into a beautiful woman.

Ana reacted without thinking. "Katrine, no." Her voice sounded harsher than she meant.

Katrine jumped, but Berdine and Sophie put their chins in the air, their expressions defiant. Berdine said, "Only a bit of fun showing Katrine what a beautiful woman she already is." Katrine's eyes were round, and her luscious red lower lip looked close to a pout.

Ana paused, taking in the scene. She felt alarmed at the implications this might have for Katrine. Her mind searched for the right thing to say. *It would be ungrateful to make too much of this. We depend on everyone's goodwill. But Katrine won't be safe for long in this environment. Berdine wasn't much older than Katrine. Some girls may have started at a young age. Katrine looks beautiful and all grown up.*

She took a deep breath and began again. "I know you meant no harm. My mother worked in your profession, but I've lived so many years in a convent school and then in service at Saint Thomas." She reached out to touch Katrine's cheek, saying, "Katrine, you are beautiful." If her words were forced, the ladies didn't seem to notice.

To Berdine, Ana said, "I'm sorry, it was just a shock. I don't judge you, but please don't judge me." She nodded, and they answered her with smiles of relief.

Ana turned and left the room. *This time disaster is avoided, but how long until the next liberty leads my precious Katrine down the wrong path? I can see why my grandmother sent me to convent school at Katrine's age. I need to pray about this. As if Eric isn't enough incentive to leave.*

Turning back to the task at hand, she thought Sister Mary Clare was right. *Hard work is helpful when you need to find the right path.*

Chapter Forty-Five

The Brothel
Kempten, Germany
May 1937

Visions of Deserts Dance Across the Walls

Ana smiled to herself at the memory of Gretchen playing with her new doll, Berta, a gift from the ladies upstairs. The four-year-old was imitating Dorcus making a cheese blintz. *Gretchen's pretty observant. She has the cook's mannerisms copied exactly.* Ana was chuckling as she came up the cellar stairs.

The large cook stood with her ear to the hallway door.

Ana froze and whispered, "What is it?"

The cook jumped and spun around. Dorcus crossed the kitchen and grabbed Ana by the arm. "Sister, you must go to the children and close the door. Hurry, but make sure you left nothing outside your room." She gave Ana's arm a little shake. "Go, Ana, and close the door." Ana headed back down the stairs as Dorcus called after her, "And for God's sake, keep the children silent."

Ana's heart was beating. With every pulse, her anxiety

increased. At the bottom of the stairs, she stopped, closed her eyes for a second and took a deep breath. *Father, your peace, please?* Sister Mary Clare, Sister Freda and Father Hugo's faces flitted through her thoughts. All lost to the new Nazi policies. Both of her fellow sisters had disappeared along with the children they were helping to escape.

Ana pulled herself up short. *I can't think like that. Lord, don't let me show fear to the children.* She opened her eyes to scan the cellar. Nothing you wouldn't expect in a cellar. Before she slipped through the secret doorway, Ana took a dusty old gunny sack and shook it out over the floor before the entrance.

She turned to see her children standing like little statues watching her. They knew the look of danger, no use hiding it from them. She opened her arms, and they came to her. "It'll be all right. God can hide us just like before. Trust him." Good words, but her mind flashed scenes of horrible possibilities. "We need to turn out all the lights. We'll keep one candle so we can move around without bumping into each other, yes?" To change their focus, she said, "Let's pull all our blankets and pillows into the middle of the floor, and I'll tell you a story."

"This is like Sukkot. Papa made tents, and we all slept together on—" Gretchen's chin trembled as it always did when she spoke about her parents. One tear rolled down Gretchen's pudgy cheek. *Poor child, God sees how much you've lost.* Ana reached out to stroke her curly little head.

Deter added, "We built a hut on our roof, and we ate and slept there for seven days." A smile touched his little face but faded away as quickly as it had come. He put his arm around Gretchen and looked down at her. "Papa stayed home, and we were all together."

Ana added, "Yes, Deter, do you remember the story about families who lived in tents and traveled through the desert?" Deter nodded, his expression somber. "Those who escaped Egypt wandered in the wilderness for forty years. But our story was before that happened."

Deter's eyes weren't on his sister. He stared at the ceiling. The very walls trembled with thuds and bangs.

Ana continued. "Our story begins with a baby boy just like little Tony. God hid him from the Pharaoh. Can you guess the baby's name?"

His attention back on Ana, Deter's hand shot up. "I know this one. His name was Moshi, ja?"

"That's right, Deter. We call him Moses, but he's the same baby who grew up right under the Pharaoh's nose. The story begins with—"

Boots clomped down the cellar stairs. Ana said, "Hush," and she blew out the candle. But she continued to whisper the story to them. They were enthralled. It must have been the best story in the world, because long after the boots went back up the stairs and the cellar door slammed, they all lay in the pile of blankets in the middle of the floor. Pictures of a large desert danced across the dark room. They fell asleep while she told them about the miracles of the seven plagues God used to convince Pharaoh to let his children go free.

Much later, when all was quiet, Ana wondered why no one from upstairs told them what happened. She wanted to go up and find out, but it was much too dangerous. Better to wait for morning when she might venture out of their room. Ana tried not to imagine what would have happened if they'd been found. *Not just us. What about Dorcus and Madam Leona and all the other ladies?* She squeezed her eyes tight to block out the images, and when she opened them she saw the sleeping faces of Tony, Gretchen and Deter. Instead of panic, she felt peace. She said to herself, "Aren't we like those wandering Israelites escaping from a tyrant?"

Katrine roused at her words and gave Ana a weak smile, then closed her eyes to sleep again. The young teen knew they were in danger. It was encouraging to see strength and maturity beginning to form in her. As Ana drifted off to sleep, she whispered, "Thank you."

IT WAS dark when Ana woke. A chill in the air, the fire in the old stove now glowing coals. So, not morning yet. Must be late, though. She wondered what had roused her.

Listening, she heard Gretchen crying in her sleep. *Poor child.* For someone so full of joy during the day, little Gretchen sometimes cried in the night, especially when she missed her mother. Deter woke to comfort her. Ana didn't have to see Deter to know he was stroking his sister's hair and holding her close like a mother would. *He is only six. Mein Gott, so little to carry so much.*

"I saw Mamma," Gretchen whispered. "She was calling me. I tried to go to her, but I couldn't. Why couldn't I go? Mamma wanted me." Her little girl voice made a sound like a baby's cry. "Where is Mamma? Why can't we go to her? I want Mamma," Gretchen sobbed.

Deter made a soft shushing sound. "We'll be with Mamma and Papa again soon. It'll be all right. We're safe." The crying settled. Ana imagined little Gretchen was drifting back to sleep. *Every day has cares and worries, but the nights hold heartbreaking memories for us all.*

Ana woke again before the children and lay wondering what she should do. There was no window to measure the time by the light outside, but somehow it felt like early morning. Within minutes, the door opened. Silhouetted in the doorway, Madam Leona motioned for Ana to follow her.

Once they were both outside the room, she said, "Let the little ones sleep longer. Come, we'll go up to the kitchen." The smell of hot coffee and sausages floated from the cook stove. Dorcus greeted her with a worried look as she set two plates full of breakfast down at the kitchen table.

"Dorcus," Madam said, "stop and eat with us. The three of us should put our heads together and decide what to do next."

Ana had been holding her breath, waiting for some terrible news. Even before she sat, she asked, "What happened last night?"

Dorcus plopped down in a chair with her breakfast plate in hand. "That was a close call for all of us," she mumbled.

Leona looked tired. "Not the last one we'll have, either."

"Was it Eric?"

"No, our late-night inspection was courtesy of a disgruntled client. You remember—the man that beat our Jeannette. I turned him out and told him not to come back."

Ana's mind thought back to the large bruise on Jeannette's sweet face. She shuddered. *So that's what happened to her.* Madam Leona noticed her shudder and remarked in a whisper, "These Nazis are pigs, and the SS are especially brutal. They turned the house upside down, and I still don't know what they were looking for." Leona took her first bite of food. "Thank God, they found nothing. Not even our friendship with the commandant would help us if they found the children." She paused, staring at her plate.

"What about your connections? Is there any word on getting us out of here?" Ana could hear panic rising in her own voice.

"Not yet, but here's what I think we need to do," Leona said. "You need to go about your business as usual. Keep shopping." Ana drew in her breath to protest, but Leona continued. "The best place to hide is in plain sight. Until we find a way out for you and the children, you need to keep Eric from being another disgruntled Nazi. I can't afford more reprisals. If we become too much of a liability, we could all be arrested."

Dorcus looked at Ana. "Eat, sister." She shot a quick look at Leona. "I mean, Ana. It will do no good to worry ahead."

Ana thought, *fine advice from someone who looks as worried as I feel.*

But she picked up her fork and took a bite of breakfast, not that she tasted any of it.

Chapter Forty-Six

Market Day
Kempten, Germany
May 1937

He's Searching for Me

Ana's lips pressed together with grim determination. It was market day again. She picked up her basket and the list from Dorcus. Madam Leona stopped her at the kitchen door.

"Be pleasant to him," she said. She must have caught alarm on Ana's face. "I'm not saying you should act like one of my girls. Be your innocent self. Remember the identity we've created for you, and by all means, keep your wits about you. Many lives depend on it." She patted Ana's arm and said with a wry smile, "I hope you said your prayers this morning."

Ana put her hand over Leona's. "It's what we do best. Prayer is like breathing to us. It only stops when we're dead." She was out the back door and on her way.

It was a beautiful day. Still cold but a hint of spring was in the air. As she scanned her list, Ana planned which stall she'd visit first. *Don't watch for Herr Eric. Act relaxed. Concentrate on the shopping.* Her inner voice sounded like Sister Mary Clare, stern and cross. It made her smile.

The air around the vendors smelled of fruits and vegetables. It reminded her of her childhood living in the country with her grandmother. Her step faltered as she detected the aroma of a man's cologne. Fear flooded her. It was foolish. She was, after all, surrounded by all kinds of people. Still, she looked around, expecting to see Eric somewhere close. No, only people buying and selling.

She moved on to the butchers for stew meat and sausages. *There it is again, the same cologne.* She twisted to look around but still no Eric. Two young men loitered on the street corner. One of them looked back at her, a leer tainting his boyish features. His friend said something, and they both laughed. Ana quickened her step. *Hitler Youth.*

She waited in the crowded butcher shop while a woman argued about the price of sausages. When Ana finished her purchase, it was a relief to step back onto the street. She pulled her list from her pocket to check it one last time. *I'm done and no Eric. You are worried about nothing.* Even her heavy basket felt lighter.

The fragrance of cologne was overpowering. A hand came from behind and took her basket. Startled, she spun around, bringing her face to face with Eric. He smiled at her surprise. She forced herself to smile back but said with mocked severity, "Herr Eric, you gave me quite a start."

"You're not frightened. You are smiling." His tone was teasing, but it seemed suspicious as well.

"I'm glad it was you and not one of those rude young men." She gestured to the group of Hitler Youth. Honestly, she was. She had some idea of what to expect from him, while they were like a pack of stray dogs, unpredictable.

"Glad it was me? You see, we're making progress." He could

be charming. "Will you join me for a coffee? I enjoyed our talk last time."

Ana hesitated.

"It isn't often I can talk to a friendly person," Eric continued. "I want something ... or they do. You don't want anything, do you, Ana?"

She looked at him. There was something very sincere about his comment, and she wondered at his honesty. "That is a very sad statement, Herr Eric."

He appeared discomfited but continued with a melancholy expression. "Power is not always a blessing. It can be a curse as well."

Ana reminded herself he was used to manipulating people. "I have to get back soon, but for a few minutes..." She hesitated again, and then she said, "Ja, I can have a coffee. But I will buy my own, bitte. My grandmother wouldn't approve any other way."

Eric nodded, and they fell into step, heading for the bakery with its small sidewalk tables. It was chilly, but the sun was shining on them, so sitting outside was pleasant.

"You're not wearing your uniform again." It was a statement and a question.

"Do you approve or disapprove?"

"I think you are less formidable." She could see she'd said the wrong thing. "Friendlier," she added. *Such a contradiction—first he looks insulted, and now he looks pleased. Lord, if you don't help me, I know I'll say all the wrong things.*

When the waiter arrived, he ordered two coffees.

"Tell me something about yourself."

Knowing he would ask about her story, she drew a deep breath. She was ready. "My grandmother raised me, and we lived in the country. What would you like to know?" *Madam said to tell the truth as much as possible. I'm less likely to make a mistake.* "I attended school in the convent."

"Well, that would explain why you don't work upstairs." She

could feel herself blush, but she didn't think he was trying to embarrass her. He seemed interested. "But why would you work for a brothel?" It was an honest question, and she felt he needed an answer.

"I led a sheltered life, but my beginnings were not so conventional. My mother was a prostitute." She could see his shock and something else. Judgment? "My mother left home because she fell in love with a very charming man. When it ended, he left her in a bordello in Berlin. She came home—sick, dying, with a baby in her arms. That was me."

Ana wasn't sure how he was taking this. Something had changed in his attitude, in the way he looked at her. "My mother died soon after, and my grandmother raised me. I think she feared I would take after my mother, so she kept me very close. I try not to judge others. Lady Leona pays well, and she is a kind employer. It's enough."

She finished as the waiter brought their drinks. "You must tire of always asking people questions." She was trying to turn the questions away from herself. "I think you are someone who studies people. Does that make you cynical?"

He seemed pleased by her assessment of his abilities. "Oh, cynical, yes, but I will change my mind in your case." The hint of a sardonic smile flashed on his features.

"I heard there was a raid on your place of employment, but no one mentioned seeing you. I wondered if you have a lover somewhere keeping you away at night?"

Lord, is he interested in me for more than friendship? Be direct. "No, and if your intentions are friendship, I can offer you that. Anything else is not possible for me. Do not confuse me with my mother or my employer." Her tone was firm but not hostile.

Eric was silent. His face went blank. Then he said, "There are people who would be afraid to be so honest with me." He seemed tense as he measured his words. "I will accept your friendship."

But it was clear he wanted more, and that made him even more dangerous.

As they sipped their coffee, a man came down the street playing his accordion. On market day, strolling musicians often performed for the crowds. His little monkey danced to the music of a children's song. The animal's antics were so comical. Soon, Ana and Eric were both laughing. When the song finished, the monkey tipped his hat, and Eric tossed him a coin. The tension broken, they talked with the ease of friends.

"I've been visiting churches." He laughed at her surprise. "No, it's true. I was wondering if you would join me tomorrow." Ana closed her mouth, speechless. "What harm can come from attending church with a friend?"

"Herr Eric, you surprise me. I wouldn't think you'd be interested in church." She was smiling as she thought, *I was hoping I'd see some good in you. Is he searching for God? No, not God, she remembered. He's searching for me.*

"Ana, you're not smiling," he said. "You know, you should smile all the time. You have a beautiful smile."

Chapter Forty-Seven

Edinburgh
May 1937

July 5, 1745

Scenes of her day with Rab and Laurie floated through Fiona's thoughts. She kept coming back to Laurie's confession that he didn't love the German girl. *Thank God.* The intensity of her relief surprised her. *Why tell me?* One thing was certain: her feelings ran deeper than she'd allowed herself to contemplate. *Until now.*

It was late when she climbed into bed. She turned the gaslight down low and lay back on her pillow. She closed her eyes, but her mind replayed Laurie's voice reciting the Burns' poem. She'd followed along from the book. Laurie hadn't missed a word, but it wasn't like he was reciting the words of the poet. *No, it felt like he was saying them for me.*

She sat up in bed. *Stop it, you goose. Stop making more of everything he said.* Turning her light back up, she saw the captain's log sitting on the table by her bed, inviting her to read. *Just what I need to settle my thoughts.* She picked up the old book and read from George Ferguson's log dated July 5,1745.

I've been home for two weeks, visiting common houses and keeping my ears open. I heard the Black Captain was seen in Arbroath in June. It made me smile to hear how hated I was. Well, they thought I was John.

I've not visited any of the ladies I usually see when in port. I can't say I'm interested. Mairi's face keeps coming to mind. Tamash asked if I was feeling myself. I canna tell him. I wish I could be as good a man as he to deserve Mairi's attention. He'd have a laugh or else I'd be fighting a duel with my best mate. I canna go on like this for much longer. I'm ready to go to war. I need to fight with someone.

Fiona closed the log. *I wonder if Wee Geordie and Mairi will get together?* That brought to mind another face. She whispered Laurie's name and reached up to touch her forehead, remembering the kiss he'd placed there.

You goose, he kissed you like a brother. But his eyes said so much more. And he wants to spend every minute he can with me. That must mean something.

She looked at Wee Geordie and asked, "Do you think he feels the same way you did about Mairi?" The captain didn't answer. Fiona turned out the lamp, and the room was once more in darkness. She slid down into bed and cuddled under her comforter. One last conscious thought floated through her mind. *I wonder what the future holds for me?* When she fell asleep, a smile lingered on her lips.

Chapter Forty-Eight

House on Latimer Square
May 1937

Finding the Puzzle Box

Fiona found a light switch by the cellar door, but the stairs stayed dark even after she flipped it several times. *Either no electricity or a faulty bulb.* So she carried an old oil lamp down the worn stone cellar steps. Flickering light cast dark shadows on the cellar walls. *It's cold down here.* A shiver ran up her back. By now, she'd finished cleaning everything in the house except the cellar. It was time she started down here. She forced herself to walk around, finding a welcome surprise. Ahead of her was an old coal shuttle and a bin full of coal. She'd used the coal in all the scuttles around the house and now knew where to replenish them.

The cellar was essentially one large room. Along the far wall, she recognized the remnants of what looked to be an old kitchen with a large fireplace rigged for cooking, much like the kitchen upstairs. Above her head, hooks were imbedded in the beamed ceiling. She guessed they were for hanging game.

Along one wall, a closet constructed of rough-hewed bricks held shelves with a few dusty bottles still present. Fiona picked up one and blew off the dust. An ancient label told her whatever it contained was from 1801. She blinked in astonishment. "I have a wine cellar."

There were several windows near the ceiling, but they all had iron bars on them and were so dirty the light barely penetrated the old glass. Although the house above was substantial, the cellar wasn't as large.

She found old iron lanterns on the walls and lit them from her oil lamp. With the added light, the room didn't feel as spooky. The hair on the back of her neck pricked, and she swung around several times, expecting to see someone standing there. She was alone. "Silly. I'm not leaving until it's clean down here." Her own words were comforting. Although the underground room smelled musty and unused, it was still her home. She decided the floors needed a good scrubbing and went to get her cleaning pail and brushes.

She worked her way across the main room until she was in the far corner. She forgot her fears with the pleasure of seeing how well the old flagstones cleaned up.

By the time she'd almost finished, the hairs on the back of her neck prickled again. Her old fears came flooding back, and she stopped scrubbing, her hand frozen above the stone floor. There was a definite presence in the room. She held her breath and listened. *Only childish fear. I'm not giving in to it.* But fear was her first response when something touched her back. She started and turned around.

A voice from across the room on the shadowed stairs called out, "I knocked, but you didn't answer." It was Alec. He was standing on the stairs with a smile on his face. He cleared his throat, waiting.

"Umm," she hesitated, swallowing hard, staring at the empty room behind her. *If Alec didn't touch my back, who did?*

"I can come back later if it's a bad time..." His voice trailed off and his smile wavered.

Fiona recovered her wits and said, "No, no, you only startled me. I thought I was alone in the house."

He jogged down the steps and walked around. "So this is your cellar. It looks the same as ours. I thought there'd be old trunks full of treasures." He chuckled.

Fiona stood, her hand moving to tuck back the curls escaping from her scarf. "I think I'm done down here. Can I fix you some tea?"

Alec seemed distracted. He was studying the cellar walls as if looking for something.

"Is something wrong, Alec?"

He looked back at her. "Not at all. I'm only interested in this house." He seemed to shake himself. "I'd love a cup of tea. Here, let me get that for you."

As he spoke, he reached for the soapy water, but Fiona was putting her scrub brush back in the pail. Their hands collided. The bucket tipped, spilling the water on the flagstone floor. Most of it rushed toward an old drain, but some pooled around one stone. It drained through the cracks around the edge.

Alec seemed interested in the floor. "That's odd. Could be the stone is loose."

"Och, aye. You're right, Alec. I expect I should make sure no one trips on it." She bent to see if the stone moved, but Alec pushed past her.

"Here, let me help." He grabbed the edge of the old flagstone. It lifted. He positioned himself over the stone and slipped his fingers under the opposite edge.

"Careful, Alec, that would be very—" But even as she spoke, he lifted the stone with little effort. He stopped to peer into the cavity below. Water collected in the bottom of what appeared to be a hiding place for a small rectangle container.

"Oh my, what have you found?" She reached down and picked up a small carved box.

Alec set the stone down and snatched the box from her hand, his eyes alight with interest.

"What have we here?" He held it close, examining it. It was not bigger than a brick. Something rattled inside. The top of the box looked like a puzzle, with ornate carvings fitted together randomly. No opening was visible.

His fingers worked over the edges, seeking a way to reveal the contents. "I can't see a way this should open, but something is inside." He shook the box as if to prove his point. "Who would hide a box in the cellar floor?" He looked up with an aha expression. "It must be valuable."

"More like wee bairns playing buried treasure, aye? It appears to be a puzzle box."

Fiona reached out, waiting for him to put the box back in her hand. He kept looking at it. She could feel heat rising in her cheeks, but her hand stayed stretched out. He set the box on her palm.

Turning toward the stairs, she said, "How about tea? I think I have some biscuits." She was sure he'd try to snatch the box back at the first opportunity. *Not a chance, Alec. If it's the captain's, it would be a treasure in its own right. Imagine, Wee Geordie, she thought, if the last hand to touch this was yours. And why would you bury it in your cellar floor? You're a canny man, so you must have had your reasons.*

They climbed the stairs to the kitchen. Alec was saying, "I'm pretty good at puzzles. You should let me have a go at it. Could be something exciting."

She wasn't sure why, but the more he pushed to look at the box, the more certain she was he shouldn't get his hands on it.

WHEN THEY ENTERED THE KITCHEN, she said, "Have a seat, and I'll have tea ready in a minute." She crossed the room, opened a cupboard and put the box inside. Alec was only a half-step behind her. She could see he was crestfallen.

He didn't sit. Instead, he looked at this watch. "Thank you, Fiona, but no. I just realized I have an appointment with one of our clients, so I must be off." As he turned to leave, he popped his head back through the doorway, saying, "You know, I'm always interested in what's happening in your life. If you need any help" —he gestured to the cupboard—"ring me up." His expression was so warm and genuine, Fiona felt rotten. She'd have to stop being so suspicious. *After all, Alec had been nothing but friendly.*

Chapter Forty-Nine

On the Road in Germany
May 1937

Flight from the Wolf

Ana's mood was pensive as she walked home. *Thank you, Father. Eric let me go.* Indeed, he had let her go—he could have detained her if he'd chosen to.

She remembered his sweet face as he talked about his childhood. *What kind of man would he have been if his mother hadn't died? From what Father Hugo said, Eric had a reputation as a ruthless man, but there was genuine grief still near the surface of his heart.*

It's sad. We don't realize how much we impact young lives. Flashes of Katrine and the other children raced through her head. How might she impact their lives for good or for evil?

"Lord, is there nothing you can do to turn Eric around?" She saw him as the child who needed to be saved. *If only there could be some way to reach him without putting her children at risk.*

A delivery truck sat in the alley. She squeezed past, deep in thought as she pushed through the kitchen door. She stopped short before colliding with Madam Leona, who'd been standing just inches from the doorway.

"Hurry, Ana, leave the basket on the table. There's no time to lose."

Leona grabbed Ana's wrist and rushed down the kitchen stairs. In the secret room, the children were dressed in warm clothes with bundles under their arms, and a basket with supplies sat on their small table. A roughly dressed man of at least seventy looked relieved as they came through the door.

"We go, ja?" he asked with an encouraging nod.

Leona's gaze was so intent as she said, "There's no time to explain. Get your things. This is our chance, and we can't afford to pass it up. You leave now." Leona gestured to the odd little man, who appeared at the end of his patience. "Herr Hermann will smuggle you out in his truck."

"But where are we going?" Ana asked.

"I don't know. It's safer that way." Leona stroked Ana's cheek. Madam's beautiful eyes grew soft.

This is goodbye. Ana put her hand over Leona's. "We'll never forget all you've done for us."

The children had been standing like little statues. Leona turned to regard them. First little Gretchen, then Deter came forward to give her a solemn hug. Katrine, still holding baby Tony, hugged her. No one wanted to let go, but Leona looked up at Herr Hermann. "Go, and God keep you all safe."

Leona took Gretchen's hand and rushed them back up the cellar stairs and out into the alley. When Herr Hermann pulled aside the back flap to his truck, the smell of fish was so overpowering they all took a step back. The children made faces and protested.

"Can't we wait for the next van?" Deter objected.

"No, Deter, we must take this one," Ana said, tugging on his scarf. "Pull your scarves up over your noses. Come on, hurry, hurry." Herr Hermann helped them climb up into the truck. It was full of large crates of fish packed with ice. A path between them led deep inside.

"Move all the way to the front," Herr Hermann instructed. They huddled down in the farthest corner. The cold was as hard to bear as the odor, but Leona rushed back into the house and appeared again with an armful of blankets. She passed them up to the old man. The last they saw of Leona was a sad smile.

As Herr Hermann handed the blankets to the children, he said, "Be silent, and we should be safe enough."

Deter looked as if he might ask a question, but Ana cut him off by saying, "Thank you, Herr Hermann. How long will we be traveling?"

"We won't be there till late tonight. But I'll make a few stops for the children." For the first time, his face broke into an apologetic smile. "Sorry for the fish. But it covers other scents. The kind their dogs pick up. And not too many soldiers want to pull out fish." His kind face disappeared behind the last crate as he slid it into place, enclosing them in dead fish.

Ana looked at the brave little faces. "Never mind, we'll make the best of this, and it won't be too long." She started digging into the basket. "Let's see what Madam Leona and Dorcus packed for us."

The first thing Ana's hand hit was a torch. She flipped it on as the cover closed over the back of the truck before darkness fell. Maybe in more ways than one.

"Gretchen, we have cookies."

Gretchen smiled halfheartedly. Ana brushed a lock of blond hair out of sad eyes and scooped her up into a hug, patting her back as Gretchen buried her face in Ana's shoulder.

Katrine was holding baby Tony, but she appeared more like a child needing to be held. All remnants of makeup had long since washed off. Her woman child was as innocent as ever. Tony whimpered. Deter sat with his knees pulled up to his chest. Trying so hard to keep his face expressionless, he said, "We will be all right. God will keep us safe."

Ana drew in her breath. *I should have said that. But maybe it was better coming from Deter. A good thing to begin this journey with.*

"You're right again, Deter. God has been watching over us all this way." She reached out and ruffled his hair to remind him he was still a child.

The engine rumbled to life, and they moved. Deter's words seemed to quiet everyone but baby Tony, so Ana looked in the basket of supplies and pulled out a bottle. Within a few minutes, Tony was slurping down liquid comfort.

"It looks like we have enough for lunch and dinner." Ana put a hand to her mouth. *My rosary.* "Oh no! I forgot to pack my things." Her next thought was both a relief and a worry. *We've escaped Eric, but what will he think when I'm not there to go to church with him? I didn't tell Leona or Dorcus.*

Katrine smiled. "I packed all your things in with my own."

"I don't know what we would all do without you." And it was true. Traveling with small children would have been a lot harder without Katrine's constant help.

After twenty minutes, the truck came to a stop. Thank God, the baby was asleep. They all listened, trying to hear what Herr Hermann said to a soldier. A dog began barking. The soldier said, "Out of the truck, old man. We have orders to search everyone." Ana began praying this terrible odor would protect them.

Herr Hermann seemed untroubled. He chuckled. "Of course, of course. I hope you like fish." It seemed forever before the old man undid the lashings holding the back cover secure.

"Mein Gott. That smell is horrible." The children snickered. "Are you sure the fish aren't bad?"

Ana heard some scuffling, and the old man must have pulled a fish from its icy bed and stuck it in the soldier's face because a disgusted voice said, "Get it away from me."

Herr Hermann said with good humor still in his voice, "It's

how fish smell. If I take too long with this shipment, it will go bad. Some of these beauties are headed for Herr Goring's table. I'm sure he would be upset if they spoiled before we get there, but do your search. Only I'll need help to pull them all off the back of my truck. I'm an old man, but you're a sturdy lad. Should be nothing for you."

There was silence for a minute.

"No one could stand that smell. You can move on. Go ahead, old man. Move on." The children covered their mouths to stifle the giggles as Herr Hermann took his time getting back into the truck.

Two hours later, the truck turned, and the road became very bumpy. Branches were scraping the sides and roof. It came to another stop. The children became still and waited until the lashings were being undone and Herr Hermann called out, "It's all right. No one is near. It's time to stretch your legs and get away from the fish. He shifted the crates with the strength of a much younger man, and his wizened face appeared as a crate was lifted out of place.

Deter greeted the old man with admiration. He said, "You are much stronger than you let the soldier believe, Herr Hermann."

The old man tapped his temple. "It is how you use your mind that counts." He helped them off the back of the truck.

Ana judged the time to be somewhere around two in the afternoon. She found a large, flat rock to use for a table and spread out half the contents of the basket, holding enough back for later. They were all quiet as they munched on bratwurst, cheese and fresh bread.

"How much longer will it take us to get there?" asked Gretchen with a mouth full of bread.

"You shouldn't speak with your mouth so full," Herr Hermann said, adding, "We will be at our destination by half-past eight."

"Where are we going?" Gretchen pressed.

Deter cut in. "He can't tell you that. It would be dangerous for you to know. Isn't that right, Herr Hermann?" Deter seemed impressed with the old man.

"I can tell you one thing. We are going into the lair of the lion, but a very strong and good lady will protect us. Like before, we will hide you right under the nose of the Nazis. It is safer this way, but only if you continue to do as you are told." Herr Hermann stood. "We must be on our way, so let's get our things together. Deter, you should be in charge of making sure every crumb is picked up. We don't want to leave any clues we were here."

Deter said, "Right. Gretchen, finish your cookie. Oh no, don't stuff it all in your mouth." He rolled his eyes at his sister's antics. Katrine and Ana chuckled, reassured that Gretchen would always be Gretchen.

They packed up as Deter kept watch for any errant crumb or bit of cheese that might give their secret lunch away. Satisfied at last there were no clues to their presence, he followed the others back into the truck.

Ana tried to pass the afternoon with guessing games and a story. It seemed forever before they once again pulled off the smooth main roadway into a rutted lane. This time, Herr Hermann impressed upon them that they must stretch their legs, relieve themselves and eat. The children were too weary to eat much, so they pressed on.

Funny, Ana thought, *we're all getting used to the fishy smell. And with the blankets, we're not even cold.*

They started drifting off to sleep. Ana still had no idea where they were or what their destination would be. She'd become accustomed to the sound of the main roadway under the truck's tires, and whenever they turned into the woods for a rest, the truck bumped over the uneven ground. She could hear the gravel crunch. *This sounds like a drive. Oh, Lord, are we near the end of our journey?* They must have moved a few hundred yards more when Herr Hermann pulled the truck to a stop.

A voice greeted him but with accented German. Ana was sure the man speaking must be a Frenchman. They spoke for a minute, but she had trouble picking up what was being said.

Katrine whispered, "This would be a good time to pray." Ana almost jumped. She'd thought everyone else was asleep.

"My very thoughts," she answered.

Herr Hermann started the truck again and pulled slowly forward. The engine seemed to echo, giving Ana the impression they had entered a large building. When he stopped and turned the engines off, she held her breath. Katrine clasped her hand and held on.

Once again, the old driver came around to the back of the truck and pulled open the tarp. Light flooded in as he called out, "It's all right, children. It's all right. We're safe now. Come wake up." He began moving boxes.

A woman's voice called up to them. "I will take good care of you, but you must be quiet as little mice." Her accent was most definitely French.

Chapter Fifty

Rab's Hoose
Edinburgh
May 1937

Unlocking the Puzzle Box

Fiona walked Alec to the back door. After he left, she pulled on the door handle to test the lock. The door was solid. *The thing is, I locked this last night.* She shivered, remembering the fright she'd had when Alec called to her from the dark stairs.

She rubbed her arms and pulled herself back to the present, looking over her shoulder. The lure of the puzzle box called to her from the cupboard. After an hour of failed attempts trying to open the box, she decided to wait until the afternoon to call on Rab's help.

When she set out for his house, she brought a basket of biscuits and her newfound treasure. Laurie answered the door. His auburn hair fell across his forehead. For a moment, she wanted to brush it back. His smile was welcoming, and she answered him with a grin of her own. Fiona realized they hadn't said anything. He was standing looking at her with those intensely blue eyes. *Must have been only a few seconds, but it certainly felt longer.*

"You look pleased about something," he teased.

She tried to hide her embarrassment by holding up her basket. "I've brought biscuits and a puzzle. Is Rab at home?"

"What? You didn't come to see me?" His tone was playful. He peeked into her basket and said, "I'm very good at puzzles."

"I'm sure you are, and you're welcome to have a go at it. I've been trying to open it all morning, and it's beyond me, so I thought maybe Rab could help."

"Come in. My grandfather had his nose in the paper all morning, working on a different kind of puzzle."

Rab was coming out of the sitting room when she entered. His face lit up when he saw her. She hadn't known Rab long, but already she considered him a close friend. "Well, this is a treat. You came in time to save me from a boring afternoon with yon grandson." He chuckled. The tension between him and Laurie had dissolved over the last week. "Seems he's given up his wild living to spend time with me. So ye saved us both." Rab winked, hitting Laurie's elbow with his rolled-up newspaper. She knew Rab was pleased at the turn their relationship had taken.

She held up her basket and said, "I've something to show you. I brought biscuits if you have tea?"

"Right you are. Let's sit in the kitchen." Rab led the way to the back of the house. The kitchen was much the same as her own. She set her shortbread biscuits on the table and pulled out the puzzle box. The size of a brick, the wooden box was covered in ornately carved panels. The pattern appeared to form twisted knots.

Rab drew in a sharp breath. "Och, aye, ye du have a puzzle. Where did ye find this treasure?"

Fiona explained about Alec coming in unannounced and her tipping over the wash water.

Rab said, "Ye say it were buried under a shallow stone?" She nodded in reply. "May I look?"

"Oh, aye, that's why I'm here. I tried all morning to work the puzzle, but I can't open the box." She shook it lightly, producing a slight rattle. "See? Something is inside."

Laurie had been standing beside her so quietly she almost jumped when he asked, "Did you say your back door was closed and locked when Alec surprised you?"

Fiona shrugged. "Yes, but I must have been mistaken. I thought for sure the door was still locked from the night before. I hadn't been through it all morning."

Laurie's tone was a touch stern. "I'd feel a lot better about you staying in that old house all alone if I knew you were careful about the locks."

She near bit her tongue to keep from saying, "And who do you think you are to tell me how to behave?"

Laurie must have seen the flash of anger in her eyes, because he smiled ruefully. "I know. Not my place to say, but I've found it hard not to think about you all the time. Guess I'm just a bit worried about you."

Her anger dissolved, leaving her cheeks flaming hot, but for a much nicer reason.

Laurie continued. "You said he grabbed the box from you—he was interested in it then?"

Fiona answered, "Yes, but when I took it back and offered to make him a cup of tea, he said he had to go meet someone. He left right away."

Rab looked as concerned as Laurie. "What du ye make of that?"

Laurie's face took on a serious cast. "Alec has ulterior motives, and we'd best find out what they are."

Fiona looked from Rab to Laurie, a bit nonplussed. "I haven't anything anyone would want. Besides, Alec's been nothing but nice to me. I don't think he meant anything." Then she remembered how the hair on the back of her neck stood up when he surprised her and the strong feeling she shouldn't let him near the box.

"Aye, well, that may be, but Alec is an odd character, has been since he was a lad. He rarely does anything without a motive," Rab said. "Laurie may or may not be right but best keep yer wits about ye." Rab turned his attention to the box. "I've seen a box like this once afore when I was a lad. This box is verra old. In fact, I'd say likely belonged to yer captain." He took the box from her hand. His forehead furled in concentration as he turned it over, studying all sides. "Can I no open it then?"

"Please do," she said.

Rab began moving the tiny overlaid panels. At first, they were a bit sticky and hard to move, but gradually he was able to move them with ease. Laurie put the kettle on to boil. They were still studying the panels when the kettle began to whistle.

"Rab, if you move that one to the left ..." Laurie suggested. Rab's hands moved the carved panels around the box until a picture of a compass rose formed. But the sequence was not progressing easily. They were eating Fiona's shortbread when the last piece clicked into place.

Rab placed the box on the table in front of Fiona. "Yer treasure, sa ye must open it."

She stared for a long minute. *The last hand to open this could have been Wee Geordie's.* She took a deep breath and drew the box closer.

Laurie gave her arm a slight squeeze. "It won't bite. Go ahead, open it."

Her hands trembled as she lifted the lid. Her puzzle box held a badly mildewed leather pouch. The leather was thin, like a woman's kid-leather glove, but no longer soft or supple. It seemed to crack and flake away as she picked it up. Fiona carefully slid her fingers inside the pouch and pulled out a blackened pendant and chain.

Rab watched her intently. He rose and went back into the butler's pantry.

"Looks old enough," Laurie said. "When was the captain alive? Around the time of Prince Charlie? That would make it almost the middle of the eighteenth century. Couldn't be that old, could it?"

"Oh aye, likely is," Rab said, returning with silver polish and a soft rag. He filled the sink with soapy water. "We'll wash the pendant off first and ge it a bit o' polish." Taking it from Fiona, Rab slid it into the water, gently scrubbing away the mold and dust.

She peered over his shoulder. "Why, the center is a stone."

"Aye, if I'm right, there's a smoky amber quartz in the center. Looks more a Cairngorm plaid brooch before it were a pendant." Pointing to the metalwork, Rab added, "See here? It's a compass rose around an amber quartz." He said with amazement, "That's a very unusual plaid brooch."

His hands were ready with a drying cloth. He brought it to the table and began using the polish to bring back the beauty of the carved silver broach. "Oh, aye. See here? A wee dagger would have fit through here to pin the brooch to a man's breacan-an-feileadh, ye ken, a plaid."

He turned it over in his hands. "Looks like it's been made into a pendant. I think he must have added the chain to give it to a lady. It was no a lady's beginning wi."

The revelation of its history hit her. She remembered seeing this broach holding Wee Geordie's plaid in place in the painting. *It belonged to the captain.* Then she remembered something else. "It's Mairi's. The captain, I mean Wee Geordie, gave it to her as a promise. I was reading about this in his log. And he's wearing it in my painting. But why bury the pendant in the cellar?"

"I canna tell ye, but he were a canny man and must have had his reasons." Rab handed the pendant back to Fiona. "If yer a mind to sell this, I'm sure it would bring a fair amount of money."

Laurie took it from her hand, putting the chain over her neck. "A bit large for a woman, but it looks bonnie on you." His smile was so appreciative, tears glistened in her eyes. *Is he looking at me the way you looked at Mairi? Oh, Geordie, I know you loved her so, and I fear I'm losing my heart to Laurie.*

Her fingers moved over the Cairngorm. The silver was carved in a Celtic knot around the compass rose. "Da told me the Celtic knots are ancient. They can represent eternal things like the past, present, future. I don't think I could ever sell this. I know what it meant between Mairi and Wee Geordie. It's worth far more than money to me."

Rab said, "I remember being told that a compass rose represents God guiding us on a spiritual journey. Yer captain had a reason for burying this in the cellar and in a puzzle box ta boot." He winked at her. "I love a mystery."

Chapter Fifty-One

Kempten, Germany
May 1937

A Wolf in Sheep's Clothing

Eric stopped as he passed the shop window. *I look like any other husband or father on his way to church. This disguise could prove useful.* He caught the reflection of an older woman smiling at him. Eric focused on the storefront. A baby basket with plastic dolls dressed in pink and blue filled the window. His first inclination was to glare at the woman, but he thought, *I can look innocent.* He turned and smiled at the old crow, tipping his hat and giving her a sweet "Guten Morgen." *Damn, but I'm good.*

A slight frown crossed his clear, open expression as he thought, *Ana sees me even beneath the mask.* He didn't like that, and yet it attracted him all the more to her. *She doesn't judge me, accepts who I am.*

At first, he'd seen the expected fear. *Everyone's afraid of the SS. When she asked about my life, she was genuine, interested. It's been a long time since anyone cared about me.* An uncomfortable thought.

How much power can you have over someone who cares about you? He shrugged and turned away from the safe Eric's reflection. *I'm not safe. Safe is not a good recommendation for an SS officer.* He shook his head. *Still, I want to be this one time for this one woman.*

He glanced at his watch and quickened his step. *She said to come to the back door. She doesn't come and go from the front door.* Madam insisted, lest anyone think Ana worked upstairs. That rankled him. *SS don't go to back doors unless we're hunting. But nice, safe men had no problem with back doors.*

He stopped before knocking. *Here I am, Eric Braun, SS officer, at the back door to a whorehouse.* Taking a deep breath, he tried to expel the anger that rose. Eric rapped three times and waited. He could hear running feet. He thought of Ana running to catch the door and composed his features. Cleared his thoughts. The door lurched open.

A heavy-set woman with dark hair glared at him. "Ja?" she demanded. Eric looked her over. She must be a cook or maid. She wasn't a prostitute.

Once again, he reached for the mask, took his hat off and said, "I'm here to take Fraulein Ana to church. Can you get her, bitte?" He bowed. Humility was difficult for him, but he could manage it. The man in the suit would be polite.

Confusion crossed the woman's fat features. Then she seemed to decide. "Fraulein Ana left employment here yesterday." The woman moved to close the door. "Auf wiedersehen."

The cow is closing the door in my face. He stuck his foot out to stop her. A hint of the real Eric slipped past the mask. "Bitte, Ana is expecting me."

She cracked open the door. "She had a family emergency. It was very sudden."

This is unthinkable. "Did she leave any message for me?"

The cow shook her head. "Nein, nein. It was very sudden. Her grandmother."

"Then can you tell me where her grandmother lives?"

She squinted with a sideways glance. "You are her friend and don't know this?" He almost struck her for her insolence. The woman raised a brow as if waiting for his answer. Then she rolled her eyes and said, "Ana shared nothing with us. Just did her job and kept to herself. In the country somewhere."

Eric stepped back. He was stunned, disappointed, angry—but most disturbing, he was speechless. The fat woman slammed the door shut. *I could kick your door down, you bitch.* He turned and looked back down the alley, contemplating going to a church without Ana, but even her name made him feel terrible. He loosened his tie. *I have to get out of this jacket. No use. I am a wolf, not a sheep, not today, maybe never again.*

Chapter Fifty-Two

Germany
May 1937

Madame la Comtesse

Ana stretched her arms over her head. She wasn't ready to leave the cocoon of warm blankets. Sleep waited to see if she'd yield once more while thoughts floated through her mind. There was a dream-like quality to last night. *We were all so tired, cold and smelly in our dark hiding place. Then there was light and noise. And many hands helping with the children.* Ana remembered seeing a beautiful, petite woman of about thirty. She had a heart-shaped face, creamy skin, large almond-shaped chocolate eyes and her dark brown hair piled up in a chignon. *For all her delicate appearance, she was in charge, making sure we were bundled off to our beds with the least amount of noise possible.*

Ana opened her eyes to look around the small bedroom. *It's been weeks since I've had a restful sleep or a comfortable bed. But it's been weeks since I slept away from the children.* With that thought, she swung her feet out of bed, feeling the need to make sure they were all right. She found clean clothes and dressed.

Ana emerged from her bedroom and followed the corridor into a main room. She looked around for the children but didn't see them. A hand touched her arm. A lovely woman welcomed her with a French accent. "I am Marie. La comtesse left instructions for you to have a bite to eat. After, I'll take you to her."

Ana nodded her understanding. "The children, please. Where are they?"

Marie clucked her tongue. "Les enfants are all still sound asleep." She indicated a plate at the kitchen table. "Eat. You must be hungry after your long drive in that awful truck."

So, she knows about us. Herr Hermann said we'd be hiding right under the Nazis' noses. Ana was full of questions, but the omelet set before her was amazing. Between bites, she asked, "Is there a count as well?"

"Mais oui, of course." Marie left her to her food without further explanation. Soon she returned to ask, "If you're ready, I'll take you to la comtesse."

Ana rose and followed her, trying to take in her surroundings as they passed through several rooms and down a short hall. Marie paused at the end of the hall to rap twice on a door.

A feminine voice called, "Enter." Marie opened the door to a beautiful golden room decorated with spring-like floral fabrics and wallpaper. The woman from the night before sat at a small table in front of a wall of windows. Warm brown eyes regarded Ana with compassion, motioning for her to come have a seat.

"I am so glad you are awake, such a terrible hiding place. The conditions in Herr Hermann's truck quite scandalized us, but he assures me they were necessary to keep you all safe." The comtesse added, "I'm Isabelle. Please have a seat, and we will get to know each other, no?"

Ana discovered the lady of the house was actually a Lady in her own right. Though she was French aristocracy, she was called

Isabelle by everyone. There was something wistful in her expression. They sat together in her solar. Isabelle explained, "My staff came with me from France. They dote on me." She shrugged.

Ana asked, "And there is a monsieur le comte?"

Isabelle didn't answer right away but looked out the window at the pastureland and horses. "Mon comte is an excellent businessman. He's away much of the time, and when he's home, we entertain. It's good for business, you understand. But hard on a marriage." The comtesse described her lavish dinner parties. "Even the Fuhrer has sat at my table." Isabelle wrinkled her nose in disgust. "A most unstable individual. But no less powerful. He reminds me of a French story my nurse used to tell me—*The Emperor's New Clothes*. You know this story, oui?"

Ana laughed despite herself. "He doesn't parade around without his clothes?" she asked.

"Mon Dieu, no. But if he did, I'm sure no one would be brave enough to say a word. He's a ridiculous man." She made a face to show her disdain. "So small and not very good-looking. Yet he holds the power of life and death for everyone in Germany. And if he has his way, he will hold that power over the world."

Isabelle was quiet for a while. They sipped strong coffee.

Ana had one question on her mind. "Can I ask why you take such a chance for me and the children?"

Isabelle radiated pride and courage. "Because it is right. Because God would want this of me, and because I am French and not afraid of this little upstart." Ana smiled at the spirit the comtesse showed.

"Well, I thank you for helping us. And I pray God will bless you for doing this." Ana held up her cup. "This is wonderful coffee."

"Naturellement, it's French. Come, let's check on les enfants." They walked back to the servants wing. As they came into the common room, it was full of people getting ready to serve lunch.

Gretchen and Deter sprawled on the floor working a puzzle with other children.

It made Ana happy to see them play, but it worried her. "Is it safe for so many to know what you do?"

"We are all French here. My people came with me when I left my home in the wine country. We grew up together. These are their children. You mustn't worry. They're not like the Germans. We all do this together."

Just then, baby Tony started wailing. Katrine was struggling to hold him. Katrine looked up at Ana. "I think he's hungry." A large table was being set with food.

Isabelle's face lit up at the sight of the Gypsy baby. "Mon petit chouchou," she cooed. Then to Katrine, "May I take him for an instant?"

Katrine looked from Ana to the comtesse with uncertainty. "He's quite a handful right now." But she brought him to Isabelle. Tony reached for the comtesse with a crumpled face, sliding into her warm embrace. His little head rested on her shoulder, and he quieted.

The other women in the room laughed. Cook turned to Ana and said, "Madam loves les enfants. Bonne chance. Oh, pardon me. Madam loves the babies. Good luck getting to hold your own infant."

"Oh, he's not my child."

Isabelle looked up. "But he is so young. Where is his mère?"

"His mother was a Gypsy. She came to a service at Saint Thomas. When service was over, we found baby Tony but no mother, only a note asking us to care for him." Ana stroked his dark curls. "Gypsies aren't doing much better than Jews in Germany."

She told them each of their stories. Tears filled Isabelle's eyes, and she translated as Ana talked. "I'm the last of the Sisters of Saint Thomas." Isabelle drew in her breath in surprise and said something in French. Ana could see shock on all their faces.

The comtesse said, "It has been so very long since any of us has seen a holy sister. We are all Catholic here. It is an *honneur* to help you."

Cook came over and put a hand on Ana's arm. Her German was halting, but the meaning was clear. She welcomed Ana and the children and asked if Ana would bless their food.

Chapter Fifty-Three

Edinburgh
May 1937

Tam

Laurie stopped once again to peer out his front window toward Fiona's house. *A storm's blowing in. No chance she'll be pulling weeds, probably not walking to town today either. Twenty-four hours since I saw her.*

Rab passed him a paper under his arm. "Ye don't need an excuse to visit wi a friend."

Laurie grinned. "You're right. Think I'll pop up the street and see how she's doing." He ignored Rab's chuckle and grabbed his jacket.

They spent a rainy afternoon in front of her fire, sipping chocolate and talking. *God, she's a good listener. And cheek, the things she says, always seeing the funny side.*

It became an afternoon ritual for the rest of that rainy May. He helped her with projects. Sometimes they went for walks. He marveled at her strength. Once he said, "You talk about God like he's a person, a friend. I want to be that good a friend."

Her smile was tender. "We are friends."

Yes, friends, he thought. But those words were like a lead weight in his heart. *I'm just her friend.*

The month had gone far too fast for Laurie. It was heart-wrenching to think he would leave for Germany on the early sailing tomorrow morning. Visions of Marguerite still came to him while he slept. She always looked perfect, seductive, and yet somewhat aloof. When those dreams came, he woke in a sour mood, angry at himself for using Marguerite and her father to get ahead. Confused, at sea, frustrated, all good words but not enough to describe his feelings.

More often, another form invaded his dreams these days and occupied much of his thoughts. Not the sleek cultured Marguerite but that short bundle of determination. *Her clear expression. Her tender heart. Fiona was simply what you saw. No pretensions or hidden agendas.* He could imagine her by his side for the rest of his life. Laurie stopped himself. *You're leaving. No choice now. Bernie's counting on you to find those children.*

He stood on Fiona's front steps, trying not to step on the small black dog at his feet. This would be the last visit before going to Germany. He bent over and ruffled Tam's head. Rab had acquired the three-year-old Scottish terrier from an old friend who'd passed away. It also turned out the dog was a true Highlander, stubbornly running away from a neighbor who'd tried to care for him. He always returned to the house he'd shared with his first master. Rab had promised to find Tam a good home far away from his old one.

Laurie had to admit Rab had the right of it. *Fiona needed protection, and the dog needed a kind-hearted and patient master.* The poor dog's eyes were listless, and his tail hung down, every bit the picture of someone in mourning. He hoped Fiona would welcome this furry friend.

Laurie knocked again, wondering, *Why don't I take Fiona in my arms? Tell her ... Tell her what?* He shook his head. It always came back to this. He had to do the right thing. See Marguerite face-to-face and make sure of his feelings. *There's a fair amount of eating crow in admitting I was wrong about the job, about Marguerite, about everything. Am I ready to make that decision?*

He'd been questioning his feelings for days, but somehow he knew the answers could only be found in Germany. *If I'm going to break it off with Marguerite, I need to do it right, but first I have to find those children.*

His mind wandered over the possibilities. *Even if I give up Marguerite, the job, everything, what if Fiona doesn't feel anything but friendship for me? Could Alec have a chance with her while I'm gone?* It always came down to this one last thought. *No, I have to be sure that with or without Fiona, I'm making the right decision.*

The door opened and there she was, looking as if she'd been cleaning in some far corner of the house. A scarf covered her dark curls. A smudge graced her perfect nose. But her smile was radiant, her dimples so deep they were almost hidden. *Was he imagining she only smiled that way for him?* They'd been standing there not saying a word for at least a minute. It was his turn to be uncomfortable. He held her gaze, and it felt like he was holding her. It wasn't just that his body responded to her—Marguerite had done that much. His heart was so full when he looked at her that he couldn't turn away.

She blushed a rosy color and looked down. It was then she saw Tam. "And who is this handsome laddie?"

"If you're talking about me, thank you for the compliment, but if you're talking about my friend here, his name is Tam."

She bent and ruffled Tam's hair as he had done a moment ago. This time, the dog wagged his tail and put one paw up for her to take. "Welcome, Tam. Would you and yon master like to come in for a bit of tea?" To Laurie's astonishment, Tam crossed the threshold, his ears pricked forward and tail wagging furiously.

"Well, it seems I should have brought a dog long ago. You've never welcomed me so fondly." If he judged the look on her face, she was on the verge of a saucy answer. At least until she remembered what she must look like. He knew because her hand went up to the scarf on her head and pulled it off.

"Cleaning again? I must say you are fetching in headscarves," he teased, taking the scarf from her hand. He reached out to wipe the smudge of dirt on her nose. She stepped back, her dimples deepening when she realized what he was doing.

"Come in. I'll try not to slosh my scrub bucket on you," she retorted.

"I come bearing a gift that I hope you'll accept." She cocked her head to the side, and so did Tam. It was so comical he laughed. "Can we have tea? I want to tell you a story first."

She smiled in reply and led the way to the kitchen. Over tea, he told her about Tam.

"Does Rab no want to take him?"

"He says the dog needs a complete change. Rab is much like his friend Willy. And Tam here needs someone who won't remind him of his first master. We both hoped you would take him." Laurie held his breath. He couldn't tell her he hoped the dog would protect her when he was gone. Or how worried he was about her being alone when Alec could show up, even with a locked door.

Fiona had been looking at Tam. She slipped off her chair and sat on the floor. "Would you like to come live with me?" Tam cocked his head to one side and barked one loud reply.

Fiona looked at Laurie in surprise and back at Tam with delight. "Aye, well, I think he's agreed." Tam put the same paw up for her to hold. "We'll get on well together, Master Tam." She took the paw and shook it. Ruffled his dark little head again. "I've never had a dog. I've no idea what to feed him or anything."

"We'll take care of that. You, me and Tam can walk into town today, and we'll pick up everything you need." *Besides*, he thought to himself, *it's a good excuse for spending time together.*

The walk to town turned into a full day. They laughed at Tam's antics. Laurie talked about the job in Germany. "The Germans are quite good shipbuilders, and Voss is co-owner of a world-renowned firm in Hamburg. I'd like to think he was impressed with me, aside from Marguerite's influence." Laurie smiled. "But Voss wouldn't know I was alive if not for Marguerite."

Fiona looked at him with admiration. "Your grandfather said you graduated a full year early and at the top of your class. That would make any employer take notice."

Laurie shrugged. Before, he might have made some smart comment, but her compliment meant something to him.

She stopped in front of the monument to the famous Scottish writer Sir Walter Scott. Her expression was so serious. Scott's statue looked down at them, the writer's own dog frozen for all time as his silent companion. Tam also stopped, sitting at their feet, regarding them with the same searching gaze as the marble dog above him.

Fiona said, "Are you sure the wonderful job and beautiful wife aren't what you still want?"

His answer was swift. "I'm more sure every day." The truth. No struggling with decisions; it was there all along. He felt a weight lift off his shoulders. The truth was standing before him, smiling up at him.

Fiona pulled her gaze from his, and they fell into step again, moving with the crowd up the hill into Old Town. He talked for a while about how much the world was changing. A government could arrest people without explanation. Tam kept pace, avoiding the feet of passersby.

They continued on to the windswept battlements of Edinburgh Castle. Even in the outer courtyard, the view was amazing. She asked, "Do you have any idea how to search for those children?"

He looked out over the city and sighed. "I don't know. It seems like an impossible task."

She put her hand on his arm. "I'll be praying all the while for you, and Rab will too." Her intensity radiated through her warm touch. "My da always said nothing is impossible with God on your side." Looking into those deep brown eyes, he could almost believe it.

When the one o'clock cannon boomed the hour, Tam spun around. His whole body jumped with every bark. It was time to change the guard. Stomping feet and clanging rifles echoed across the courtyard as they walked back down High Street.

Fiona said, "I suppose we should get Tam's food and go back. You must have packing to do, and Rab will want to spend time with you too before you leave."

He put his hand over hers before she could take it away and folded it in his own. "I know of a great little cafe. Would you stay out longer? The owner's a friend of mine."

"Aye, we'd like that very much, wouldn't we, Tam?" The dog cocked his head again and gave that same uncanny answer of one loud bark.

"It's settled." Laurie still held Fiona's hand. His fingers curled around hers. They found a pet store and talked to the owner about what to feed her dog. Tam was interested in everything in the store. They shared a moment of total amusement as he sniffed a bin full of balls.

Laurie held up a bright red ball. "Right, laddie, should we have one of these as well?" Tam's tail wagged with anticipation. "Guess we have one more thing to add to our purchase."

Fiona bent and patted Tam. When she looked up at Laurie, pleasure radiated from her sweet face. He thought, *I always want to remember how happy she looks just now.*

He led the way through Old Town and down an arched passageway with an old black-and-brass sign reading, "Lady Stair's Close." It led to a small open space between buildings with a narrow view of the city beyond the alley. Fiona looked up to see the blue sky above. She turned around, charmed by the novelty. The little alley had several small shop fronts. Across the way, a yarn shop was closing for the day. Green ivy climbed the sides of the stone-walled buildings that enclosed the space. An old black lamppost stood at the center of the close, but most amazing was the aroma of fresh baked bread and steak pie that filled the air.

In front of them, a sign above a door said, "Jock's Steak Pies." Laurie let go of her hand to open the door. His friend was serving steak pies and bread to a couple by the window. Looking up, the chubby little waiter hurried over. "It's grand ta see ye, Laurie."

"Jock, this is my friend Fiona and her dog Tam. Do you think you could feed us some of that wonderful steak pie I can smell?" Tam barked once again. *Does this dog understand everything we say?*

"Weel not, so as ta say that my eatery is goin ta the dags. I must feed this one, too, or he's liable to make a row." And without missing a beat, Jock turned and showed them to a table in the corner.

Chapter Fifty-Four

Edinburgh
May 1937

A Perfect Day

Laurie dawdled over his meal, trying to stretch out their time. They talked about almost everything. Laurie stopped her once and said, "You lost everything when you lost your parents." He searched her face. "Weren't you bitter? How did you get over being angry at God?"

Her eyes were tender, sympathetic, but she shook her head. "In a way, I keep my parents with me. It's all the little things I remember them saying. At times, it's like Da is standing next to me, giving me advice." Seeing hurt and loss come to the surface, he regretted asking the question. "And they gave me a strong faith." She put her hand over his. "You were much younger when you lost your parents. At least you've always had Rab."

Yes, I had Rab, but I wasted so much time resenting him. "We had a good relationship when I was a lad. He taught me to fish. The sea was his life, and I loved it. Guess that's why I ended up being a marine engineer. He and my grandmother were more like second parents to me. Their house was warm, welcoming. Not that home wasn't."

Lost in thought for a minute, he said, "I never stopped to think that Rab lost my grandmother in that same epidemic that took my father—Rab's only son." He shook his head. "I was just angry—at God, at my mother, at Rab, at everyone. I was a thirteen-year-old boy. My mother must have been beside herself with grief. Rab too, for that matter." *There's so much I regret.* "She asked Rab to come live with us. Good thing, because she died just one year later. She was—that is, she was frail after the sickness left her."

"To lose her too, that must have been so hard."

Laurie grimaced. "You wouldn't have known it to look at me. By the time she died, I'd built a wall around my heart. Sometimes I wonder if she gave up on life. Maybe if I hadn't been so difficult…"

Fiona reached out to take his hand. Her eyes were so full of compassion. "You were a hurt child. I'm sure she knew that."

They talked about his school and Marguerite. The new job. They even discussed the political outlook for Germany. Fiona worried her fork in the steak pie and said, "I'm thinking things in Germany are worse than what the papers say."

He stopped himself from rolling his eyes. "You've been talking to Rab." She nodded. "Until now, I'd have made some smart comment. Marguerite says Germany is doing well. The economy is better than it's been in years."

"I think we have to assume it's only doing well for some Germans."

"Yes, my conclusion as well." He frowned into his food. "I never doubted Marguerite, and I put down everything Rab said."

Fiona's opinions about the world didn't stray too far from Rab's. "I don't understand how the world can look the other way. Hitler's policies on racial purity have already cost many their lives. Even in Canada, I heard how Germany treats people who disagree with Hitler. I'm afraid for you to go there, but I am more afraid for those children. They're lost without you."

She saw war on the horizon. He discovered she was well read and contemplative. Her education might not match Marguerite's, but her mind was quick and full of insights.

They walked home, and he helped her in with Tam's food. It was awkward leaving her. It felt like he needed to say something more. She walked him to the door and reached out to take his hand. Her touch sent a charge through his body. Laurie pulled her to him and held her tight. She responded without hesitation. Her arms went around his neck. As he leaned down to kiss her, she stretched up to meet him. Her lips were soft and yielded to his. As the kiss deepened, she melted into him. He pulled back, shaken by the powerful emotion.

She searched his face. But what could he hope to give her at this last moment? He bent and whispered in her ear, "Wait for me till I figure this out." Then he turned and left. He couldn't bear to look at her face. It might have told him how she felt. *No, if I knew for sure that she wanted me as much as I want her, I don't think I could leave.*

In the early morning, leaving proved harder than Laurie expected. He'd have felt much better if there'd been some reason to see Fiona again, but none came to him. *At this hour, she will be asleep.* He'd had his chance, and it was probably better to leave things as they were.

Rab called out, "Yer taxi is here. Are you sure you don't want me to come see you off?" His grandfather's eyes were very bright. Laurie reached for his hand, but the old man engulfed him in a hug. "Ye know I love ye, son. If ye need my help, I'll always be here for ye." Rab's voice cracked a bit.

Laurie's throat closed with emotion. He hugged Rab back and held him for a long moment. "I know. You can pray for me."

"Always do, always do."

"Rab—" He hesitated. "Watch out for Fiona and keep an eye on Alec."

Rab stepped back, his big hands still holding Laurie's arms. "Ye can depend on that."

They shook hands, and he was out the door, down the steps and into the back of the taxi. "Leith, Custom House Quay, please," he said, and the driver pulled away. A dense fog hung over the road. He could only make out the shadow of the house at the end of the street, but he strained to see any sign of light. He told himself, don't look back, but his eyes held on until Latimer Square disappeared.

Chapter Fifty-Five

Leith Docks
Scotland
May 1937

Wait for Me

The front door shut behind Laurie. "Wait for me." His words echoed through Fiona's thoughts, chased by "until I figure this out." She touched her lips. *It was only a kiss, but it felt like so much more. A promise and he was gone.*

"You stupid goose," she said aloud but added quickly, "Och, Tam, not you. I'm stupid." He gazed back at her with those wise eyes. "He's leaving in the morning. I won't see him again for a long time." Her face crumpled, and tears spilled down her cheeks. "Tam, I'm certain I love him. What if he chooses the good life and the beautiful wife instead of the poor girl and the big house?" One sob escaped. Tam stretched up, little black eyes studying her face. He set one foot on her leg, and she sank to the floor. Her hands ran over his coarse black hair, comforted by the solid warmth of him. There in the hall, she sat with Tam and cried until exhaustion overtook her.

"Guess you'd know about grief, wouldn't you, laddie?" His head settled in her lap. Soulful eyes looked up at her. "All right, we both need to get some sleep." Fiona patted him. "Let's go to bed."

Her steps were heavy as they climbed the stairs to her chilly bedroom. She lit the lamp and the fire. As she got ready for bed, Tam wandered about inspecting his new home. She set a large pillow a few feet from the fire and patted it for him to lie down. But when she turned to climb under the covers, she found him on the bed waiting for her. Tonight of all nights, she was glad of the company. Before she turned out the lamp, Tam seemed to notice the captain's painting. His attention focused on the image of Wee Geordie. She watched the dog cock his head to the right and left. His ears pricked forward as if he was listening, and then he barked once.

"You're a strange dog." She reached for him, but he was already settling on the coverlet by her feet. Fiona looked into the captain's eyes, imagining what he might have said to the dog.

She snuggled under the covers, and the full weight of exhaustion settled over her. But instead of sleeping, her mind raced through memories of Laurie. The first time they'd met. Fixing her back door. His smile seemed to dance before her eyes. She turned over again and again until she fell asleep.

Laurie came to her in her dreams dressed like the captain. He handed her the necklace. "It's yours, lassie," he said, or was that the captain who spoke to her? In her dream, they seemed to be the same person. When he kissed her, it was all Laurie. Warmth spread through her body. She ached for him and woke herself, calling out his name as he faded from her arms.

It was dark, and she was cold in her room. She stuffed the pillow over her head, mad at herself for not speaking up. *I should have told him I love him. He's risking his life and doesn't know.*

She pulled the pillow off her head. Two shiny eyes were inches from her face. She jumped with fright and nearly knocked Tam off the bed. "Sorry, Tam, sorry." She gathered him close to her. It must have been what they both needed, because they fell asleep in the warmth of mutual comfort.

At daybreak, a wet nose nudged her hand, followed by a whimper. Fiona rubbed the sleep from her own eyes, glancing at the clock. "Tam, tell me you're not an early riser?"

He wagged his tail.

"I hope that's not a yes."

One bark followed. "All right, laddie, but you'll need to wait until I put some clothes on ta do your business." She dressed in under five minutes and took Tam out to the kitchen door. An old stone dike enclosed the garden. It was enough space for Tam to take care of his necessaries, so she left him to it.

She had filled the tea kettle when she remembered Laurie would leave soon. Longing and sadness washed over her once again. She remembered her dream. *I should have told him I love him.* The voice of reason argued back. "He didn't say that to you; he just said to wait until he figures it out."

Tam scratched at the kitchen door. Once inside, he knocked her over as he raced past her toward the front of the house. She found him at the entry door. His leash lay on the floor where she'd left it the night before. "Och, Tam, what is it you want now?"

He barked at her, then at the door and then at the leash. Turning circles in his impatience, he stopped and stared at her with those wee black eyes. Her heart quickened as the thought came to her. They were up so early she could make it to the docks before Laurie's ship sailed.

"You are a canny wee laddie. A grand idea." Fiona raced back to her bedroom. As an afterthought, she went to her diary that sat on the dressing table. She slipped the small photograph of her and Aunt Tyna into her pocket. If Laurie was bound for Germany, she could at least remind him of what he was leaving behind in Scotland.

She was ready to leave fifteen minutes later. Tam kept up a steady pace, but even walking as fast as she could manage, it was a farther walk than she'd realized. The fog had moved in overnight, and she was thinking she'd lost her way. Signs of a waterfront emerged from the dense haze. She smelled the sea. Gulls flew overhead. Then ghostly looking warehouses appeared.

She saw a black taxi sitting next to an ancient stone building. She rapped on the passenger window. The cabbie stepped out of his motorcar. "Can I help ye, miss?" he asked, touching the brim of his cap.

"Is this the Edinburgh dock? I have a friend sailing for Germany this morning."

"Bless me, miss, this be Leith. Yer no in Edinburgh any longer."

Fiona knew she'd been walking for a long time, but she couldn't have walked all the way out of the entire city. "What?"

"No worries, lass, these docks have stood for hundreds of years, so even though this is Leith, it's still where anyone leaving Edinburgh by sea must sail from."

He pointed to the left of the building where a gate led out to the dock. "Through the gate, and anyone should be able to direct you. You'll want the Mauritania. She's due to sail in under an hour."

He answered her puzzled look with, "I took a chap here earlier this morning."

"Thank you." She smiled. The thought struck her that wee Geordie must have sailed from here as well.

People packed the dock on the other side of the gate. Fiona screwed her brows together as she searched the crowd. *I don't see Laurie anywhere.* "I hope this wasn't a bad idea," she said to Tam.

People queued in front of an official-looking man with silver-rimmed glasses perched on the tip of his nose and a clipboard in hand. Fiona joined the line, wondering if she was in the right place or had she missed his sailing altogether?

Her eyes kept scanning the crowd, so it startled her when the little man asked, "Name please, madam?" He glanced down at Tam with a skeptical look on his face and added, "We have no pets booked on this sailing."

"Oh, we're not sailing. We're, that is—" She drew a deep breath and started again. "I'm here to see a friend off. I just wondered if he's already boarded."

"Name?" He was all business.

"Laurie, I mean Lawrence MacKenzie." The man ran his finger down the list and looked up.

"Sorry, it appears he's already checked in. I'm afraid you've missed him." He sounded sympathetic, but that only made her more embarrassed. Fiona chided herself. *It was wrong. I shouldn't have come. He would have just thought I was chasing after him.* But she still felt miserable that she hadn't been able to see him one last time.

Fiona forced a smile. "That's all right. Thank you." Her inner voice was not so kind. *I came all the way here for nothing. I need to get out of here.* Her disappointment was so great she bit her lip to keep from crying. *You stop it, no tears.* She was pushing back through the flow of passengers when a hand touched her shoulder. Before she could react, Fiona was spun around and pulled into Laurie's arms.

Tears spilled down her cheeks. She wanted to bury her face in his chest, but his hand tilted her chin up. He was kissing her, at first gently, then fiercely, claiming her for his own. She couldn't think of anything but him. The world around her disappeared, and she was alone on the docks with Laurie. If people were staring, she didn't care.

When their lips parted, he kissed the side of her cheek and whispered in her ear. "You came. Oh, God, I wanted to see you." He pulled back from her to look into her eyes, and she saw his eyes were bright with unshed tears.

"What made you come? I was standing on deck watching all the activity, and there you were. How did you get here?"

She reached up to brush tears from her cheeks. He took her hand, kissing it, and her wet cheeks. She gulped in air between hiccup sobs, forcing out her words.

"It was—it's Tam's fault." For the first time, Laurie looked down at Tam. The Scottie dog sat staring up at them, his tail wagging tentatively.

Laurie bent down and roughed his head. "Thank you, Tam. I owe you for this, laddie." Tam's tail began to wag furiously.

Then Laurie was holding her close again. "I've so much to say." She started to speak, but he stopped her. "No, let me get it out. All the way here, I knew I didn't want to leave. I don't want to leave you. Not now. Never. I don't care anymore about the big break. I'd be happy to join Bernie at Scotts shipyard. He said he could find me a place. You are what I want. Not Germany, not Marguerite."

She was crying, but smiling so broadly her cheeks hurt. Before she could answer, he rushed on. "We haven't known each other very long, but if you say yes and marry me, I'll pull my trunk off that boat. In fact, they can have my trunk. Just tell me, do you feel the same?" He was searching her face. Confusion stalled her response. Then she realized he didn't know.

"Yes, yes, I love you, Laurie." The words were out before he was kissing her again. Then she pulled back. Something he said troubled her. She couldn't think what could spoil this perfect moment.

He'd said Bernie. His friend from school. The thought of those missing children flooded her mind. *I love him so, but can I tell him to forget Germany? Oh, Da, how can doing the right thing be so hard?*

Her father's voice came to her as clear as if he whispered in her ear. "Is your happiness worth the lives of two bairns?"

No. He has to go if we're going to have a life together. It's got to start out on the right foot. Fiona looked into Laurie's eyes and said,

"What about those children? I want you to stay, but we can't just leave them alone out there."

If I said nothing, he would stay, but what would happen to them? She waited. *What have I done? Why did I have to remember those bairns?* Indecision seemed to cross his face, but she could tell when resolve set in.

He ran his hand through his hair. She loved that simple gesture. "Of course not. I'm not sure what I can do, but you're right. I have to try." The Mauritania's whistle blew once. It was time for him to board. "But promise you'll wait for me. I'll do everything I can to find those bairns so I can get back to you."

"Yes, yes. And you'll find them. I know you will." Fiona pulled the photograph from her pocket. "I wanted you to have this to remember me by while you're away."

He took it from her. "That's you and your mother?"

"No, it was taken a month before I left Canada. It's my Aunt Tyna with me."

He looked at her image with such love, then slid it into his jacket pocket. "Thank you. I'm glad you brought it, but your face is all I think about these days. I love you." He pulled her close again. "God, why didn't I see it until now? I'll write as soon as I get there." He kissed her, demanding more from her, and she responded with equal passion. Her whole body felt charged with energy. Then the whistle blew again, and the little man with the clipboard called to him to board if he was sailing.

He fished in his pocket and pulled out a pound note. She shook her head no as he pressed it into her hand. "I want you to take a taxi home. It's safer. Let me take care of you. I love you." He kissed her again, then turned to run up the boarding ramp.

He stood on deck watching her as the ship slipped from its mooring and motored out into the waterway. Fog closed in around him, swallowing him and the boat. Fiona looked down at Tam. "Thank you, laddie, you were right to bring us here." She dried her cheeks and turned to find a taxi home.

Chapter Fifty-Six

House on Latimer Square
Edinburgh
May 1937

The Ghost Horses

A warm glow enveloped Fiona as she remembered the heat of Laurie's kisses on her lips, the strength of his embrace. When he'd pulled her so close, she'd dissolved into him. *Did a taxi bring me home? I can't remember.* All that was real about her day was standing with Laurie on the dock. The deep timbre of his voice. The words he'd whispered in her ear. She replayed the scene a thousand times, amazed he loved her and how much she loved him.

Yet I sent him away for the sake of the children. What did I ask of him? It was exhausting to think how many things could go wrong. *Will they arrest him if the authorities find out he's looking for Jewish bairns? What if he gets there and decides he wants Marguerite? No, that's not possible.* There it was again, his last words to her: "I love you." She smiled to herself, riding her emotional rollercoaster to the heights. "I love you too, Laurie."

She climbed the stairs to her room. It was late, and she felt happy but exhausted. Tam led the way, ready to sleep himself. She didn't correct him when he jumped on her bed and settled near her feet. Before she turned out the lamp, she looked up at her captain. His smile seemed so tender. *You're pleased too?* She smiled back. The glow of the dying fire lit the room as she drifted off to sleep.

It must have been hours later, because the bedroom was cold and dark. A sound stirred her from sleep. Tam was sitting at the foot of her bed staring up at the captain. The dog's ears pricked forward. His eyes intent, he cocked his head to the side and barked once, just the one eerie bark. He stood, his attention shifting to the front of the house.

She heard it as well. The horses and carriage were back. She slipped out of bed, and Tam jumped down to follow her. He was running back and forth, following the sound. She tried to pick him up, tried to show him the empty street through her window. He was squirming and wouldn't be held.

The team was louder. Close. She listened to the creaking leather, jingling harnesses and the sound of horseshoes on the cobblestone square. When she put Tam down, he ran for the door and barked once again. She grabbed her robe and slippers and opened the door to the hall. He ran toward the back stairs, barking frantically. She followed while throwing on her robe and sliding her feet into the slippers as he moved toward the window at the end of the hall.

The fog must have cleared, because the moon shone on the kitchen garden and stables. This time, it wasn't a silent scene. The kitchen door banged shut. Her heart raced with the realization. *Lord save us, someone's been in my house.* Tam took off barking as loud as he could down the servant stairs to the kitchen. She was right behind him, and they reached the back door together. She pulled it open, and Tam ran through. The gate to the small garden stood open. The dog darted out to the stable yard. Something told Fiona to stop. A warning. Tam stopped barking. He listened, his body tense, ears pricked forward. The sound of the horses had faded, and the mews stood silent. The stall doors were black shadows in the old stone structure. He barked again, but she wasn't listening to him. Instead, she was thinking, *This time I know I closed the garden gate and locked the kitchen door.*

Stepping back to the doorway, she called, "Tam, there's a good lad. Come back to me." He had stopped barking, standing still in the deserted courtyard, listening and sniffing the air.

"Tam, come." She worried he might run away, but he came at her second call. She stepped forward and closed the garden gate behind him.

He did his business, then scratched the ground with his back legs and gave one last humph. When he was back inside, Fiona closed the door and locked it. A minute later, she wedged a kitchen chair under the door handle. All Tam's agitation vanished.

Panic seized her. She wanted to run up to her bedroom and barricade herself inside until morning. Instead, she took a deep breath and steadied herself. Da always said, "Best to face your fears head-on, or they'll rule your life."

She looked down at her wee dog. "Well, now you've heard the horses and carriage, but so has our visitor. It seems our ghost horses and your barking frightened someone right out of the house. But I think we'll have a look around." His tail wagged.

She found a torch and flipped it on. As an afterthought, she picked up the cast-iron poker by the kitchen fireplace. "Right, laddie, if anyone's still here, you bite him, and I'll whack him with my poker."

They checked all the lower rooms while Tam remained by her

side. His calm demeanor told her all was well. By the time they climbed the stairs to the second floor, Fiona was sure Tam would have warned her if anything was amiss, so they went back to bed.

Chapter Fifty-Seven

Rüdesheim am Rhein, Germany
May 1937

La Comtesse

L a comtesse bounced Tony on her hip as she walked with Ana into the servants' great room. She said, "I can see you are thinking of something that makes you happy. It's good. You don't smile enough." She added, "We French are less serious than you Germans."

"Oh, la comtesse."

"Isabelle, if you please. Even my people only address me formally in public."

Ana smiled. "Look how well my children are doing. Only two weeks, and they've forgotten we were running for our lives." She spread her arms wide. "Look, they're just children."

They stood in the great room where the servants ate and visited. Gretchen squealed as a little girl tagged her. And the chase was on. The five other children, including Deter, fanned out to avoid Gretchen's tag. No adults scolded them for running around the room. Mothers and fathers went about their work with indulgent smiles on their faces. "It's a miracle. They are acting their age."

Ana was still smiling, but her heart felt a tug of melancholy. "There wouldn't be so much suffering in this world if we were all less serious." She smoothed back Tony's dark curls. "He likes you. You must remind him of his mother. She was a dark-eyed beauty."

La comtesse said, "I can't stand the idea of not holding him ever again." Tony took his fist from his mouth and patted Isabelle's cheek. They both laughed, but Ana saw the longing in la comtesse's eyes.

Isabelle said, "He could be French. He looks like my own brothers." She put a hand on Ana's arm. "I've been wondering. How would you feel if I find a way to keep him here with me?"

Ana drew in a breath. "But you can't be serious. Too many people could give him away. Then you'd all lose your lives."

Isabelle looked down as if considering something. She said, "Oh, but I am serious. My people and I are in this together. Let me tell you why." She motioned to Etienne, her tall, lanky steward. "Etienne and I were best friends as children. We were always getting into trouble. If there was mischief, count on us as instigators." The baby pulled at Isabelle's necklace. Ana was about to stop him, but la comtesse smiled and lifted it for him to see. His sticky fingers pulled it into his mouth.

"We came here all together. It was the only way I could bring myself to leave France. Most of my people were married before me, but still they moved their families to stay together. You see, I took all my friends with me. We have a good life here, but we also have a very French life. When the economy changed for the better, my husband was gone more and more. Business," she said with a Gallic shrug. "The first time the refugees from Hitler's racial policies started coming to the kitchen for help, it was a year-and-a-half ago, and we gave them food, a place to sleep for a few nights."

"What did your husband say?" Ana asked.

"Oh, he is a good man, but I didn't tell him." Isabelle wrinkled her nose. "It was better he didn't know. If he knew, he might have stopped me, and how could I turn them away? They were people, non? Families, children." She shook her head. Etienne was tickling his three-year-old daughter, and the other children were climbing all over him, trying to draw him away.

When Ana looked back at la comtesse, there was pain etched on Isabelle's face as she continued. "We had a friend, Stephen Meyer. He was our veterinary physician. He had delivered a foal for us. The delivery was difficult, and the mare was a favorite of mine. A week later, he had dropped by to check on the mare when his son Jacob came running up. The boy was young, only five, and he was near to hysterics. It seems the Gestapo had paid an unexpected visit to Stephen's house. His wife Marlene was home alone with Jacob and his little sister. Marlene was very pregnant with their third child. She sent Jacob out the back to find his father. I still remember the terror on the boy's face. Jacob was shrieking, 'The Hitler men, Papa, come quick! Mamma needs you.'"

Baby Tony reached for Ana, but when she tried to take him, he gave her a silly grin and wrapped his arms around Isabelle's neck. It was for the best. La comtesse seemed to take comfort from holding Tony.

"We told Jacob to stay behind, but he was having none of it. Jean, our gardener, had to carry him into the house, kicking and screaming. Pauvre enfant, he was terrified. Stephen said we'd best not come, but of course we went with him."

Ana could tell the comtesse was seeing it all again as she continued.

"When we got there, the Gestapo had Marlene and little Rachel outside. Men were tearing apart their house, searching."

"What were they searching for?" Ana asked.

"We never found out." La comtesse shook her head. "I remember they were throwing everything out in the yard. Marlene was terrified, and Rachel was wailing." Isabelle gave baby Tony a kiss on the head.

Ana asked, "Were they Jewish?"

"He wasn't Catholic, but otherwise I never thought to ask. Stephen came on the scene first. He tried to stop them, to find out what they wanted. They said he was under arrest. Crimes against the Reich. When he asked what he'd done, they hit him with the butt of a rifle and knocked him unconscious."

La comtesse took a ragged breath. "We stepped in, trying to stop them. Explained he was our vet. They said Stephen was a Jew.

"I told them I was la comtesse, and my husband was very influential." Isabelle shook her head sadly. "Nazis are very snobbish, and I acted the part well. I told them my husband would have them punished for this." She shook her head again. "They don't care. Nobility means nothing to them. Even when I said the Fuhrer was often my dinner guest, they just sneered."

"They didn't know who you were?"

"Oh, they knew. I think they hated me more because of my title. They didn't believe Hitler was my dinner guest." Isabelle gestured toward her steward. The man had children hanging off both arms. But la comtesse was seeing another memory. "Etienne tried to help Stephen, but they punched him in the stomach and told me I'd best get my man out of there or they'd arrest him, too."

Isabelle wiped away a tear. "I learned later the Gestapo hold a man's whole family guilty if he's accused of a crime. They ripped Rachel from her mother's arms and tossed her in the back of their truck. When one of them drove away with little Rachel, Marlene screamed." La comtesse shut her eyes. "Mon Dieu, I can still hear her screams. The men pushed her down and kicked her hard in the stomach many times."

Ana reached out to hug Isabelle, but la comtesse shook her head, saying, "They took Stephen, too, and left. Marlene gave birth to a stillborn baby boy and died herself only a day later." La comtesse was silent for a long moment.

Ana knew such things were becoming more common, but it was still hard to believe men could be so evil. "Where did they take your friend and his daughter?" she asked.

"Oh, I had my husband look into the matter, but for all his influence, he never found out what became of Stephen and little Rachel. He discovered a neighbor had accused Stephen of making his prize cow sick and told them Stephen was a Jew." La comtesse shrugged. "It turns out Stephen was a Jew, at least somewhere in his background. That's all it takes."

"And the little boy?"

"He's here with us. Etienne has become his father. The funny thing was, no one came looking for him.

"After that, when people asked us for food, we realized what they were running from. Then one day Etienne came to me. He said we had to find some way to help these people. I agreed, but how? Mon Dieu, there are so many of them trying to escape to safety outside of Germany. He was the one to make contacts. He will always find others willing to make mischief with him."

Etienne stood up with four children attached to his arms and legs.

"We helped as many as possible get out of Germany. It hasn't been easy, but it is very rewarding." She looked around the room. "We all decided this together. All my people loved Stephen and his family, and not one person here would have it any other way."

Ana said, "I, for one, am very thankful, but it's so dangerous."

"Mais oui, but after all, that is life."

"Ana," Gretchen giggled. "Help us."

Ana shook her head. "You're on your own, Gretchen." She realized Gretchen had spoken to her in French. "Amazing how quickly they're learning French," she said to la comtesse.

"It's easy for children, and it may help them when they leave." Isabelle paused, adding, "I've heard from my husband. He'll be coming home in a month. We'll have to move you sooner than I was thinking." Isabelle reached out and put a hand on Ana's arm. "Don't worry. I'll have Etienne speak to his contacts and find you a way out of here."

"They'll hate leaving here."

"Oui. It is good to hear them laugh." Isabelle's expression turned hopeful. "Will you consider leaving Tony with me if I can work it out?"

Ana shook her head, but the look in Isabelle's eyes stopped her. Anguish, loss, loneliness all came to mind. Ana's heart hurt in sympathy. She remembered Herr Beckmann's wife and how bitter the woman was over the loss of her own baby. Yet Frau Beckmann had never even looked at Tony or picked him up when he cried.

Ana said, "There are so many reasons that would be dangerous. How could you work it out?"

Isabelle kissed Tony's dark curls. "I will think of something, or perhaps God will make a way." She seemed to cuddle Tony all the closer.

Deter ran around the room with a boy about his age. They jumped into the fray, and the children became a giggling mass of little arms and legs. "You would never know Deter is the same somber little man who came here with me. He looks like any other six-year-old boy."

La comtesse chuckled. "It is good for Jacob as well. It's helping him heal."

Ana's eyes widened to realize the little boy playing with Deter was the boy in Isabelle's story and a Jew as well.

"And your Katrine." La comtesse nodded toward the window seat. Katrine was talking to her new friend. "She is becoming a young woman. A romantic. But what fourteen-year-old girl isn't, do you not think?"

Ana said, "I've only just learned Katrine speaks many languages." They stood watching the two teenagers. "The young man is the gardener's son, isn't he?"

Isabelle nodded. "He is so shy. I'm surprised he had the courage to talk with her." The cook called them all for the evening meal. They sat down at the table and spoke about ordinary things.

Chapter Fifty-Eight

Hamburg, Germany
May 1937

Arrive in Germany

Crumpling his copy of the telegram, Laurie tossed it overboard. He smiled, imagining Fiona's face when Rab brought her the ring. *I should have been the one to give it to her.* He wanted it on her finger, as much a reminder that she was his as it was a reminder that he belonged to her.

As he watched the Mauritania dock, he saw Marguerite from the deck. His heart gave a jump. *Oh my God, I'd forgotten how beautiful she is. That's why I fell for her. She looks like a movie star.* Marguerite could have walked off any set in Hollywood with her white suit and fox stole. Her pale blond hair fanned out over her shoulders. Red lips smiled as she found him with her eyes. Even her father came to meet the boat. His old self whispered, "Can you really walk away from that?" But his answer back was one word only: "Fiona."

On the trip over, Laurie had thought about how he should

proceed. *No matter how I come at the problem, the only chance I have of finding the children is continuing with the facade.* He felt like a traitor to take advantage of this man's goodwill. Regret for deceiving Marguerite plagued him, but the lives of those two young children would have to assuage his guilt. So he disembarked with his best smile in place.

She threw her arms around him. "Darling, I've missed you so. Really, did it have to take so long to leave that dull, cold city?" He'd left his heart in that dull, cold city, but before he said something he'd regret, he kissed her. "Well, I forgive you now that you're here," she said.

Stepping past her, Laurie heartily shook her father's hand. "Thank you for coming, sir. I look forward to working for you." After all, he'd been looking forward to that—*the chance of a lifetime* —even if it would be short-lived.

"Next week will be soon enough for you to get started," said Herr Voss. "Marguerite has plans for you until then." Herr Papa smiled indulgently at his daughter.

"Yes, and they begin right now." Marguerite took Laurie's arm as she guided him past passengers lined up to go through customs to an official waiting to clear him. *So this is what wealth and privilege feel like.* The old Laurie could get used to this kind of treatment. But the new Laurie was more than a little embarrassed.

The passengers looked on with odd expressions. They appeared fearful, and when he made eye contact with the other travelers, they glanced away. Some people were being taken out of line and searched. But the little man waiting to stamp his passport and travel documents just smiled nervously at Laurie.

"The reason for your visit?" he asked, looking more at Herr Voss than at Laurie.

Marguerite spoke before Laurie could. "He's my fiancé and will be working for my father."

Damn, I don't remember asking her to marry me, he mused. *And the squid wrapped its tentacles around the swimmer and pulled him to the bottom. Just like that.*

Awkward. But what can I say? Hey, wait till I ask you? I didn't realize I was signing a contract for marriage. But if he'd been honest with himself, it was always understood. *In Edinburgh, she was always a little aloof, but now she's so excited to see me. What am I doing to her? She cares for me. I'm walking all over her and her father, still using them to get what I want. How is that a noble cause?*

Laurie jumped from the loud smack the man made when he stamped the paperwork. The little man snapped to attention, his hand in a salute, giving an exuberant, "Heil Hitler!"

Evidently, this behavior was not unusual to his future father-in-law, because they passed the customs official without comment.

Laurie whispered in Marguerite's ear, "Hey, is that kind of thing common?"

She simply smiled and nodded and, patting his arm, said, "You'll get used to it." There was something different in her manner. She always appeared so confident, but here she was, the master of her world. More like royalty. The crowd parted for them as she led the way.

He couldn't help comparing Marguerite to Fiona's humble nature. Marguerite still had his arm as they came to a limousine. The porter put his trunks in the boot, and they slid into the luxurious leather interior. "We found you a nice little flat not too far from us." She sounded coy and saucy, so he wasn't sure what to expect.

The limo headed out of the city. It was beautiful here. Wide, tree-lined streets. Occasionally, he glimpsed large country houses through the trees. They drove up a crushed rock drive which curved around until a large brick home came into view. The lines were stately and elegant. The white trim looked newly painted on this three-story mansion. Marguerite was watching his face, pleased with his appreciation. "This is my home," she said, pride written all over her beautiful face. "I love it here, and you will too."

"Yes, I can see you do." He leaned over and kissed her cheek. Being with her was still heady. He'd given his heart to Fiona, but all his other senses were battling the seduction of Marguerite and her world of wealth and privilege. *What is it about Fiona that made me think so little of Marguerite?* Even now, with Marguerite sitting next to him, Laurie's heart was hundreds of miles away.

They pulled past the main entrance to a garage that was more like a small house with lots of large doors. The second story appeared to have living quarters. *So this was her surprise.* He glanced over at her and caught her grinning like the Cheshire cat. It was going to make looking for those children harder. He fixed a pleasant expression on his face. "Aren't I staying in town? A small flat?"

She beamed. "This is a small flat, and I said nothing about living in town. Besides"—her lower lip pouted enough to look tempting—"I want you close to me, and I thought that's what you would want too."

"You know it is, sweetheart." He kissed her but only quickly. *This is getting worse by the minute. How long can I live with myself? Worse still, I'm cheating on someone no matter what I do.* He wasn't sure if he could last long enough to get those children back to their family.

Chapter Fifty-Nine

House on Latimer Square
Edinburgh
May 1937

A Ring

Once again, a wet nose roused Fiona from sleep. This time, it was well into the morning. "I'm sorry, laddie. You've been patient long enough." Tam covered her face with thankful kisses. She giggled. "Tam, stop. I can wash my own face."

She dressed, and soon they headed for the back stairs. As they came down the hall, she remembered last night's visitors. A bad dream or did it really happen? The chair was still wedged under the kitchen door handle. It hit her hard. The horses, the door slamming. It had all been real.

After letting Tam out, Fiona sat at the kitchen table. *Did Tam hear the horses, or did he hear someone in the house?* The idea of an intruder was alarming. *I'm not afraid of the horses, but a prowler is another matter.*

It was too much to sort out on her own. She wanted to visit

Rab as soon as possible, and with that in mind, she rushed through her morning with a sense of urgency. He was a good friend and the voice of reason. *But how will I—should I—tell him about Laurie, about the dock?* She shook her head for the hundredth time.

A loud rapping brought her to the front door. There Rab stood with a telegram in his hand and his arms open wide. Fiona walked into his embrace. He said, "Laurie sent me a telegram from the ship. He's told me yer to be his wife." Rab kissed the top of her head. "I'm that happy for ye both. Ye dinna ken how happy I be."

Large tears rolled down her face. She'd been wondering if the day before on the docks was real as well. *It's all true, and Laurie wanted to tell his grandfather right away.* Relief washed over her. "I was coming to tell you myself. I wondered how you'd take the news." She gave him a thankful squeeze, then wiped a tear from her cheek. "I'm not a prime catch. No money, just a big house, and of course"—she looked down at Tam, waiting at her feet—"a wee dog." She pushed the door open further, adding, "Come in, and we'll talk."

And they talked. At first, they talked about her and Laurie. Sitting at the kitchen table, she told him about Tam waking her early and the trip to the docks. "I'm not even sure why I went. Just to say goodbye, I guess." Rab pulled a small box from his pocket.

"Laurie asked me ta gi ye this." He slid it across the table to Fiona. "It was my Daisy's. He said he wanted ye wi a ring on yer finger and no mistake." Rab chuckled. "That is, if ye dinna mind it comin' from my own wife's hand."

Fiona was crying again as she opened the box. It contained an older style silver ring carved in a Celtic knot surrounding an amber quartz much the same color as the stone in her pendant.

"I think, truth to tell, Laurie does na want yon Alec ta come callin'."

She put the ring on her finger, and to their surprise, it fit perfectly.

"Rab, I love it, but are you sure you want to part with this?"

"Gladly, with hope you both have as happy a life together as it were for me and my lass." Rab's voice had grown husky.

She reached over and hugged him again. "I'll always remember that and thank you."

They talked on, but soon she told him about the happenings in the dead of night—the whole of it from when the ghost horses woke them until they came to the empty courtyard.

"An ye say there was a bang like the door slamming?" Rab asked.

"Yes."

"An yon kitchen door were locked the night before?" he asked again.

"Yes, I'm sure it was. I hadn't been out that way since the morning before, and I know I closed the gate." She waited as Rab stroked his chin. "Well, what do you think?"

"You and yer laddie should come stay wi me," he said decisively.

She shook her head. "No, Rab, but I thank you for the offer. I feel as if I must stay here. I'm not sure why. Call me crazy. I just feel it."

He put his hand on hers. "I think Tam is a guid companion. I've nae doubt at all he'll let ye know if anything's amiss." He reached down and gave the dog a pat. "Aye, won't ye now? All the same," he said to Fiona, "let's have a look at yer locks and windows. We'll make sure yer hoose is secure."

Chapter Sixty

Headquarters

Kempten, Germany

June 1937

Another Assignment for the Wolf

Eric bumped shoulders with a man on the street who said, "Hey there, watch where you're—" The man's words cut off when he made eye contact with Eric.

No masks today. He turned from the man's fearful expression with a smirk on his own face. *Yes, they should be afraid. All of them.* From somewhere deep inside he heard, *even one petite young woman.* Two weeks since Ana had left and no word, nothing. He'd looked for her on market day, only to leave disappointed and angry at himself for wanting to see her again. *And I'm not going back to ask that fat cow of a cook.*

Eric took the stairs to his quarters two at a time. He was through the door and ripping off his new suit when a knock stopped him.

He flung open the door, ready to vent. "Telegram for Herr Eric

Braun." A boy in a Hitler Youth uniform thrust the message forward. As Eric took the note, the boy's hand shot up in a salute to the Fuhrer. Eric pushed the door shut before he heard the familiar, "Heil Hitler."

It was from his friend Michael. "Got you a transfer to the SS in Hamburg. Stop. This is a big promotion. Stop. You owe me. Stop. Orders are already at headquarters. Stop. See you soon. Stop. Michael." Eric read the message again. The wolf's leer returned and with it came his confidence. *I always come out on top. Michael's not likely to do me a favor unless he needs something. That's all right, too. I'll make this pay off.* He slapped his leg with the paper. *Wonder how the commandant feels about my promotion.*

He pulled out his uniform, dressed and packed his bag within fifteen minutes. *I'm done pretending.* He left his ordinary suit on the bed.

As usual, Eric found Commander Akermann at his desk, even on a Sunday morning. Eric knocked once at the half-open door.

"Ja, ja. What is it?" Akermann looked up from a stack of paperwork. A frown crossed his pudgy face. "So, Herr Braun. You wasted no time coming to gloat." Pulling Eric's orders from a drawer, the commander slid them across the desk. "You must have influential friends. Who receives a promotion after failing at a task?"

There it is again. He's talking about the nun and those brats.

"I didn't fail at anything." Eric stood ramrod straight, his chin up in defiance. "May have been delayed, but I'll find them. In the meantime, I'll see if I can find something to say about your command when I reach headquarters in Hamburg. They might find my suggestions helpful." Eric expected a horrified look on Akermann's face, but the man only looked tired.

"I thought you'd come at once. Your orders say to report by this evening. A car is waiting for you downstairs." Commander Akermann sighed as he turned his attention back to his paperwork.

It was hard to feel the elation of victory when people failed to play their part. Still, Eric was glad to leave this place behind. *That cow of a cook will have to wait. I won't forget her.* He smiled slyly as he turned to leave. *I forget nothing.*

The driver made a quick stop for Eric's bag, and they were on the road. The scenery sped past, but Eric's thoughts lingered on what might have happened to the nun and children. *I'm positive they are no longer in the area. I am the wolf, and I will find them. It's only a matter of time. After all, don't I always come out on top?*

Chapter Sixty-One

Carinhall, Germany
June 1937

Laurie's Introduction to German Society

Marguerite looked beautiful. Everything sparkled from the diamond earrings to the luminescent sequins on her white evening dress. There was an excitement about her he hadn't seen before. She was saying, "Everyone will be there. I can't wait to introduce you." She held Laurie's hand as they sat in her father's limousine. He'd only been in Germany a little over twenty-four hours, and his social calendar already appeared to be full.

"Who is everyone, and why are they so important?" *This is the real girl. These are the people who matter to her. At school, she was always so reserved. Hell, getting her attention was a challenge. More like a badge of honor when I captured her.*

"Laurie, don't be so exasperating." Her lips pressed together in concentration as she straightened his bow tie once more.

"These people are important to the future of the Reich. It wouldn't hurt for you to cultivate their friendship."

She's anxious, worried. He wore his crooked smile. "Not to worry, baby." He slid his arm around her. "I can behave when I have to."

The limo turned down a long driveway, giving him his first glimpse of their destination. With a low whistle, he said, "Would you look at that? Is this the Fuhrer's house?" *This estate makes Herr Papa's place look like a summer home.*

"No, silly, Carinhall. It belongs to Hermann Goering. His first wife was a baroness. She died."

"That's too bad." Laurie wasn't sure what to say to her brief history lesson.

"His new wife, Emmy, is an actress."

A servant in livery was waiting to open their car door. As they slid out of the auto, Laurie remembered what he'd heard about Goering. The man was an aviator during the last war, an ace of sorts. Now part of the inner circle, Goering had the ear of Hitler.

They mounted stairs to an ornate entry hall. Laurie's gaze was everywhere. Without warning, it lingered on Marguerite's blond hair, how it hung in perfect golden waves down her bare back. Her beauty was hard to ignore. A butler took his overcoat, and they moved with the other arriving guests toward a reception line.

Herr Voss signaled them out of the crowd. "MacKenzie, this is one of my contemporaries in shipbuilding." Herr Voss turned to a dower-looking man of some sixty-odd years. Like Voss, the man was overweight, with heavy jowls and a frown that belonged on an English bulldog. "Herr Dorfman, my newest engineer and Marguerite's fiancé, Lawrence MacKenzie, straight off the boat from Edinburgh University."

The older man's eyes lit up. He extended his hand with enthusiasm. "Well, they turn out some excellent engineers in Edinburgh, and I have heard you're one of the best." Laurie shook the man's hand, flattered by the compliment, but he couldn't stop from thinking, *odd to see a bulldog smile.*

"Why, thank you, sir. I very much appreciate your comments." To Herr Voss, he added, "I sincerely hope my employer agrees with you." They all laughed, and Laurie joined in, if a bit nervous.

"Nonsense, lad. He's been telling me all about you."

His future father-in-law slapped him on the back. "You're a real prize, my boy. New ideas, fresh blood. It's what we need."

Laurie wondered if Herr Voss might have had a bit too much schnapps already. *How does he know if I'm any good? I just got here.*

Before Laurie could reply, Marguerite tugged on his arm, guiding them into the main salon. He'd never seen so many diamonds and furs. "When do the king and queen arrive?" he whispered in her ear. She gave him a playful swat but was already moving toward someone she knew.

Laurie paused a moment to take in his surroundings. *I read somewhere Goering styled himself a cultured man, but this is overdone. Everything is gold, gilt and polished silver.* Laurie stopped to study a painting. *The light and color—must be an old master. Looks like it belongs on the walls of Buckingham Palace.* His mind wandered back to his arguments with Rab over the state of affairs in Germany. *Marguerite was certainly right about the German economy. Hitler's been good, at least for commerce.*

But it was the people who bothered him. They looked so garish. Many of the men were in uniform, their medals shining in the candlelight. The women looked like royalty. Diamonds glistened from their necks and wound around their wrists. *There must be a fortune here in jewelry alone.* But all the window dressing in the world couldn't hide the hardness in their faces.

"What?" Marguerite was looking up at him with a proud expression. "Isn't it too wonderful? Did you ever think it would be like this when we were back at school?" She wrinkled her perfect nose with delight.

He answered her honestly. "No, baby. I never imagined I'd feel this way."

She was pulling him over to meet another blond beauty. "Hildie, this is my fiancé, Lawrence MacKenzie." She turned to Laurie, saying, "These are her friends, SS-Hauptsturmführer Eric Braun and SS-Hauptsturmführer—I mean Captain—Michael Muller."

The officers clicked their heels and made slight bows. Since no hands were extended to shake, Laurie inclined his head in acknowledgement. He was still feeling a bit chafed every time Marguerite said fiancé. She was saying, "He's a bit of a rogue but smart, just graduated from Edinburgh University with honors in engineering."

Hildie extended her hand. Laurie was guessing she didn't expect him to shake it by her startled expression. She held her clutch purse over her mouth as she said something in German to a young SS officer. Hildie's escort snickered, but by the smug expression on the young man's face, Laurie was guessing the joke was on him. Marguerite seemed to take it personally. She flushed and moved on to the next introduction.

When Laurie asked what was so funny, she answered, "Oh, nothing." Marguerite was smiling, but it looked forced, and her color was still high as she explained, "Hildie expected you to kiss her hand. You should have, you know."

No, I didn't. By the fifth introduction, he was becoming quite good at hand kissing. Laurie was a great fan of American films, and they did it all the time in the movies. Like Errol Flynn in *Charge of the Light Brigade. Maybe I should've taken up acting.*

After a while, the novelty wore off. When the dinner bell rang, Laurie was feeling not so much like a dashing actor. A bit more like a prize poodle being shown off to all of Marguerite's friends.

He started wondering what it was she saw in him. *It couldn't have been my academics.* She wasn't even an engineering major. He'd never stopped to wonder why she'd picked him from all the other lads. Now the thought plagued him. *Yet she picked me, and her father gave me this amazing chance. And now Bernie has someone in just the right place to find those bairns.*

At dinner, they sat next to some regular-looking people. He realized Marguerite and her father didn't know he'd been brushing up on his first-year German. They only spoke to him in English. He could pick up a word here and there, often catching the drift of their discussions. But someone must have said something to the people sitting next to them. They spoke in English most of the time.

"We just moved into our new home. You must come and have lunch with us. The china is exquisite. You can say a lot about the Jews, but they have good taste in most things."

Not sure what the woman meant, Laurie asked, "Did you have help from a Jewish clerk in picking out your china?"

"Heavens no, Herr MacKenzie. There are no Jewish clerks. Well, at least not anywhere I would shop." She was aghast at his lack of knowledge. "The china came with the house."

"I apologize, madam. That kind of thing must be rare. At least it is in Scotland." Her snobbish reaction offended him.

Marguerite put a hand on his arm and leaned over to whisper in his ear. "They moved into a home after the Jews who owned it were arrested."

He looked at her. "Not the whole family? Might they not come back and want their things?"

Marguerite said, "No."

Laurie remained silent for the rest of the dinner, just listening to the other dinner guests. After the comment about the china, he learned to hide his shock and horror at what passed for a pleasant dinner conversation.

Laurie remembered talking to Rab about an article on Aryanization of German businesses. Something about Jewish-owned businesses being taken over by Aryan Germans as far back as 1934. He'd paid little attention to what was happening outside his own world. Now he realized that homes and possessions were being confiscated. *And I thought Rab was exaggerating.*

He learned a lot about Germany by listening to dinner conversations. These wealthy Germans seemed to adopt an expression of boredom. They accepted the new rules governing Jews and the church, laughing off the loss of life and liberty for those subhuman—a term he realized referred to anyone who wasn't pure German. He wondered, *What does that make me?*

Down the table, Hildie's escort Eric said, "And could you believe the woman hid her jewelry in the baby's diaper?" Such a contradiction. How could someone who looked like a fresh-faced laddie be a part of all this?

"Well, you've had more experience chasing down babies, haven't you, Eric?" his friend Michael seemed to joke. The table was silent for just a moment. Laurie looked at Eric. The eyes never lie, and these eyes were deadly. Funny, he'd not noticed it earlier. There was something scary about this bloke.

A sweet grey-haired grandmother said, "Those Jew babies must have tough hides." They all laughed. It was sickening. Fortunately, Laurie had taken to playing cards during his time at school. It got him in trouble more than once, but he was pretty sure he'd mastered the poker face—an American expression he'd picked up watching films.

When he was sure his features were neutral, he glanced over at Marguerite. She was chuckling at their joke. He stared at his plate, looking anywhere but at his beautiful Marguerite, afraid she'd see the disgust in his eyes.

After dinner, she excused herself to touch up her makeup, so Laurie wandered through the salon. A servant handed him a drink. It was quite by accident he overheard a conversation between Marguerite's father and a black-uniformed military commander.

He picked it up as Herr Voss was saying, "Ja, I had him checked out as soon as I saw how Marguerite felt about him. His bloodline is very pure. Even with his dark looks, his family on both sides are descended from Viking stock. Warriors. Sailors. Then, too, his professors said he was top of his class. A brilliant engineer."

Flattering, but disturbing as all hell. *Voss went to speak with my professors. Makes a bit more sense since the last time I spoke with Professor Finlay, he asked if I was sure I wanted to work in Germany.*

The commander didn't seem as impressed as Marguerite's father. "He's foreign. An outsider. You should think of this before you let them marry. She should marry a German."

The noisy crowd blocked the rest of what was said. Laurie thought a lot about that small piece of conversation. *It shouldn't surprise me a wealthy man would check out a perspective suitor, but checking my bloodlines is more like dog breeding than I care to consider.*

Laurie found a corner and leaned against the wall, watching the other guests. *He's right. I am an outsider.* His mind drifted back to one of Rab's arguments about living in Hitler's Germany. *I thought he was being ridiculous. I'm not so sure Rab wasn't spot on.*

Chapter Sixty-Two

Voss Marine
Hamburg, Germany
June 1937

A New Job and a New Friend

Voss Maritime Engineering was a leading shipbuilder in a country known to put fine ships to sea, so when Herr Voss informed Laurie a week later over dinner he'd start his new job in the morning, Laurie grinned, saying, "Thank you, sir. I'm looking forward to that."

Marguerite exploded with objections. "Papa, I had plans for tomorrow. Couldn't he go another day?" When she pouted, Laurie thought the old man might give in to her as he often did.

"No, my love. I have a new project, and I want this young genius of yours to get started on it."

She said little through the rest of the dinner.

Thankfully, even her downcast looks didn't discourage her father. At the close of their meal, Herr Papa turned to Laurie. "We'll be leaving at 6 a.m. sharp. You'd best get plenty of rest."

The meaning was clear, so Laurie excused himself and, with a kiss on the cheek for Marguerite, left the room. He didn't get as far as he'd hoped. Her chair scraped the floor as it slid back, and she was at his side within a few seconds.

"Laurie, stand up to him. He can't interrupt all our plans." She was peevish but still looked beautiful.

"He's my boss. It's a new job. I want to make a good impression." He patted her hand as it rested on his arm. "But don't worry. We'll have plenty of time together."

She looked up at him with those big blue eyes. Her mouth pushed into a pout, inviting a kiss. He leaned close, her breath soft on his lips, and kissed her, savoring her passion and waiting for his own to rise within him. He lingered, searching for the rush he'd felt with every kiss.

No, it's gone. As he pulled back, he looked at Marguerite's expression. *She doesn't notice the change. Her face is flushed and ready for more. I've been so sure this was what I wanted.*

What this affluent German social caste was really like had even quenched his physical attraction for her. He marveled at the freedom he felt.

Herr Papa rescued him with a call from the dining room. "Herr MacKenzie, don't let my daughter twist you around her finger or you'll be no good to me."

Laurie smiled at the warning. *Ironic coming from the old man.* Marguerite's eyes were still closed as he drew back. He kissed her forehead and turned to leave the house. *If there's any chance of finding those children, she needs to think things are the same.* It didn't mean he'd have to feel good about doing this.

Laurie discovered he had a personal sense of honor, though hidden for years under anger. Before, money and success, plus the need to prove himself to his peers, had driven him. That had all ended on the docks of Leith. He was honor bound to find the children so he could end this pretense. The sooner the better but right now Marguerite's social contacts were giving him an invaluable education which he hoped to turn into information leading to the children's whereabouts.

He wondered, *How long will Herr Papa look kindly at me as a perspective son-in-law? With the political climate, Voss must feel pressure to send me packing.*

Laurie tried to think about his next step. *The problem is I have no bloody idea what to do next.*

Fiona's words floated through his consciousness. "I'll be praying for you. I know you'll find them." He missed her. From seven hundred miles away, he felt her encourage a smile onto his weary face.

Laurie hadn't had time to himself all week. Thanks to Herr Papa, he could finally sit and write letters home. He pulled out the small picture Fiona had given him and propped it on the desk in front of him as he wrote. His words reached out to her.

I love who you are. He sobered, wondering, *Does she still feel the same?*

He took his time with one letter to Fiona and one to Rab, trying to describe the macabre culture, the garish people. On impulse he wrote to Fiona, "You are my compass rose. Like Rab said, you are a constant reminder that God is guiding me on a spiritual journey. I need that because it's unbelievable how dark it is here. Those children count in the scheme of things."

Even dogs are of more value to these people.

It was near midnight when he finished both letters. Writing had purged him of the horror he'd been carrying. He found himself exhausted and ready for sleep.

As an afterthought, he enclosed his letter to Fiona in the envelope to his grandfather, remembering how frightened Bernie's family had been about getting word out of Germany. With that done, he fell asleep.

It seemed he'd just closed his eyes when his alarm rang out the hour of 5 a.m. He groaned and rolled over to hit the clock off the nightstand, but his hand touched the letter. He realized in this culture of deceit and intrigue, even a sealed letter addressed to his grandfather wasn't safe to leave behind. *I'd better take that with me today and find a place to mail it.* He was awake and ready by six, waiting in the drive by Herr Papa's auto.

The firm was impressive, all he'd expected and more.

"We're working on both military and commercial projects," Herr Voss informed. "For now, you will be working on special projects. Your work will be compartmentalized."

Laurie nodded, though his inner voice told him, *You mean you don't want me to know the complete picture, so this is a military project.* His face paled as a question hit him. *Could they think I might be a spy?*

On the job, the other employees smiled and shook hands but remained aloof. Before the midday meal, Herr Papa said, "I've promised Marguerite she could luncheon with us." *So, she managed to get her way with her father.*

While Herr Voss took an important phone call, Laurie wandered back to his new desk.

"Name's Terrance Mulligan." A short man of about thirty something with a distinct Irish accent clasped his hand and shook it vigorously.

"Laurie MacKenzie. Pleased to meet you." *After a week with only Germans, it's good to speak with someone from home—well, near enough, anyway.* "Do you work here?"

"Ten years. I married a local girl and came to work for this firm. It's a fine company," Terrance said, with a bit more volume than necessary. Laurie looked around, but no one seemed to even notice their conversation.

He asked, "I've got some time to kill. Do you have a few minutes? I have questions, and you might help me out."

Terrance rubbed the back of his neck. Laurie watched him. *Is he worried about talking to me? Should I just say skip it?*

Terrance shrugged. "Why not." He turned to a man passing by

and said something in rapid German. Then he gestured to Laurie. "Let's take a walk, shall we?"

As they walked alongside the dry dock, the little man pointed to the latest project for the Fuhrer. "We're not supposed to say, but the latest ships aren't seagoing." He winked. Laurie looked but saw only the outside of a large building. He wanted to ask more, but Terrance seemed to take great care of where he was when he said anything.

Laurie stopped him. "This is great, and thanks for showing me around, but if I'm putting you in a bad spot, I understand. If you point the way, I'll go back to my desk."

Terry answered with a conspiratorial smile. "This should work great." They were standing next to the steel works. Large doors were open in the old brick building, giving them a view of workers covered in leather protective gear as they moved enormous cauldrons of molten steel. Heat radiated from the building. It was hot and loud even thirty feet away.

"A bloke can't be too careful. I don't want to be overheard. It's not healthy." Terrance added, "First why don't you tell me how you landed this job?"

Laurie ran his hand through his hair. *I'm not sure how much I can say to a perfect stranger. Come to think of it, that's probably what this guy is feeling.* He smiled sheepishly. "I see what you mean. It's hard to know what to say and who to say it to."

Terrance just smiled. Then he asked, "Got a cigarette on you?"

Laurie pulled out a pack, and they shared a light. He took a long drag. "So, this is how it happened." He told Terrance about school and Marguerite. And about meeting Fiona and the differences between the two women. Laurie talked about Marguerite's social schedule and feeling like a prize poodle, not sure why he said so much. "Look, I know it's daft telling you all this, maybe even dangerous, but I'm all alone here, and I needed to talk with someone." Terrance was just a guy, but he wasn't German, and right now Laurie needed a friend. He stopped short of saying anything about the children, ending with, "Besides, you have an honest face."

They both chuckled, and Terrance said, "My mum might disagree with you. She always said I had guilty written all over my face." He sobered and added, "Sounds to me like you're in the wrong place. You should be back at Scotts shipyard. In fact, if you make it back there, could you put a word in for me? I'm not staying here."

Terrance looked around again. "Listen, be careful who you tell things to. It's not safe. People disappear around here. Neighbors. Friends. Family. And it's like they were never there. Someone new lives in their houses. Drives their autos. Runs their businesses. You should leave, lad, and the sooner the better. This isn't a great opportunity. It could be a deadly mistake." He ended with his gaze locked onto Laurie.

Laurie decided. "I've something I have to do first. And I could sure use some help. Then, yes, I can put a word in for you at Scotts. I'll head back as soon as I get this done."

A worker was walking toward them from the main offices. Terrance said, "Let's have dinner together. You know, talk about home." His volume was up again. "As soon as you settle in, next week."

"Right." Laurie glanced over his shoulder.

The young man slowed as he approached them. "Herr Voss says you're to go back in the office. Fraulein Voss is here. Bitte, I mean please."

Laurie nodded to the lad and turned back to Terrance before following him. "See? She doesn't realize I'm a Scot, not a poodle."

Chapter Sixty-Three

Arbroath, Scotland
June 1745

The Captain's Log Before Charlie Lands

Fiona propped up the pillow on her bed, settling herself to read a bit. The captain's log sat open on her lap. She read through the list of visits to call on the clans loyal to Prince Charles. She read about when the young prince landed with his ships and men from France. A fiery cross would light up the Highlands, calling the clansmen to their chieftains. There would be a mass gathering at Glenfinnan.

The captain wrote, "Ah, and won't that be a grand sight ta see?" Most of the next page was a list of dates, lairds, and the number of men they could muster.

Fiona sought the next entry with Mairi's name. "There are English garrisoned all over Scotland, and some clans are loyal to King George, so a man canna be too careful. And I thought smuggling was a risky business. The intrigue of governments is even deadlier."

Wee Geordie stopped again to see Mairi before Prince Charles landed. He knew they would be in the thick of fighting soon because he wrote, "I am compelled to see Mairi's face again—to know arrangements are in place for her safety. There'll be fighting soon, and I'm not sure how things will go. I've got to see her before then."

Fiona read on until she found an entry for June 25, 1745. The Tearloch put into Arbroath. The captain wrote: *"We are well aware of the small garrison of soldiers and the tariff officials at the Port of Arbroath. We've made a habit of coming into port aboard a skiff while the Tearloch stays well away from English eyes. The port master and his men are no so observant at the end of the week. They like their ale and a wee visit to the local pubs."*

Fiona felt sleep heavy on her eyelids. She slid the book to her nightstand. Tam was curled up at her feet, already sound asleep. She smiled at the captain's painting as she turned out the light. She snuggled under the covers and was asleep within seconds.

In her dreams, she was a silent observer as Wee Geordie and Tamash rowed out from the Tearloch.

Tamash pointed to the red cliffs north of Arbroath. "The fisher folk in Auchmithie are the only ones able to see the Tearloch tonight."

Fiona looked up to the small village hugging the clifftops. He was saying, "And they're all snug in their beds, narrie a candle still flickers."

The skiff scraped rocks, and both men jumped out to pull the small boat up onto the shale. The public house was only a few yards up the beach. Fiona felt the cobblestone street under her feet.

The Seaman's Rest stood at the very north end of the town past the breakwater. It was a good-sized building with large public rooms on the first level and rooms to rent on the second. Family quarters were in back. Tamash stopped to stare at the inn with pride. "Geordie, ye ken it were a fine thing ye did, helpin' my da to build the Seaman's Rest."

As they crossed the stable yard, Fiona looked around. *You helped him build all this? There's more to you than I ever guessed.*

Geordie just smiled. "I had my selfish reasons."

"Those reasons wouldn't be no so tall"—Tamash held his hand up shoulder height—"and have fiery hair would they?" He had a broad grin on his face.

But Geordie stood for a moment looking at the darkened windows. "It appears all are abed, Tamash. Do ye think we've come too late?"

"Nay, my da and sister should still be up."

It was late, but Tamash's father answered their quiet knock with, "Who be ye to knock on my door at this hour?"

"It's Tamash, sir," and before Tamash could say another word, the door was flung open. His da grabbed him by the arm and pulled him in, motioning for them to follow and quickly.

He clapped them on their backs and said, "It be that glad I am to see ye. Och, but yer a sight for a father's eyes."

Tamash laughed and said something, but Fiona could tell Geordie didn't hear him. Mairi stood in the kitchen doorway with a candle in her hand. She looked unreal in the warm flickering light. Golden threads sparkled in her long red hair. Her honey-brown eyes twinkled at the sight of Geordie. His voice cracked a bit as he said, "Hello, Mairi." Fiona had to look away, for he had such a look of longing it made her heart ache.

Mairi beamed all the more. "It's happy I am ta see ye again, Geordie." She turned to the fire and stirred up the coals. Her long red curls tumbled over her shoulder. Fiona heard him catch his breath at her beauty. "Are ye both hungry?" she asked.

Tamash answered for them. "Nay then, lass, we've just come ta see ye afore Charlie comes hame."

"It's soon?" his da asked. To Mairi he said, "Gi us some ale and glasses. There's a good lass."

As Mairi turned to fetch such, Geordie said he'd help her. Fiona followed along, and as soon as they were out of hearing, he added, "Lass, yer a bonnie sight ta see."

Mairi blushed famously. "Will there be fighting soon?"

"Aye, that there will. I wanted to know that ye and yer da were safe afore it started. Do ye mind?"

She reached out and took hold of his hand fiercely. "Och nay then, Geordie, for it would break my heart if I dinna hae a chance ta see ye as well."

Tamash and his father sat with their ale at the table and talked about who would answer the call. Wee Geordie and Mairi sat by the fire.

Geordie said, "I've much collected for Charles' war chest. Many of the Highland lairds and chieftains have added to the box. But I'll no deliver it till I see how things go."

"You have yer doubts about success?" she asked.

"Aye, well, the prince has many character flaws, and he seems far more Italian or French than Scots, but he has some fine men to advise him though some near him are doubtful. Mairi, if not the prince, then who will unite the clans?"

She reached for his hand again. "It's a fine thing yer doing. But success or no, I trust ye to know what's right."

Wee Geordie's smile was so tender as he said, "The confidence you have in me makes me feel the need to be the man you see. I hope I shall not disappoint you."

Fiona wanted to stay in the dream, but the scene faded from her mind as she roused from sleep.

Chapter Sixty-Four

Rüdesheim am Rhein, Germany
June 1937

Horror at Night

"Can I have a word with you, sis—I mean, Ana?" Etienne asked. The tall steward looked uncomfortable not addressing her by her calling. Ana smiled at him and was rewarded with an amazingly boyish grin. Imagining this man as a young boy making mischief would be easy.

He motioned to her from his office door. "If you have a minute?" She followed his tall, lanky form into his crowded little office. Ledgers and paperwork sat in piles on his desk and on every other open space, giving her the impression of organized chaos. This was, after all, a working farm and a country estate, and it clearly took a good deal of management.

Etienne picked up a pile of books from the only other chair. She sat as he intended and watched him close the door with his foot. He turned, having nowhere to set the books, so she offered to hold them. When he set them on her lap, he seemed distracted.

She wondered what was so difficult for him to get out, but he shrugged his shoulders and said, "I think it would be good if you came with me to meet my contact. If the opportunity presents itself, we must move on it." He waited for her response.

It was a bit of a bombshell. *I knew this was coming but so soon?* She looked out his only window at the view of her children playing in the field beyond the barn. When Etienne cleared his throat, it caught her off guard. Sympathetic eyes told her how much he understood.

"With le comte coming home, there will be dinner parties once again. They probably wouldn't pay any attention to servants' children, but if we can avoid the risk, it would be safer for us all. It's dangerous to stay any longer than necessary."

She swallowed that old familiar acid taste of fear. "Most certainly. I would be happy to come with you. When do we go?"

"I was thinking we'd visit him under the cover of darkness." Etienne's expression was impish. "Can you be ready to slip out at ten tonight?" He smiled. "I hope you don't mind going alone with me? It's better that it's only the two of us. A man and woman alone at night..." He blushed. "Well, if we're seen, people will draw their own conclusions."

"And Marie, will she mind?"

"Marie knows already. She suggested it."

"Tonight then." Ana rose, books still in hand, and turned to the door. Remembering, she replaced the pile on the chair.

AT TEN SHE found him back in his office, his desk lamp on. It appeared he was going over a ledger. When she rapped on the half-open door, he looked up. "Good, you've saved me from working on these." He picked up a stack of receipts and glanced down at her feet. "Sister, you'll need a jacket and some stout shoes."

Before she said anything, he added, "I'm sure there are mud boots and a jacket by the kitchen door. You look about the same size as my wife, and she leaves hers there. I'll meet you in five minutes."

True to his word, he was waiting in an old truck when she came through the kitchen door. They drove down a country lane that seemed to wander this way and that. Etienne pulled off the road down a two-track path. Again, he pulled off the track to a wooded glade. A well-worn path led farther into the trees. He was silent for most of the drive, so Ana was startled when he turned off the engine. He was already out and around the truck, motioning for her to follow.

"It's so dark out here." Ana pulled her collar up. "Did you bring a torch?"

He looked up at the full moon. "There's enough light. Let your eyes adjust. You'll be fine but stay close to me."

They walked quite a way through the trees before coming to a clearing. A brook ran through the center with a bank that rose on the other side. He turned to her. "Take my hand."

His fingers closed around hers, startling her. *I haven't held a man's hand in years.*

If he could see her face, it must be showing her surprise because he added, "We French have a reputation with the ladies." Ana could make out a roguish grin again. He shrugged. "If anyone sees us, they will think I have a meeting with a secret lover." There was a chuckle in his voice. "They won't know my Marie would kill me if I even thought of looking elsewhere. French wives have a reputation, too, you know."

"Not sweet Marie." She smiled at the look of chagrin on Etienne's face.

"You should know, sister, looks are often deceiving." His voice became very serious. "From here on, no talking. Walk where I walk and try not to break any branches."

He was all business as he scanned the clearing before leading her across the brook. They climbed rocks up the bank and avoided any soft dirt. It wasn't too much farther when she saw lights through the trees.

Etienne reached out to stop her. Perhaps one hundred yards across an open field sat a farmhouse and an old barn. A military truck was parked in the drive. In the glare of its headlights, at least a dozen soldiers stood with rifles at the ready. A large man was being hauled from the house. Etienne's grip on her arm tightened, and she looked up to see the grim expression on his face. Her own heart began beating wildly as she watched the scene unfold.

A soldier pushed the man to the ground. Another man, who must have been the officer, emerged from the house. He shouted orders back inside and to the men by the truck. There was a sudden flurry of action as more soldiers rushed inside.

Ana saw for herself the Nazi policy for searching. The men threw chairs and dressers out of the house. The soldiers seemed bent on destruction rather than on finding something. She could hear glass breaking and furniture crashing.

From their hidden spot, Etienne and Ana watched as the officer looked toward the barn. Etienne tensed. The officer ordered his men to surround the small structure. Without warning, the prisoner stood and bolted.

Ana put her hand over her mouth to keep from crying out. But she realized the man must have known he could never escape. Caught off guard, a soldier fired once into the farmer's back, knocking him to the ground. The officer in charge was angry. He began screaming in the shooter's face. Abruptly, he turned toward the barn and shouted at two of his men to bar the barn door.

The soldiers brought petrol from the truck. Men went back into the house. Within minutes, the house was on fire. Next, they doused the barn and set it aflame.

"Mon Dieu," Etienne whispered. He put his arm around Ana's shoulders, drawing her further into the cover of the trees.

Screams erupted from the barn. Ana pushed forward again, wanting to help even though she knew those same flames would consume her, but Etienne held her back. They heard the cries of small children.

She turned her face into the rough fabric of his coat. Silent sobs wracked her body. Her eyes closed against the sight. But the sounds still reached out to her. Women, children, and men were crying for help. She looked up through her tears. The soldiers stood around watching the fire and making what sounded like small talk as they smoked.

"Animals, my God, they are animals." She spoke aloud without meaning to, but the screams drowned out her voice. All too soon, the screaming stopped. She heard only the pop and crackle of the fire.

"We go now." Startled by Etienne's voice, she looked up to see anguish distorting his face. Fear was there as well. *If the SS have found Etienne's contact, are they close to finding la comtesse?* A shiver ran up Ana's back. *If we'd arrived earlier, we would have joined those poor souls in the barn.* Etienne turned, his strong arm on her shoulder.

He led her back through the woods. They didn't speak again until they reached the truck.

He gripped the steering wheel. "How can God let this happen?" He spit out his anger.

She knew he wasn't angry at her. *We people have a habit of blaming you, Lord, for the evil we do.* She watched grim determination take the place of anger as he started the truck.

She thought of the crying Christ on the cross at the convent where she'd attended school. *The sisters told me the Lord was weeping for our sins. I'm sure these men are among those the Lord weeps for.* Ana said, "I feel so sorry for them."

"Especially the small ones in the barn." Etienne replied. He shook his head as if he could wipe away the memory of what he'd seen.

Yes, there were small ones in the barn, but I was thinking about the men who stood by and let them burn.

Chapter Sixty-Five

Hamburg, Germany
June 1937

An Ally

Laurie found the work interesting, even challenging. The pace increased every day for a week. Herr Voss commended the men over the loudspeakers. "Well done. We finished our project on time and under budget." The men cheered and clapped.

Terrance was all smiles as he stopped at Laurie's desk. "Well, how was your first week on the job?"

"I learned a lot. Not like school, though, much harder. Say, now that things are settling down, would you like to get a pint after work?" He looked around. Was it his imagination or did the room get quieter?

"Sure you can get free of the boss's daughter?" Terrance grinned. "That'd be great. Only, why don't you come to my house for dinner? Lydia's a splendid cook." Under his breath, he added, "It's safer to talk there."

Can I trust this guy? I've only known him a week. If I see him at home with his family, I'll know if he's real or just putting on an act.

Laurie pushed his doubts aside. He needed someone he could trust, and, after a week of observation, Terrance seemed to be a regular guy.

He made a quick call to Marguerite. "You can't be serious," she objected. "This man isn't the kind you should be associated with."

"He's a nice guy. I like him, and he's from home." This social snobbery was wearing on his nerves.

"But don't you like my friends? They all love you. I wanted us to take in a cinema with Hildie and her new captain. Afterwards we could talk, just the two of us, over coffee. There's a great little bistro around the corner." Marguerite had changed to her injured tone. *Well, why not? It always worked on her father.*

"Look, baby, you'd like this guy. He's married to a local girl. And, after all, he is a senior engineer. I can learn a lot from him." Laurie waited. His heart felt as if a net was being thrown over it. The phone line went silent. *If she wants me to yield, it's not going to work. Not this time.*

"Why don't you come with me? You could get to know his wife." He was certain of her reaction, but for a moment he wondered if she wanted to be with him, or was it all about control? Silence again. *Oh Lord, what did I do? If she says yes, how will Terrance feel about having the boss's daughter to dinner?* He held his breath and waited.

Marguerite must have thought it over but said, "No. That's all right. We can talk later."

Laurie rang off and realized he'd been perspiring. He took out his handkerchief to wipe his brow. *How could I have been so blind? Did she think she was so beautiful she could lead me around like a dog?* Once again, Fiona's smiling face flashed through his thoughts. *It's hard not to compare them. They're so different. But then, I'm different too.*

After work, Terrance came to find him. "I'm ready when you are."

Laurie gathered his things. "Say, I hope this won't put your wife out?"

"Not at all. She'll love having company." Terrance gave him a wink.

After two weeks in Germany, you, my lad, are the breath of fresh air I needed. They were out the door and on their way in no time. After a twenty-minute tram ride and a three-flight walk-up, they entered a homey apartment that smelled like heaven. Laurie inhaled the scents of baked bread and pot roast. Terrance nudged him. "I told you my girl can cook."

Most of the German women Laurie had met, those in Marguerite's circle, were stylish. Hard. Superior. He was astonished to find Lydia was a sweet person. She was also very pregnant. She greeted her husband with a kiss. Terrance's four-year-old son raced into the room, nearly knocking Laurie over.

"Papa, you're home."

Laurie watched as his new friend lifted his son into a big bear hug while the lad planted kisses on his father's cheeks. Laurie's heart ached with longing for a life with Fiona and lots of bairns. How had he changed so much in such a short time? The answer was simple. Fiona.

"Herr MacKenzie, my husband has said great things about you." Lydia offered her hand to Laurie. He wondered if she expected him to kiss it. But no, she shook his hand, giving it a gentle squeeze.

Terrance set his son down and turned him to face Laurie. "Young man, this is my friend, Mr. MacKenzie."

A small hand extended. Laurie bent to take the hand and shook it with as much dignity as the child seemed to give him.

"Good to meet you, sir. My name is Richard."

"Your English is great." Laurie was impressed.

"Thank you, but we only speak English at home. Papa says that's what we Mulligan's do."

Laurie looked up with approval at Richard's proud parents.

The dinner was without question the best he'd eaten since arriving in Germany. It was plain cooking. He'd had his fill of fancy dinner parties and rich meals.

Later, Lydia put Richard to bed while he and Terrance stayed at the table over coffee and strudel to talk. Their conversation had danced around during dinner of home and ordinary things. It was as if each man was taking the other's measure.

Terrance said, "Hitler's done wonderful things for Germany. The people loved him. But then things changed, slowly at first. By the time we became alarmed, it wasn't safe to say anything. Three months ago, Lydia's friend gave birth to a baby with a severe cleft palate. The state destroyed the baby and sterilized my wife's friend. Lydia is petrified about delivering our child."

She returned to the table and slipped her arm around her husband. "When church leaders spoke out about my friend, our pastor was arrested and beaten. Our church is watched now. This is not the Germany I grew up in. It's not where I want to raise my children." Terrance kissed her cheek, and she cleared the table.

"You see how it is. I know we should leave, but the police keep tabs on every move we make. The more so because I'm Irish, and if you're a member of certain churches, they watch you closer."

Laurie shook his head in disbelief. "Good God, they'll be following me, too?" *How the hell am I supposed to smuggle children out of Germany when I'm being watched?* He heard Fiona's voice, whispering, "God will help you." *Well, that's hard as hell to believe.*

He swirled the coffee in his cup, feeling his emotions spin as well. "Fiona and my grandfather say God will help me, but He didn't help your wife's friend, and He's not helping you get out of here is He? I've never been much for church. I know there's a God. I guess He hasn't bothered with me much either." He looked up, expecting Terrance to comment. Instead, he saw compassion in his eyes. Understanding.

Laurie was sinking, and he blurted out, "I came here to find two children. They are cousins of a school friend. Jews."

Terrance frowned. "It's not likely they're still alive."

If Terrance isn't a straight-up guy, this will end my stay in Germany, maybe even my life, but I'm already in over my head. "Wait, let me tell you the whole story. If I can find them and get them home, I can help you and your family while I'm at it." Laurie launched into the contents of Bernie's letter. He'd committed it to memory. As he finished the story, silence hung in the room.

Terrance said, "Looks like the Almighty might have had his eye on you all along."

"I'd like to call my grandfather. How do I do that without being overheard? I'm going to need a bit more direction and a plan to get us all out of here."

"Sure, I can help you with the phone call." Terrance added, "One more thing. We'll be praying for you."

Laurie rolled his eyes. "Thanks, that's what my grand-da says, but I'll need some practical help."

"You might be surprised, me lad o."

Chapter Sixty-Six

Latimer Square
Edinburgh
June 1937

His Father's Man

Alec was already in his robe and slippers when he popped his head into his father's study to say goodnight. *What's this, a visitor? The man with a hooked nose. So, Father engaged the dodgy bloke again.*

Without explanation or even an introduction, his father said, "See that you're in early tomorrow. We have an important client first thing."

"Anything you'd like to tell me about ahead of time?" Alec let a hint of frustration creep into his voice.

"Just do as I say. I'll inform you when I want you to think." His father flipped a hand in Alec's direction, commanding him to get out.

As he closed the door, Alec heard the mystery man mumble something. Before the door latched, the old man snapped, "No more excuses, Jones. Get it done or I'll—" The door was solid and muffled the rest.

It bothered Alec as he sipped a brandy in the front sitting room, hoping for a moment of peace to replace the turmoil in his thoughts. *I'd say Father's still after the treasure. Not having any luck, old boy?* Alec smirked. *Hope the old man fails miserably. Wouldn't it be even better if I found the captain's treasure box first?*

Alec heard a door close, so he walked to the front windows to get another look at Jones. The street was dark and deserted. Then movement caught his eye, and he looked toward the end of the square. A dark figure darted under the archway that led to Fiona's stable.

Alec set down his drink. He craned his neck to see if the figure would return. He was sure it was his father's mystery guest. After a minute of waiting, he cinched his robe tighter and slipped out the kitchen door. His only plan was to come around Fiona's house from the other side. He snuck undetected from behind thick shrubbery bordering their property. It was dark, but his eyes adjusted.

"Damn." He stifled a cry as his slippered foot stepped on a sharp rock. *I'll have to be a bit more careful.* He stopped short as he came around the far end of the hedge. Jones, still dressed in the dark trench coat, slipped a key into the lock of Fiona's kitchen door. *I wonder how often Mr. Jones has visited Fiona's house?* Alec smiled at the irony. He'd taken the key several times to explore the house. *It's lucky we didn't bump into each other.*

"That means even though Father gave this bloke his key"—Alec's face lit with revelation—"he still hasn't found the treasure yet. Good."

He crept closer. *What if he finds it this time?* His throat tightened at the thought. *I can't take that chance. Got to think of a way to keep him out of her house. If I make a noise, will it scare the man off?*

But although the handle turned, the door didn't move. The man moved to a window, but that seemed secure as well.

Fiona must have been taking precautions. Well, good for her. I like her spirit. She's stopped Father's schemes. All five-foot-two of her.

The dark figure opened the coal scuttle and peered in. *Good God. He couldn't be —*

Before Alec could finish the thought, the intruder went feet first down the chute.

A bark sounded from somewhere in the house. Alec jumped. *She has a dog? When the bloody hell did that happen?*

Jones clambered back up the coal chute. Alec couldn't help a low chuckle. The man's face matched his black coat. The moon shone on wide, disembodied eyes. Jones coughed. He stumbled as he scooped up his hat and took off running around the side of the house.

A light came on in the upstairs hall window, accompanied by more barking. It was time for Alec to retreat. As he made his way back to his own kitchen door, he thought about what this might mean. *It won't be easy to sneak in there anymore.* A smile spread across his face. "Good thing she calls me her knight in shining armor."

How to proceed—maybe a romantic dinner out, some flowers. It's not like I'm unable to turn a lady's head.

Chapter Sixty-Seven

House on Latimer Square
Edinburgh
June 1937

Highland Warriors Now and Then

Tam barked fiercely. He scratched at the bedroom door, and when Fiona rose to open it, he raced down the dark hall toward the kitchen stairs.

Fiona charged after her wee Highland warrior. "Och, Tam, don't go so fast, or we'll both break our necks."

This time Tam ran between the kitchen door and the door that led to the cellar. That was frightening enough. It felt as if she were being invaded, but she couldn't tell from where. There was no use listening, because all she could hear was the wild wee beastie at her feet. "Wist, Tam, I canna hear anything."

But there was no use trying to quiet him. She lit the lamps in the kitchen and tried to peer out the window. It was dark outside, nothing more.

She checked the newly installed locks. Stout deadbolts were

still in place and locked. Rab had even insisted on an iron bar across each door. He'd also made sure the windows were secure short of breaking glass. Still, there was nothing to shake her confidence like her wee Highland warrior ready to do battle.

Tam was sure someone was just beyond the door. The question was which door? Fiona thought again of the coal chute. *Would someone want in badly enough to slide down that dirty hole? Perhaps.*

Then, just as suddenly, Tam stopped barking. He cocked his head to the side and listened. She did the same. Silence. He humphed and scratched his back feet, satisfied he'd chased off his adversary.

He started toward the stairs and looked back to see if she would follow. *Who is the pet, and who is the master?* Still, she followed him up the back steps and down the hall. *Think I'll leave the lights on just in case my wee fiend decides on another flight of frenzy.*

By the time she reached her room, Tam was once again curled up on her coverlet. *Well, even if he felt sure he could sleep, she was sure she couldn't. This house was always going bump in the night.* It might have been the ghost horses again, but she hadn't heard them. Besides, her inner voice told her Tam had the right of it. Someone had tried to get into her house.

She added a bit more coal to the fire. In the flickering firelight, the captain seemed to invite her to spend some time with him again. She smiled and pulled out his book. The gaslight gave her room a warm glow, and the fire made her room cozy. It always felt as if he sat with her as she read. More and more, she loved and respected this distant relative as an ever-closer companion.

Last time she'd read about Wee Geordie posing as the Black Captain while smuggling clansmen and weapons to the gathering places. She scanned through the pages, looking for Geordie's impression of his prince.

"I will gee ye this," he wrote. "Though he is young, Charlie has a knack for gathering men to him. He arrived in Arisaig, and within a month he gathered enough support to raise the standard at Glenfinnan. It made my heart swell wi pride to see so many clansmen with one word on their lips: Freedom. Though notably absent were the border clans.

"I've nae doubt the battles will be brutal, odds overwhelming, but we're fighting for our freedom, and none will fight sae bravely. English George has the advantage in numbers and weapons. His armies are well disciplined and well fed while the Highlanders are poorly fed, poorly clothed, and poorly equipped. We must pray for guid leadership."

Fiona looked up at the captain, imagining the scene as he painted it for her. She found her place and read.

"While I've been able to keep the Tearloch disguised as my brother's ship, the Turace, myself and my crew were with Prince Charlie when he took Perth. We heard the English sent Sir John Cope and troops to hold Perth. But the English commander thought it better not to meet Charlie and his three-thousand-strong Highlanders. I still canna believe it, but Cope rode instead for Inverness. We took Perth to the cheers of the people. Nothing can stand in our way. After Perth, we crossed the Forth near Stirling and were on our way to Edinburgh.

"I heard from my house servants the city was in a panic. Some said it should be defended at all costs, but soon calmer heads prevailed, and a delegation was sent to Charles. Charles demanded that the city surrender or he would attack at once. He knew nine hundred Highlanders under Lochiel had been smuggled into the city. In the end, Edinburgh surrendered without a fight, and within a few hours, Prince Charles rode to Holyrood and proclaimed his father James VIII king of Scotland.

"I write this so I'll never forget what happened next.

"We were wild with victory. That night I took Mairi to a ball at Holyrood. Och, she looked grand wi her golden curls flying to the reel. Her eyes sparkled as we danced the night away. And before I gave her back to her brother, I asked her to be my bride. I've faced raging storms and powerful enemies and risked my life repeatedly, but I've never feared so much as to face her with my heart in my hands and wait for her answer.

"'Mairi,' I said, 'I ken fine I'm not as guid a man as ye deserve, but I dinna think I can face the future without ye by my side.'

"I'll not long forget that terrible moment when she looked at my trembling hands. A single tear slid doon her cheek. My heart hit my stomach, but it rose again when she looked into my eyes with all the love I'd hoped to see.

"'Aye, Geordie, I'd be proud to be yer wife.'

"I kissed her and cared not a whit for the tongues that would wag in the mornin'. Mairi was mine, and that was all that mattered—that and facing her brother and father. I'm nay sae certain I'd let a prize as precious as Mairi go to a scoundrel, a smuggler, like myself."

Fiona closed the captain's book. Her mind drifted back to the docks at Leith and the look in Laurie's eyes when he told her he loved her and asked her to share his future. It had been three weeks since he'd left, but it felt like forever. Mairi managed the wait for Geordie, and he was in constant danger. "Laurie," she spoke his name aloud. "I know you're in danger and cannot come back to me till you find those bairns, but know I'm waiting, my love. I'm waiting."

Chapter Sixty-Eight

Hamburg, Germany
June 1937

The Phone Call Home

"**D**idn't I say payday's the best time to come in here?" Terry said with a verbal swagger.

"Not exactly a private place for a phone call, is it?" Laurie tried to keep the sarcasm out of his answer. The room was full. "Everyone from the office is here."

"Don't you get it? That's why it's perfect." On their way to the bar, Terry called out for two glasses of beer. As he put some money down, he turned to Laurie. "The one thing you don't want to do is stand out. See, everyone's here."

He cast his gaze around the room. In the same tone he used with little Richard, he said, "We're going to have a nice drink. Then you go toward the back. There's a washroom there. There's also a back door."

He smiled as the light dawned on Laurie's face. "Go to the

right down the alley and around the corner where you'll find a pay phone. It's a side street so not much chance anyone from work would notice the call." Terry accepted their beers and handed Laurie his drink.

"Here's to the scoundrel in both of us."

Laurie chuckled, taking his drink and saluting his Irish friend.

Terry looked down as if pondering the color of his beer. "Did you get the coins for the pay phone?" he asked, just loud enough for Laurie to hear.

Laurie answered with confidence. "No worries. With all the change in my pockets, I must weight two stones more."

They kept their conversation casual. True, they were speaking English, but the subject, home and family, was likely repeated all around the room.

Terry glowed. "I tell you, I don't know what she sees in me. She's beautiful. Good mother, great cook and all the rest. That makes her perfect."

Laurie slapped his friend on the back. "You're right. I don't know what she sees in a scoundrel like you." He chuckled at Terry's mock offense. "But then I don't know what my girl sees in me, either." He lifted the remains of his drink. "Here's to women who love scoundrels."

They downed the last drop. Then Laurie excused himself to move through the crowded room while Terry ordered another round.

Laurie walked casually. No *need to look nervous*. After all, he was just visiting the water closet. The men's room door opened, illuminating the dark hallway as a co-worker emerged. Laurie almost collided with the large man.

"Hey there, Sigwald." He reached out to steady the other guy. "Had a bit too much already?" He smiled his crooked grin as Sigwald patted his arm.

"Du bist ein guter Bursche," the big man slurred. Laurie was pretty sure he'd just been called a good guy, but Sigwald had downed a few too many.

The big man added with a silly expression on his youthful face, "Obwohl du ein Ausländer bist."

Did he say even though I'm a foreigner?

"Well, thanks, bloke." Laurie motioned to the door to the loo. "Is this the toilet?" he asked in halting German.

"Ja, Ja," Sigwald answered.

Laurie visited the toilet before he hit the alley. Sigwald had startled him, reminding him of the effect a stein of beer had on his bladder. Then he cracked open the men's room door. The hallway was smoky but deserted. The back door was a few steps away.

He pulled out a cigarette and made his way into the fresh night air. The door closed behind him. He paused to get his bearings. The alley was little more than a narrow walkway between two buildings. Through the half-open door on the opposite wall he could hear pots clanging, mixed with the sound of commerce. A restaurant maybe. Rubbish bins of discarded food lined that side of the alley. His foot kicked a bottle as he moved off to his right.

Wee glowing eyes peeked out of one can. Rats. He hated rats, but the four-legged kind were harmless. They reminded him of those black-suited military types. Friends of Marguerite. Not so harmless.

He lit his cigarette and strolled toward the street, his mind coming up with something convincing to say if he was stopped, but he wasn't. And there was the pay phone, just as Terrance said. No traffic and no stores—apartments lined this street. Laurie drew the tobacco into his lungs and blew out slowly, taking a moment to look around.

Lights were on here and there in the flats across the street, but no one watched him. The phone, which was unusually private for a public phone, was located next to a large oak tree.

His composure returned as he felt the coins in his pocket. There was no light in the booth, but a nearby lamppost gave him enough light to see what he was doing. *A bit more luck, God. That's all I need.*

Before long, an operator was asking him for the number. Then he heard the scratchy connection go through. The line rang three times. He could imagine his grandfather in his favorite chair with the paper in front of his nose. The phone didn't ring often, so it would startle him. Four rings and still no answer. At five rings, Laurie began to lose hope.

"Hello." Rab's voice sounded a world away.

"Rab, it's so good to hear your voice." Tears stung Laurie's eyes. He couldn't believe how much he'd missed his grandfather in just three weeks' time.

"Och, Laurie. Thank God it's you." Rab's voice cracked. "How are ye, laddie? We've been that worried about ye. We got yer letters yestereve."

Laurie was stunned. It seemed a long time since he'd written those letters.

"I canna believe it's you."

"Listen, Rab, I haven't much time. It's crazy here. I don't know how long I can take it. God, I miss you and Fiona. How is she? Tell her I love her. I want ta come home." He gulped in air. "How —how was she when you gave her grand-mam's ring?" Laurie closed his eyes, imagining the scene as Rab described it.

Rab ended with, "She loves ye, laddie, and there's no doubt about it. But you've been given a job, right?"

Laurie couldn't answer. His throat was clogged with emotion.

"Aye, to that end, son, I've been talking to Bernie. He says the girl who watched his niece and nephew was from Bavaria—a little town called Mittenwald. I've been thinking. Bavaria is still largely Catholic. That saying, the Church might be the first place to start."

Laurie cleared his head, trying to take in what Rab was telling him.

"I suppose ye could find out what churches are in that area. I know ye can do this."

"But, Rab, what if I can't?" Laurie's question hung in the air.

"Ye know, son, the Lord will guide ye." Rab was silent. Static filled the trunk line. "Ye must seek him for yerself. If ye call out to Him with the gift of yer heart, He will meet you there."

Laurie balked at his grandfather's words. So much rebellion, so much anger at his parents' deaths, had built a wall between him and his grandfather's god. *What if even God can't scale the wall?*

"Rab, if—" Laurie pushed on, "when I find them, I have a friend with a wife and a bairn. They're helping me, and we need to get them out of here with the children." He waited, half-expecting his grandfather to object. "He's Irish. I'll write to you about him. A good guy. He believes like you." Laurie paused. "I think."

"We'll make it happen. No worries about that." Rab's voice was firm. Warm. Laurie remembered the times he'd climb into his grandfather's lap as a wee lad when his parents were still alive. Rab told him stories by the firelight in his small Highland home. Then later, at the house on Latimer Square, he'd held Laurie in his arms, comforting him when his parents no longer could. He realized the older man was constant. Strength. Love. Support.

"I think I can call you again at the same time next week." An urgency to get back tugged at Laurie. "I can't talk for long. Terry says I'm being watched." He heard the quick intake of breath from his grandfather. "It's all right, Rab. They watch all foreigners. Can you have Fiona with you next week? I'd like—" He couldn't get the words out. "I need to hear her voice."

"Ye have my word on it, son." Then, mysteriously, as overseas calls sometimes do, the line went dead. Laurie tried to rattle the receiver button but nothing, not even the annoying static.

Rubbing his hand through his hair and over his face, he took a deep breath and exhaled. It was time for his game face. He couldn't let his expression betray the emotions rolling through his heart. He retraced his steps to the back door of the beer hall and thought, *Now I'll need that second pint.*

Chapter Sixty-Nine

Rüdesheim am Rhein, Germany
June 1937

Finding Light on a Dark Night

The trip home was silent. Etienne looked dark and angry like a storm ready to break. Ana felt her own storm rising. Icy fingers touched her heart. Dark winds pushed thoughts through her mind. *I never thought I'd have four children. This isn't the life I've chosen. What if I fail? We could all die. Maybe everyone who helps us will die. If God was taking care of us, what about all those people who burned to death in the barn? Was God watching from above? Did you even see what those men did?* But God was silent. Her prayers floated in the air unheard.

When they pulled up to the kitchen entrance, Ana opened the door. She couldn't bring herself to look at Etienne or say a word in parting. By the time she reached her room, the shaking had begun. She didn't undress. Instead, she sat on her bed and pulled close the surrounding blankets. Alone. Afraid. Evil seemed to watch from the darkness.

She'd started wearing her rosary again, cold next to her skin. She pulled it out. As her fingers ran over the beads, she prayed. It was familiar. Comfortable. Without conscious intent, she whispered the Lord's prayer.

"Our Father."

Whose father? Mine? Tony's? Katrine's? What about Gretchen and Deter? Are you their father, too?

"Who art in Heaven."

Are you here with us? Or do you stay far away from this world only looking down at us from heaven?

"Hallow'd be thy name."

Your name? Emanuel. God with us. Yes, God with us.

"Thy kingdom come—"

But this kingdom belongs to a demon. A madman. Evil has taken over the hearts and minds of weak men.

"Thy will be done on earth as it is in heaven."

She shook her head. *I can't imagine that's happening.* Then she remembered Madam Leona and the old man with a load of flounders and five souls in the back of his truck. The comtesse. All the people here. Etienne. The farmer tonight. *He gave his life to do your will.*

"Give us this day our daily bread."

We are here in this place for now. Today, we are safe and fed.

"And forgive us our sins as we forgive others."

Forgiveness? For what I saw tonight?

"I feel sorry for them." She whispered again what she'd said to Etienne. *I remember the weeping Christ.* Once again, she thought of what old sister Maria had said: "He cries for the sins of men, the lost ones." Ana answered aloud, "I don't know if I can forgive them." Another bead slipped through her fingers.

"Lead us not into temptation but deliver us from evil." *That's the thing. To stand against evil, not to take on one of its many forms: bitterness, fear. Not to listen to the lies.*

Ana sighed as her personal storm passed. Her tiny room was

washed in moonlight. She rose to open her window. A light breeze caressed her cheeks. The estate seemed to sleep peacefully. She leaned out her window to look up into the black night sky covered in millions of tiny points of light. *Beautiful. Even in the darkness, He gives us light.* From here, each star seemed like such a small point of light, but there were so many of them. Together, they were brilliant. *Then that's all you are asking me to do. Add my light to this dark time.*

She curled up on her bed and snuggled into the warm blankets. Her storm having passed and peaceful sleep overtaking her, Ana finally found rest.

Chapter Seventy

Edinburgh
June 1937

Don't Tell Rab

Tam's cold, wet nose nudged Fiona's hand. She struggled to get back into her dream. "Not now, Tam." She groaned and rolled over and pulled the covers up around her neck. She felt him move. Warm breath floated past her face. He was watching her, waiting. She opened one eye, squinting into his eager black face. Full morning light filled her bedroom.

"All right, all right, ye wee beastie. And who was it that kept us up last night barking at nothing?" Her mental fog lifted. *That was wrong. It had been something or, more likely, someone.* Two black eyes stared at her with intent, willing her to get up.

"I'm up," she said, reaching out to pat his head, which only encouraged him to demand more.

"Up, up," he seemed to say, barking and laughing at the same time. Well, it seemed like laughing with his mouth open in a doggy smile. His body quivered with excitement as he hopped around her coverlet.

Fiona put on her slippers and dressing gown and walked Tam down the hall. *Well, that was wrong, too.* She walked while he ran ahead. Tam paused at the kitchen stairs, encouraging her to speed it up with an impatient bark. Then he was gone. She called out, "Och Tam, ye'll break your wee neck flying doon the stairs."

She opened the back door to peek out, but Tam was having none of it. He shot past her into the small kitchen garden. He had business to take care of.

Everything looks so different in the light of day, she thought. *Nothing to be afraid of.* She looked around, but there was no evidence of her midnight visitor. *It's hard to imagine why anyone would want into my house.* She bit her lip. *If only Laurie was here. But he isn't.* Then she thought of Rab. *I have Rab both as a friend and soon as a grandda.*

Thirty minutes later, she was in the front hall hooking Tam to a leash when a knock startled them both. She unlatched the door and turned her attention to Tam, who was barking furiously. "Rab, I was just coming to see you."

"It seems your new dog doesn't like me much."

Alec stood on her doorstep with hat in hand. "May I please come in, or will he have my ankles for his breakfast?"

Her eyes widened. "Why, Alec, yes, of course, come in and welcome." Tam's barking had stopped, but it appeared Alec was right. Her dog didn't like him much. "It's Alec. He's our friend." As if saying that would make her dog more agreeable. Tam only humphed in acknowledgement and moved to stand between her and Alec, never looking away from the tall stranger.

"Were you going out?" Alec sounded so disappointed. "Would you have a moment to visit with me first?" He bit his lip, his brows drawn together in concern.

"Are you all right, Alec?" She looked up into his normally friendly face.

"Might we have tea?"

"Tea sounds grand." She smiled. "Haven't had a cup yet myself, and I could really use one."

"Understandable. You were probably up half the night." His smile was sudden. "You know, your face says everything. That beautiful arched brow just asked how I'd know that." He turned and closed the front door. "That's why I've come."

He walked past her toward the kitchen. Fiona stood in stunned silence. *How in the bloody hell could he know that?* "Alec—how—you weren't. I mean, of course you weren't, but how?"

He smiled apologetically. "No, I wasn't trying to break into your house."

"Well, of course you weren't, but how do you know about my night?"

"Tea, please, and I'll tell you everything." He turned to walk in the kitchen's direction, and Tam followed. She could feel her inner kettle on the boil with frustration. Instead, she blew out her building steam and thought, *Fine then. Tea first but I'll not wait long.*

Tam sat and watched with doggie ears pricked forward whenever Alec spoke.

Another five minutes and the tea was ready. Alec sat at the table across from her.

"Well, out with it. I've waited long enough. Tell me what's on yer mind."

"It's a—" Alec broke off mid-sentence, his attention focused on her hand. She watched his expression change, reminding her of a fox on the hunt.

"You found the war chest," he said, grabbing her hand to look closer at Laurie's ring. Just as quickly, Tam stood, body tense, emitting a low, rumbling growl. They both looked over at her wee protector. Alec released her hand.

"No, Alec, I haven't." Tam sat again, silent but still alert. "I'm not even looking for the war chest." She watched his reaction. Confusion and frustration passed over his features. Then she added, "I'm engaged to be married."

He scooted his chair back. His mouth opened but failed to produce a single word. She'd never seen this smooth, cultured man so surprised. He said with a substantial amount of incredulity, "To whom? You've only been here a few months."

"Laurie."

Alec composed his features. He sat staring at a point beyond her face.

"This was Laurie's grandmother's wedding ring." She twisted it on her finger as if touching the ring could draw Laurie nearer.

"Of course I'm happy for you." His mouth turned down, belying his words. "You know he doesn't deserve you."

She disagreed. "Alec, I know what—"

He put a hand up to stop her. "No, Fiona. I'm happy for you." His tone was sincere. "Still—" he brushed at a bit of Tam's fur clinging to his trousers—"I thought he was engaged to a foreign girl." Alec leaned back in his chair and looked up, considering something. "What was her name? Marguerite? That's it. Didn't Laurie go off to Germany with her? Something about the chance of a lifetime," he added with a chuckle. "Sure he doesn't have a girl in every port?"

He sat up, changing the subject, not giving her time to respond to his last stinging comment. "Fiona, may I use your water closet for a moment?"

"Do you know where it is?"

He nodded and disappeared back down the hall.

While he was gone, she sipped at her tea. *What's wrong? He's acting so strange, out of sorts.*

When he returned, she said, "I know all about Marguerite." She thought to herself, *Don't say any more. I'm sure he doesn't mean anything.*

Warmth radiated from his face, so sincerely. "Seriously, Fiona. I am happy for you." He sat and stirred his tea, studying the swirling liquid. "I hope we can still be close friends?"

This man is so hard to read, but yes, I want to be his friend. "You were the first friendly person I met here in Edinburgh." She reached out and touched his arm. "Alec, can you tell me what's wrong?"

He took a deep breath and then launched into his explanation. "My father and I, we've never been close. It was different when Mother was alive."

Fiona realized she'd never thought about the absence of a woman in their home. "I'm sorry. I know what it's like to lose a parent. Has she been gone long?"

He said flatly, "She died in the same influenza epidemic that took Laurie's father."

She shook her head, dismayed.

"Let me guess. Laurie didn't mention that, did he?" It was more of a statement than a question. "Laurie and I have never been friends." Alec shrugged, crossing his arms and looking down his nose. "We don't move in the same circles, didn't go to the same schools, but even if we had, I'm a few years older. Oh, I don't know why. Maybe it's our social standing, or even maybe it's my money. He just never liked me much. Can't say that's all his fault."

Alec focused on her little guard dog, still on duty, watching Alec for any signs of trouble. When he glanced back at Fiona, she saw such hurt on his face she felt sorry for him.

"But then, I don't think I have any real friends." He gestured toward Tam. "Even your dog doesn't like me."

"Oh, he'll be all right once he gets to know you."

"I hope so, but I'm glad you have him. It's not him liking me I'm worried about." Alec sucked in a breath and then pushed on. "I think, no, I'm sure my father's having you watched."

Fiona put a hand to her open mouth. "Alec, why would he do that? I have nothing but this big old house."

"Last night I came downstairs to say goodnight and interrupted a meeting my father was having with someone I couldn't quite place. It bothered me. Later, I was at the front of the house drinking a glass of—" he paused—"warm milk, just looking out at the square trying to place where I'd seen that chap." He sat forward. "Then I saw what looked like the same man sneaking around the corner of your house." He took her hand again. "Fiona, he was trying to get into your house."

She shook her head in disbelief. "But why? What could I possibly have that your father would want?"

"It's the pursuit of more. My father"—he stressed the word with a sardonic smile—"will never have enough. Nothing is good enough. Lord knows I've never been good enough. I wondered what he wanted when he tried to talk you out of keeping this house." Alec slapped his leg. "I know where I've seen your prowler. He was in my father's office the day you arrived. I remember because he's not the sort of client my father serves."

Tam stood and started barking.

"No, Tam, quiet." The dog sat with a humph.

"When I saw him sneaking around the corner of your house, I was worried about you," Alec continued, "so I cut through our back garden. He was already in your stable yard."

Fiona put a hand to her neck. *So it is true. Someone is trying to get into my house.* "But why?"

"I have my suspicions. It was your dog that scared the man away. My god he's loud for such a small dog. Quite comical. The man tried to go down your coal chute. But when your dog started barking, he climbed out and quickly disappeared."

Alec looked over at Tam. Once again, Tam started a low growl. Fiona moved to hush her dog, but Alec said, "Don't stop him. I think it's a good thing he doesn't like strangers. It just might save your life."

She stood. "You think your father would have me killed?"

"No, not intentionally, but the man he's hired looks rather unsavory."

She sat again.

"That day you were showing the antique dealer your things, I realized what he wanted. He believes the captain hid his war chest somewhere in this house."

Rab's words echoed in her head: "Yer uncle was obsessed with finding the treasure."

That's not something I want in my life. "I don't care about finding the chest."

Alec leaned in, gripping her arm. "Oh, but you must. Don't you see? You'll only be safe when it's found." His body tensed like a cat ready to spring.

"I can't say I don't believe there is a war chest, because the captain talks about it."

Tam was growling. Alec's grip on her arm tightened, and she pulled away.

All his attention focused on her face. "He does? What does he say?"

"So far, he talks about giving it to Bonnie Prince Charlie." She realized she spoke of the captain in the present tense.

"But he wrote about the chest?" Alec's eyes fixed on some inner picture. His voice sounded dreamlike. "It exists." Then he turned to her, his voice urgent. "You must find it. You'll never be safe from my father until you do."

"I wouldn't know where to start. Besides, it belongs to the captain. I don't want to get into some obsession with buried treasure. From what I hear about my uncle, it didn't do him any favors. He lived here all his life and didn't find the war chest because the captain didn't want him to have it."

Alec gave a short bark of a laugh. "You do realize how silly that sounds. The captain is dead these many long years. You talk about him as if he was living here with you."

She thought of the painting and the log. "I feel he does," she admitted.

"Think on it then? I'd be happy to help you look. I'd think this captain of yours would want you to be safe." He smiled. "I couldn't live with myself if anything happened to you."

He looked at her so tenderly, she thought, *How could I have misjudged this caring man?*

Alec cleared his throat and swallowed hard. "One thing. Please don't tell Rab about any of this. It's embarrassing that Father should stoop so low. They don't think much of us. I don't want to make things worse."

She hesitated, feeling something was off with his request. "I won't do anything to make matters worse." *Not quite a promise but the best I can do.*

Chapter Seventy-One

Rüdesheim am Rhein, Germany
June 1937

In the Light of Day

When Ana rose, it was already mid-morning. She was a little surprised no one woke her. *Of course, if everyone knows what happened last night, no wonder. They must be as frightened as I am.* In the light of day, it all seemed so unreal. *But it was real.*

The screams of those people trapped in the barn still echoed through her thoughts. A single tear slid down her cheek. She wiped it away with a shaky hand, amazed she had any tears left to cry.

As she brushed her hair, she stared at the reflection in the mirror. Blank, red-rimmed eyes stared back at her. Her curly black hair was now just below her earlobes. *I look so much older than twenty-two.* Sun glinted off her brush handle, and it sparked her memory.

All those points of light. What did He say to me? Yes. I just have to be one point of light in the dark sky of Germany. Funny how it still steadied her to think of God's simple direction. The girl in the mirror smiled a little. Ana took a deep breath and went searching for her children.

Gretchen and Deter were playing with the other children in the servants hall. It was another rousing game of tag. Gretchen ran right into Ana as she rounded a corner.

"What's this?" Ana hugged her little angel.

Gretchen giggled. "We thought you would sleep forever."

Brushing a curl out of Gretchen's eyes, she answered, "And I can see you are being so quiet, letting me sleep so long."

Serious Deter came up behind his sister. "Did we wake you, Ana?"

She mussed his dyed-blond locks. "Not at all. I'd have to have ears like God to hear you all the way from my room." She added, "You should play. Go on, it's all right." The two were back in the game before she could turn away.

Katrine was helping in the kitchen, talking with her new friends. *Katrine has an ear for languages. Her French is getting better all the time. You wouldn't know she's only been here a month; she fits in so well.* Ana passed by the kitchen door, lingering long enough to hear their topic of conversation. *I guess it doesn't matter if you're French or Chinese when you're a teenage girl talking about young men.*

She jumped at the tap on her shoulder. "La comtesse asks if you could join her in her sunroom for coffee?" Marie was a personal maid to Isabelle, and Etienne's beautiful wife. She put a hand on Ana's arm and added, "Are you all right?"

"Thank you, yes. A bit shaken but I'll get over it. How is Etienne?"

Marie smiled sadly. "He won't say much, but I'm afraid he's very upset. He worries something he did might have caused that terrible visit to his friend." She shook her dark curls. "Mon Dieu, I still cannot believe. But I'm keeping you. Etienne and la comtesse are waiting for you." She moved into the kitchen, calling for a tray for la comtesse.

By now, Ana knew her way around the estate, but the closer she came to the solarium, the more anxious she became. She felt for her rosary, her fingers worrying the beads. She thought of the burning barn and shuddered.

There's an actual chance we could bring down the same terrible fate on all these people. Will they turn us away? Where will we go next, Lord? How will I keep my children safe? She paused with her hand on the door. Closing her eyes, she leaned her forehead on the polished wood. *I will trust you. I will. No matter what's next. Just keep these people safe, please.*

Ana knocked once. Isabelle's voice sounded strained as she called out, "Entrez!"

In contrast to her thoughts, the room was awash in beautiful sunlight. La comtesse sat at a table with baby Tony on her lap. Etienne was making him giggle with delight as the big man popped his head back behind a napkin. They both looked up and smiled. Ana's legs felt wobbly, and she let out a tremendous sigh. A tear slid down her face, and she returned their smiles as relief flooded her.

She stammered, "Sorry, it's just that I don't know what I expected. Last night was so terrible, and I'm—I mean—I thought you might blame me for putting you in danger after all you've done for us."

Isabelle got up and came straight to her with baby Tony still on her hip. She engulfed Ana in a three-way hug. Ana let out another shuddering breath and began to cry as if she hadn't cried all the tears in the world last night. La comtesse held her tight. Even baby Tony patted her. Baby drool hit her arm as he leaned in to plant a sloppy kiss on her cheek. Then he leaned into Isabelle, and she got a sloppy kiss right on the mouth.

Ana brushed away her tears and smiled despite herself. "My goodness, he is teething, isn't he?" Etienne rose from his seat and handed her a napkin.

La comtesse said, "Another tooth broke through last night. Come, my dear, have a seat. We have some talking to do."

Another wave of panic hit Ana, and she wrung her hands. Her eyes darted between Etienne and Isabelle. *Oh Lord, for a minute I thought they would keep us. Where will we go?* "I know. We need to leave, and I don't blame you." Ana wiped her tears. "I couldn't bear it if anything happened to any of you."

La comtesse drew back in shock. "Mais non. Nothing of the sort. We need to be very careful. It might mean you need to stay longer. Just until we have another connection to get you all out of Germany."

Marie entered, carrying a tray of strong coffee and sweet rolls.

"Je vous remercie. Thank you, Marie. Let's all sit down and talk this out."

Chapter Seventy-Two

Hamburg, Germany
June 1937

The Hunting Weekend

Laurie squinted into the setting sun. *This country is beautiful.* He walked up the drive to the Voss estate. He'd begun using the excuse of wanting to stay at work longer so he could take the bus home instead of riding with Herr Voss. It gave him some measure of freedom. Time to think, too. On his ride home he'd watch the ordinary people—children playing, neighbors stopping to chat. Then there was the other side. Large estates, lavish decor and all the opulence he'd once dreamed of.

He found his co-workers were regular guys. They were worried about making the rent or proposing to their sweethearts. Then there were the German people who considered themselves above all that. The Nazis. They weren't ordinary at all. And what passed for polite dinner conversation sent shivers up his spine.

It's like a children's story my mother read to me. I've gone down the rabbit hole and come out in a land that isn't at all what it seems. It's dangerous, even toxic.

Edinburgh is just as beautiful this time of year. No hidden plans to do away with Jewish businesses. Simple—everyone just trying to make a living. No hidden agendas. Like Fiona. He groaned, feeling homesick.

If I were with you, Fiona, we'd already be married. Her face floated in his imagination. *She's come through such loss, but there's no hatred, no selfish desire in her. Fiona's strong, beautiful, and unshaken in her faith. I'm coming to believe those are all rare gifts. Not much of it to be found here.* Laurie sighed, letting go of the images filling his mind.

Anger burst through him. "What the hell am I doing here? It's been more than a month, and I still have no idea how to find those children." *How long does Bernie expect me to try, and how long can I keep Marguerite thinking I still care for her?* He was feeling the distance between them. Laurie knew at this rate it would only be a matter of time before she became fed up with his long hours at work.

He heard Rab's voice again. "God will help ye." Laurie shook his head in disbelief. "Why would God help me? Did He hear me when my father died? Did He have to take my mother too?" For just a moment he was a fourteen-year-old boy again lost in grief when his mother died. He could feel his chest tighten with emotion. "Everyone said it was God's will when my mum died. No, God's never shown much interest in me. Why would he help me now?"

He rounded the last turn, and the big house came into view. *There she is. Beautiful Marguerite. Waiting for me.* He lifted his hand to wave. *The worst of it is, I think she cares for me.* In a flash of memory, he pictured Marguerite at the last dinner party laughing at a story of a young Jewish woman who tried to hide her jewelry in her bra. Later, when they were alone, he asked, "Why were they searching her? Did she steal the jewelry?"

Laurie remembered her exasperation at his question. She

snapped, "Yes, she was stealing from the Reich. Everyone knows the Jews grow rich on the backs of the German people." There it was, the same phrases used by the Nazi party. Could this cultured, beautiful woman be so gullible as to accept all this without question? *There has to be a real person under all her charm, someone who cares for others.*

Marguerite's smile broadened as she came to him. "I have wonderful news. We're invited for a weekend in the country."

Laurie's throat tightened again. *The last thing I need is another weekend with Nazi society.* "Sorry, baby, I don't think I can make it. Your papa has me working on a special project."

"Oh no you don't. My papa has already said we can all go." Again, her lower lip pouted, begging to be kissed. He tried not to notice and gave her a kiss on her cheek instead. She was saying, "He's taking too much of your time." She linked her arm in his as they walked back to her front door. "I'm going to have a talk with him."

"Marguerite, no, you can't." He let frustration creep into his voice. "He's my employer. Don't you see? I've got to show him what I can do." *Could she sense his panic?*

Her face grew serious. "Darling, you shouldn't try so hard. I'm sure Father's pleased with you. It's a big change, but you are doing well. I just need to see more of you." She smiled so warmly.

It's hopeless. His heart hurt at what he was doing to Marguerite.

"Well, at least it's settled. You're all mine for the weekend." She appeared pleased at her victory.

On the way down, Herr Voss explained, "The first day there will be hunting."

Laurie raised an eyebrow as he turned to Marguerite.

"Not the ladies. Just the men. You do hunt?" she asked.

"It's an odd time of year for that, isn't it? This is fishing season." Laurie waited for further explanation. When it didn't come, he said, "Well, I haven't hunted since I was a boy, but not to worry, I can handle myself."

Herr Voss said, "I hope so. It's important for you to fit in. Make conversation when you can—most of them speak English. These are business connections, so it's more than just a weekend away." He beamed with pride. "You'll do fine, my lad."

It was a long drive. Marguerite entertained him with facts about the castle. He was listening half-heartedly when she said, "It's been in the same family for eight hundred years. You'll meet the count and countess. They're quite nice. We've attended this weekend several years in a row."

They drove through wooded foothills. He tried to be aware of his surroundings, but all he could see was forestland. Even after they turned off the main road, trees seem to form a wall on either side of the drive. There in front of him, a castle stood on a small rise.

The car drove over an ancient-looking drawbridge into a court-yard. Stone towers with pointed tiled roofs reached for the last of the day's light. White-washed stone and red-timbered beams gave the house a medieval look. The woodlands that rose behind the castle looked as ancient as the stones of the old building. It was something out of a storybook.

Herr Voss was saying, "The family uses this as a hunting lodge or summer home. Beautiful, ja?"

The weekend party was quite the social event. The host and hostess were very pleasant Germans, proud of their heritage. They clearly enjoyed showing off their home. Although there were the ever-present serious military types, Laurie felt a note of excitement in the air.

It wasn't until dinner that things seemed to settle. Dinner was formal in a large room lined with windows overlooking beautiful gardens. Chandeliers and cut glass reflected the lights of what must have been hundreds of candles. Even the china glowed with its golden rims.

The conversation was lively. Laurie felt someone staring at him. He scanned the guests around the table. A sweet grandmother sat on his right with Marguerite on his other side. Herr Voss and another gentleman sat across the table. Past a woman with far too much makeup sat Marguerite's friend Hildie. She smiled when his eyes met hers and said something to the man next to her.

Oh, it's her friend from the parties. The young captain's light blue eyes were looking back at Laurie. *Eric Braun—he's always wearing a smug, superior expression when he looks at me. I don't like him much, but I don't think he likes me either.* The man made a small salute and chuckled at some private joke. Laurie nodded slightly in reply.

The older woman sitting next to Laurie said something so quietly he wasn't sure if she was talking to him.

"I beg your pardon, did you say something to me, madam?"

She spoke just loud enough for Laurie to hear. "You should be careful of that one."

He turned to see a petite-framed, white-haired woman. For all her size and advanced years, she looked quite regal. He imagined she would be at home in a throne room.

"Sorry, Herr MacKenzie," she continued. "I've been watching you all evening. You must learn to perfect your poker face. You don't like him much, do you?" She smiled sadly. "And you're askance at this lot, aren't you?"

Laurie looked around, surprised at her directness, but she continued, "No one pays much attention to you when you pass sixty. I doubt they'd listen if I shouted at you." She chuckled and took a sip of her wine.

Laurie couldn't help smiling back. "That could have its advantages. You seem to know me. Excuse me, have we been introduced?"

She looked up into his eyes with a direct gaze. "I'm the

Countess Dorothea Grafin Lehndorff." She mimicked the Nazi air of superiority, chuckling a little before adding, "but my friends call me Dolly."

"I'm most pleased to meet you, Countess."

"No, you may call me Dolly." Her eyes twinkled with mischief. "That unpleasant young man staring at you is Eric Braun."

"I know. He seems to be at every dinner party we go to."

"Well, yes, he would be. Likes to be with men of power." She turned in her seat to face Laurie. "You are quite the topic of gossip. Handsome young Scot. You're the fiancé of Marguerite Voss. Her mother was a Scot, you know." Dolly frowned. "She died quite young. A shame, really, a fine woman. Not like her daughter. Marguerite looks like her mother, but her father brought her up." Dolly turned back to her meal.

Laurie couldn't think what to say to Dolly's frankness. He took another sip of soup.

"Your eyes tell all."

Is she speaking to me or herself? She seemed intent on her soup.

Slightly affronted, he said under his breath, "I thought I was getting good at my poker face."

"Not hardly." She was taking bits of bread and breaking them into the soup. Not what he thought a countess might do. After a minute, she said, "I see honesty in your eyes. I like that, but it can get you killed in this group."

"Please call me Laurie. And thank you. I will work on my poker face."

"A bit of advice, Laurie. I see you studying the other guests, but if you want to know something, watch the older servants."

He hoped for more conversation with Dolly, but she turned to the guest on her other side.

Sitting to his left, Marguerite tapped his arm and leaned closer, speaking next to his ear. "What did the countess say?"

"Not much. She said you look like your mother."

Marguerite put her hand over her mouth and whispered, "She must be eighty if she's a day. Dreadful old woman. Her family is extremely wealthy and well-placed. But she's too outspoken." She looked directly into Laurie's eyes, warning him. "Not someone we want to be around."

Laurie's frown deepened at Marguerite's comment. *I like the countess.*

After dinner, the men excused themselves for brandy and cigars in the library. As they were leaving, Laurie cast an eye to Marguerite. The last thing he wanted was to sit in on another conversation about the superiority of the Germans. He'd rather join the ladies for a chat and gave her a pleading look, but she pushed him toward the door. He shuffled along with the other men.

Then, to his surprise, a small hand reached for his arm. "Oh, Herr MacKenzie, would you be so kind as to help me up the stairs?" Dolly's voice was loud enough for the other guests to hear. In a softer voice, she said, "I had to take pity on someone so desperate." She smiled up at him.

"Thank you." Following her lead, he said loudly, "I'd be happy to help you, Madam Countess." When he looked over his shoulder, Marguerite shot him a disapproving glare.

"You know, I think you and I have common ground for a friendship."

"I'd like that, Dolly. I'd like that very much."

At the top of the stairs, Dolly stopped to catch her breath.

From below, a deep voice called up to him.

"Herr MacKenzie?"

Laurie looked over the banister to see Eric hailing him from the lower hall. "We leave at first light. I'll be looking for you in the courtyard." The German smiled a smile that wasn't a smile, clicked his heels and did the "Heil Hitler" salute.

"I'll be there." Laurie continued to himself, *you self-righteous, smug, son-of-a-bitch.* To Dolly he said, "I don't even know why he doesn't like me."

"I'm afraid Eric Braun could be a dangerous enemy." She looked up at him. "Those SS types don't like foreigners much, especially ones they can't cow. Watch yourself. If I remember right, my room is down the hall." She patted Laurie's arm. "You be careful tomorrow."

Chapter Seventy-Three

Germany
June 1937

An Accidental Shooting

L aurie jogged down the main staircase and out the front door, stopping outside. Even with the early morning light, thick fog hid the drive. Grey, disembodied shadows of men appeared then disappeared again as tendrils of fog swirled around them. *So, they've already gathered?* He recognized a few of the men and called, "Morning."

Barely able to see his own feet in the morning mist, he walked down the front steps and onto the crushed rock. *They'll cancel the hunt. We can hardly see each other.* As if in answer to his thoughts, his host, Count Something-or-other, came around the side of the house with six hounds, beautiful dogs.

Herr Voss walked up behind Laurie carrying two rifles and handed him a gun and a handful of cartridges. "I'm counting on you. Don't have to remind you, do I? You know what side your bread is buttered on." Voss gave Laurie a good-natured elbow in the ribs. "These people control government spending. More money, more ships. Simple as that."

Laurie tried not to bristle at the old man's instructions. "Thank you, sir, but how will we hunt with the fog so thick?"

He looked around at the muted outline of trees beyond the courtyard. He estimated twenty feet of visibility.

"Come, come, my boy. You're no stranger to fog. What do you Brits call this? A pea souper?"

Obviously, the rest of the party saw no reason to cancel. Men gathered in twos and threes until all were present. The hunting party walked down the drive about a quarter of a mile. The castle was well out of view, shrouded by the dense fog.

Laurie heard the rumble of a motor approaching. Within minutes, a box truck pulled up. Everyone else seemed to expect the arrival. Grim faces watched as one of the group flipped open the back canvas covering. Two armed guards sat inside. Between them slumped a hooded figure.

Eric stepped forward. "Get out," he commanded. The men roughly dragged the figure to his feet and pulled him to the tail-gate. Instead of helping the person down, they pushed him off the back. He fell with a crack that sounded for all the world like a bone snapping. Even with the hood, the cry of anguish was unmistakable.

Laurie looked at the other men in bewilderment. Pleasant and amiable dinner guests now wore hard, unyielding expressions. In the grey light, their faces reminded him of stone. They didn't look at each other but focused solely on the hooded figure now kneeling in the gravel.

Eric pulled off the hood to reveal a lad of around seventeen. "I've arranged some sport to make our morning more chal-lenging."

He undid the bindings on the prisoner's hands. One arm hung useless at an odd angle, revealing the location of the broken bone. Laurie stiffened with outrage at the condition of the lad. It was hard to see the human behind the swelling and bruises covering the boy's face. Curly red hair hung over downcast eyes.

Laurie looked around the group again. "What did this boy do to be beaten so badly?" he asked Herr Voss. It was Eric who gave him an answer.

"This Jude was trying to run away with his Aryan sweetheart." Eric's lips curled in disgust. "The girl is being re-educated." There were chuckles from some of the men.

"This is absurd. He looks as Aryan as any of you." Laurie's pulse was racing. He pushed damp locks from his face. One of the dog handlers, an older man, caught his eye with a direct gaze. The man moved his head slightly. No.

Is it a warning or my imagination? Whatever was meant, it gave Laurie cause to think. *If I say more, it might only make matters worse for the lad.* He took a deep breath and exhaled slowly.

"His grandfather was a Jew." Eric's pronouncement was more than a statement of fact. It sounded like a death sentence.

Once again, panic rose in Laurie's chest. *It's a bluff, right?* "So, what does that mean? You can't be serious?" He looked from man to man until Eric came to stand in front of him, his face mere inches from Laurie's.

"What? Do Scots have such weak stomachs?" he asked in English. Looking over his shoulder, he added for the others in German. "Well, Scottish men wear skirts, after all."

Laurie was pretty sure he'd translated that word for word. His temper flared, but he said nothing. Once again, the smug SS officer's face was inches from him.

With a short laugh, Eric said, "Didn't those tea-drinking English conquer you Scots?"

To hell with it, this guy is done baiting me. Laurie smiled as he answered back. "And haven't the same lot beaten the Germans and the French in more recent history?" He followed good advice from a new friend. He narrowed his eyes and gave Eric his best poker face. "At least our defeat was a matter of money and leadership. There is no fiercer fighter than a Highlander."

Eric answered back loud enough for only Laurie to hear. "We Germans are unequaled in battle."

The glint in Eric's eye told Laurie he'd touched the man's sense of pride. Eric turned to the boy, and Laurie mentally translated his German. "It seems our British friend doesn't understand German honor will not tolerate Jews who corrupt the master race. Have you learned your lesson, young man?"

With what appeared to be utter relief, the boy nodded vehemently. "Ja, mein Herr. Danke, danke."

Laurie looked toward the castle, wishing he could walk away. When he turned back to Eric, he saw a challenge. He was sure Eric wasn't a safe person to turn his back on, so he fought to stay rooted in one spot. He could see the urge to run in the lad's eyes.

Eric said in a flippant tone, "You are free to go, Jew." The boy looked from face to face. "Get up, Jew, go." The young man stood, but he, too, seemed hesitant to turn his back on the group. Slowly, he backed away, looking everywhere at once.

A loud shot cracked the silence. Laurie jumped as Eric fired his pistol into the air. The boy took off at a dead run through the brush. Laurie watched as the servants stopped the dogs from giving chase. A nervous titter rippled through the surrounding men. From what conversation he could catch, Laurie thought they must be waiting for the fog to clear a bit before continuing their morning hunt. *But what are we hunting for?*

Herr Voss leaned close to Laurie. "See, my lad, we Germans are not so hard-hearted as you might think." Laurie looked at his boss with a half-smile. *I wonder if he knows how relieved I am.* "Right you are, sir. Well, while we're waiting, I was wondering if we might talk a bit about the new project?"

Another shot rang out. Eric stood apart from the group, his pistol still held skyward. He announced, "The hunt is on."

The dogs became restless, pulling at their restraints. A servant picked up the discarded hood and gave each hound a moment to catch the scent.

Eric said, "It's the smell of fear, Herr MacKenzie. Every Jew reeks of it."

Laurie looked into Eric's eyes. They were calm, as if he'd commented on the smell of fresh baked bread.

"You really intend to hunt that boy?" He couldn't help sounding incredulous.

Eric smiled his answer, turning to follow the others. Herr Voss pushed past Laurie to join the pursuit, calling over his shoulder, "We gave the Jew a head start. What more could he expect?"

Laurie froze. *God, what the hell do I do now?*

"You could go back to the house." An older servant stood directly before him. "Of course, you would embarrass your employer and come under SS scrutiny."

"I'm sorry. Who are you?" He didn't add, "And why should I listen to you?"

The little man's wizened face smiled sadly.

This, then, is the world I'm saving those children from. Bernie, I'm so sorry.

The servant continued, "Or you could join the others and appear to be one of the group. It's a big decision. The question is, what's at stake?" Laurie looked into the man's eyes. They seemed to reflect all the horror he was feeling. "If you follow them, you might help the boy."

Laurie was astonished at the man's suggestion. "Do I show everything I'm thinking?"

The servant was compassionate and understanding as he nodded. "My mistress, Countess Lehndorff, said to watch over you."

"You've taken such a risk talking to me like this but thank you. It's what I needed."

The smile widened, spreading over the wrinkled old face. "We

Germans are not all like these men. I remember a time when honor meant protecting the helpless."

Laurie nodded as the man's words sunk in. He thought of those two children facing all this alone. Before he left, Bernie had given him a small photograph of the bairns. Their faces were burned into his heart.

"Thank you." He loaded his gun. When he looked up again, he saw the servant motion for him to follow as he disappeared into the trees.

Laurie's legs felt rubbery as he took his first step. He'd seen the faces of evil and knew he couldn't turn his back and remain the same man. *I have to admit that servant was God sent.* He allowed himself a momentary rueful smile at the irony of his last thought. *Maybe He can help me find a way to save the lad.*

The group had a good start on him, but with every step, an inexplicable conviction grew stronger that God could help him save Deter, Gretchen, and maybe this boy, too. Again, the old servant appeared to wait for him ahead in the trees.

For an old man, he sets a brisk pace. Laurie was determined to keep up. In the fog, branches suddenly materialized, hitting his face. His heartbeat increased when he realized the old servant was nowhere in sight.

He kept trudging on, trying to keep the same course. He remembered the castle sat in a large forest. *It's possible I could get lost out here for a long while.* His throat tightened at the prospect. He began to hear men's voices. They were well ahead of him, still hidden in the mist and thick brush.

Movement behind him made his nerves jump. A hound appeared out of the fog. Mist closed behind her. She came alongside, matching his stride for a minute, and then she moved a little faster. *If I can't see the servant, at least this dog will bring me to the others.* He stepped up his pace to keep up with her.

Fog swirled around his feet, and he stumbled over a stump in the path, nearly dropping his gun. The hound stopped, waiting for him. She ran ahead, then back-tracked, eager for him to catch up.

"All right, girl. You lead, and I'll try to keep up. I wish you could tell me what to do when we find them." He shook his head at the absurdity of allowing this animal to guide him. But when she left the path, Laurie followed.

For a while, it was him and his four-legged companion. She made no noise at all, but he crunched branches with every step.

Someone called out, "Over here." It sounded a great way off to his left. He held his rifle at the ready and waited. Then a hound bayed.

Laurie moved in the direction of the noise, but the dog blocked his path. Intelligent chocolate eyes stared up at him. She made a low woof and moved off to his right. He was sure he'd been told to follow her lead.

He whispered, "All right, girl. I'm following you. Hope you know where we're going."

Visibility was getting worse, but the dog moved with urgency. He almost tripped over her as she stopped again to sniff the air and listen. She crouched, placing her feet carefully. He tried to copy the care she took with every step.

In a dozen steps, she froze in place, her nose pointing just ahead. Through the trees, the mist melted enough so Laurie recognized Eric standing in a small clearing. Beyond him, another shape crouched in the bushes.

Eric hadn't spotted the lad. It was as if Laurie's whole world balanced on this one moment. He whispered a quick prayer. *If you're listening, help me save this boy.* Laurie's gaze flicked back to the boy and collided with an instant recognition. The lad jumped up to run. Laurie brought his gun up and pulled the trigger.

A solitary cry of pain told Laurie he'd hit his mark. All at once, the party of hunters seemed to converge. Eric was lying on the damp leaf-covered forest floor holding his arm, the blood already soaking his jacket sleeve.

"Oh Lord, I'm so sorry. I didn't mean to shoot you. I was aiming at the boy, and you just got in front of me." The bullet had only grazed Eric's right arm. "Och, and it's your shooting arm. I'm sorry. I guess I'd best leave off hunting when I can't see what's ahead of me clearly."

"You shot me." The German sounded incredulous. "Are you crazy?" He spit out his words. "Do I look like a Jew?"

"Well, you'll have to admit that laddie looked no more Jewish than you. Can I help you up?"

Eric batted Laurie's hand away. "I can get up on my own." He stood. His right arm was covered in blood. A servant took a quick look at the wound, then pulled out a handkerchief. "Never mind that. Get after the boy." Eric's face was red with anger.

"Better get back to the house, MacKenzie." Herr Voss looked embarrassed but said, "It was just an accident. Too much fog."

Eric began a steady stream of German. The words came too fast for Laurie to translate.

If I didn't know better, I'd think he's disparaging my manhood and intelligence. Of course, I can't say I blame him.

Herr Voss patted Laurie's shoulder. His boss looked disgusted with Eric. "You'd think you did it on purpose, the way he's carrying on."

"About the boy?" Laurie queried.

"I expect he's long gone."

Laurie tried to appear disappointed.

"Not to worry. For a Jew in Germany, there's nowhere to hide. They'll pick him up later." Herr Voss slapped him on the back. "That was a good try. I'm proud of you." He winked. "They know you haven't hunted since you were a boy. It was hard to see out there. But you tried to kill the Jew." He shook his head. "Now you're one of us."

Laurie focused on the castle coming into view through the mist. He was stunned into silence by Herr Voss's words.

"I don't mind telling you now how much they disapproved of

my bringing you here." A proud grin spread across Herr Papa's face. "You showed them all. They'll trust you now." He slapped Laurie on the back. "You're a gifted engineer. You'll make a fine son-in-law and a good Nazi."

Laurie felt the sting of his last words. *Not a Nazi, never that.* His stomach roiled with disgust.

Herr Voss called to a servant to take their rifles. If Herr Papa thought it odd that Laurie was mute, he didn't show it. Instead, he was already walking off to rejoin a group of his friends.

Laurie's hands were shaking so badly he had to stuff them in his pockets. He jumped when a voice close behind him said, "You weren't aiming at the boy, were you, sir?" The older servant moved up to walk next to him.

Laurie glanced sideways. "I have excellent aim." They shared a secret smile. "What will happen to the boy? Did I merely postpone his death?"

"Perhaps. But there are still men of conscience in Germany. I think you are one of those."

"Thanks for sending me the dog. She helped me find him."

"What dog? All the hounds were with the handlers." The servant took out a handkerchief and rubbed the back of his neck. "I can't think how they missed the trail."

"No, there was a dog. She's the russet-colored hound."

"If you say so."

Everyone entered the castle at once. Eric held the makeshift bandage over the wound on his right arm. "Get the hell away from me." He spit out the words as another servant rushed in to help.

Their host stepped forward. "For God's sake, Braun, you're dripping blood all over my floor. Go with my man. He'll get you cleaned up."

Laurie moved behind the group and slipped into a room off the main hall. He shut the door, savoring the quiet. Two large chairs faced an inviting fire. The sound of the wood crackled and popped in the small sitting room. A decanter filled with an amber liquid beckoned him from the sideboard. It took him two strides to reach his goal. His hands wouldn't stop shaking as he poured himself a drink. Behind him, the door opened and closed. Laurie froze.

"Laurie?" The heavily accented voice belonged to his new friend Dolly. "I just spoke with Rutgar." Laurie turned to see concern written on the tiny woman's face. "Come by the fire. You must be so cold."

Yes, he was cold, but it was the kind of cold you get from shock. He moved to sit in one of the wingback chairs. Dolly went to the sideboard and poured herself a drink. With the decanter in one hand and the drink in the other, she joined him in front of the fireplace.

"He told me everything. Horrible. Horrible. What's becoming of us as a people?"

They sat in silence for a long time, Laurie staring into his drink. His hands were calmer now, but his eyes blurred with unshed tears. He tried to gain control before he spoke. Dolly reminded him of his own grandmother. He wished he was a boy again and could curl up in those safe arms.

She was saying, "It is dangerous to trust just anyone. I understand this. I live with it daily." She smiled sadly. "I will do what I can for the boy."

He looked up at her. He had to be sure of her. So much depended on the right decisions. "My grandfather is a believer."

"And you?" Her question hung in the air.

"I've been frustrated with Grandda for all his comments about God. After my mother died, the last thing I wanted was to be like my grandfather."

He closed his eyes. The entire scene flashed through his thoughts. *Those regular-looking men, their faces hardened into masks of hatred. Hatred for that poor boy.* "He was only a boy, you know. Only a scared lad."

"From what my man said, you had help there."

"I wanted to run, but he—you said his name is Rutgar? He said something that made me think I might help. It was so hard to see anything through the fog." He regarded her, judging how she might take what he was going to say next. "Then the dog came along. She guided me right to the place. The boy was there and Eric, too. It all happened so quickly."

"How good a shot are you, Laurie?"

"Excellent. We didn't hunt much, but my grandfather took me shooting—target practice." He smiled. "After my parents died, it was one of the few times I enjoyed being with him."

"You hit your mark?"

"Thank God."

"That is my point, young friend. Do you think you can trust God and me to help you with whatever it is you're doing in Germany?"

Laurie looked at Dolly. Weighing her reaction, he said, "I'm looking for two children. Jewish."

She smiled. "I knew it. I knew you couldn't be interested in that dreadful girl and her father. My friend would roll over in her grave to see what her beautiful child has turned into."

Laurie sat up straight. "Of all the lads at school, she chose me. And with her came this wonderful opportunity. You know. Not just the beautiful rich girl but also the advance in my career."

He was ashamed to meet her eyes, waiting for her to be appalled. When she didn't speak, he looked back to understanding eyes.

"I met another girl. She was good. Real. Kind. And everything got so complicated." He sighed. "I was going to break it off with Marguerite. My friend came to me thinking that I was coming here and asked me to look for his cousins. Only by then I didn't want to come."

"But you did."

His voice was flat. "I felt I had to."

"And this girl? What's her name?"

"Fiona." Saying her name out loud warmed him.

"What did Fiona think?"

"She said she knew I would find them. God would help me."

Dolly's expression was gentle. "Like He helped you today?"

Encouraged, he said, "I feel like we've been friends for a long time, Dolly."

She reached over and patted his hand. "I know people. Let me help you find those children and get home to the right girl."

There it was, reaching out to him. Hope. "I'd like that more than you'd ever imagine."

Dolly poured them both another drink. "Now, my young friend, tell me everything you know about these children, and let's hope the Nazi beast has not swallowed them up."

"The letter said that Herr Faber, his wife and two children were living in Bamberg. The boy is only six. His name is Deter, and the girl is four. Her name is Gretchen. The couple hired a nanny, a young girl from a farming family in Bavaria. Neighbors wrote to my friend's family just after the Nazis came to the Faber home and arrested the couple. The family lived in that home for years. They were well-liked. Neighbors were all shocked but too afraid to say anything. Within days, a new family moved into the home." He shook his head. "I still can't get over that part. A family just moved in and took everything—furniture, family heirlooms, everything."

"And the children?" Dolly asked.

"That's the thing. Everyone in the neighborhood thought the children had been taken, too. But then Nazi officials went around to all the neighbors, asking for information about Deter and Gretchen. The family who wrote the letter said they were roughed up a bit but told the police nothing."

"Did they have any idea where the children were?"

"They think their Bavarian nanny must have taken them on an outing."

"They didn't return?"

"No. I'm not sure how, but she must have been warned about the Nazi raid because she and the children didn't come back home."

"So, how do you know they're still free?"

"I don't, but officials are still asking everyone in the neighborhood if they know anything about the children."

"Bavarian you said?"

Laurie nodded.

"Do you have a picture?"

Laurie nodded again and slipped his wallet out of his pocket. He pulled out the worn photo Bernie had given him before he left.

Handing it to Dolly, he said, "That's all I have, and I do not know where to start."

Dolly smiled at the sweet children in her hand. "They must have had help. The boy has Jew written all over his face. The girl is better. Perhaps she could blend in. But not the boy. If they are still alive, someone is hiding them." She looked up at Laurie. "Not so hopeless as you might think."

She fell silent, staring into the fire. Her eyes closed. The silence stretched on. Laurie thought the old girl had fallen asleep. Then a beautiful smile spread across her face.

"Let me do some digging. I'll be in touch. You might need to take that beautiful Marguerite on some day outings."

Chapter Seventy-Four

Edinburgh
June 1937

Only a Dream

Fiona stood alone in her kitchen washing the dishes, hearing Alec's voice again in her thoughts.

"Don't you see? You must find the chest. You'll never be safe from my father until you do."

She mentally argued back. *The chest belongs to the captain.* She dried the last dish, putting it back on the shelf, and paused. *I don't believe that treasure will be found until the captain feels the time is right.*

She answered herself aloud. "That's a crazy thought." But she was sure it was true.

By late afternoon, Fiona was settled in her bedroom armchair. It was her favorite spot to read the ship's log. With a cup of tea on the tray next to her and her wee furry friend lying over her feet, she was ready to seek advice from Wee Geordie. She found her place and read:

"It is rumored Prince Charles is planning on staying in Edinburgh for at least a month. And since Mairi agreed to be my bride, I'm determined to make her mine before she regrets her decision. We've obtained a special license at no small expense in bribes, and this Saturday we will be wed at her home church in Arbroath. My servants are making the hoose ready for its new mistress. I canna believe my guid fortune to have such a bonnie wife for my own."

Fiona smiled up at the captain's portrait, happy for him. "I wish I had a picture of Mairi," she said. "Well, never mind. I see her through your eyes. Does Laurie love me like you loved Mairi? I hope so."

Her armchair felt so comfortable. She leaned her head back from the warmth of the fire and closed her eyes.

Mist swirled around her. She looked up through the trees, only seeing shadows of the foliage. She moved along quickly, feeling the wet ground under her feet. A dense hedge lay in her path, but she pushed through. Laurie stood there. She couldn't remember how to make words, but it was good just to walk together for a time. Then she smelled danger in the air.

She moved faster, willing him to keep up with her. He was making so much noise tramping through the undergrowth. When she heard him trip, she turned back to see him already getting up. *Wait for him. Wait. There it was again. Danger.*

We must hurry, Laurie. It's almost too late. She moved ahead, and he followed her. Men were yelling a great way off through the trees. A hound bayed. He had the scent. She knew he was smelling a fox.

Laurie stopped. For the first time, she noticed his gun. Somewhere in the back of her mind, she thought she must be dreaming about the captain fighting with the Bonnie Prince. But when Laurie turned in the direction of the voices, she blocked his path and looked up into his eyes, willing him to come with her. They were close.

After a moment he followed. She tried to tell him to be much quieter by placing every step with exaggerated care.

The acrid smell was overwhelming—evil, fear, and something else. Musky, fierce, feral. When she came to the clearing, she stopped. A man with an angelic face stood there, but she knew his intent was evil. A boy was hiding in the bushes. The scent of blood and fear was strong on him. He was hurt. She froze; her whole body quivered with tension. *Stop the man.*

Fiona jerked awake, the blast of the rifle ringing in her ears. Her heart pounded inside her chest. She grasped the arms of her chair and willed her breathing to slow. *It's nothing, just a dream. But Lord, if Laurie's in danger, protect him please.*

Chapter Seventy-Five

Edinburgh
June 1937

A Trip North

I t isn't a good idea to dwell on dreams, Fiona reminded herself for the fifth time. *They're random, probably influenced by something I saw or read. But I can't shake it off. Mum always cleaned when she worried —something about disengaging your mind but keeping your body busy. It always helped her.*

Fiona was up at first light cleaning her unused bedrooms. The idea was to turn out the rooms: wash curtains, dust, flip mattresses. Tam followed her from room to room, chasing the broom or mop and sliding across the wet floors as she gave them a thorough scrubbing.

She hadn't slept well last night though she had no more dreams about Laurie. *I can't remember having any dreams at all, but I can't shake the feeling he's in danger. Prayer helps, but even then I can't seem to say more than, "Please help him."*

Tam heard the knock before she did. She'd scrubbed herself

into a corner when he ran across the floor, his little legs making lots of motion but not much progress. By the time he reached the bedroom door, he was up to full speed and barking up a storm.

Fiona tiptoed over the wet surface. When she arrived at the front door, Tam's barking had settled. He sat with a wagging tail, waiting for her to let his friend in.

Rab's warm smile greeted her. When his open arms welcomed her into a bear hug, her tension eased. She'd never known either set of grandparents—they died long before she was born—but she loved this old man like he was her own grandfather. *Thank you, God, for putting him into my life.*

He patted her back. "Och, lassie. Whatever can be wrong? Yer hugging me like I've been gone ta war."

Her eyes felt moist as she drew away. "I'm glad to see you, that's all." *I won't worry you over my silly dream.* She patted his arm. "I feel like we're family already."

"If yon grandson gets half as warm a welcome, he'll ner leave ye."

Rab came in, and she closed the door.

"I've come with an offer to take ye and this wee lad on a small trip." Fiona and Tam both cocked their heads to the side. Rab chuckled. "I think yer spending too much time alone wi yer dog. But we'll take him with us all the same. I want to travel to Peterhead to make my arrangements about the boat."

Hope flooded her heart. "Has there been word from Laurie?" She held her breath, wishing for good news.

"Nay then, lassie, not since he called the other night. I want ta be ready to move with haste when he needs me is all."

"When do we leave?"

"And I thought I'd have ta talk ye into it. Well, we could leave as soon as you can be ready. Pack what ye need for a few days."

"I could be ready in less than a quarter hour."

Rab's smile was her answer. He turned to leave, calling over his shoulder, "It can be brisk up north. Bring some warm duds. Oh, and some dog fuid for the wee man."

Fiona threw some things in a small bag and sorted out which coat and gloves to take. She realized she needed to make the house as secure as possible. Moving from room to room, she checked windows and tried locks. Before she could finish, a strange sound drew her back to the front of the house.

Rab sat in a grey Bentley, looking pleased as he pushed on the OOHGAA horn. When she opened the front door, Tam barked back, doing his happy dance.

"Rab, I didn't know you owned a motor car. She's a beauty."

He stepped out, pride shining in his weathered face. "I don't have occasion to take her out much, but she's been a fine car for many years."

Chapter Seventy-Six

Edinburgh
June 1937

One Step Ahead of Father

OOHGAA. "Bloody hell." Alec's temper was raw. His frown deepened as he glanced toward the bedroom window. He was late. He looked back at his mirror long enough to straighten his tie. *Working until the wee hours of the morning and for what? A junior clerk could have done this brief. Damn the old man.* Mimicking his father's voice, Alec spoke to his reflection. "See that you're in court by half past ten." He couldn't shake the thought plaguing him since he rose. *Why does father give me all the menial work? Haven't I proven myself?*

OOHGAA. Alec stomped to his front window and squinted through the sheer drapes. The scene below halted his mental rant.

"Hello. What have we here?" He parted the sheers a bit, giving him a clear view of Fiona's front steps.

His lips quirked into a half smile. "My God, that auto is as ancient as Rab." Catching sight of Tam, he added, "Oh God, the dog." His frown returned as he watched the beast hop around with obvious excitement. But when Tam danced out of the way, Alec caught sight of an overnight bag.

"Well, it appears they're going somewhere overnight. All three of them." He smiled again and looked around the square.

No sign of the mysterious stranger. So Father has no idea Fiona's house will be vacant tonight. Ironic, isn't it? I'm usually at the office by now. This could be a game changer.

He glanced at the brief sitting on his desk. His grin widened. "Well, old boy, thought you'd put me in my place again, didn't you? Looks like this is my lucky break."

His mind flicked back to his last visit with Fiona, including the quick trip to the downstairs water closet and the window he'd left unlatched. *That war chest has got to be somewhere in her house. It has to be. And if she won't look, so much the better. This way, she won't even know when I find it.*

He looked at his wristwatch. "I'd better get going." He gathered his papers and put them in his leather case. Tossing his hat on, Alec whistled as he went down the back stairs toward his father's auto.

Chapter Seventy-Seven

Traveling North
Scotland
June 1937

Mairi's Diary

They traveled from Edinburgh to the newly opened Kincardine bridge. Rab said, "Did ye ken this be the longest bridge in Scotland?"

Fiona shook her head. "No."

"An engineering wonder." He winked. "Cut our travel time to the north. I used to drive sixteen miles further west to cross the river at Stirling."

"How long will it take us to get to Peterhead?"

"Oh, a fair bit." Rab seemed secretive.

Once over the new bridge, they turned inland, driving north to Perth.

Fiona had never been there, but she remembered reading in school that Perth was called the gateway to the Highlands. Blue mountains provided a breathtaking backdrop to the forested rolling hills. As they drove the city's cobblestone streets, she looked at the old buildings and thought about Prince Charlie's welcome there.

The captain said the people lined the streets, cheering. If she closed her eyes, she could see the scene as Geordie described it. Everyone thought there would be a great battle right there, but the English General Cope pushed his men to Inverness rather than meet Charlie's three thousand Highlanders. She was glad this beautiful town had been spared. It lay peaceful in the morning light, snuggled into the winding River Tay.

They drove east from Perth, and she began to see the water again on her right. Rab pointed to it, saying, "That be the Firth of Tay." But her mind was wandering back to Wee Geordie's log. She could see the land as it must have looked when Prince Charlie led his army across Scotland.

Rab broke into her daydreams, replacing Highland warriors with one impish boy as he continued his story about Laurie's antics as a lad. Soon she found herself laughing and wondering if they'd have a son. "Sounds like you spent a lot of time together."

His smile faded. "Oh, aye. Mind, he wasn't always at war with himself. While his parents were both alive, he was a happy lad. He's smart, quick to learn things. Sees how things fit together. That's what makes him such a guid engineer. After his da and mam both were gone, well, he lost his way." Rab's smile faded. A grimace spread across his weathered face.

"I tried." He shook his head, his eyes fixed on the highway, but she suspected he was seeing memories more than the road. "He was so angry."

Deep lines creased Rab's forehead. She realized with a start he must be in his late sixties. He always looked so vital. She never thought of his age.

She reached out to touch his arm. He put his hand over hers. "Then he met you." Rab smiled again, and the years seemed to fall from his face. "Answered prayer, lass. That's what ye are."

The road followed the Firth of the River Tay as they traveled east and north. Winding through the town of Dundee, the land rose up from the waters of the Tay. Stately homes sat on the hillside above the road. She was thinking about what a wonderful view they must have when Rab asked, "Did I tell ye about my fishing boat?"

"No, you haven't."

"Well ..." He started with a description of The Elspeth. Before she realized it, they were past Dundee. Her stomach growled, and Tam was getting restless.

Her stomach growled again. Rab gave her an amused look. Fiona blushed and said, "I'm famished, and I think Tam could use a walk."

"A wee bit more, and we'll stop for some fude."

At last, he pulled into a seaport town. "I think I found something that will please ye. We'll stop here for tea."

They rolled through the town with an impressive view of the North Sea. Blue and yellow paint brightened the stucco of the old buildings, but many were constructed of grey or rusty sandstone. They looked more like monuments to the past than thriving businesses. But the people on the streets and the signs of active commerce said otherwise.

The car rolled off the main road and drove past an ancient-looking harbor when she asked, "What town is this?"

"Arbroath." He glanced at her sideways.

Fiona gave Rab a double take. "Arbroath?" Her heart began racing. "The same as Mairi's father's inn?"

"The very same, lass." He winked. "The very same."

Rab drove past the harbormaster's office to the end of what looked like the business section. From here she could look out to sea. The afternoon sun broke through the clouds, reflecting off silver waves far out on the horizon.

They passed the breakwater, and the land beyond the road appeared to be all beaches. In the distance, she saw tall cliffs as the land curved, protectively sheltering Arbroath from the worst of the North Sea storms. *Could this be the shale beach where Wee Geordie and Tamash pulled their skiff up on top?*

Rab pulled his Bentley to the curb in front of a time-worn building. The sign above the weathered door said "The Seaman's Rest."

So this is Tamash's father's inn. They went here together, he and Wee Geordie, to talk about rebellion and to see Mairi. Without conscious thought, Fiona opened her car door and stepped onto a broad brick walkway.

Wee Geordie's past. Here it was on the corner, near the port. She stood gazing at the old inn. It felt like 1745 instead of 1937 as she reached up to rap on the door. Rab put his hand over hers. She jumped with a start. She'd forgotten he was with her.

Shaking herself out of the past, Fiona looked around for her wee dog. Tam sat at her feet. A blush spread across her cheeks. "I imagined this very place."

"I ken, lass. Not to worry. There's history here. Yer history." *Yes. It is my history.*

The three of them entered a small foyer with a desk in front and stairs curving up to what must be the rooms above. Tables and chairs filled the rooms on either side of the desk. One half seemed more of a pub with its large bar and display of whiskey bottles. Sunlight filtered in through the small pane glass windows. Flames crackled in an old stone fireplace that dominated the end of the other room.

A chubby little man in his mid-forties with a shock of curly bright-red hair framing his round face approached them from the bar. He had his hand out before he reached Rab.

"And ye would be Rab MacKenzie."

They shook hands, and Rab turned to her.

"Fiona, I'd like ye to meet Hamish Ferguson. He'd be a cousin of sorts. Ye share a great, great, great, great grandda." Rab looked pleased with his calculations.

"Aye, that would be about right. I am pleased to meet you." Hamish extended his hand to her.

"I don't understand," she said, taking his hand.

Rab patted her shoulder. "When you told me about the inn owned by Mairi's father, I remembered seeing this place on my way up to Peterhead. I gave Mr. Ferguson a call and arranged our visit."

The little man chimed in. "Name's Hamish to you. It's no like we're strangers, ye ken. We share the same blood, and that makes us family." His chubby face beamed. "Come have a seat. We've much to talk about."

He led them to a table by the roaring fireplace and then stood back, looking at Fiona. "If there were any doubt at all, it's gone forever." Hamish directed their attention to an old painting on the far wall. "That is Mairi, just after she was wed."

Fiona stood and crossed the room to the wall with the windows. On a paneled section hung a beautifully framed painting.

Hamish stood beside her. "It could be yerself. The hair's a different color, but the face. Well, lass, you bear a striking resemblance to our Mairi."

Her eyes widened in disbelief. "I always knew I was related to the captain, but he seemed more like a friend. But seeing Mairi..." Her throat clogged with emotion. "It's like looking in a mirror."

Rab was standing by her other side. "No wonder Wee Geordie's watching over you, lass." He slipped an arm around her and gave her a squeeze.

Hamish scratched his jaw. "I beg yer pardon. What's that yer sayin' about Wee Geordie?"

Fiona smiled with delight. "I'm happy to give you a few surprises as well. We do have a lot to talk about."

They talked long into the afternoon. Hamish fed them a wonderful meal—genuine Arbroath Smokies. The smoked haddock was delicious, covered with melted butter and lemon and served with chips. The real feast was what he could tell her about Mairi and her captain. "I am myself a direct descendent to Tamash. That would be—"

"Mairi's brother." She pointed at Hamish. "I know Tamash. I know about him. He was a good friend to Wee Geordie."

She grew serious, afraid to ask what she wanted to know. "I'm reading the log and fitting what I can remember from history in school with what he's talking about." She blushed a little.

"I know this sounds terrible, but I skipped ahead to the last few pages, and it ends suddenly. Geordie says the Tearloch was at sea during the last battle at Culloden, but what the English did to the Jacobites after was horrible. What happened to Geordie and Mairi? I mean after Culloden." It was like waiting to hear if a friend had died.

"Aye, lassie. Wee Geordie was guid at hiding his identity. They left for a bit to trade in France." Hamish gestured to Mairi. "Our Mairi was a bonnie sailor, but when her father died, they came back here to run the inn." He winked. "Him and Tamash kept their hand into smugglin' with the inn as a respectable facade. It was quite profitable, as ye can imagine."

"Oh, I'm so glad." She covered her mouth, embarrassed at her sense of overwhelming relief. "It's so good to hear they made it through everything." She reached out to take Hamish's hand. "I feel you are family."

"Well, lass, we are that and more." Without saying another word, he left the room.

She looked at Rab. "Did I say something wrong?"

Rab had been quiet through most of the conversation. He sat scratching Tam's head. "It looked ta me like he thought of something. Just wait, lass, I'm sure—"

But Rab didn't finish because Hamish returned carrying a small book. He held it with reverence and placed it in front of Fiona.

"It was Mairi's diary. I found it years ago and have often read through it. That would be why her portrait hangs on my wall. She was a fine woman and wise. She loved her husband and wee bairns, but she loved God." He touched the cover as if he were saying goodbye. "I ken she'd want ye to have her words."

Shaking her head, Fiona objected. "No. Thank you so much, but I can't. It's yours and too much for me to accept."

Rab put his hand on hers and squeezed. "Aye, but I'm thinkin' it's what she'd want."

"Exactly." Hamish smiled. "It's what our Mairi would want."

Chapter Seventy-Eight

Germany
June 1937

Some Direction from Dolly

Herr Voss received a call. It was all very secretive, but judging from Herr Papa's deep worry lines, something had gone wrong with his pet project. Thankfully, they needed to return to Hamburg at once. Laurie knew only pieces of the project—something experimental and military. Marguerite pleaded with her father to let them stay, but he was insistent Laurie would be needed at the yard.

She pouted and stamped her foot, then capitulated when her father offered a new dress for the next party. Still, Laurie was sure she was doing everything she could to delay their departure. Herr Papa was getting more and more annoyed.

You go right ahead, baby, make Papa suffer. Take as long as you like. I want a word with Dolly before we leave.

Laurie threw his things in his case and hurried downstairs.

Luck was with him. He recognized Dolly's personal servant Rutger.

"Where might I find the countess?"

"The back garden, mein Herr." His wise old face held the hint of a smile.

Dolly was sitting alone on a garden bench. She looked up from her reading. "Ah, Laurie, I heard you'd be leaving early." She smiled at his surprise. "I told you it pays to talk to the servants. They hear everything. But I'm so glad we have a few moments alone before you leave. I had a thought. You should go to the hometown of the children. You said they were from Bamberg?"

"It might be dangerous to talk with the neighbors."

"Oh, no, not the neighbors. You said the nanny was Bavarian, no?"

Laurie nodded.

"Many young women come from the farming areas in Bavaria to find work in the towns. A good percentage of those girls are from religious homes." She reached out to take his hand. "Laurie, you must be careful. It is not safe to talk to just any clergy. The pope himself is trading the support of his bishops for more influence of the Catholic party in the Fuhrer's government."

"That seems hard to believe."

"Hard to believe, yes, but also sadly true." She shook her head. Her eyes seemed a bit too bright. He could see how much this impacted her personally.

"I'm Catholic. My mother was from France. I know the parish priest at Saint Martins. There's a good chance my friend will remember the girl. If so, he might have information that will help you find what happened to the children."

She passed him a slip of paper. "I've written him a note. It will be as dangerous for him as it is for you. This will let him know he may speak with you. Take your girl with you. She should give you excellent cover."

"Thank you, Dolly. I never expected you to be helpful so soon, but I have just one question." Laurie felt foolish for asking, but Marguerite didn't seem interested in anything but lavish dinner parties. "How do I talk Marguerite into visiting this town?"

"Marguerite spent the weekend complaining about how much you're at work. Well, tell her you want to spend a day with her. This town is beautiful, ancient. Tell her you've heard about it. A romantic day alone. She'll jump at the chance." He objected, but she smiled at him. "Laurie, remember your poker face." She winked. "Take my word for it. She'll love the idea."

THE CAR WAS ready and waiting. Laurie stored his case in the boot. Herr Voss stood by the bonnet, looking at his wristwatch. Laurie shoved his hands in his pockets. He kicked at a bit of gravel next to his shoe.

"Would you like me to go see what's keeping Marguerite?" It wasn't something he wanted to do, but waiting was wearing on his nerves, too.

"Nein. She's likely to dig her heels in, and we'll be waiting for another hour." Herr Papa sighed and shrugged, his hands limp at his side.

Laurie nodded. His arms folded across his chest. He leaned on the front bumper. *This could have been my fate.* A life of waiting on this beautiful, spoiled woman flashed before his eyes.

Both their heads shot up as a commotion came from the front door. Two servants carrying Marguerite's bags walked down the steps and across the drive to the car. *Oh Lord, they look frustrated.*

Laurie's thought was barely formed when the hostess and Marguerite came out the door. His fiancée smiled sweetly, saying something he couldn't catch, and kissed the older woman on both cheeks. Laurie smiled, thinking they'd misjudged her mood.

Marguerite's face changed to a scowl as she headed for the car. *I'm guessing the ride home will be tense.*

Marguerite fussed and fumed at her father. When the old man

snapped, "Guter Gott, Marguerite. That is enough. Not one more word from you." She clamped her mouth shut and settled for an icy glare at the back of his head.

Why didn't I see this side of her in school? The German countryside slid past, but Laurie's thoughts were back in Scotland.

Fiona, I've known you such a short time, but you are better than this. Rubbing his hands over his eyes, he pretended to nap. *I'd give anything to be back at home this very minute.*

He thought of walking on Castle Hill, how warmth spread through him as Fiona's fingers curved around his hand. He remembered the stiff breeze blowing a dark curl into her eyes—how he ached to reach out and brush it away.

As they drove into town, Herr Voss had his driver drop them both at the shipyard. Laurie watched the car move away. *Marguerite will have to have her temper fit without an audience, thank God.*

Laurie relished having something to puzzle out. Another place to put his thoughts. Herr Voss needed all hands on board, so what was previously compartmentalized was now explained in detail. Voss was bidding on a government contract for a flying bomb, a sort of airborne torpedo.

"What do you think Herr Hitler will need these for?" Terry whispered. They were pouring over wiring schematics, looking for a problem with the guidance systems. It wasn't a question. They both knew Hitler was looking at all of Europe with greedy eyes.

Terry got home every night, but Laurie slept on a cot in the corner of the large office. He could get more done when everyone left for the day. The room was quiet, and he could think. By Thursday, it appeared they had the problem solved. He ventured a moment alone with Terry and asked, "Are you all right helping them make flying bombs?"

Terry shook his head. "At least Britain's not at war with Germany, not yet anyway. I don't see any way around it. We have to do our job."

Laurie looked his friend in the eye. "But when we leave, we need to give the program a setback."

Terry nodded. "We'll have to do a bit of reverse engineering." He winked and gave Laurie the hint of a smile.

Herr Voss came to Laurie at lunch, and Laurie tried not to look guilty. This man had given him a chance, believed in his abilities, and he would pay him back with a catastrophic failure for his pet project.

Instead, Voss slapped him on the back. "You've earned your pay packet for the week. Go home, lad. Go home before my daughter kills me for keeping you at work."

It was the perfect opportunity to put Dolly's plan in motion. "Thank you, sir. I was wondering if I could take Marguerite on an outing. Bamberg is supposed to be beautiful."

"Mein Gott. Ja, take her. I'll even give you the motor car."

Chapter Seventy-Nine

Edinburgh
June 1937

Night Visit

It was dark and quiet. Edinburgh was tucked in for the night. Alec waited until midnight to sneak over to Fiona's house with a six-foot stepladder. The trouble was, on this side of the house the ground fell away, leaving the ladder a good four feet short of the first-floor bathroom window. It didn't seem insurmountable. After all, he was tall. As he climbed to the top rung of the ladder, he realized it was much harder than he had originally thought. He tried to get one leg through the window first, almost losing his balance. The only answer to his dilemma soon became clear.

Bloody hell. He leapt upward off the ladder, hoping momentum would do the rest. The thrust sent the ladder tumbling to the ground and Alec rocketing through the window. The bottom of the tub came up quickly, and his face smacked on the porcelain. He lay in a crumpled mess, rubbing his injured nose and staring up at the window. *Well, shit, at least I'm in, and I never intended to leave that way, so what does it matter?* He listened for a minute for fear he might have drawn someone's attention, but all was quiet, so he hauled himself out of the tub.

With Fiona gone, the house was his to search, and he knew where to start. He whispered, "The log."

Moving through the dark house was easy since all the houses on his square were identical from the front. Even the interior layout was like his own. With moonlight filtering through the window in the entry hall, he could just make out the main staircase. He remembered that Fiona's bedroom was in much the same space as his own room.

Why is she so secretive about the damn log unless it's telling her things? Things she wants to keep from me. He pushed open her bedroom door to find the silvery moonlight throwing everything into dark shapes and shadows. He waited. The room felt off. Eerie. As his eyes adjusted to the dim light, a table, chairs, and her bed came into focus. Nothing more. Nothing moved.

His heart raced with the thought that someone else was there with him. He stepped back into the shadows, listening and controlling his breathing. After a few minutes, he decided his imagination was getting the better of him—it was only a big empty house. After wiping the sweat from his forehead, it took only a few minutes to locate the log.

It sat on a small table near a chair. *This is all going very well,* he thought. *And why not? I deserve a bit of good luck. Might as well light the lamp and read the book. The sooner I discover its secrets, the sooner I'll be on my way to a new life. If Father's man is watching, for all he knows Fiona's up late. A fire might be nice.*

He stoked the coals and lit the fire, settling himself into Fiona's armchair with the log. But even with his education and interest, he found it slow reading.

"It is rumored Prince Charles is planning on staying in Edinburgh for at least a month. And since Mairi agreed to be my bride,

I'm determined to make her mine before she regrets her decision."

After thirty minutes, Alec found his eyelids drooping. He scrubbed a hand through his hair. *This reads like a goddamn romantic novel.*

He rubbed his dry eyes and closed them for a minute.

He was charging through the house, searching everywhere. A basket-hilt sword swung at his side in its scabbard. As he passed a mirror, he caught his reflection wearing a red English uniform. The servants cowered from his advance. Their fear made him feel powerful. In the dream, Alec knew what he was searching for and was positive it was here somewhere. He turned over beds, sent dressers crashing. An uncommonly large man stepped in front of him. Light glinted off the warrior's blade. His stance was wide, blocking Alec from his goal. A grin spread slowly across the shadowed features. Alec looked up into the cold, dead eyes of a sea captain.

With a roar, Alec pulled his sword free and held it at the ready. He lunged forward, meaning to strike his opponent first. His blow was blocked, and the shock traveled down his arm to his chest.

The ringing of steel blades woke him with a start, knocking the log off his lap. The room was dark.

I must have drifted off to sleep. Don't remember turning out the lamp. He rubbed his arms. The light from the fire sputtered. The room was chilly. He was stiff and stretched his limbs, then halted.

A faint jingling caught his attention. It came from a long way off but was moving closer to the square. Alec peered out the window. Fog rolled in from the sea, and the square held it like a blanket.

There it is again, only closer. It sounds like a team of horses. As he listened, he could hear their hooves on the cobblestones. He strained to see through the mist. Nothing swirled in the fingers of fog. But with every minute, the sounds grew more pronounced.

Louder. Moving right at him. He swung around to look at the chair. *Could I still be sleeping? Still in a dream?*

Faint glimmers of light from the coals cast shadows over the painting above the fireplace. The Black Captain watched. Alec peered through the gloom as he imagined the same cruel grin he'd seen in his dream taunting him from the painting. The captain stared at him. Alec couldn't drag his eyes from the face.

A horse whinnied, pulling his attention back to the window as metal wheels scraped over the stones below. He pushed his forehead against the glass. *So loud.*

He expected to see a carriage with a team of horses emerge from the fog. But only sound moved below—creaking leather and jingling harnesses coming around the side of the house.

Alec tripped over a stool as he raced to the bedroom windows above the archway. A vibration traveled under him, and the horses snorted, but he couldn't see anything. *It's him, isn't it?* Alec's attention fastened on the captain, who was frowning down at him. He moved to the chair. Dead, cold eyes moved with him. He couldn't look away even with everything in him telling him to run.

He scooped up the log and backed out of the bedroom, watching the captain's eyes move with him to the door. He glanced over his shoulder at the hall. The sound of the horses moved to the rear of the house.

With every ounce of courage he could muster, he ran to the back stairs, feeling like the captain was right behind him. The window at the end of the hallway overlooked the back garden and stable yard—they were empty. No horses or carriage. All quiet.

The hair pricked up at the nape of his neck in warning something was following him. *It's just my imagination. Nothing more than a spooky dream.* His head turned to look back down the hall. Mist swirled in the darkness. He squinted. The white filmy shape of a man took form. *The captain.*

As Alec stood transfixed on the landing, the sweet smell of decay drifted toward him.

You're dead. Not real, not real. He clutched the log to his chest.

"I'm not afraid of you," he shouted as the captain glided toward him. "You can't stop me from finding your bloody war chest."

But his heart was pounding. Every instinct commanded him to flee. Without conscious thought, he turned to run down the kitchen stairs. His eyes were wide open and head swiveling back to see if the captain was on his heels. His feet missed a step and sent him stumbling over the last few stairs. At the kitchen door, he threw back the bolt and shot out of the house. It wasn't until he closed the door to his own room that he realized he still clutched the captain's log.

Chapter Eighty

The Northeast Coast of Scotland
June 1937

Spirit of a Smuggler

The smell of fresh baked bread—heaven to her senses—sent a rumble through Fiona's stomach.

Rab glanced over his shoulder to the basket sitting on the back seat. "Deilia's bread smells wonderful. Shall we stop for an early lunch?"

Fiona smiled. "Great idea."

They were on their way back from Peterhead. Not for the first time, Fiona found herself amazed at the love and admiration she had for her friend, soon to be grandfather. Rab still kept his Highland home intact. He'd walked out the door the day of his wife Daisy's funeral and, though he'd been back many times, in his mind Daisy was always waiting for his return. Her things were just as she'd left them when the influenza hit her hard.

Rab had picked up a bit of cross-stitch still sitting on the table. His eyes were bright when he'd spoken of her. "After she died, I left to help Jean, Laurie's mum. I suppose if I ever came back here to live, I'd get 'round to doing something with her things." He exhaled. "This way, it's like she's still here."

Laurie's face floated through Fiona's thoughts. *I want to be loved like that.*

She looked out the passenger window at grassy fields stretching to touch the icy blue North Sea. The road here was far above the shoreline. Rab pulled into a wide space and parked the Bentley.

"Ah, it's beautiful here." When Fiona opened her door, Tam took off through the tall grass, running with abandon.

"Do you know the name of the castle?" She pointed across a green field to ruins that seemed to spring from a huge mossy rock. The closer they came, the more she realized the castle and the field were not at all connected. A steep trail led from the grassy knoll to the beach below.

"Is it on an island?"

"No an island, really. Most of the time, there's a beach." Rab handed her an old plaid, and she spread it on the ground. "Tam, laddie. Come get some water." Rab poured a bit from a flask into a small bowl. A black ball of fur streaked toward them. Ears were plastered to his head, his doggie teeth looked bright white with his mouth open wide in a doggie smile. A long red tongue flew to the side like a banner in the wind. He slid to a stop and flopped down beside them, panting to catch his breath.

Rab unwrapped several slices of gammon, handing her some of the ham.

"Yon is Dunnottar Castle." He pointed to the ruin as he took out his knife to cut off a chunk of cheese. "Yer uncle told me an interesting story about the place you'll not find in any history book."

She took the cheese, breaking off a piece for Tam.

"Once it was a fine fortress with sea caves on the windward

side. Large enough for a small boat to land. They say tunnels lead straight up ta the keep."

"Was it intact during the captain's time?" Fiona stared out at the grey rock, trying to imagine it as it might have looked.

"Oh, aye. It's rumored Prince Charles hid from the English in those walls." Next, he handed her a slice of Deilia's bread. "After Culloden, the prince and his closest men left the field to the Highlanders. They could see the tide had turned against them." Rab shook his head in disgust. "They deserted the very men who'd risked everything to protect them."

"Wee Geordie was right about Prince Charles."

"That's the rub." Rab took a chunk of ham and cheese. "Yer uncle said the captain had given the prince the chest in hopes it would help the men."

"They were poorly equipped and supplied. I remember that part."

"By Culloden, they were tired, fiercely cold, and hungry. It was axes and swords against English Edward's muskets and well-fed troops." Rab looked at the castle. "Charlie didna use yer captain's war chest for Scotland. No for the lives of the men left dying on the battlefield. He had a mind ta take it wi him back to France."

She poured them both a cup of steaming tea from the thermos. "But how did the chest come back to the captain?"

"The Black Captain was first a smuggler. He knew about the sea caves at Dunnottar. When he heard where Charlie was hiding, he came by night. They said he made it all the way to Prince Charles' bedroom. Held a dirk at his throat and demanded his chest back."

"But how did he get away?" Fiona looked back at the castle. It was a fortress even now, a sentinel to the austerity of this land.

"Well, the laird of Dunnottar were no too happy that the prince was such a coward. I dinna know all the details. But the captain left wi his chest and a promise it would never be used for selfish purposes."

She squinted at him, interrupting his history lesson. "I think you and Laurie are more like my captain than I am."

"Oh, aye? And how would that be?" Rab arched a bushy brow.

"Do all Highlanders have a smuggler's heart?"

"No a smuggler's heart, just a heart, lass, just a heart. And we're no too fond of bullies."

A cloud passed over the sun, and shadows fell across the sea beyond the castle. In her imagination, she pictured the Tearloch waiting for her captain to return with the war chest. As the cloud moved on, a brilliant light sparkled off the waves. A ship was making its way where she'd imagined the Tearloch a minute before. She put a hand up to shade her eyes. "Do you see that? It wasn't there a minute ago and now…" She pointed.

"The sea's like that. It can play tricks with your eyes."

"From here, the ship looks so small."

"No small. They're comin' in wi their catch. She's the same size as the Elspeth." His friend Kevin captained Rab's boat.

Her mind drifted back to the night before, sitting at Kevin and Deilia's table as they told them about the missing children. Kevin's face grew dark with anger. "And they can move into your house and take everything? No one will stop them? Just because they were Jews?" He was incredulous. But Deilia dabbed her eyes, asking question after question about the Jewish children. There was no doubt of their help. The four of them laid their plans far into the night.

Rab ate his sandwich for a minute and then said, "It's not that we love smuggling, mind. It's that, when we're doing what we must"—he chuckled—"well, we must do it and damn the cost."

Fiona mused, *The captain did what he must and damn the English and even the Bonnie Prince. Rab and Laurie will do what they must to get those children to safety and damn the Germans. It all seems right to me. Maybe I have a bit of the spirit of the smuggler as well.*

Chapter Eighty-One

Hamburg, Germany
June 1937

A Visit to Bamberg

Laurie held Marguerite in a warm embrace, speaking against her cheek so she wouldn't see his face. "I've been working way too much, but your da has given me the entire weekend off. Let's spend some time together, just you and me. I heard Bamberg is a beautiful little town. We can take in the sights."

There I got it all out. He pulled back to look at her face and had to smile at her obvious delight. Relief washed over him. "Have lunch and talk?" *Dolly was right.*

She grasped his face in her hands and guided it down to kiss him. When their lips parted, she was flushed with excitement. "I'd love it. When can we leave?"

"I don't have to be back at work until Monday."

Marguerite deflated. "Oh no, Saturday's Wagner's opening at the Music Hall. Everyone who's anyone will be there, and I bought our tickets."

He tried not to show his disappointment. Opera was not on his list of fun Saturday nights. *I'd rather sit through one of old Professor Peabody's dry lectures than attend the opera. I have to find those children and get out of this place before it kills me.*

A thought occurred to him. "We could leave tomorrow morning if you'd like? If one day is all we have, we'll make the most of it."

"Wonderful." She straightened his tie and kissed him on the cheek. With a speculative squint she said, "I was thinking you were only interested in my father's job, not his daughter." But the pout that followed was playful.

Laurie wrapped his arms around her again and gave her a hug. "I'm sorry, lass." He kissed the top of her head and wondered how long he could keep her from seeing his heart—*if she hasn't already guessed.*

Chapter Eighty-Two

Rüdesheim am Rhein, Germany
June 1937

The Count

Shocked, Ana asked, "You told your husband about the children?"

Isabelle put an arm around Ana. "I told him some of our servants have family visiting." She shrugged at her deception. "I do this not from fear of what he'll say but to protect him from a dangerous truth."

"I'm not so sure how that works at confession," Ana commented with the ease of someone who'd grown to be a friend.

"I told him a visitor brought an orphaned baby boy with her. A sister had died and left un nourrisson, an infant. The father was unknown." She shrugged again. "Not such a rare thing, is it?" Isabelle hurried her next words. "I told him I want to keep the baby."

Ana drew in her breath. "That was risky, wasn't it?"

Isabelle's smile softened with all the warmth of a woman who

knows she's loved. "He said he can't wait to meet his new son."
La comtesse glowed.

When he arrived, the count was not at all what Ana expected.
Phillip was in his middle years, a good ten years older than his
wife, a handsome man with sandy-blond hair and kind eyes. It
was plain to see he adored Isabelle. Just as la comtesse had
assured her, the count accepted baby Tony. It was more like love at
first sight. He played with Tony on his lap and tickled tiny feet,
sending Tony into squeals of infectious laughter.

She felt sure Tony would have a place in this family forever.
Ana sighed and watched Deter and Gretchen set the table in the
servant's quarters. *Lord, how will we help the other three?*

La comtesse appeared at her side with baby Tony on her hip, a
permanent fixture these days. "What will the count say when he
sees Deter and Gretchen?"

"I told you, he will say nothing." She smiled at Ana's apprehension. "Not to worry, my dear. We'll all get through this. We
just have to be careful." She handed Tony to Ana and pulled
papers from her pocket. "Look." Taking the baby back, she said
again, "Open. Look what my count has already accomplished."

Ana unfolded the paperwork. It was official-looking documents. Her mouth fell open. A birth certificate for Thomas
Anthony. "This is for baby Tony?"

Isabelle nodded. She was radiant with happiness.

"Well, comtesse, your count is an amazing man." Ana shook
her head in disbelief.

"He said it was easy since I rarely leave the estate. A simple
matter."

"Do you think he could help the rest?"

La comtesse shook her head. "Non, mon amie. My count
doesn't ask about them, and I won't tell him. It is better this
way." She patted Ana's hand. "Look what God has done already.
He will find a way, no? That being said, we will have some enor-

mous challenges. The count will host a large dinner party—more of a weekend."

Ana felt the blood drain from her face. "When?"

"At the end of the month. These will be dangerous times, but I know we can get through this." She reached out to wrap her free arm around Ana. "I have asked our family priest to come baptize my new son, Thomas. I think he will encourage us all." The baby squealed at something, then giggled at their startled faces.

"See? He likes his new name already."

Chapter Eighty-Three

Latimer Square
Edinburgh
June 1937

Alec's Not Crazy

Alec tossed the captain's log on his bed and flopped down. His heart beat wildly. *Think, man. There are no spirits, no ghosts. You spooked yourself is all.* The adrenaline melted from his body. Overcome with exhaustion, he closed his eyes for a minute, just to catch his breath, and dozed off.

He was being chased down Fiona's hall; the air was rancid with decay. When the ghost caught hold of his sleeve, Alec startled awake, sitting bolt upright with a strangled scream still in his throat. Trying to settle himself, he scrubbed his hands over his face and through his hair. *Right, sleep is out of the question.*

The moonlight shone on his room and the captain's log. He flipped on his light and picked up the old book with a renewed sense of hope. *This could work out better than I thought.* He read. At dawn, he was still reading. He rubbed his dry eyes. The search for clues was slow. *Give me a boring legal brief over eighteenth-century dialect any day.*

The light crept across his floor, reminding him the morning was passing without a single breakthrough. He slammed the log closed, cursing. "God help us. Barely a mention of the chest."

He glanced at his clock. *I'll need to send word to the office. Half past nine, so Father must have left already.* Alec shook his head. *He didn't bother to find out why I wasn't ready.*

The thought stung, but maybe it was for the best. Alec opened his bedroom door just a crack to make sure the hall was empty. Then he jogged down the stairs and stopped at the library door to listen before slipping in.

A quick call to the office: "So sorry, I'm ill. Cancel all my appointments, please, and notify my father."

The secretary didn't bother to ask why I needed her to tell my father I was ill. The old man isn't the sort to hide his feelings. I expect everyone knows what he thinks of me. It was a weight of shame that Alec always carried. *Something has to change, and that log is my best hope.*

Back in his room, he sat on his bed and picked up the log once again. He thumbed through the pages, frustrated with his lack of progress. He blew out a long breath. His head fell back on the pillow. Sleep stole over him, and he was dreaming again.

"Well, my boy, I'm proud of you. You're a bright lad, always said so." His father beamed with pride as he patted Alec's back. "How will you spend the money?" Avarice gleamed in the old man's eyes. "I could use a full partner at the firm."

"I plan to start my own firm." Alec patted his father's shoulder, watching the old man's face fall into a frown. "I'm moving to London at the end of the week. Sorry." He shook his head. "Just business. Nothing personal, you understand."

Bright afternoon light flooded his bedroom, creeping under his eyelids. Alec struggled to stay in the dream. Despite the deep sense of satisfaction watching his father taste defeat, the light pulled him back to the task at hand. He rubbed his eyes, called for tea, and read the log again.

This time, he picked up a notepad and pen and took notes. In the space of a few pages, he was onto something. The daring raid on Dunnottar Castle gave him hope. But just as quickly, the Black Captain's oath that the war chest would never be used for selfish purposes confounded him. Near the end of the log, Alec discovered a page missing, clearly torn from the book. He sat up, a wicked grin slowly spreading across his face.

"So, our little Fiona isn't the innocent she pretends." He flopped back onto his bed. "Bloody hell. Laurie wins again—the girl and her money."

He swung his feet off the bed and began pacing his room. He had to bend her to his will. Once the treasure was his, he wouldn't need the girl. Until then, it was war.

Friday, he called in to work claiming illness once again. He spent one more day in his room, not being able to sleep or eat anything. Cook came to the door, trying to entice him, but even she gave up.

The log ended without further mention of the war chest. The fate of the chest must be on that missing page. Alec reviewed it again. *I was reading the log and fell asleep. I heard horses and a carriage.* The truth hit him hard.

"I heard them," he said aloud. "They came into the square, then to the back stables. I'm not crazy. If the horses and the captain's ghost are real, then Fiona must know." He ran a hand through his ragged hair. "She has to. She lives there." He brightened. "If she has the missing page, it could be she's too afraid of the ghost to find his treasure."

Late in the afternoon, he heard barking. A door slammed. Talking. Alec looked out his bedroom window. He wiped his eyes, willing them to focus.

"They're back." His heart skipped a beat. He shot a quick look at the captain's log, still lying on his bed. "Good God, I have to put the log back in Fiona's bedroom." He watched long enough to see them all go into Rab's house.

If I hurry, I can get it back and she'll be none the wiser. Alec shoved his legs into his trousers as he hopped toward his bed and stuffed his feet into his shoes. He snatched up the book and ran down his own back stairs and ignored the servants' startled looks as he flew past them in the kitchen.

Thank God I left the back door unlocked, so getting back in won't be a problem. He raced up Fiona's kitchen stairs and down the hall. As he tossed the log on the chair, he could feel the captain's eyes on him but willed himself not to look. He ran back out the way he'd come. With no key, there was nothing for it but to close the door and leave it unlocked. *Let her think Father's hired man has been in the house. It might even draw her closer to me.*

Chapter Eight-Four

Bamberg, Germany
June 1937

Father Ignatius

The day turned out to be beautiful. White clouds floated across a deep blue sky and the warm sun fell on Laurie's face. He sighed and looked at his watch.

Marguerite's idea of spending a day together is far different from mine. This was the fourth shop he'd waited outside while holding her packages. Lunch was a litany of who would be at the opera and what they'd be wearing.

His mind drifted back to walking the battlements of Edinburgh Castle with Fiona. He remembered just standing with her hand in his, looking out at Princess Street and later sitting at the cafe with Tam at their feet. *We talked for hours.*

When the shop door opened, he shook himself back to the present. A clerk carrying a large hatbox and two more bags trailed behind Marguerite.

"I hope all those packages will fit in the boot, or should we tie those to the roof of your papa's auto?"

She grimaced. "Oh, Laurie, don't make fun of me. I found the perfect dress for tomorrow night. It's all little sequins…"

He stopped listening as the clerk piled the packages into his arms. It didn't matter that the girl gave him a sympathetic smile along with the bundles.

He was closing the boot when Marguerite said, "Look. There's Marta." She waved at a young woman down the street. "We were friends as children. Come on, I want her to meet my handsome fiancé." She was already turning to cross the street when Laurie grabbed her arm.

"Wait. I need to stretch my legs a bit. You go see your friend. I'll take a stroll up the street and visit that old church."

"You can't be serious?"

She's quite homely when she frowns. I wonder if she'd do it so often if she could see how distorted it makes her face?

"Rab loves headstone rubbings," Laurie lied. "I'll see if I can borrow some paper and charcoal."

She rolled her eyes. "Well, suit yourself."

He didn't look back as he wandered up the street. Instead, he studied the medieval architecture of white-washed buildings with colored crossbeams and red-tiled roofs. The river Regnitz flowed through the center of town. Old bridges spanned the waterway.

He stopped to read a sign that said, "Old Town preserved from the Eleventh Century." *It's a beautiful village.* Unfortunately, on many buildings red Nazi banners hung from the windows of upper floors. They looked like claw marks rending bloody wounds on what should have been a tranquil setting.

Laurie chanced a look back down the street to see Marguerite enter a shop with her friend. He let out his breath and felt his shoulders relax. *Was I worried she would want to make a stone rubbing?* He smiled at the absurdity of the vision as he opened the door to the ancient chapel.

The church looked hundreds of years old. White walls and gold accents reflected the light from high paned windows. To one side, candles flickered below a statue of Mary holding the broken body of her son. Laurie caught a whiff of incense, sweet but not overpowering. The peace of this place filled his heart.

He walked down the aisle and slid into a pew, bowing his head. He sank onto the kneeler, his knees fitting perfectly into the worn depressions.

Lord, here I am. His thoughts were halting. *Before Germany, the last time I talked to you was when my mother died. I didn't think you heard.* His eyes grew moist at the recollection. Then feelings, memories, tumbled over him. Times when all seemed stripped away from his life. Times that made him feel helpless and alone.

"This wasn't why I came," he whispered, trying to interrupt the flow of his thoughts. But all his wrong steps spread out before him—the callous words spoken to his grandfather, the gambling, the drinking. All of it overwhelmed him. "I have no right to any help." His own voice was barely audible.

The tide of his feelings shifted. He saw times he'd shared with his parents; the love they'd had for him and for each other. The face of his grandmother smiling at him floated through his thoughts. And Rab. Always Rab.

He remembered coming past Rab's bedroom, the door ajar. Laurie could see his grandfather kneeling next to the bed. He was startled when he realized the old man was praying for him. The last words he'd spoken to his grandfather that night had been so terse, so insulting. He remembered being disgusted as he moved down the hall at the old man's weakness.

He felt shame at the memory, but something more rose within him. Rab was faithfulness itself, a rock, someone who would never give up, never leave, no matter what Laurie did. In that moment, it felt like a warm blanket covered him. A soft whisper said, "Not alone. Never alone."

Laurie jumped as a hand touched his arm, and he looked up at a pleasant, balding old man in priest's vestments.

The man said in German, "I'm Father Ignatius." His smile was kindhearted.

Laurie wiped his sleeve across his eyes, pulling himself away from something he still wasn't sure he understood back to the present.

He answered in English, "Father, you're just the man I wanted to see." He patted Dolly's letter, still folded into his jacket pocket. "Is there someplace we can talk?"

The priest nodded and led Laurie back to a comfortable office. The room was bright with the afternoon sun shining from windows that looked out to a beautiful little courtyard. Father Ignatius motioned for Laurie to have a seat on a small sofa, but instead of sitting behind his desk, he pulled an old ladder-backed chair over to sit in front of him.

"I have a letter of introduction from a mutual friend." Laurie handed the priest Dolly's letter.

As the older man examined the envelope, a smile touched his face, making it look much younger. In perfect English, he asked, "You know Dolly?"

"We haven't known each other long, but she's already been a good friend to me. Please read her letter, and then you can decide if you want to talk to me."

The priest pulled glasses from his pocket, holding the letter to catch the light. After a few minutes, he looked up. "You trust Dolly?" Laurie nodded. "As do I. Tell me your story, son."

Laurie recounted the contents of Bernie's letter, adding some of how he came to be traveling to Germany.

Father Ignatius considered. "No, tell me your story. Dolly says God is up to something with you. Why are you here?" Laurie looked into honest eyes so like his grandfather's. They demanded an honest answer.

Leaning his elbows on his knees, he dragged a hand through

his hair. "I came for a great job and a beautiful girl. At least, that's how it started. Now I don't want the job or the girl. I just want to find these bairns and get back home." There was so much more he wanted to say. "I'm not even sure where to start. It's upside down. Everything I thought was important isn't anymore."

Laurie talked about the change in him since meeting Fiona. Then, when he'd decided to stay in Scotland, Bernie's visit had changed his course again.

"Father, let me ask you a question. How do you know when God hears you? No—how do you know when he's telling you something?"

The old priest shook his head. "That's the question, isn't it? It's different for everyone, but it's the same for all of us. It's the same because it never goes against God's character. Do you know many people who say they know God?"

"My grandfather and Fiona. You can see it in their eyes. They never give up. They care about what matters. But why would God help me? I'm using this man and his daughter, and I was always going to use them. But I didn't feel bad about it until now. It's still wrong. If I leave, I leave those children. I can't walk away."

"You say you're wrong to use them." Laurie looked at the man through tortured eyes. "I think you can't give up on those children because God is talking to you.

"Look, we're all someone's man. Jewish children call the Nazis Hitler's men. Before you came here, it sounds like you were a man who served ambition, money and success. Now, whose man are you?"

"I'm not sure. How can God use someone with such a dark heart?"

Father Ignatius sighed and smiled. "That lets out the whole human race. The human heart is full of all kinds of evil. The Lord didn't come for the perfect. He came for those who would answer his call." The priest patted his shoulder. "I can help with the children."

Laurie looked up, startled. He'd forgotten his reason for coming.

"Their nanny was a young lady from a parish in Bavaria—Saint Thomas. The brother there was a good friend of mine."

"Was?"

Father Ignatius shook his head. "He sent the girl to me when she was hired by a Jewish couple. It was a good job. Good family, sweet girl. The day the parents were taken, she had the children on an outing. A neighbor caught her before they returned home, and she brought them to me. I helped her get them back to Saint Thomas."

"Where is Saint Thomas?"

"They're not there. Father Hugo got word the SS were in his village. He'd been helping other children, and I guess that must have reached loyal party members." The priest shook his head again. "He sent the last four children out with a young sister."

"And you're certain Deter and Gretchen are with her?"

Father Ignatius nodded sadly. "I spoke with Hugo several months ago. He told me of his worries for these last four children."

Laurie sat forward in his seat. "What happened?"

"There was a young SS officer tasked with rounding up all the stray children. Father Hugo died during questioning. They say this young man looks like an angel, but he has the heart of a demon—Eric Braun."

Laurie sat back in his chair, unable to believe what he'd heard. "I know this man." His throat closed around the words he spoke next. "Did he find them?"

"No, but I know they're no longer in Bavaria. I heard the nun took the children to stay with a farmer. They say the wife turned them in, but the farmer got them away before the SS made it to their house. Herr Braun was so enraged he burned the farmhouse to the ground."

"He can do that? Just for helping a sister and some children?" Laurie shook his head in disbelief. "What happened to the wife?"

Father Ignatius paused, a sadness spreading across his weathered face. "No one knows. She disappeared. I don't think she told Braun anything. I would have heard something if she had. The farmer came home to a smoldering house. No wife, but his barn was untouched, poor man. He's still looking for her. He sent word through the churches." Father Ignatius shrugged.

"I expect she went back to her parents, but at least she didn't tell the Nazis anything useful." The priest touched his cross and frowned. "There are still good people in Germany. Our friend Dolly is one of them. If I find anything out about the children, I'll send word to Dolly. We keep in touch. If I know her, she's already contacting the people who would hide them. And it is four children—your friend's two, a Romani baby and a Chinese girl. The sister's name is Ana."

Both men jumped at a sharp rap on the office door. Father rose and opened the door to an angry-looking Marguerite. Her face hardened as she looked from the priest to Laurie.

"I think it's time for us to leave." She turned on her heel and walked back through the church.

Laurie flushed with embarrassment. "I'm sorry, father—"

The priest put out his hand. "Go with God, my son." His handshake was firm, warm, encouraging, and he had a twinkle in his eyes when he said, "Dolly was right about you. God is up to something."

Chapter Eighty-Five

Latimer Square
Edinburgh
June 1937

Returning Home

There was a strength and permanence about the old grey stones of her home. Relief washed over Fiona as they drove into Latimer Square. All the way here, she'd worried they might not make it back in time. It was Friday afternoon, and Laurie promised to call them this evening. The setting sun gave everything a golden glow, reflecting her mood. Soon she'd be speaking with Laurie, hearing his voice. *I'll know how he's doing, and I can tell him how much I love him.* It suited her just fine when Rab stopped his Bentley just in front of his own steps.

They had a quick meal next to the phone for fear of missing the ring. Fiona sat with Tam at her feet and the telephone on the table next to her.

She looked up when Rab came back into the room with a tray

of tea and biscuits. She could feel excitement building and beamed with pleasure. "Laurie's call"—she glanced at her watch—"should be any time now."

Rab set the tray down, handed her a cup, and then settled in his favorite chair, his own cup in hand. "Well," he said with a satisfied smile on his face, "we can tell our Laurie everything's in place. As soon as we get word, Kevin will have the Elspeth on her way to pick me up. I'll set to work getting the supplies we need, and we're off as soon as it's all aboard."

She felt like a child begging but couldn't help saying again, "I want to come with you."

Rab shook his head. "No, luv, it's too dangerous." He put down his cup and leaned toward her. "I'd no want to explain to my grandson why I risked yer life."

They were both tired from the long drive. The clock on the mantel ticked off the seconds, then minutes, then hours. She found it hard to swallow her disappointment. Worrying at Laurie's ring, she asked, "Do you think he's in danger?"

"There's any number of reasons for him not calling. We canna think the worse." Rab rubbed his temples and looked at the clock once more. "Come on, lass. I'll walk ye home. It's no likely he'll call this late, and we've had a long day. Best get some sleep."

She smiled weakly and rose to follow. When he wasn't looking, she dabbed away a single tear. *Last time I saw Laurie, he wanted to stay here. Oh, God, I sent him away to find the children. Why did I tell him to go? If I never see him again, it will be all my fault.*

Rab carried her bag up the street and insisted on coming in to check the house before leaving. He rattled all the windows. Coming to the kitchen door, his hand jerked back.

"Do ye remember locking this?"

She came around to look at a closed but unlocked door.

"I must have been in too much of a hurry when we left." Squinting her eyes in concentration, she said, "Though I thought I locked it."

Rab rubbed the back of his neck, considering what she'd said. He shot the deadbolt into place. "Well, we'll take another look through and make sure nothing's disturbed."

I wish I'd told Rab about Alec's visit. It just never seemed like the right time to bring it up. Now it'll be like I'm hiding things. Still, he should know. "Rab—" She hesitated as they turned to leave the kitchen.

"Aye?" He looked so weary.

"Oh, it's nothing. We'll talk tomorrow." He smiled, and she followed him as they made a thorough check of the house.

Later, when she brought Mairi's diary up to set next to Wee Geordie's log, she noticed the log was in the wrong place, sitting on her chair. She spun around, almost expecting to find an intruder. Nothing. Just Tam and, of course, the captain. *Could I have left the book on the chair? No, I'd never do that.* Because of its antiquity, she'd been very deliberate with its care.

Her heart started beating faster as she noticed her ribbon marker was missing. She set the diary and the log on her night table and looked up at the captain. *Someone's been here in my room.* She wanted to run back to Rab.

"Tam, you'd tell me if someone was here, wouldn't you, boy?" The dog jumped up on her coverlet and turned around three times, then settled himself to sleep. His answer was obvious. All was well, at least for the present.

She knelt to set a flame to the fire and warm her room. Once again, she pulled her hand back at the evidence of a recent fire on the coal grate. Stunned at the audacity of her intruder, she thought, *Whoever it was sat in front of my fire.* She sank back to sit on the floor, frustration and anger welling. *And they made themselves comfortable while reading.*

She hugged her knees to her chest, feeling violated and looking around as if someone was still watching her. But Tam was already sleeping. It was quiet, and she was overtired.

Laurie, I wish you were here. She decided to just lie on her bed and wait for morning. Sleep if she could. But sleep overtook her as soon as she placed her head on the pillow. Fiona slept the deep, dreamless sleep of exhaustion.

Chapter Eighty-Six

On the Road to Hamburg
Germany
June 1937

An Uncomfortable Silence

"I don't understand you." Marguerite spat out her words. "You can't talk to just anyone. Not all the churches are Reich approved."

They were driving back to Hamburg. Laurie asked, "Reich approved?"

"Most of the churches are coming on board with the Fuhrer's church doctrine but not all of them. And especially some of the older clerics." She gave him a disgusted look. "Why weren't you getting your stupid stone rubbings?" He tried to think what to answer. "What could you have to say to that old man?"

"He was an interesting old fellow. We were just talking."

Marguerite rolled her eyes in reply, then said nothing. Her silence became alarming as it stretched through the rest of their journey. He caught her casting sidelong speculative glances in his direction, but even with several attempts at conversation, she kept her thoughts to herself.

It was late when they returned, and she gave him a kiss good-bye. It was passionless, just the kisses he'd been giving her. Patting his lapel, she said, "You will try to find my friends interesting tomorrow night?"

"I find some of them interesting."

But Marguerite turned away to leave him standing alone in the drive. He shook his head. His feet felt like lead as he climbed the stairs to his apartment. He needed to shut the craziness out for a little while.

Laurie thought about visiting Terry. He looked at his watch. It was already too late. Even for their normal stop at the pub on pay packet day.

"Payday." He groaned. *I forgot what day it is. I was supposed to call Rab. Fiona.* Even the thought of her flooded him with so much longing. He plopped on the bed, sitting with his head in his hands. His throat was clogged with emotion. *I missed my chance to hear her voice.*

I can't imagine how this day, my life, could get much darker. He was alone in a foreign country among people who would kill him if they knew his plans. He lay back on top of his bed, wanting to shut out the thoughts. As he drifted into the welcome oblivion of sleep, he heard a quiet whisper. *Not alone.*

Chapter Eighty-Seven

Rüdesheim am Rhein, Germany
June 1937

A Baptism

The comte and comtesse were radiant at the baptism of their new son Thomas. Everyone gathered in the small chapel on the estate grounds on Thursday morning to celebrate a mass in honor of the occasion. Etienne and Marie stood as godparents to the child. And no one was happier than Ana, Katrine, Deter and Gretchen. Baby Tony had found his forever home. God was good, and he would help them all to a safe place.

The ladies had been cooking for days to serve a lavish luncheon. Not for dignitaries, but for Isabelle's family disguised as servants. It was a very French celebration with tables set up around the gardens. The wine flowed, and the children ran in the grass and played games.

One small woman caught Ana's eye. She looked like royalty in her dress and bearing. The woman's face beamed with love. Ana guessed this must be a close family friend or relative.

Ana caught sight of Katrine strolling with a young man. When a hand reached out to touch Ana's arm, she turned, expecting to see Marie. Instead, the small regal lady looked up at her with bright blue intelligent eyes. A face that must have been beautiful in youth.

"Hello, dear, my name is Dolly."

Ana curtsied, because it seemed like the right thing to do with this woman. "My name is Ana, madam." The woman extended her hand, and Ana took it, wondering if she was expected to kiss it out of respect. Instead, she received a warm squeeze and a smile to match.

"I see several unfamiliar faces here since my last visit."

"I've only been working for la comtesse for a short time."

"And the children?"

Ana's face must have betrayed her alarm.

"My dear. You must hide your feelings better than that."

Her expression was still kindly, but Ana felt like running until the woman said, "It's all right. I'm a close friend of the count and la comtesse. We old families are all close. Most of us are related." She tapped her head with two elegant fingers. "We remember the old days. When honor and country and yes, even God, meant something."

Her eyes shone. "I think God has brought us together today, dear sister." She continued to hold Ana's hand as she turned and led the way to Isabelle.

The count was bouncing baby Thomas on his knee. A string of baby drool decorated his papa's trousers. La comtesse laughed at her husband's delight in his new son. She hesitated as she looked up at their approach. She stood and came to meet them. "Dolly?" She looked from her friend to Ana and back again.

"Isabelle, we need to talk. I'm sorry, dear, it cannot wait."

"But of course." La comtesse turned and whispered something in the count's ear.

"What? You think I cannot take care of my own son without

your help?" He sounded gruff, but his eyes twinkled. Ana thought the comte looked years younger as he played with his son.

Ana looked back at baby Tony. "I'm so happy for you, Isabelle."

"Could there be a happier day?" La comtesse glowed. As she passed Etienne, she said, "Etienne, could you join us for a few minutes?"

He looked concerned as he followed the women to the solar. With the doors closed, la comtesse gave her full attention to her friend. "Dolly?"

"My dear, if I am right, I have met someone looking for Sister Ana and her children."

Ana drew in a sharp breath. *So, Eric is still searching for us.*

She cast a quick glance at la comtesse. Isabelle appeared to study her friend, but she hadn't denied that Ana was a holy sister.

Dolly waited a minute before she continued. "I'm going to tell you about a young man I've promised to help." She spread her hands wide. "Then, if I am wrong, we can all go back to the party. But if I'm right, we can make plans to get them all to safety." Ana's pulse quickened. Could this be the help she'd been praying for?

All but Dolly sat. "The young man is Laurie MacKenzie—a Scot. An engineer just graduated from Edinburgh University. He went to school with Marguerite Voss. You remember, her mother was a Scot as well." She shook her head. "A beautiful woman, inside and out. If she could see what's become of her daughter, she would find no rest in Heaven." Dolly sighed. "But I digress.

"Laurie took a job offered him by Herr Voss at his firm in Hamburg. The girl tells everyone Laurie is her fiancé. I think that was his original plan, but before Laurie left Scotland, he fell in love, and it changed his life."

Ana wanted to interrupt but waited instead for the story to unfold.

Dolly continued, "A friend came to him after he'd decided not to take the job. This friend had a letter telling about the arrest of his cousins in Germany and how the children were missing—Deter and Gretchen."

Ana gasped. Dolly's sharp eyes caught the slip. She nodded with confidence. "His friend, a Jew, thought Laurie was going to Germany, you see. And he did, but for one reason only, to find those children. I'm afraid Germany was not at all what our young man expected."

La comtesse said, "A dangerous thing to ask of a friend, is it not? Tell us how you know all this."

Dolly launched into a description of the hunting weekend. They all sat transfixed.

When Dolly finished, she spread her hands wide. "You tell me. Have I not helped find places for your rescued ones to go? Am I still your trusted friend?"

La comtesse rose and crossed the room, folding Dolly in a warm hug. "You are my cherished friend."

She cast a glance at Ana and Etienne. They met her direct gaze with a slight nod. "Now we will tell you what we know."

Chapter Eighty-Eight

Hamburg, Germany

June 1937

The Opera

Laurie shook his head in disbelief. *On Saturday nights, I've always been a pub kind of guy, but I'll have to admit this opera is amazing. Not something I'd ever expected to say.* The rich baritone of Bockelmann held him spellbound. He leaned over to Marguerite. "These seats must have cost a pretty penny."

He noticed her stiffen and clench her jaw. *There was a time not so long ago when you laughed off our differences. Now I can't do anything right. I think you'll be glad to see me go.*

Even though his thoughts were tinged with regret, he had to admit it was for the best. He'd never wanted to hurt her, but Marguerite's sudden coolness made him wonder. *What's behind your change toward me?*

Once again, she raised her opera glasses, but this time she wasn't looking at the stage. Instead, she surveyed the audience.

He noticed her stop at Herr Eric Braun. She lowered her glasses and nodded. Braun acknowledged her with a charming nod of his own.

Laurie wanted to say something to warn her away. *I know it would be best if you're disappointed in me but not this. I don't want to drive you to this monster.* Instead, he only said, "A dangerous man."

"Nonsense. He's a soldier in the Reich." She looked over at Laurie. "He's someone you should cultivate as a friend. Herr Braun is climbing to the top." She glanced back at Eric and smiled seductively.

Sarcasm dripped from every word as Laurie said, "The man hates me. Can't think why. After all, it was an accident. I'm an excellent shot, but there was too much fog to see anything."

He hoped his lopsided grin conveyed the pleasure he took in winging the SS officer. She rolled her eyes in response.

It was Laurie's turn to consider the audience. The furs and glitter were everywhere. Marguerite looked beautiful tonight, but so did everyone else in the audience.

As he looked around the music hall, he locked eyes with his new friend Dolly. He was surprised he hadn't noticed her before since she was sitting in a box across from them on the same level. She looked at Marguerite and then at the door to her box. Laurie was sure she meant for him to excuse himself.

He leaned over to whisper in Marguerite's ear, "Excuse me, I need to use the convenience." She scowled but said nothing.

Laurie slipped into the hall and made his way to the far side of the theater. Dolly hurried toward him, her hand stretched out.

"Mein Gott. I thought you'd never see me. I've been staring at you through the whole first act." She took his arm when he reached her. "This way."

Dolly led him down the stairs to the intermission lobby. To a waiter she called out, "Two champagnes, please." She spoke under her breath to him. "If we're drinking, they'll think we're bored with the music." Her eyes twinkled. "I wouldn't have taken you for the opera type, but you were transfixed. Like it, did you?"

"Yes, it's different from what I expected."

She laughed louder than necessary. In a whisper, she added, "No matter what I say laugh now and, whatever you do, don't show any surprise."

He chuckled in response. "Madam, you amaze me."

"Good. You're getting the hang of this. I found your children."

He was stunned. Relief flooded his body. His smile cracked his face in half. And when he laughed, he felt pure joy and something else. Thankfulness.

"I've a friend near Rüdesheim am Rhein. She invited me to her new son's baptism on Thursday. The thing is, he's not—"

"He wouldn't be Romani, would he?"

"Why yes? But how do you know this?"

"I took Marguerite on that little outing you suggested. Father Ignatius told me about a nun traveling with a Gypsy baby, a Chinese teenage girl, and two children—Gretchen and Deter."

She took his hand in hers and squeezed it, her eyes shining with delight. "I've seen them, all of them. They're being cared for by my friend near Rüdesheim am Rhein. In fact, her new son looks very much like a Gypsy baby. But we need to get the others to safety as soon as possible."

He wanted to hug her right there in the middle of all these people but, knowing that would only draw attention to them, settled for kissing her hand. "Thank you, my friend. Thank you."

Dolly patted his shoulder. "Had enough of the lovely Marguerite, have you?"

"I'm positive Marguerite suspects I'm up to something. Our relationship has cooled." The noise level in the hall rose. The intermission must have begun.

"How soon can you get them out?" Dolly asked.

"It will take at least two weeks to arrange things. Where is this town?" He struggled with the pronunciation. "Rüdesheim am Rhein?"

"Good news. It's on the Rhine. You said your grandfather has a fishing boat. He should be able to get all the way to the village."

Laurie looked toward the swell of noise. People were moving down the staircase into the atrium. At the top of the stairs, looking down at them, was Marguerite, her one brow arched with speculation. She said something to someone out of Laurie's line of vision. Eric Braun stepped up to the banister and looked down at them. Laurie did a brief salute but couldn't wipe the cheeky smile off his face.

Eric offered his arm to Marguerite, and they moved down the staircase.

Dolly said under her breath, "You be careful of that man."

"Oh, I am. I am." Laurie fixed his smile on his fiancée as they approached. "There you are, beautiful. Look who I found."

Eric clicked his heels in the standard Nazi pretentious bow. "Madam, so good to see you again."

Dolly inclined her head in acknowledgement. "Herr Braun and Fraulein Voss. I'm afraid I took advantage of your Herr MacKenzie. I'm shaky on the stairs, and I asked for his help to get down." She patted Laurie's arm again and ignored the dagger looks from Marguerite.

"Quite all right. He's more the nightclub type, I'm afraid," Marguerite countered. A definite slight intended.

"Not at all. I may be the newest fan of the opera. I quite enjoyed the first act." Feeling protective, Laurie moved to stand between Marguerite and Eric Braun. They chatted until the bell was rung, announcing the start of the second act.

Dolly asked, "Oh, Herr Braun, would you be kind enough to help a lady up the stairs? I'm afraid I've taken too much advantage of Herr MacKenzie."

She looked up at Eric with a sweet expression on her lovely face. He clicked his heels and offered her an arm.

Laurie turned to Marguerite with his own arm extended. She rolled her eyes, looked around, and smiled through gritted teeth. She said loudly enough for his ears only, "Really, Laurie. I asked you to stay away from that old dinosaur."

"Oh, baby, you can't ask me to say no when a lady needs help down the stairs." He knew his smile was no less forced than hers but no matter. His new acting career was about to end.

Laurie's mind wandered through the rest of the opera. He needed to talk to Rab. Thank God for his grandfather. Fiona's soft brown eyes came to mind. The way she looked at him. Which led to her mouth and the promise of a kiss. He wondered if they could be married as soon as he got back.

If this trip has taught me anything, it's that life's too precious and perilous to wait for happiness.

"Laurie, are you even listening to me?" Marguerite broke into his thoughts.

"Sorry, what did you say? I was puzzling over a problem," he lied.

"You're all about work."

And I used to think you were so cute when you made that pouty face.

He was about to say something when he noticed Eric across the hall. The man wasn't watching the opera. His eyes were on Marguerite. Laurie couldn't read his expression. Speculation. It sent a shiver up his spine.

He reached over and put a protective arm around her. Leaning close to her face, he said, "I wasn't thinking about work. I was thinking about you."

Her father's auto and driver were waiting for them as they exited the opera house. Laurie helped Marguerite into the back seat and slid in beside her. She looked at him with a serious expression.

"Where's the old Laurie?"

"I'm right here, baby."

"No, not really. You were such a rogue at school, so attentive, not so serious working all the time." She turned her attention to the window.

Guilty. He had changed. How could he answer her? He could feel the change in her as well.

He snapped back, "You've changed, too."

"I have not." She rose to his challenge. Her words spit at him.

He was riding the wave of frustration. "You only care about getting your way or what dress you're going to wear or who's watching you." His words sounded every bit the accusation he intended.

She snapped, "Well, if you acted like you cared about me, maybe I wouldn't find interest elsewhere."

The truth stung, but his mouth was disengaged from his brain as he said, "You mean Eric?" His tone changed to a stern warning. "He's a nasty character. You're going to get in over your head if you think you can control him with your pouts and looks."

She was silent the rest of the trip, a statue looking out the window. He wanted to say something, but he couldn't call back his words. Truth had a way of sticking to people. Like her words stuck with him now.

She's right. I'm not the same guy I was in school. It's hard to even remember what that guy was like. All the old Laurie cared about was how to get ahead or pay off a gambling debt.

Finally, he whispered, "You mean I'm pushing you into all these parties and the whole Nazi doctrine?"

She shot him a quick look. "Don't be silly." Bitterness laced every word. "This is who I've always been. You just didn't see me. All you saw was my father's job."

Truth was out there, and it stuck once again to him. *What now?*

He reached across the seat to take her hand. His voice was low and clogged with regret. "It's not what we thought, is it?"

Her answer was in the small squeeze she gave his hand. "No. No, it's not." He could feel her disappointment.

"What do you want me to do?" he asked, fearing what she'd say next.

"Oh, Laurie, I don't know." She looked into his eyes, and for a moment, he remembered loving her. But it was just a flicker of light. Fiona was the sun at noontime.

When they pulled to a stop in front of her house, the driver opened her door, and she left without another word.

Chapter Eighty-Nine

House on Latimer Square
Edinburgh
June 1937

Telling Rab

Fiona woke, still dressed, her bed undisturbed. Da called that kind of rest the sleep of the dead, but she felt anything but rested. With morning came light. Things looked better in the light of day. But not this day. She was still shaken by her late-night discovery and something else too. Guilt plagued her.

I never intended to keep Alec's secret. I lied. That was wrong. But her greatest fear came because she knew it was wrong to keep the secret from Rab. *It's the same as saying I don't trust him.*

An inner voice argued back. *It never seemed like the right time.* The argument continued. *No, you goose. You rode all the way to Peterhead and back. There were plenty of right times. You just didn't want a long discussion about all this unpleasantness. I've missed my parents so much, but since meeting Rab and Laurie, I haven't felt so alone. No matter how you tell him, he's going to be hurt by your lack of trust.*

Tam followed her through morning chores. By mid-morning, she realized there was no point in putting it off. *I need to tell Rab, and I need help. Someone was brazen enough to sit by my fire and read the log. Who knows what they might do next?* She grabbed her coat and headed for the front door.

She peered outside. Leaves and small branches littered the empty square. The cobblestones were still wet from an overnight rain, and the wind had sharpened. Guilt washed over her once again. She almost closed the door, wanting to retreat into the safety of her own house. *No, it's not safe here anymore, is it? Oh Lord, have I ruined a wonderful relationship before it's started?*

Tam tried to push past her, but she said, "No, laddie, this is something I must do myself." She bent to scratch behind his ear. "But you stay and keep the scoundrels from coming in, right?" Tam backed up and sat with a humph as Fiona slipped out the door. She secured it with the key, comforted when the bolt slid into place.

The Frazers were gone. She'd watched them leave this morning. Her eyes scanned the empty square. No sign of Mr. Frazer's hired man. She straightened her back and set her course for Rab's front door, rapping twice. She could hear his footfall.

"Och, Fiona, I was just thinking about ye."

This man cares about me. She hesitated, knowing she was going to disappoint him.

He broke the silence. "Come in, lass, come." He motioned her in but turned to answer the whistle of a teakettle. "We'll have tea." It wasn't a question, more like a mid-morning ritual.

She followed him to the kitchen. He was already busy putting out the cups and brewing a pot of rich, dark tea. She sat down and thought, *What a comforting smell.*

He put a cozy on the pot and brought it to the table. "Would ye like some biscuits…" His voice trailed off. "What is it, luv? Has there been another intruder?"

His worry for her safety brought tears to Fiona's eyes. She bit her lip, but it was no good. She was crying and couldn't stop. Rab was out of his chair and at her side, kneeling on the kitchen floor, drawing her into a loving embrace.

"No, Rab." She took a breath. "No new visits."

"Och, lassie, I'm sure Laurie's all right."

Fiona held up a hand to stop him. "No, it's that I didn't mean to keep this from you." He drew back to look at her. Another breath and she said, "It's only—he asked me not to say anything. I'd only make matters worse." The guilt overwhelmed her again, and she blurted out, "I knew it was wrong. Da always said a secret from someone you love is the same as a betrayal."

Rab reached for his chair and slid it over to hers. He sat and, taking her hand in his, looked into her eyes. She felt like he could see straight into her soul. She couldn't tear her eyes away or hide from his examination. *Da said the eyes are a window to the soul. Rab's eyes say he's safe. They say he loves me.* The corners of her mouth relaxed into a hint of a smile. She took another deep breath.

"Alec came to see me before we left." She steadied herself. "He said his father was having me watched. The watcher's the one getting into the house. He means to find the war chest."

Rab let out his breath.

"He says the only way I'll be safe is for me to find it first."

"An Alec told ye that we didn't like him. We would tell you not to trust him."

She nodded as a tear slid down her cheek.

"An Alec's right about one thing. I dinna trust the lad. There's somethin' not right about him. I could see it from the time his mother died. Ye ken we lost Laurie's parents around the same time."

Rab shook his head at the memories. "Mind, I think the poor woman died years before. It was never a happy household. And yon laddie was so lost without his mam."

He stared past her, and Fiona realized how hard it was for him to talk about the influenza epidemic.

"It left its mark on all of us. Laurie was never the same, but Alec—" Rab paused. "Well, in his da's eyes Alec always fell short, couldn't please him." The silence stretched out. "What do you think? Shall we hunt for the chest?"

Her reaction was immediate. "No. I'll honor the captain's wishes. That chest won't be found until it can take care of the helpless. I know that's what Wee Geordie wanted."

"There's my girl." Rab grinned.

Fiona's arms flew around his neck. She squeezed him tight. "Thank you, Rab. Thank you for understanding."

It was a watery smile she gave him, but the weight of worry lifted. "What should I do?"

"Aye, well, first off you and yer wee laddie are moving in wi me." She protested, but he stopped her. "Nay then, it's for the best. I will na worry about you if yer here. And you said no one's going to find the chest until Wee Geordie wants it found."

She nodded.

"Let's go collect everything you need." They rose without even a sip of their tea. Rab reached over to clasp her hand. "And Fiona, yer not to think yer ever alone. I'm yer friend, and I already feel as though I'm yer grandda as well."

Chapter Ninety

Hamburg, Germany
June 1937

A Friend to Stand with Me

Laurie was relieved to get back to work, but come Monday morning, additional problems replaced the success of last week. It was past noon when he finally talked to Terry in private. They shared a cigarette out on the pier.

Terry blew out the smoke with a sigh. "It's been a bugger of a day so far." If Terry was a picture of exhaustion, his eyes were as sharp as ever. "So, what's up? And don't bother saying it's nothing."

Laurie shook his head. "Remind me never to play cards with you." He looked around and whispered, "We found the children."

Terry's response was immediate. "Grand." He clapped Laurie on the back. "They're all right then? 'Cause I have to say, me boyo, I didn't really think they were still alive. Jews are disappearing daily."

"Aye, well, we still have to get them out, so I'm going to need help to call my grandfather again."

Terry was nodding. Laurie added, "That's the good news. Here's the bad news." He shoved his hands in his pockets and gazed at the harbor. "Marguerite's had it with me. She's really pissed off all the time. Acts like she's suspicious." He described his weekend.

"First off, laddie, you are hiding something from her. She may know something's up. The ladies have a sixth sense about that sort of thing. Or she might feel put out a bit, you know. It doesn't mean she thinks you're a spy or something. Hey, with all the long hours we put in, maybe she's worried you've found a lassie in town."

Laurie scrubbed a hand over his face. "Well, whatever's causing it, I get the impression she's about to send me packing." He grimaced. "Actually, it's a relief her feelings have cooled. I didn't set out to hurt her even though I always intended to use her."

He looked down at the old boards of the pier. "At any rate, I don't know how much time I have. Can you help me call Rab tonight?"

"No worries, we'll go for a pint after work." Terry's grin was impish. "With any luck, the old man will have us working late on this additional problem and give us the perfect excuse."

Laurie noticed a man dressed in a black suit standing in a doorway. "Is it me, or does that seem odd to you?" He motioned with his thumb toward the building.

Terry looked past Laurie. "That's the welding shop. Not the place you'd wear a suit to work. I don't remember seeing that bloke before."

Something felt off. Laurie could see the same uneasiness in his friend's eyes. Terry threw his cigarette in the water, and they turned to go back to work.

At day's end, the whistle blew. Shift change began. The engineers office emptied, leaving Terry and Laurie still at work poring over plans. Herr Voss called out to them, "Don't worry about that. You've both done well today. Go home to your family, Mulligan. Come along, MacKenzie."

"Ah, sir, if we might stay awhile, we've almost figured out this problem."

They looked up at their employer. The older man stuffed his hat on his head.

"My daughter will have my hide if I keep you here much longer." He chuckled. "Stay if you like, but you remember to tell her it was your idea." Herr Voss shook his head. "To think my best workers aren't even German."

They'd given Herr Voss the truth. He and Terry had figured out this latest problem, and they'd almost come up with a way to put some major bugs in the system. Enough to make it harder for German missiles to hit European targets. They took advantage of the empty offices to lay their plans.

"First things first. Find out from Rab how long it takes a fishing boat to cross over to Germany and make its way down the Rhine."

Terry had moved to look out the window. He stood relaxed, but then he straightened and moved to one side. His attention focused on the shadows across the street.

Laurie asked, "Will you be able to leave, say, in a week or two at the most?" The lack of an answer made him turn from the wall calendar. "Terry?" He came to stand next to his friend, but Terry blocked him from the window.

"The bloke we saw in the shipyard." Terry's voice was not much more than a whisper.

"In case you haven't noticed, they're all lads in the shipyard."

"No, idiot. The bloke in the black suit standing havin' a smoke in the doorway."

"Aye, I remember." Laurie peered past Terry's shoulder. A

match flared, lighting the features of the man in the black suit. "I'll be damned. It's the same guy."

Alarms went off in Laurie's head. If he had to guess, he'd say Eric Braun held grudges and was having him watched.

"Maybe your girlfriend is on to you after all."

"No, I don't think she'd turn me in to the police." Laurie puffed his cheeks out. "There's only one person I've pissed off enough to have me watched." He rubbed a hand over his face. "Now how will I call Rab?"

Terry put his hand on Laurie's shoulder. "First, we'll have a drink or three. How are you fixed for change?" Laurie shrugged.

Terry stuffed his hat on his head. "No worries, I've got a pocket full." He handed Laurie a fistful of coins. "I save them for Richard. He likes his da to pull a coin from his ear. I love to see his face. Every time, it's like the first time I showed him the trick."

As they headed out the door and down the stairs, Terry explained his plan. "We're celebrating, right?"

Laurie thought he knew where this was going.

Terry continued. "We'll have a few pints, and I'll be a bit of a distraction. It's a good thing you have an Irishman for a friend. If there's one thing everyone believes about an Irishman, it's his love for the drink."

"That's not the Irish—a Scot could drink yon Mick under the table any day."

By the time they hit the street, they both appeared to be in their cuffs. Better to throw the watchers off. A drunk wasn't likely to be up to mischief. They started an argument about which country produced the best whiskey.

Monday night and the beer hall wasn't crowded, but there were enough workers to make it comfortable. They sat at a table closest to the toilets and the door to the alley. Laurie called for two pints, and they kept up their lively discussion about Irish whiskey as opposed to its Scottish counterpoint. The man in the black suit came in and took a seat not too far away.

Terry leaned in to his friend. "SS, wouldn't you say?" Laurie nodded his reply, then Terry restarted the friendly argument. "Well, there's Jameson's label for one."

"Aye, I'll give ye that, but if you've no tasted Talisker's single malt, you've no tasted guid Scotch." Laurie elbowed Terry, who glanced up as the pub door opened. Another man in a dark suit entered and sat with their watcher. "Am I seeing double, or are there two blokes in dark suits?"

"It's their uniform, or do they just all go to the same tailor? What say we kick this up a notch?" Terry said in a loud voice, "Can we get another couple of pints?" He corrected himself. "Bitte."

A pretty barmaid delivered their drinks with a saucy smile in Laurie's direction, looking back over her shoulder as she moved away. They downed their drinks, telling jokes and laughing while watching the blokes watch them. After an hour, the two suits looked bored and disgusted.

Terry leaned in close. "I think we could make our move anytime. I'll get the next round." He rose, hitched up his trousers, and staggered to the bar. On his return trip, he spilled most of Laurie's beer on the table. Laurie stood to brush off his pants. His friend slurred, "Sorry, mate."

"And isn't it just like a Mick to spill his drink when a Scot would nay waste a drop?" Laurie laughed and headed down the hall toward the water closet. With a glance over his shoulder to make sure the Black Suits weren't following, he was out the back door. In no time at all, he held his breath while listening to the scratchy connection as the operator rang Rab's number.

"Hello?" Rab's voice sounded so clear, as if all static had left the line.

"Rab? Rab? It's me, Laurie." Tears welled in Laurie's eyes.

"Och, it's Laurie," he heard his grandfather call out.

"Rab, I've found them. I've found the children. Do you hear me?"

"He's found them," Rab repeated. "Och, that's grand, son. Smashing." With some noise in the background, he thought he was losing the connection until he heard Fiona's voice.

"Laurie?"

"Fiona, my God, you have no idea how much I've missed you." His voice caught.

"Not half so much as I've missed you." She was crying; he could tell.

In his mind's eye, he could see her standing there—her long black hair and beautiful brown eyes. "I want to be there with you. I want to hold you in my arms and never let you go." Peace washed over him. *This is right. She's right.*

"That's all I want too. I feel so terrible I pushed you into going there." A little sob punctuated her words.

"No, luv. It was the right thing to do, and I'm bringing out some others. I'll explain later, but Fiona, it's bad here. If I can't get them out, they might all die."

He had to pull himself back to business. He only had so long before one of his watchers came looking for him.

"I love you. God, how I love you. You were right. He helped me. I don't know why, but God has been helping me. But I have to talk to Rab. I haven't much time, and we need to arrange for the Elspeth to come get us."

"Rab, he needs to talk to you. Laurie, I love you with all my heart. Come home to me soon."

Before he could answer, Rab was on the line. "Aye, I'm here, laddie." His voice sounded husky.

"Rab, there are more coming out than just two children. I have an Irish friend, his wife and wee son, and there's a Chinese girl, a baby and a nun."

He explained about the sister bringing the children from a parish in Bavaria. "I realize it's a lot to take in, but I can't leave

464

them. If I'm going to make it out, I have to bring them with me." He closed his eyes and took a deep breath. "Rab, it's bad here—dark, so dark."

By the time he returned to the beer hall, it was all arranged. The Elspeth would take a little more than two days to make her way from Peterhead down the coast to Leith. Then another few days past England and another two or three days across the Channel, plus time to stop and pick up Terry and his family at his sister-in-law's home in Düsseldorf before motoring further down the Rhine to get Laurie.

Laurie slipped in the back door through to the men's room in time to see Terry stumble into a pretty blond barmaid, spilling her tray onto the floor. Laurie crossed the room to help his friend up. He wanted to laugh at Terry's performance. *He's having too much fun playing tipsy.*

"Come on, my friend. Let's go home." Laurie looked around to see the watchers still in place. *Thank you, God, if you could just keep helping me 'til I get everyone to safety and see my girl again.* But to Terry he said, "We'll catch a taxi."

Chapter Ninety-One

Edinburgh
June 1937

The Last Straw

Aside from being unable to catch Fiona at home, the week had gone well for Alec. His cases were going splendidly, and his father was in an uncommonly good mood. Alec was crossing the outer office to hand over some documents for re-typing when his father and a dapper-looking gent of about forty stepped into the room. They both had the satisfied look of two men who had concluded a lucrative business deal. Alec thought, *Nice to see the old man without a scowl on his face.*

Thomas Frazer cleared his throat and said, "Attention everyone."

The room quieted. Alec turned to look at his father. Something was afoot.

"I want to take this opportunity to introduce my new partner." Everyone smiled and a small applause followed. His father held up his hand to still the room. "This is Sir Michael Penbrook the third. He will join us starting next week as my full partner, taking over the firm when I retire." Heads swung round to Alec.

"Oh, Alec, I'm going to need you to move to the smaller office. Can't have a full partner without a proper office." More applause as the two men shook hands.

Why, Father, why? Alec's world seemed to close in on him and tilt sideways. He felt as if his father had slapped him in the face. Heat rose in his cheeks.

That's it. Father's cut me off. He never considered me as more than an errand boy, an underling, another employee.

He turned on his heel, papers still in his hand, and walked back to his office. *Correction, my temporary office. I'm about to settle in the storage room. Will the boxes be staying, or will the old duffer ask me to move them to the attic? Well, you devil, I won't do it.*

Alec left the papers on his desk and picked up his hat and overcoat and walked out of the office. Silent stares followed him, but he didn't care. *This is bloody humiliating. I'm done trying to please the old Clootie. You'll regret this, old man.*

Alec headed down the stairs and out onto the busy street. He walked. People pushed past him, but his legs carried him on. He didn't know where he was, didn't care. The breeze whipped his coat around him and threatened to send his fedora flying. He pulled his hat down and lowered his head into the wind.

By mid-afternoon, he stood at the entrance to Latimer Square looking at the three houses: his father's house, well kept, looking as opulent as it must have done two hundred years ago; Laurie's house, showing signs of much-needed repairs but still a fine old home. But the house at the end, that was another matter.

It looks neglected, abandoned. Yes, it looks abandoned. He marched up to the front door and knocked. *Nothing. Where the hell is Fiona?*

Alec waited and turned to look at the square. *In all the time I've been trying to catch Fiona at home, I've never once heard her blasted dog bark.* He scowled. *I wonder.*

Alec marched down the square to Laurie's house. As he rapped on the front door, a fierce barking came from the other side of the door. When the dog quieted, the door opened, and Fiona stood before him.

"Oh, Alec. I'm sorry. Rab's gone. But you're welcome to come in if you'd like." She looked up into his face, concern flitting across her features. "Is everything all right?"

"Where have you been?" he snapped. "I've been looking for you for days."

She flushed. "Rab asked me to move in with him," she stammered. "Alec, someone's been in my house." The color in her cheeks rose. "I had to tell Rab about your father's man."

Alec clamped his mouth shut. He was sure he'd scream at her if he said anything. *Just breathe, old boy.* It was a full minute before he could calm his features. "I wish you hadn't done that. I suppose he's going to help you hunt for the war chest." He remembered the missing page in the log. *Unless you already know where it is.*

"No, Alec. I'm not looking for it, and neither is Rab." There was something in her eyes. She was direct, even forceful.

He drew his breath in. "You've already found the chest?"

"No. I'm not looking, and I have no idea where it is." Her voice softened. "It's not meant to be found until there's a need. The captain said so in his log."

Alec threw his hands in the air and exploded. "Rubbish. How can an eighteenth-century sea captain decide who is worthy of his treasure?" He rolled his eyes. "Come on, you're a smart girl. Don't tell me you believe in fairy tales and ghost stories." He stopped short, thinking of the specter of the captain chasing him down the upstairs hall. *But I'm bloody well not letting a ghost ruin my future.*

He calmed his voice and adopted a pleasant expression. "I can help you find this. Let me help you as your good friend."

A low rumble erupted from her dog, who stood at her feet.

Alec glanced down into fierce little eyes. The beast's fang teeth were exposed. Alec backed up and almost fell off the step.

"I've appreciated your friendship, but I'm not looking for the chest."

"Come on, Fiona. I'm only thinking of your safety."

"Alec, my decision is firm. I won't go on a treasure hunt." She looked defiant, angry. "And when you see your father, tell him to keep his man out of my house or I'll call the constable."

That was the last thing he expected from her. He let out a growl of frustration. Her dog started forward, but she stopped him with her leg. Alec could see he'd frightened her.

"I told you Rab doesn't like us. Did he put this into your empty little head?" He realized he'd crossed the line and tried to apologize. But she stepped back and swung the door closed.

Alec roared at the closed door. "You can't treat me like this. I've been your friend."

He hit the doorframe with his fist hard enough to dent the wood, warranting some rather loud barking from the other side of the door. The bolt slid into place.

She actually locked the door on me. That's the last straw.

Chapter Ninety-Two

Hamburg, Germany
June 1937

An Unexpected Invitation

Laurie dropped Terry at his flat and then spared no expense in taking the taxi all the way back to the Voss residence. The front door swung open as the taxi pulled up. Marguerite stood on her steps, staring down her perfect nose. She watched him pay the driver with her arms folded and her expression grim.

"Laurie, we're having our dinner late." She walked toward him and then halted a few feet away. "Ew, you smell like a brewery," she said, her voice accusatory. "You've been out with your Irish friend, haven't you?"

"It smells worse than it is. I had a pint of beer spilled on me by accident." Her father came to the door. "We managed that problem, sir."

"Well, I had no doubt. You work well together. Come in, lad. Cook will have something to say if we keep dinner any later."

"I can't, sir. I have to change. Someone spilled a pint of beer on me."

Herr Voss laughed. "We can stand the smell of good German beer any day, Ja, Marguerite?" He motioned Laurie through the front door, patting his back with congratulations. At the table, Herr Voss went on extolling Laurie's achievements while Marguerite scowled.

During coffee, Voss pulled out an embossed envelope. He handed it to Marguerite. "Thought you might want to see this."

She tore open the seal and scanned the contents. "Another dinner party," she said, tossing it to Laurie.

He picked up the card, stumbling through the pronunciation. "It's from Phillip Graf von Kessler."

Herr Voss explained. "The comte and comtesse are hosting a party at the end of the month."

Laurie felt a jolt of panic. *Just about the time I'd planned on getting the children out.*

Marguerite interrupted his thoughts. "Don't worry, Laurie. No hunting this time." She was taunting him. There was a nasty undertone to her words. "Perhaps Laurie would rather stay home, Papa. I don't think he likes our dinner parties."

Laurie's mind raced over possibilities. *I'm not sure if this is good or bad news.* He looked at his beautiful Marguerite. She met his gaze with defiant eyes. *Is she trying to provoke me into an argument? How much does she know?*

Herr Voss looked at his daughter, frustration lacing his words. "Nonsense. Rüdesheim am Rhein is ancient and beautiful—some of the best wine growing country in Germany."

Laurie's heart skipped a beat. *This couldn't be the same place the children were hiding. Or is this part of Dolly's plan?*

Her father was saying, "It's just good business. We'll all go and that's that. Marguerite, make sure you respond with the three of us attending."

Laurie stood. "Well, thank you. I think I will retire early so I'm fresh for tomorrow." He didn't look back as he left the dining room.

As he walked up the stairs leading to his apartment, he decided he would send Terry to see Dolly. With watchers on his tail, he couldn't risk a visit himself, but he needed some advice.

If it's not part of Dolly's plan, postponing the Elspeth might be the safest course of action, all things considered.

Chapter Ninety-Three

Hamburg, Germany

June 1937

Even Your Friends Are in Danger

Terry didn't come to work Tuesday morning. Laurie chuckled at the thought. *Our next argument will be who can have a pint or three without a bloody hangover.*

After work, he went to check on him. The door to the Mulligan apartment stood ajar. Still, he rapped on it and called out. "Terry? Anyone home?"

Pushing it further open, Laurie moved into the entry hall. From his vantage point, he could see someone had ransacked the apartment.

"Terry? Lydia?"

He had to be careful where he stepped. The floor was littered with their possessions. Someone had slashed the sofa, and it looked like they'd taken a club to their radio. *My God. What happened?*

In the kitchen, drawers were pulled out, their contents strewn over the floor. Laurie jumped back when he stepped on one of Richard's toys and it made a loud squeal. The sound echoed in the quiet apartment. *It feels deserted.*

"Why, God, why?" he whispered in a desperate plea. *It's because of me, isn't it?* He could barely breathe as he moved through Terry's home.

The china hutch lay across the dining room table, dishes left shattered on the floor. Laurie's heart was beating so fast he thought it would burst from his chest as he neared little Richard's room. Even toys lay in pieces across the floor.

Remember what Father Ignatius said. Eric flew into a rage and burned the farmer's house. Oh God. It appeared every room had suffered destruction at the hands of ... Who? Braun? A thought struck him. *No blood.*

A shred of hope, not much to hold on to. They were gone. Perhaps taken. Laurie retraced his steps back to the third-floor passageway.

Across the hall, a door unlatched and swung wide open. Terry stood there, still in his rumpled clothes from last evening. His eyes were red and puffy. His hair was uncombed. He put a finger to his lips before Laurie could react and pulled him into the strange apartment. He took a last look in the hallway and closed the door with exaggerated stealth.

Laurie threw his arms around his friend, relief flooding him. "What happened? Where are Lydia and Richard?"

"My neighbor said they came while we were at the pub." Terry's face broke. His eyes screwed shut, but the tears ran down his cheeks as he shook his head. "I don't know where they are."

Deep worry lines etched his boyish face. "I went to the police station, but they wouldn't say anything. They wouldn't even come see the vandalism in our apartment."

He rubbed the stubble on his chin, looking beyond Laurie. His eyes glazed. "Has to be the SS." He looked back at Laurie. "God, she's eight months pregnant. And Richard must be scared to death." He sniffed and wiped his face with his sleeve.

"I'm so sorry, Terry. This must be because of me."

Laurie was at a loss for words. *What kind of place is this? Even my friends are in danger. I haven't even done anything yet.* "You have to stay away from me."

Terry was quick to respond. "Not on your life. I'm getting my family out of here. We're coming with you no matter what."

"I'll talk to Dolly and see if she can find out anything about Lydia and Richard." Laurie looked around. "Whose apartment is this? Are you safe here for the time being?"

"Frau Dortchmyer. She's a good egg, a sweet grandmotherly type. She let me sleep on the couch. Said she would ask around, but I'm afraid there isn't anyone to ask."

"I'll come by tomorrow. We'll see what Dolly can find out."

They stepped into the hall and were greeted by a squeal. "Da!" Richard launched himself at his father, hugging him and planting kisses all over his face. Lydia was coming up the stairs. She looked so weary, her face pale and strained. Terry opened his arms, and she crossed the hall into his embrace.

For a minute, there was only silence as the little family held each other. A sob broke from Lydia. She held her husband and buried her face in his shirt. Laurie didn't want to intrude. Still, the threat from prying eyes was a genuine possibility. He motioned them back into the neighbor's apartment.

They sat on the couch, Lydia crying. Richard's arms stayed wrapped around his father's neck. Finally, she looked up. "They were asking me questions about you, Herr MacKenzie." She shook her head. "I said nothing. Not one word except you were a co-worker and had come to dinner once."

Little Richard's head popped up. "They were nice, Da. They said I could go to Hitler Youth and wear a uniform and everything." He held his father's face in his hands. "Can I go, Da?"

Laurie shook his head. "Lydia, I'm so sorry."

She rose from the couch and crossed the room. "No, Herr MacKenzie. Get us out of here. This is no longer my home. They kept questioning me all night." She broke down crying again and turned back to her husband. She looked down, color coming back to her cheeks. "They wouldn't even let me use the toilet."

Laurie offered, "Let me help set your place back in some order."

"No, I'm going to take Lydia and Richard to her sister's in Düsseldorf until we meet your grandfather. Can you talk to Herr Voss? Just say my wife is having problems with her pregnancy. Tell him I need some time off to take care of her." Terry stood and grabbed Laurie's arm. "We'll be there as you planned. Don't let me down, MacKenzie."

"I won't, Terry. I won't."

Chapter Ninety-Four

Edinburgh
June 1937

Rab Makes Arrangements

Tam ran to the front door, barking with excitement, wiggling with pleasure. Fiona watched him with a sense of relief. That could only mean one thing. *Rab's back.* Early this morning, he had gone to make arrangements for the Elspeth's mooring and supplies.

Rab came through the door and bent first to scratch Tam behind the ears. "I will miss ye, laddie, when ye leave." He looked up at Fiona as she came in from the kitchen. "He's splendid company, isn't he?"

"That he is and a good watchdog as well." She bent to rough Tam's head, but her face was serious when she looked up at Rab. "I had a visitor just an hour ago. Our Tam was ready to take him on."

"Och, well, I can only guess that would be Alec."

Rab straightened and gave her a hug. Hugs were becoming a

regular occurrence. It always made her feel so secure and loved. Her own parents had been affectionate. Though many Highlanders had a gruff reserve about them, not Rab. She hugged him back and then stepped away. "Something was wrong. I could see it in his face. He wasn't himself."

"Did he ask ye again about the chest?"

"Yes, he did, and why I was staying with you."

"And I can tell he was none too happy you've told me about his father." Rab was peeling off his jacket and hanging it on the hat stand.

"He was frightening. When I closed the door, I heard him hit something with his fist." She still felt a bit shaken by Alec's behavior.

Rab patted her hand. "He'll not hurt ye. I've known him all his life, and if I had to say one thing about Alec, I'd say he's a coward."

"Still, this was a different Alec. He was another person." To change the subject, she asked, "Is everything ready then? Oh, and did you think to ring up Bernie?"

"Och, aye, I must do that straight away. I canna tell him an exact time, but at least I have the date."

"Rab, can I not come with you?" Her heart ached to see Laurie. Staying here at home was hard to bear.

He stopped on his way to the telephone. "I canna put you in danger and face my grandson. No, Fiona. I know it's hard to bide at home, but ye must, lassie."

She nodded, unable to speak as a wave of disappointment washed over her. Then she looked at him through watery eyes and said, "I know you're right."

Chapter Ninety-Five

Hamburg, Germany
June 1937

A Risk I Have to Take

It wasn't until lunchtime the next day that Laurie could leave work. He told anyone who would listen to him how his girl was mad at him, and he needed to find a gift to make it up. *Figure there isn't a man alive who wouldn't understand that necessity.* Once his excuse got around the office, he took a lot of razzing of the good-natured sort.

At noon, Laurie made a quick trip out the back way and through the shipyard. It was pouring rain. He suspected even his watchers would seek some kind of cover. Still, there was no point in being careless. Lives depended on caution.

By the time he circled the beer hall block a second time, he was sure no one had followed him. Laurie slipped into the phone booth and closed the door, feeling like a spy in a movie. *At least it's dry.* Laurie tapped his fingers as he listened. Dolly's number rang three or four times.

"Grafin Lehndorff Residenz."

Thankfully, Laurie recognized Rutgar's voice.

"May I speak with the countess?"

"One moment, bitte."

Soaked to the skin, Laurie shivered. Waiting gave him a moment to look up at the apartments across the street.

Someone could be watching him even now. He shook his head at the foolish thought. *Who would call to report a stranger using a pay phone in the middle of the day?*

"Hello?" The countess sounded concerned. "Is something wrong?"

"Dolly, I need to see you. Are you free for lunch?" He'd only used this phone at night, and now he stood exposed in broad daylight.

"Where are you?"

He realized she hadn't said his name. Laurie felt hairs on the back of his neck lift. So Dolly's being careful.

"I'm on Kinderstrassa and Mullerstrassa in a phone booth."

"I will send Rutgar for you. Stay there." The line went dead. Even after she hung up, he held the phone to his ear. *Better to look like I'm talking than just standing here.* It was a full twenty minutes before a car stopped at the curb and waited. *God, this had better be Rutgar.* He hurried through the rain to the passenger's door and yanked it open.

A warm smile welcomed him. "Hello, Herr MacKenzie."

"Hello, Rutgar. Thanks, mate, for coming." Laurie's head fell back against the seat. "Bailing me out of tough spots is getting to be a second job for you."

Rutgar smiled at his response. The servant meandered through the city streets, even doubling back on his route several times. Laurie was dry by the time they were back at Dolly's.

Her house looked like a small castle—old stone and leaded windows. Like Herr Voss' estate, the grounds were private and wooded. All the same, Rutgar pulled around the back of the house, and they entered through the kitchen.

Dolly was waiting for him in her breakfast room. Its floor-to-ceiling windows looked out on a small walled garden. Even on a stormy day like this one, Laurie marveled at how much light was in the room.

"It's beautiful," he said. Her smile was genuine and caring. "Thank you for seeing me."

She waved away his thanks. "I wanted to talk with you as well. Your call was most timely." A maid set a plate of poached salmon before him. Dolly took a bite of her fish and smiled in appreciation. "You go first. What was it you needed to talk to me about? I have a feeling our concerns will be similar."

"On Monday night, my friend Terrance helped me make a call to my grandfather. We planned for his fishing boat to pick up Sister Ana and the children at Rüdesheim am Rhein at the end of the month. When I got home, there was an invitation to a dinner party with Phillip Graf Von Kessler on the same weekend."

Dolly held up her hand to stop him. "Isabelle, the comtesse, must have arranged this. I see what she's thinking. An excellent idea."

Dolly ate her lunch and listened as Laurie described finding his friend's apartment trashed. "She's eight months pregnant, and his son is only four." Dolly shook her head. The words were pouring out of him. "How can we get the children out with a dinner party going on? To make matters worse—"

She leaned forward and finished his sentence. "You're being followed."

"How—"

"A friend came to warn me. He says Eric Braun suspects you. He's having you watched. That's why Rutgar took so long on his return trip. Right now, anyone who knows you is under suspicion." She leaned forward. "You're sure you can trust your friend?"

"Positive. He's Irish. His wife is German but terrified."

"They should find a safe place to stay until it's time to go. Even Herr Voss and Marguerite will be in danger if Eric finds out what you're up to."

He put a hand over his eyes. His thoughts were racing ahead, thinking of all the things that might go wrong. *This place is getting worse by the minute.*

"We have to postpone our escape," he said.

"My friend, this is the perfect opportunity. With everyone at the party, we at least know the wolves are all occupied. We have to find a way to end your engagement with lovely Marguerite in a very public manner. You don't want Herr Voss and his daughter to suffer from this subterfuge any more than I do."

"God, no. I've been so worried about the children, I haven't thought what this could mean for Marguerite's safety."

Chapter Ninety-Six

House on Latimer Square
Edinburgh
June 1937

Alec Hunts for the War Chest

For the longest time, Alec sat on his bed staring into space, replaying his father's announcement. He remembered the looks of sympathy from the other employees. *I can hear them all saying, "Well, fancy that, the old man's passed his own son over."* A vein on his temple pulsed, shooting pain through his head with every beat.

I should have seen this coming. Father's never pleased with me. He clenched his jaw. *I've wasted years trying to earn his respect, make him proud. All that time and for what? Face facts, you're never going to please that wretched old man. The hell of it is, he's always so sure he's in the right. I doubt he considered me for a minute.* Alec didn't notice as the light grew dim. He didn't rouse himself when the room was dark.

There was only one person who loved him. *And you deserted me,*

Mamma. I remember your red eyes and the silent dinners. Maybe he doesn't like me because I remind him of you. I'm sure you welcomed death. It was your escape, wasn't it?

Alec swallowed hard. *How could you leave me with him?* His inner voice sounded like a child's. He shook himself. *Now Fiona's deserted me just like you. But death is not the only way to escape Father.*

There have got to be other options. I could go to another firm. He debated. *Yes, then I am starting at the bottom in some firm on Market Street, living in a one-room flat in Tollcross. And all the time people would say Thomas Frazer was right to choose someone else to take over his firm. Alec doesn't have what it takes.*

No, I'm bloody well not giving up this life. He won't force me to start over. I'll prove him wrong, beat him at his own game. I want to flaunt his failure in his face, humiliate him in front of everyone. Providence placed that war chest within reach for a reason. The old man wouldn't spend time and money trying to find it if he wasn't sure of its presence.

"Well, if Thomas Frazer believes it's within his grasp, I have to find it before him."

Alec thought of Fiona's house key and perked up. *If she's staying at Rab's, I have the house to myself.* He'd been sore since his fall into the bathtub, so he was stiff when he stood to cross the room. *I know where the key was, so I'll have a look-see if it's back in place.*

His house was quiet. *Must be late.* His father's office was dark and deserted. Alec found the key in his father's desk drawer. The mantel clock struck one as he slipped out.

He rapped on Fiona's back door and waited. *Capital. No barking dog so no Fiona.* The key turned, but the door still wouldn't open. "Blast, forgot about the bolt," he whispered. "I'll have to go in through the front door." The street was empty, but Alec wasted no time slipping through the front.

Right, I need a strategy. He would start with the cellar and work his way to the attic. At one time, he'd thought he'd find the chest in the cellar. His excitement grew as he remembered the puzzle box Fiona had found under a loose flagstone.

The search proved fruitless. After prying up all the loose stones in the cellar floor, he'd found nothing and was left with the job of replacing everything back to its original state.

I don't want her to think someone's still looking. The last thing I need is for her to keep better watch over this house.

When he came up for a glass of water, early morning light filled the kitchen. Alec froze. *I've worked all night.* It was like having cold water splashed on him. He glanced at the kitchen clock. *It was almost time to get ready for work.*

The question is, am I going back there? He weighed the pros and cons. *What would good old Alec do?* He knew the answer. *I'd act as if nothing of import had happened. Good sport, that sort of thing.* Appearances had to be kept up. *That's all right. It will make victory all the juicier.* He looked around at the growing light. *I'll hurry.*

Ready for work, and on time at that, Alec followed his father to the auto. The old man didn't say a word about his absence. Alec fell into a pattern of work during the day and treasure hunting at night. It gave him hope to have a plan. *I can still beat him, but I need the treasure box.*

His nightly visits began at midnight. He'd knock on walls, search for false backs in cupboards. As the week wore on, his confidence flagged. Failure marked his nights. During the day, his father humiliated him, forcing him to move into the small office and move boxes of files. The sympathetic glances from everyone in the office only fueled the fire that drove him. But success was still out of his reach.

One night, he was working on the second floor. He stopped in front of the captain's painting. He willed himself to stand and stare the man down, eye to eye.

"I will find your bloody treasure. You can't stop me. You're dead."

Moonlight broke through the clouds, giving a brilliance to the painting. Alec watched transfixed as the captain's skin took on a luminescent glow. He stepped back. Then the light was gone as quickly as it came, and the painting was shrouded in shadow. As he turned to leave, he felt the hairs on the back of his neck prickle. *I must find the chest even if it means shaking it out of Fiona.*

Chapter Ninety-Seven

Rüdesheim am Rhein
Germany
June 1937

Getting Ready for Guests

Dolly received a call from Scotland in the middle of the month with the times for the escape of Terry's family and the pick-up of Laurie's group. Before going to the weekend at the Kessler estate, the plan was set.

On the last Thursday morning in June; Deter, Gretchen, and Katrine got ready to leave with old Francois. They would stay at the gamekeeper's cottage on the other side of the estate. The old man was a favorite among the children for the wonderful stories he told.

Katrine seemed to catch enough cues to realize this was a goodbye forever. It was with a somber face and red eyes that she said goodbye to her friends. Isabelle let her hold baby Tony one last time. She cuddled him close. Tears flowed down her cheeks, christening the baby's dark curls. "I love you, little one. Remember me. I'll never forget you.

Ana circled one arm around the teen and squeezed.

Katrine wiped away her tears and handed the baby back to Isabelle. "He's found his mother." She smiled at la comtesse. "I'm happy for all of you." Then she hurried to follow Deter and Gretchen.

It was Marie's idea that Ana stay behind and accompany her into the village. Etienne would take Ana to the hideaway later. "She can come shopping with us. All those narrow, winding streets can be confusing. Certainement you'll want to know where you're going in the middle of the night."

Ana nodded. "Good idea. Can I help with the shopping?" If all went well, she and the children would be there early Monday morning. It was the perfect time. Le comte was famous for his lavish parties. He would wine and dine his guests all weekend. By Sunday afternoon, they would be on their way back home.

Etienne brought them into town in his old pickup. Ana was in awe as she passed the vineyards. "I had no idea you grew wine here."

Marie said, "Mais bien sûr. We are French after all. The climate here is very good for the grapes. Even the Germans can appreciate fine wine."

Etienne added, "We also raise some of the best warmbloods in Europe. They are Oldenburgs. You know this breed of horse?"

Ana shook her head. "I've seen them grazing in the fields. They're handsome animals." As they entered the village, she exclaimed, "It's beautiful!"

"Oui, Rüdesheim is ancient, first or second century." Marie sighed. "I still prefer French villages. But the people here aren't so different. I am content. As long as I have my Etienne and my little ones." She asked, "Do you have the list for the fish market? A nice man, Herr Dolfmyer. His shop is on Rheinstrasse along the water."

Etienne parked the truck, and they all went off to their assigned errands. Marie pointed down Marktstrasse lane. "Walk down this street all the way to the end. Turn right and you're on the waterfront. You'll see his sign. It will take us a while. Shall we meet back here in twenty minutes?" Worry flitted across Marie's pretty face.

Ana gave her friend a warm smile, saying loud enough for anyone listening, "A little longer please, enough for a short walk. It's such a beautiful day."

As she turned toward the water, Ana tried to pay attention to everything, noting landmarks that would help guide her in the dark hours before dawn Monday morning. The lanes were narrow and the shops all half-timbered. Colorful clerks stood outside their doors, welcoming shoppers.

Ana realized, *I'm leaving Germany. Will I ever see her again?* That thought hung in her mind as she embraced the town with her eyes. *I love German villages—cobblestone streets, flowers in window boxes, and chubby-cheeked children playing. I'll miss you.*

Ahead of her, she could see the sun sparkling on the river. *I smell fresh bread. It's unmistakable. So, there's a bakery on the corner.*

Marie had given her simple instructions. At the end of the street, Ana turned right to follow the river toward the fish market. Little docks spaced several hundred feet apart jutted into the Rhine River. Fishing boats bobbed next to each small quay. She noticed double train tracks between her and the water. A large warehouse stood by the water's edge. All this she tried to imprint on her memory.

The bell above the door rang as she entered Herr Dolfmyer's store. It was cool inside. Ice-packed tables displayed rows of fresh fish. The clerk wiped his hands and greeted her.

"Can I help you, Fraulein?" He was a stout man with a fisherman's apron stretched across his middle.

"Herr Dolfmyer, bitte." She'd been told to ask for the owner since he was used to their arrangements.

His smile broadened. "I'm Dolfmyer."

"Die Gräfin Kessler has asked me to give you this list." He took the list and scanned its contents.

Ana added, "She asks if you can deliver on Saturday morning, bitte?"

"You are new." The man's gaze was appraising. It was the same in all small towns. Villagers tended to be suspicious of anyone who didn't belong to the tight little community. It wasn't a question, more an observation. Herr Dolfmyer continued. "Ja, I will have her order ready on time."

"Danke." Ana turned to leave. *Seems easy enough. Just down Marktstrasse to Rheinstrasse, and the water is straight ahead.* She was pretty sure she could find her way even in the dark.

As she walked along the esplanade, she could see a small park ahead of her at the water's edge. She found a quiet bench beside a pond. Old growth beech and oak trees towered above her.

Ana closed her eyes to her beautiful surroundings and waited for peace to enter her heart. Only vaguely aware of the noise outside the little park, she didn't open her eyes until she heard truck engines pass. Two military cars and a transport truck rolled past her and parked along the tracks. Alarm shot through her, and she rose to go find Marie.

"Ana. Ana, wait." It was Eric's voice. *No, this can't be happening, not when we're so close to freedom.* She stopped and looked up at the beautiful clouds floating across the blue sky. *If I pray for your will and open my eyes to see his face, what does that tell me, Lord? Oh, Eric.*

Chapter Ninety-Eight

Rüdesheim am Rhein, Germany
June 1937

Unexpected

"Ana, Ana." Eric was sure he'd glimpsed her. He hurried through the busy market crowd. The urge to push people out of his way was almost overwhelming.

"Ana."

He called out once again, his hand in the air like a drowning man reaching for the surface. He saw her stop, and for a second he thought she might run. Then she turned toward him. Her smile was warm, even radiant. How could he have imagined she'd deserted him, when here she was clearly glad to see him? He was out of breath when he caught up with her.

"Eric, how are you? I'm so sorry to miss our time together. Did you get my message?"

"Ja, your grandmother. That cow of a cook said she was ill."

Her expression blanched.

The memory of how he'd felt when he'd lost his mother

washed over him. He saw those same emotions reflected in her face.

"That woman wouldn't tell me where you'd gone." He worked for control as rage flooded him.

"But, Eric, she didn't know. I left in such a hurry I'd not said more than why I was leaving."

Usually when I'm angry, I see fear in other's eyes. Not so with Ana. The thought made a warm spot in his stony heart.

"She is better? Your grandmother is better?"

Ana looked down and sadness filled her eyes. She shook her head. *No, he thought. It must have ended badly.* "Walk with me. The park is beautiful, and the day is perfect." He took her arm and guided her on the path. "This will be like old times. We can talk. Ja?"

But they were both silent for a while. He glanced at her, noticing how long her rich, black hair had grown. Thick curls covered her shoulders.

"Your hair is much longer."

Even as he spoke those words, something bothered him about how short her hair had been the last time they'd met.

Ana reached up and pulled at an unruly curl. "I think it is messy this way."

"I like it."

"Tell me how you've been."

He looked at her, searching for deception or pretended interest, but he didn't see any. He told her—not the dark things, just about his new position and chance for advancement.

"Are you happy, Eric?"

Her simple question took him aback. He stopped to look at her, searching his heart for the answer.

"No."

Her eyes seemed to see into his thoughts. Eric looked away, staring at the path. He was in danger of being open, even honest. She'd undone his defenses with a simple question. At the edge of the park, he heard an engine start. The commander must have concluded his business. *We only have moments left.*

"Ana. I can't lose you again."

She gave him a tentative smile.

"I mean, you are my friend, Ja?"

Her smile deepened. Then he heard someone call his name. "I have to go, but meet me here on Sunday. I'm here for a dinner party at the Kessler estate, but I can get free for a bit on Sunday. At one, Ja?"

"Eric—"

"No, I must see you."

His name was called one last time. He reached for her hand, and she gave it to him willingly. One squeeze and he let go. He jogged to the edge of the park and turned. She was still standing looking at him. He wanted to keep the memory of how she looked and never forget her simple beauty.

Michael poked Eric in the ribs. "Why don't you introduce me to your friend? She looks too innocent for you."

Eric frowned at Michael's leer. "Not on your life. She's just a friend but not your type."

"Since when did I have a type? I'm a man of many tastes, and she looks delicious."

He snapped, "Shut up, Michael."

His friend gave him a hard look. He knew Michael could be dangerous if provoked but so could he.

Michael said, "She's not your type either. Too innocent."

They sat in silence. Eric wasn't sure why he felt so annoyed at his friend. *I'll never introduce you. You're not a safe guy for Ana.* Eric shook his head at the irony of that thought.

Chapter Ninety-Nine

Rüdesheim am Rhein, Germany
June 1937

Ana's Reaction

Ana watched as Eric joined several other officers. He saluted and climbed into the front seat of the military car, giving her a discreet wave and a sweet smile. She felt numb. Only a moment ago, she'd worried about leaving Germany forever. Now she was worried they'd never make it out. *How can this be? Isabelle can't be aware that Eric Braun was attending her dinner party. She would have warned me.*

Ana took a deep breath, remembering her sincere interest in Eric. She'd felt God was after this man from the moment she'd met him. Whenever they were together, she could see the young boy Eric must have been before his mother died. *If only there was a way to reach that child. That was God's heart for Eric to save him from this darkness.*

The soldiers loaded back into their truck and drove away. Only then did she feel the deep, bone-chilling fear creep over her.

Put one foot in front of the other and walk to meet Marie, she commanded herself. But with every step, the grace in the park drained from her. On this beautiful warm day, Ana shook with an inner cold. She crossed her arms and hugged them to her body to keep from collapsing.

Ahead, Etienne's old truck was parked along the narrow street in front of a small toy shop. Marie straightened from where she leaned against the truck door. She spotted Ana and waved. But her smile faltered as Ana drew closer.

Only a few more steps, and I'll be on my way. But where?

"Mon Dieu!" Marie grabbed Ana's arm. "What has happened? You are as white as a ghost." She guided her friend to a bench.

"I can't go back to the house. But I must. Oh God, what do I do?" Tears rolled down Ana's cheeks.

"Tell me what has happened."

And Ana did. She told Marie about the man who had chased them from Bavaria, about Father Hugo, about meeting Eric in Kempten, and she told her about her walk in the park.

"Funny how sometimes God gives you what you need but only for as long as you need it." Ana smiled through her tears at Marie. "Unimaginable peace and even God's love for this despicable person flooded me until he walked away. Then it was gone. I had only my own feelings." She took hold of Marie's hand. "And I'm so afraid, Marie. What should I do?"

Etienne was coming down the street. Marie leaned into Ana. "We go, but the back way. No one will see us. We must talk to la comtesse and think about what to do next, non?"

Ana nodded. "Ja, she'll know."

Chapter One Hundred

Rüdesheim am Rhein, Germany
June 1937

Courting Old Money

"Why are you even bothering to come?" Marguerite glared at Laurie. "There won't be any strange old women to befriend you, only important people—my people." They stood at the auto door waiting for her father.

"I'm sorry if it annoys you, but I find all people interesting. You can't always want to talk to people because of their positions or the power they wield." He reached out and touched her arm. "I promise I'll be the perfect gentleman."

She rolled her eyes and looked away.

"Except with Herr Braun."

Marguerite cast him a look full of daggers.

"The man is pure evil, Marguerite. Be careful around him."

She put her hands on her hips and leaned toward him. "Jealous?"

He looked into her beautiful eyes, trying to convey his

concern. His voice softened. "He's dangerous. I want you to be careful around him."

Her features hardened. "Laurie, you used to like a little danger. What's happened to you?"

Herr Papa appeared at the door. As they drove, Marguerite's hurt and resentment filled the air between them. Halfway to their weekend, she thawed and began talking about her favorite topic—who was coming to the weekend away. Laurie tried to listen to Marguerite's chatter about the Graf and Grafin Kessler without appearing too interested.

Herr Voss extolled the advantages of this business connection. "The Graf—the count—is one of a few in the aristocracy with money to invest. Even the Nazi Party courts his favor."

Being included with the inner circles of Nazi power was heady for Herr Voss. He looked sideways at his daughter. "You must be on your best behavior."

Score one for the old man. Laurie's thoughts were not unkind, just a matter of observation.

Marguerite opened her mouth to say something and shut it. Instead, she continued her litany of who's who.

"My hairdresser said they have invited many of the top-ranking party officials." Something in her tone changed as she said, "I hear Eric Braun will be attending."

Laurie kept his gaze out the auto window, watching the countryside slide by. He turned to see her looking at him. Her expression reminded him of a cat playing with a mouse.

If I ever felt bad about deceiving you, I am feeling much less guilty with each passing day. To think we might have been married. An involuntary shiver ran up his spine.

She looked over at him and smirked, satisfied to have his attention with this small jab. He wanted to tell her how thankful he was she'd shared this side of her personality.

I still have to exonerate Marguerite and her father when I leave. No matter how rotten she is, I can't put their lives in danger.

The long ordeal of riding in the car with Marguerite and Herr Voss was over. They turned off the main highway down a country lane. As used to opulence as she was, Marguerite still caught her breath. "Isn't this beautiful?"

He had to agree with her. The house with its spires and terraces resembled a small fairytale castle. Even the outbuildings, while not as old as the house, still belonged in a children's book.

Horses poked their long necks out of some stalls—intelligent dark eyes regarded them with mild curiosity. As they pulled to a stop before the main entrance, young men in liveries came to open their car doors.

Laurie focused on Marguerite. *She's glowing with avarice. This is what she wants from life. It's beautiful. And so is she. But her beauty is only a shell. From what Dolly told me, the people living in this splendor are wealthy in other ways. To save even one life at the risk of all this, well, that says something.*

Count Kessler was a kindly-looking chap of about forty. He exuded a good-natured warmth. His lovely wife was younger and beautiful. La comtesse had the look of a woman who knows she's loved. So far most of the German women he'd met were aloof and superior. But this woman was open and friendly. She looked like someone who didn't mind mixing with the servants.

She reminds me of Dolly. When the couple came out to greet them, la comtesse balanced a pudgy baby on her hip. Herr Voss was formal with a slight bow and stiff introductions, but their host and hostess were warm, relaxed, and even charming.

"So happy you could join us. This is my beautiful wife Isabelle and our son Thomas." The baby cooed and drooled, flashing two front teeth in a baby smile.

His wife added with a thick French accent. "We are so happy you could come." Laurie noticed the comtesse didn't hand the baby off to a servant but held him possessively. *You can see how she loves children,* he thought. Then it hit him. *The baby's almond-shaped chocolate-brown eyes, much like his mother's, passed for French but showed little of his father's lighter Germanic coloring.*

Could this be the Romani baby traveling with the holy sister and the other children? This is one very brave woman.

He stepped forward, extending his hand. "Lawrence MacKenzie, sir, madam." He copied his employer's slight bow.

If his name or the fact he was a Scot struck a familiar chord, it wasn't clear. For a moment, Laurie was taken aback. *Dolly said it was all arranged.*

It dawned on him that the arrangements were made with la comtesse. He was impressed anew. *This is one brave woman.* His thoughts were interrupted as their hosts turned to go back into the house.

"Paul and Andrae will show you to your rooms. Please rest as long as you like. Only a few guests are arriving this evening, so dinner will be informal at seven."

They left the comte and comtesse in the entry hall and followed their staff up a winding staircase to the second floor. Andrae showed the hall to the left, but Paul said, "Mr. MacKenzie, your rooms are up one more flight."

Laurie followed with only a moment's glance backward. Marguerite didn't look at him or even comment. *It's ridiculous to feel slighted since I plan on leaving her, but I guess I'm only human.* She had distanced herself from him in every way. He nodded to himself. *It's for the better.*

Paul led him to a sunny room at the front of the house. As he turned to leave, he handed Laurie a note.

"From la comtesse. When you are ready to respond, pull the rope." Paul indicated the fine-braided cord next to his bed. "I will come back for you within minutes."

Laurie stared down at the scrap of paper. It held a single line of elegant cursive: *Monsieur, please have tea with me as soon as you can.*

He looked at the bell pull and decided to see la comtesse while

Marguerite was still unpacking. He gave a good pull on the cord and paced as he waited for Paul to return.

After months of frustration and pretending with Marguerite, it's ending. I'll be back with Fiona in a matter of days.

He walked to the window and looked out. The drive and the front entrance were three stories below. He leaned his head against the window encasement and closed his eyes. He was standing once again on the docks at Leith with Fiona. The wind whipped her hair around, but she reached up, brushing the hair off his brow. Her warm brown eyes were shining with unshed tears. He reached for her.

Laurie jumped at the rap on his door announcing Paul's return. The servant led him down the hall to a narrow set of stairs. "I will take you down the service stairs and through the kitchen," Paul explained. "No chance any of our guests will see us."

As they came to the kitchen, everyone looked up and all activity paused for a minute before the workers went back to meal preparation. Paul and Laurie walked down a narrow hall that twisted and turned until they came to a door. Paul opened it and stepped aside, motioning for Laurie to enter.

They seemed to have passed from the service area to the family's wing. They were in a much wider hallway, but within a few paces, Paul stopped again. He rapped on a door and said something in French. La comtesse answered back with a simple, "Entrez, s'il vous plaît."

Laurie entered alone. Floral wallpaper and golden sunlight greeted him. This was a woman's domain. Tall windows overlooked a garden, but he could see horses grazing on distant pastures. All this his eyes registered in a moment, but the scene before him was anything but peaceful.

La comtesse's hand rested on the shoulder of a young woman. The poor woman sat hunched over, cradling her head. Laurie wondered if she'd been crying.

When the girl looked up, it felt like the room tilted sideways. She was so like Fiona. Curly black hair—her eyes were blue instead of brown—but she had the same delicate, heart-shaped face. La comtesse indicated the young woman. "Monsieur MacKenzie, this is Ana. She has brought the children safely from Saint Thomas in Bavaria."

Ana rose, brushing one lingering tear from her eye and said in English, "Very pleased to meet you, Mr. MacKenzie. Thank you for helping us."

"I'm sorry, sister, it's just you look so like someone from home." He felt a blush creep over his cheeks. "But I beg your pardon; has something gone wrong?"

La comtesse motioned for Laurie to have a seat, and they all sat at the little breakfast table. "How much do you know about the situation?" she asked.

Laurie began, "Well, that Sister Ana—"

The young nun broke in. "Just Ana, please. It is safer for all concerned."

"Sorry, of course. That Deter and Gretchen were out with their nanny when their parents were taken. The nanny took them back to her home in Bavaria. Nuns gave them shelter at Saint Thomas. I know a nun got them out of the area before the SS came asking questions. I'm afraid that's about all I know."

La comtesse added, "One man has been pursuing them across Germany."

"Yes, that bit as well. I've met him—Eric Braun." Laurie grimaced. "A very dangerous character."

Ana interrupted. "A tortured soul. But yes, very dangerous. I got to know him while we were hiding in Kempten. He didn't know who I was, of course. I left that town and came here to escape him. Today, he saw me in the market square."

Laurie asked, "And he still doesn't know you have the children?"

"No, but he wants me to meet him in the village on Sunday

afternoon." Ana looked at la comtesse. "It's dangerous for you if I stay here."

Isabelle explained, "It seems our Monsieur Braun accompanied his commander as one of his aides. We didn't realize he would be attending."

"I only just learned he'd be here from Marguerite," Laurie said. "Her hairdresser seems to know who's doing what." He added, "I think Braun's been having me watched the last few weeks. He doesn't like me." Laurie's mouth curved up. "I shot him once."

La comtesse gave him a rueful smile. "So you are the one who shot him."

"He thinks it was a hunting accident. I only winged him, but it stopped him from killing a young man. It was all I could think of."

"Dolly told me the story, but I didn't know this was the same man hunting our children." She stood and paced. "It is unfortunate he's here, but I think we will just have to keep a very close eye on him." She stopped and turned to look at Laurie. "I imagine he wouldn't like you much after that, but why is he watching you?"

"I'm not sure. It could be because I'm foreign and don't fit in. When I took this job, Marguerite assumed we would be married. Now even she thinks I'm unsuitable. That's all right with me. No offense intended, but it's crazy here. I'm only staying for those children. They're cousins of my school friend."

"You are quite right, monsieur. It is crazy in Germany. If not for my Phillip, I would take my people and go back to France. Your friend, he's Jewish?"

Laurie nodded. "Bernie said he wouldn't be welcome in Germany. That was an understatement. From what I can see, being Jewish gets you killed in Germany."

Ana spoke up. "Even helping a Jew is enough to get you killed."

Laurie gave the young nun an encouraging look. "My grandfather is on the way, but he won't be here until the wee hours on Monday morning." They were all silent for a few minutes.

La comtesse's gaze drifted to the window and the garden beyond. She was thinking. When she turned back to Laurie, she said, "I think I have a plan. Mr. MacKenzie, do you think you could continue to be frustrating to your Marguerite?"

His grin was lopsided. "I expect I could frustrate anyone without half-trying."

"That, Mr. MacKenzie, could be a valuable asset." For the next thirty minutes, she explained her strategy.

<h1 style="text-align: center;">Chapter One Hundred One</h1>

Edinburgh
June 1937

Rab Leaves

Fiona buried her face in Rab's coat. His arms gave her one last squeeze. She inhaled the faint smell of his soap and shaving cream. Her heart ached with a sense of loss even though he wouldn't be gone long. He'd become the grandfather she'd never known. Now he was sailing to Germany. To danger. She worried that the men she loved would never return.

One by one, tears escaped her eyes and rolled down her cheeks. *I won't cry. No, not now that Laurie is coming home.* She brushed them away as Rab pulled back to look at her.

"Lassie, I promise ye it weel be a right." She nodded her head, not trusting her voice to sound positive.

Rab planted a kiss on the top of her head. "Ye dinna ken how much I care for ye. You bide here, aye?"

She nodded again.

"An keep this wee beastie with you. He's a braw wee laddie. He'll let ye know if anything's amiss."

"I will, Rab. I will."

She gave him one last watery smile.

"Ye can trust me to bring your man back, aye?"

She kissed his cheek.

"I do, Rab."

Then he was gone, and she stood alone in the kitchen listening to the front door close. Tam looked up with concern in his doggie eyes.

She bent to pat his head. "It's all right, Tam. He'll be back soon."

She wondered how she would get through the days. *Praying, but I need something to keep my hands busy.* She'd been cleaning Rab's house for days. It had helped her while they waited for the Elspeth.

She walked to the front room. Outside the window, a gust of wind blew leaves up the street. Her own house sat at the back of the square, dark and empty.

Well, there's getting my house ready for guests. As long as I stay the night here, I don't see that spending the days there could be dangerous. "Besides," she said aloud to Tam, "I'll take you with me." The dog wagged his tail.

She went in search of a tablet and pen. *The first thing to do is make a list.* "Rab said the wife was expecting. I wonder if I could afford a cradle. There's a bed in the smaller bedroom, so the wee lad could sleep there."

Her mind was spinning on, thinking about how to make her home welcoming. *I'll need supplies for meals. I should do some baking. Goodness, this list has filled my days already. I hope I can get it all done by the time they get back.*

She grabbed her jacket and picked up Tam's leash, intending to start by pricing a cradle. *And a short walk will clear my mind.*

"After all," she said, patting her dog, "you could use some

exercise." Before she knew it, her feet carried her all the way to Leith.

She wondered if the Elspeth was still in her moorings. But no, Rab and Kevin were gone. Then she realized where she was standing. *I remember the last time I stood here. It was right here he said he loved me.* She closed her eyes and tried to imagine Laurie's arms around her. Tam bumped her leg with his nose, bringing her back to the present. Her wee Scottie looked up at her, a question in his eyes.

"You're right. We need to get going."

As she walked up the hill toward Edinburgh, her feelings settled. She reached in her pocket for a handkerchief and felt a folded paper, her list. The walk had helped settle her fears. It was time to put her plan into action.

Fiona smiled as she thought about Wee Geordie. *I never expected to follow you in the smuggling business, but I think you'd approve of this cargo.*

The afternoon light faded as she finished her shopping and walked home to Latimer Square. A cradle would be delivered the next morning, and her first day of waiting was coming to a close. She whispered, "Lord, please keep Rab and Laurie safe, and bring them home to me."

Chapter One Hundred Two

Rüdesheim am Rhein, Germany
June 1937

A Plan All Along

The sound of engines drew Laurie to the bedroom window. Two military jeeps and a small troop transport rolled to a stop in front of the entrance. *Well, well, Herr Braun and company have arrived. What's with the armed men? Alarming, but everything the SS does is calculated to intimidate.*

Laurie pulled the sheer privacy drapes aside to give him a better view of the drive below. Once again, liveried servants came out first to open doors, followed by the comte and comtesse. Baby Thomas was not present.

Just as well. Why give the buggers a chance to notice how Phillip's son shows none of his father's light coloring?

He couldn't hear what was being said three stories below, but all present appeared cordial. The troops—about twelve men— disembarked and followed Paul around the side of the house. Laurie suspected he was taking them to an outbuilding. Eric, his commander, and another man he recognized from parties disappeared into the main hall.

Laurie glanced at his wristwatch. Ana should be on her way to the gamekeeper's cottage. *I wish I had time to go with her. It would be nice to meet those children. But that will have to wait for the wee hours of Monday morning. In the meantime, I need to become as difficult as possible.*

He flopped down on the bed and stared up at the ceiling and muttered, "Funny, throughout university I was accused of being damn infuriating. Never gave it a second thought. Planning how best to aggravate is definitely harder."

He started turning over ways he might antagonize Marguerite without being too obvious in his efforts. *That's the rub. If I try too hard, it'll look put on. No, it has to look like Marguerite gets fed up and sends me packing.*

The scene with la comtesse rose before his eyes. His pulse quickened as it had then. When the sister looked up, she was so like Fiona. He pulled out the small photo of Fiona and her aunt in Canada. His eyes misted as he stared at her, and he whispered her name.

It can't be a coincidence that Ana looks like my Fiona. His thoughts wandered back to something Rab often said. *Nothing is hidden from God. How often did he tell me God had a plan for my life? If God knew Fiona and Ana looked enough alike to be sisters, could he be showing me this was his plan all along?* The thought was comforting.

Laurie murmured to the photo, "You are my compass rose guiding me through this path back to you." He closed his eyes, and sleep took him home to his Fiona.

It was seven when he came down to dinner. As expected, Eric was present. But it was disheartening to see how Marguerite played up to him. *She's made her choice—power and prestige. I just wish she wouldn't choose him as well.*

Eric sat at the other end of the table, yet he spoke loud enough to be heard above the other dinner conversations. "Herr Mackenzie, I hear good things about your work."

Funny how the man sounded sarcastic even when his words were compli-mentary. Laurie matched his tone. "Thank you, Herr Braun. And what is it you do exactly?"

There was nervous laughter at the table. Laurie caught the glare directed at him from Marguerite, but Eric's face showed only mild amusement.

"I am a soldier in the Reich. Not to worry if you haven't heard of us. After all, the north of Scotland is still primitive, Ja? Even the men wear skirts. I'm surprised you didn't wear yours. You have a skirt, don't you, Herr MacKenzie?"

Heads swung back down the table to Laurie. Eric's commander was observing their conversation with only mild interest, but la comtesse had the ghost of a smile on her beautiful lips.

Oh, laddie, you'll have to stop using the same tired jabs. "You should travel more, Herr Braun. You wouldn't believe how civilized we've become. We actually hunt for prey more challenging than young boys. But then, he did get away, didn't he?"

Herr Voss, sitting next to Eric, choked a bit on his food, but the rest of the room went silent. Every eye shifted to Eric, but his face was a well-schooled mask. The young Nazi let out a loud laugh. Laurie thought he heard a collective sigh. *Are they so afraid of this baby-faced man they all held their breath?*

Count Kessler started a conversation with Eric's commander about the German economy. People began talking to each other. Laurie took a drink of his wine. He made eye contact with Eric and raised his glass in salute. Herr Braun's expression revealed only sardonic amusement. Eric returned the salute. Laurie's eyes drifted to Marguerite. Her mouth was pulled into a thin line. *Looks like I've put steam in her kettle. Let's hope when she blows her whistle she has an audience.*

Chapter One Hundred Three

In the Woods
June 1937

The Gamekeeper's Cottage

I t was late afternoon when Ana arrived at the gamekeeper's lodge. The lodge was built in a small clearing deep in the woods, far from the main house. A shaft of late afternoon sunlight lit the scene like an old master's painting. She thought it looked like a cottage right out of one of Hans Christian Andersen's books.

Old Francois had brought the children out earlier and spent the day telling Deter and Gretchen stories. He left for the estate soon after Ana arrived. She was a little surprised when Gretchen begged, "One more story, please?"

The old thatched roof and flagstone floors made it the perfect place to tell them the story of Hansel and Gretel. Even at this time of year, the thick stone walls kept the interior of this one-room cabin chilly. The children lay on mats before the fire. They snuggled into their blankets and waited for Ana to tell them one last story. Late afternoon light faded, and darkness settled over the forest around them. The children looked sleepy. By candle-light, Ana painted pictures in their minds about the brother and sister who strayed from home. When she came to the part where the wicked witch captures Hansel, Gretchen said, "Oh, did the Nazi men help her?"

Ana shook her head. *Maybe I should have picked a different story.* "Gretchen, there are no Nazi men in this story, and just wait until you will see how the children outsmart the witch."

When she finished, Ana's tone turned playful. "Well, I would eat this candy cottage, wouldn't you, Deter?"

"Ja, I'd eat a Schokolade door." Ana could almost see visions of chocolate doors on Deter's face.

"Ja and the windows in peppermint sticks. I'd eat that first," Gretchen chimed in.

"You both would eat the house down around us." Ana tickled them until they giggled. Pulling the covers up around their necks, she kissed their heads. "Go to sleep. You can dream about smart, brave children who end up with tummies full of candy."

"And trick all the bad Nazi witches," Gretchen whispered as she closed her eyes.

Ana rose and crossed the room. Katrine was making hot chocolate. She set a cup on the table before Ana.

"I heard what Gretchen said." Katrine smiled. "We're leaving, aren't we?"

Ana nodded. "God willing. We leave here on Monday morning at three. A man has come from Scotland to rescue Gretchen and Deter for their family. He will take all of us back there."

Katrine asked, "All the way to Scotland?" Then she looked toward the window. "But we're here because the Nazis are close, Ja?"

Ana sensed fear had entered their fairytale cottage. "Ja, very close." She, too, looked toward the window. "We should close the shutters on all the windows." And Katrine rose to help. It felt better until Ana thought of all those people who had died locked in the barn.

Yes, but God has brought us this far. She hugged Katrine. "I know it's hard to leave your friends."

Katrine stopped her. "I will miss them and baby Tony—I mean Thomas. But Ana, you're my family too."

Here was encouragement from the very person she meant to encourage. God always gives us what we need. But once again she remembered the farmer shot protecting the people in his barn. A small voice in her heart warned, *Sometimes He requires a great price to protect the objects of his love.*

Chapter One Hundred Four

Rüdesheim am Rhein, Germany
June 1937

Endings and Beginnings

By Friday morning, the house was alive with activity. From his window high above the drive, Laurie watched the steady stream of guests arriving. He'd looked for Marguerite at breakfast, but she wasn't present. At lunch, there was still no sign of the lovely Marguerite, so he wrote a note apologizing for his behavior the night before and asking if she was avoiding him. He wasn't sorry, and the note was a touch sarcastic, but it was hard to antagonize someone if you weren't in their presence. He asked Paul to deliver it for him, but there was no response from the fraulein.

In the afternoon, Laurie went for a stroll to the horse barn. During dinner conversation on Thursday, he'd heard la comtesse was a well-known horse breeder. The barn was huge, with stalls and turnouts down the one side of the aisle and two larger foaling stalls on the opposite wall. He stopped to admire a mare and new foal. The mare came to sniff his hand over the stall door. Her head bobbed, and she nickered. Laurie wished he had something to offer.

"She's a sweet girl."

The voice came from behind him.

"Bonjour, it's Herr MacKenzie, isn't it?" A tall, slender man was coming down the aisle. With shirtsleeves rolled up and bits of hay on his pants, it was easy to see that this man was at home in the barn.

"Sorry, hope it was all right. I needed to—say, how did you know my name? I don't think I've seen you before."

"Etienne." The man extended his hand, and Laurie shook it gladly. "It wasn't hard to guess with your red hair. You look like a Scot."

"And you, monsieur, look so French."

"Thank you."

The man came to lean over the stall door. The mare nuzzled Laurie's arm. Etienne slipped his hand into his pants pocket and pulled out a peppermint.

"She loves these. Here, take one."

He handed Laurie the small red-and-white striped candy. Laurie held his hand out, and she took it with the barest touch of her velvety lips and turned to tend her baby. "She is a beauty," Laurie said in admiration.

"I hear there is a small matter of ending the relationship with a certain young woman." Etienne grinned. "In matters of the heart, I thought you could use some advice from a Frenchman."

Laurie had to chuckle. "I've always been good at frustrating women, just never on purpose."

"The trick is to chase her while you do those things you know she hates, non?"

"Well, thanks for the advice. It's worked for you, has it?"

"Mais non. My Marie would kill me if I even looked in another's direction." His smile was infectious. "We French know these things." Etienne looked around and said in a low voice. "I will be taking you all to the village on Monday morning."

Laurie sobered. *This funny, friendly guy will risk his life to help me.* He turned and extended his hand. "Thank you for your help." *It seems so little to say for someone jeopardizing everything.*

"You are most welcome. Bonne chance, Monsieur MacKenzie." Etienne glanced past Laurie to the barn entrance. "And here is your opportunity pour chasser la jeune femme."

Laurie turned to see Marguerite enter the barn on the arm of Eric Braun. He knew it would take a minute for her eyes to adjust to the dim light, so he turned back to Etienne. "Thanks, and it's Laurie."

Laurie called as he approached the couple. "There you are, my love. Well, well, Herr Braun, you don't waste much time moving in on another man's girl." He delivered his insult with an insolent chuckle.

"I'm not so sure Marguerite wants to be your girl."

Eric was playing it very cool. No hot temper or explosion. Still, his words were sharp as knives as he said, "She was telling me about your odd behavior. I think she's wondering if you have another girl."

Laurie looked at Marguerite, and, to give her credit, she looked guilty. Her other hand came to rest on Eric's arm as if to stop him.

"I was saying you are always disappearing to talk with some odd person. Was that the barn hand you were talking to? After all, Laurie, anyone would wonder what interests you in servants and old women."

"He seemed like a fine fellow. Knows a lot about horses. You should talk to him. You could learn a bit more about breeding— horse breeding, that is." He was standing close enough to touch her. Before she could respond, he reached out and pulled her into his arms, kissing her soundly. As the kiss deepened, she yielded to him. The chemistry they once shared flared to life. He had just enough time to think, *Etienne's advice seems to have backfired,* when she pulled back and slapped him on the face.

She stepped back to Eric, her face flushed. "Laurie, you are the last person to talk about good breeding. Your behavior is outrageous." She took Eric's arm. "Let's leave him to his interesting servants."

Eric said nothing, but Laurie could see the speculation in his eyes as the couple passed him to leave through the far end of the barn.

Etienne came to stand next to him. "Very French of you, if I say so."

Laurie rubbed his cheek and smiled a lopsided smile. "On the contrary, we Scots are quite good at getting our faces clouted." The two laughed, but Laurie turned serious. "She's been telling him I'm acting suspicious. Looks good for her, but I'm not sure it helps us get the children out undetected."

"The SS are always suspicious." Etienne clapped Laurie on the back. "We will get you out safely."

Chapter One Hundred Five

Edinburgh
June 1937

Missed Connections

Fiona jumped with surprise when the telephone rang. "Hello?" She could tell right away it was an overseas connection.

Even with all the static, the caller sounded desperate. "Hello, is Robert MacKenzie there?" She was sure she recognized a slight Irish brogue.

"He's at sea," she answered. *What did Laurie say about calling? This could be a trap of some kind. Or what if there's been an accident?* But the voice sounded much relieved when he spoke again. "And you must be the beautiful Fiona."

"This is Fiona." She was guarded as she asked, "Is anything wrong? Who is this, please?"

"Laurie might have mentioned me, but I'm Terry, his Irish friend.

"Yes, of course he's talked about you. But Rab should have picked you up this morning."

"We made it late to our meeting place with Laurie's grandfather. We had a small bump. A seven-pound bump, very pink with lots of blond hair."

Fiona relaxed. *This isn't a trick. I can hear the proud papa in his voice.*

She laughed. "I take it your wife had her baby. A girl?"

"A beautiful girl just like her mother."

Fiona grew serious. "Oh dear, that's wonderful, but I see your dilemma. Do you know the next stop? Rab would have gone on to the second meeting since he can't be late." Her mind was running over Rab's schedule. "He must be there by four on Monday morning."

"Right, if you hear from him, tell him we'll meet him there." She could hear the worry in his voice. "With any luck, we'll see you soon." The line went dead.

Fiona sank to her knees and prayed with all her heart for everyone involved. *What have I started by sending Laurie to Germany? Lord, don't let anyone get hurt.*

Fears seemed to press in around her, crowding out her prayers, making her feel hopeless. Tam had been watching her. He nuzzled her with his head, one paw resting on her leg. She hugged him close.

"You're a comfort, Tam, good boy."

Then she thought of a scripture her father used to say when she was afraid and hopeless. It was as if she heard his voice saying, "Remember, love, it says in Isaiah 41, 'Fear thou not; for I am with thee: be not dismayed; for I am thy God: I will strengthen thee; yea, I will help thee; yea, I will uphold thee with the right hand of my righteousness.'" She sighed. "We just need to stay busy, don't we, Tam?" She scratched behind his ear. "And trust God."

Chapter One Hundred Six

Rüdesheim am Rhein, Germany

June 1937

Chassant une Femme

Laurie spent Saturday afternoon looking for Marguerite. He decided not to act intoxicated. The smell of alcohol on his breath and a whiskey-drenched handkerchief in his pocket should give the impression he'd been drinking all afternoon.

She wasn't at lunch, but an hour later, he found Marguerite sitting with the ladies in the salon. Paul tipped him off. It seemed the staff was party to his charade. The young man led him to a large room but left him at the door.

"Thanks, mate."

Paul winked. "Bonne chance."

No one noticed him slip into the room. Women sat on sofas and chairs chatting. Trays of pastries and the aroma of strong coffee added to the ambiance of relaxed conversation.

Laurie came up behind Marguerite to whisper in her ear, "Come on, baby, let's talk. I hate it when you're mad at me."

With remarkable poise, she stood and excused herself. She walked past Laurie to the door. He followed, wondering which Marguerite he would see next. Once down the hall and out of earshot, she turned on him.

"Laurie, this has got to stop." With the next breath, she asked, "Have you been drinking?" She stomped her foot. "Don't you drink one more drop before dinner tonight."

Laurie reached for her, but she stepped away. He rolled his eyes and tried to placate her.

"You're mad, aren't you? What is it this time? Did I forget to notice your hair or a new dress?" He stepped into her once more, reaching for her arm and pulling her toward an embrace. "You know you can't stay mad at me." He spoke into her ear. "We just need more time together."

She was stiff. He could feel the heat rising in her face, and he was sorry to admit he was having fun playing his old self. *God, was I so obnoxious?* A hand reached out and pulled him off balance. He hit the other wall but caught himself before sliding to the floor.

"Is he annoying you?" Eric asked Marguerite.

Laurie stood and straightened his jacket. "Wait, a minute. You have no right—"

Eric was every bit the gentleman, and Laurie loathed letting him play the rescuer, but it couldn't be helped. Marguerite stopped Eric before things went further. "I'm quite all right. He— that is, we—need to get things straightened out." Tears filled her pretty blue eyes, and Laurie was sorry he had to put her through this.

Eric looked from Marguerite to Laurie, and he bowed and headed back the way he'd come.

"Marguerite, I'm sorry but—"

She cut him off. "We're finished, Laurie. I'm tired of making excuses for your lack of interest in my friends." She threw her hands in the air. "You embarrass me every time we go out."

"Marguerite—" he started to say, but she exploded.

"I don't know what you're up to, but it had better not put my father in a poor light." Her eyes narrowed as she stared him down. "Why don't you leave, find your own way back to the city? I don't think even Father will miss your boorish behavior." She turned on her heel and marched back down the hall.

She suspects me of something. Thank God, it's over. Laurie walked off in the other direction but stopped. *I don't want you either, but I don't want you to fall for a madman. I have to make sure you listen to me one last time.* He jogged back down the hall after her and grabbed her arm, swinging her around. "I know you are angry at me. I'm sorry it didn't work out with us, but please believe me in this one thing." He took a deep breath. "When I came on Eric in the woods, he was executing a teenage boy, not hunting for game, Marguerite." He searched her eyes. "His game was a frightened boy, not a criminal. The boy's only crime was being a Jew."

Her face had been blank. He wasn't sure if she could see past her anger to hear what he was saying. As his words sank in, her expression turned to horror.

"My God. You shot Eric on purpose!"

Laurie shook his head in disbelief. He'd done all he could, and now he could leave with a clear conscience. But there was still the worry about getting out of this crazy upside-down world. Even his beautiful girl wasn't at all what she seemed. Would she tell Eric her revelation? But no, she wouldn't do anything to put her father in a bad light. Laurie did something he'd done more and more often in this land on the other side of the looking glass. He said a quick prayer.

He walked to the stable, hoping to find Etienne. With his walking papers served, he needed to find a place to stay out of sight. And he'd rather it wasn't somewhere Eric might find him. *Rab will get here in a little over thirty hours.* Laurie raked his hands through his hair, trying not to think of all the things that could go wrong.

In the dim light of the barn, he searched for the sound of

human activity. The beautiful mare nickered as he came close to her stall, weaving back and forth, looking for another peppermint. He held out his hand palm up so she would see he was without a gift. She sniffed and licked his palm and went back to munching on the hay.

"No hard feelings? There's a good girl." His hand brushed her silky neck as she turned away. The foal came close to smell the man.

"Careful. Don't give that young vixen your hand. She may decide to keep some of your fingers." Etienne chuckled.

Laurie relaxed with the pleasure of being done with a distasteful job. "I know a few people who would do as much. Marguerite says she's finished with me."

He glanced around to assure himself they were alone. "It wasn't as hard as I thought it would be. Kinda stings your pride, you know?"

Etienne shrugged. "Sometimes it is best to let the woman think it's her idea to end the relationship, non?"

"Well, thanks to you, Marguerite has served me notice to leave." It felt wonderful to be free of Marguerite, her father, and that whole Nazi lot.

"I can tell this is a great disappointment. If your grin was any wider, it would split your face." Etienne slapped Laurie on the back. "Come, let's get a drink in my office, and we'll decide what to do next. Oh, and try not to smile. It's best if people see how distraught you really should be."

Laurie hung his head low and slouched, but only as long as it took them to enter Etienne's office.

"I keep some whiskey in my drawer."

Laurie must have registered his surprise.

"I know, not the thing you'd expect from a Frenchman, but it seems to fit the occasion today."

Etienne pulled a half-empty bottle out of his drawer and one glass from the top of an old file cabinet. The other glass was full of pens which he dumped on his desk.

"Have a seat."

Laurie looked around at the stacks of books and papers covering every horizontal surface in the room. He could see only one actual chair, so he lifted the papers off the seat and deposited them on the floor. Etienne poured them each a generous portion and sat himself down in the chair behind the desk.

"Here's to freedom."

"Oh, no, laddie, I have a girl back home waiting for me."

Etienne's eyes widened in surprise. "I am seeing why the French and Scots have been allies through the ages." His grin broadened. "That's all right. A good whiskey needs no toast at all." They finished their glass and Etienne rose. "You get your things, and I'll take you out to meet the children. It's a good place to hide until you're ready to leave."

Laurie extended his hand. "Thank you, my friend, for risking so much for a stranger."

Etienne's handshake was firm. "Go with god, mon ami."

From the kitchen, Laurie took the servants staircase to the third floor. The hall was empty as he made his way toward his room. His head down and his posture unhurried, he shoved his hands in his pockets. Within a few steps of his room, he gave up all pretense and hurried through the door.

Once inside, he scooped everything into his satchel. He pulled his jacket from the chair and went to check the hall. He headed back the way he'd come and slipped into Etienne's office.

The tall Frenchman said, "Now we must go rapidement."

Laurie put his coat on to follow and absently felt his pocket. His jacket had a small breast pocket on the inside lining. He kept his picture of Fiona there. Close to his heart but hidden. Nothing. He turned all his pockets inside out. No photograph. He stopped mid-stride to check again. Etienne turned to look at him.

"What's wrong? We must leave. Everyone's busy. Let's go. Hurry."

"I keep a picture of my girl in my pocket. I was looking at it this morning, but I was sure I put it back."

Laurie opened his wallet, finding the small photo of the bairns, but even after a thorough search, Fiona's picture was gone. Laurie looked at Etienne.

"It was there earlier, but it's gone." He turned back, but Etienne grabbed his arm.

"You will see her soon. Not to worry. I'll have a good look for it as soon as I get back." He tugged on Laurie's arm. "We must take advantage of this opportunity."

Laurie nodded and turned to follow, reluctant to leave anything of himself behind.

Chapter One Hundred Seven

Rüdesheim am Rhein, Germany
June 1937

The Dinner Party

A small string quartet played in the great hall. Lights danced off the crystal chandeliers. Eric stood near an enormous fireplace. *It's a good place to watch the dinner guests.*

He was waiting for Laurie. *Something's off about the man. Could be that he is from an inferior race—a foreigner. He doesn't belong with Marguerite. She needs a good German man.* It wasn't the first time he'd considered courting the beautiful young heiress. The face of Ana floated across his mind.

Why compare every woman with Ana? They always come up short. Ana is... He searched for one word to describe her. *Ana is Ana, pure.* He looked around at the men and women entering the main salon. *Ana would be as out of place as MacKenzie in this group.* He nodded to his commander in silent greeting and told himself, *Don't be a fool. This is where I belong.*

Still, a wife like Marguerite would have many benefits. And

many men kept a woman on the side. Even as he thought these things, he knew Ana was not the sort of woman to become a mistress.

Marguerite walked into the room. She was so sleek and beautiful, dressed in a deep-red evening gown. It clung to her figure, leaving little to the imagination. The light from the chandeliers made her long blonde hair look like silk. She seemed to search for someone.

I hate MacKenzie. He doesn't even have the good sense to tread lightly around the SS. He's insolent and too self-assured. Maybe I hate him because he doesn't value what he has. All eyes turned to Marguerite, but when she found Eric, her smile sparkled. His pulse quickened as she walked right to him.

"Eric, you're looking handsome this evening."

He recognized this as a ploy to elicit a compliment. It wasn't necessary. *She must know how amazing she looks.*

He clicked his heels and bowed ever so slightly. "Marguerite, you are beautiful as always." The dinner bell sounded, and he offered her his arm. "Where is your fiancé?"

She made a pouty face. "I've broken off our engagement. He could be back in Scotland by now for all I care." She tossed a heavy curl over her shoulder.

Alarms went off in Eric's head. *If MacKenzie has truly left the country, I may never know what the man was doing here.* A servant came to the table as they were sitting down. The young man searched the faces and brought a note to Marguerite.

"Excusez moi, mademoiselle. Is Monsieur MacKenzie coming to the table this evening?"

"He's not here. Why?"

Eric noticed the note in the boy's hand. "Is that for our friend?"

Before the servant could respond, Eric snatched the note. He skimmed it. *Cryptic.* It said, "We missed our connection and are leaving with you." Possibilities ran through his mind, none of them good. His hunter instinct had been right. Herr MacKenzie was definitely up to something.

He asked, "Is someone waiting for an answer?"

"No, monsieur, a village boy delivered it."

Eric dismissed the servant with a nod.

"What is it, Eric? What does it say?"

He handed Marguerite the note. She scanned it and then crumpled it up. "Well, I don't care if he has another woman; I'm done with the man."

Funny how she assumes infidelity when something much larger might be afoot. He wondered if he should investigate further or let the man return to his uncivilized country. A perfectly groomed hand rested on his arm.

"Eric, tell me about what you're doing these days in the Reich." Marguerite leaned over, her shoulder brushing his. She looked up at him through thick lashes. Her full red lips pulled into a seductive smile.

He put his hand over hers. A sense of possession rushed over him. *No, I think Herr MacKenzie can wait till tomorrow.*

Chapter One Hundred Eight

Gamekeeper's Cabin
Rüdesheim am Rhein, Germany
June 1937

Is Anyone Too Far Away from God

They are so alike, Laurie thought as he watched Ana explain to the children how they would leave Germany in the middle of the night. *Her hair is shorter. The eyes are a different color, but the shape is identical. And the expression is so similar.*

Even the tone of her voice brought a flood of longing for Fiona. Laurie realized with a start that the two women had the same spirit. Gentle, yet with a firm resolve. *I've only known Ana for one short afternoon, and already I'm sure she'd do whatever it takes to care for these children.*

They had welcomed his company at the cottage. Katrine and Ana both spoke English, but his German had been steadily improving. Laurie could understand most of what Deter and Gretchen said, but Ana or Katrine had to help him with his answers. Ana was trying to settle the children for the night, but they kept asking questions about Scotland and how they would get there.

Tears welled in Katrine's eyes. "It is very generous of your friend to give us a place to stay."

"Not a place to stay but a home." He reached out to touch her arm. "A home. It's a promise. My lassie looks enough like Ana to be her twin. The best of it is she has the same heart as Ana. I know she will welcome you." *It's a lot to promise without talking to Fiona or Rab.* But he had no doubts.

He knew Katrine was worried. *No one waited for her in Scotland or anywhere. Katrine was alone.* She sat there, staring at the floor. When she looked up, she said, "You will be there too, Ana. Ja?"

Ana moved to put her arms around the girl. Laurie's chest felt tight at the sight of the pain etched in their expressions. The realization that their long flight was ending had been joyful until they started asking what would happen next.

Ana spoke in English. "God will sort things out." She kissed Katrine's head. "He's taken care of you through all these dangers. Can you not trust Him for what's next?"

Katrine wiped her eyes on her sleeve and nodded, looking up at Ana with love.

After all the children were asleep, Ana made some tea, and they sat together talking. "Tomorrow, I must make my way to the village to see Eric. If I don't, I know he will come searching for me. I can't take the chance."

Laurie had heard the story of how Eric had chased them across Germany, how he met her in Kempten and his strange attachment to her.

"I don't understand why he's interested in me."

Laurie's mouth dropped open. "Sister, don't you realize what a beautiful woman you are?" Like his Fiona, she seemed to have no sense of her feminine attributes.

She was already shaking her head. "You are too kind, but I

don't think my looks have much to do with it." She paused, searching for a way to explain. "God is calling him."

Laurie almost fell out of his chair. His tone was incredulous. "God is calling Eric Braun?"

"Is any man too far from the light that God can't reach him?"

It stopped Laurie before he could form his next objection. Thoughts raced through his mind of how far he'd been from God when he'd felt the pull of His Spirit.

"I don't understand either," said Ana, "but I know God's asking me to get these children to safety and show Eric how much God loves him."

Laurie nodded, speechless. Part of him wanted to believe Eric could find the peace he'd felt in his own heart. He hadn't done the things Eric had, but without realizing it he'd chosen a path that could have led to a life with Marguerite. *God saved me from that.* "I don't know how you can hope to change him."

"Herr MacKenzie—"

"Laurie," he corrected.

"Laurie, haven't you discovered yet we can only do our small part? The bigger picture belongs to God himself." Ana smiled. "We just have to do what we can."

Chapter One Hundred Nine

Rüdesheim am Rhein, Germany
June 1937

Eric's Conquest

It had been quite a while since he'd taken a woman to bed. Marguerite's skin was pure ivory, soft and flawless. The memory of their union still shook him to his core. They'd both had a bit too much to drink, but they knew what they were doing. And she was willing, even hungry for his attention. He had the nagging feeling she was trying to push Laurie from her mind. *But no, he couldn't be mistaken about her attraction to him. Their chemistry was heady.*

It wasn't her first time, but she was almost shy at first. *No, not at all whorish but not pretending to be completely innocent.* Eric respected her honesty. *How could MacKenzie walk away from a woman like this? Well, his loss and all that.*

Blond curls fanned out over her pillow. *Even in sleep, the woman was breathtaking.* He didn't want to leave her bed, but it wouldn't do for her papa to discover their affair, so he slipped out of bed just before dawn, congratulating himself on his conquest. He was well on his way up the ladder, and Marguerite would help him secure his place in the Reich.

His clothes were littered across the room. He gathered them and dressed without waking Marguerite. As he walked back to his room, he remembered his meeting with Ana.

Why not? I'm not tethered to Marguerite. Not yet, at any rate. He glanced at his watch. *I can catch a few hours of sleep before I meet Ana.* He slid under his covers, and as he closed his eyes, he thought of MacKenzie's note. Something about a missing connection. The oblivion of sleep engulfed him before he could unravel the mystery.

Chapter One Hundred Ten

Rüdesheim am Rhein, Germany
June 1937

Until We Meet Again

It took every ounce of courage Ana could muster to keep her appointment with Eric. She arrived early and sat on the bench, praying he wouldn't come. It was almost one thirty, and he still hadn't arrived. Ana sighed as the big clock in the village square chimed the half hour. She would leave by two if he didn't show up. She decided she would buy some bread crusts to feed the ducks who floated in the pond in the center of the park. Some cookies for Gretchen might be nice.

She was crossing to the far side of the park when she heard her name. Ana knew it was Eric. The urge to run was almost overwhelming. He called again. There was no getting around this meeting, so she turned.

He was hurrying up the path. SS didn't run unless they were chasing you. They didn't have to—no one would fail to come when they called. But as she faced him, his boyish, almost angelic face struck her once again. *Did God give her glimpses of the Eric He'd created, not the evil man he'd become?*

She found it wasn't hard at all to smile back. "I was going to get stale bread to feed the ducks." She motioned to the bakery. "I'm told the baker always keeps some for the children." She laughed. "I think we have the fattest ducks in Germany."

He nodded in reply, and they linked arms as they walked to the bakery. It was odd how companionable they could be as long as she let God lead her actions. He bought a bag of stale bread, and they walked back to the pond.

She laughed as the ducks waddled toward them. "I think they saw us coming from the bakers."

Eric's voice was barely audible as the ducks quacked loudly. "I'm afraid we'll have no peace to talk with this racket." He took the bag and flung its contents out over the pond. The ducks headed back to the water. "Shall we sit and watch them feast?" He indicated a bench near the water's edge. "There is always a dominant bird in the flock. Usually the biggest because he's the bully."

They settled back on the bench in friendly silence. Ana said, "You seem different. Has something happened?"

"I'm contemplating marriage." A shock ran through her body. Then she realized it wasn't her he was talking about.

"She's quite beautiful. An heiress." He seemed to be stumped for any further description.

"Is her heart kind?"

"That is a funny question."

She read the turmoil on his face. "I can see it is not. I wish for you a kind wife, a loving home, a good mother for your children."

He seemed to search her eyes for any deceit or lies. *He may not have realized it, but Ana was pretty sure he'd heard God's heart for his future.* She knew it didn't come from her.

"It would be a good move. My commander isn't impressed by my work so far." Eric seemed unguarded.

She wondered if his failure to capture her and the children was a black mark on Eric's record. *What an odd predicament. I would have to sacrifice myself and the children for this man to be considered a success.*

"You think this marriage would make you a success?"

Eric pulled back to look at Ana. Bright red blotches climbed his neck. "And how do you measure success?"

Ana knew she was on dangerous ground, but she answered honestly. "To be the man God intended you to be. To do good for others—that would be a success in my measure."

His face registered incredulity. "You would make a terrible SS officer." He burst out laughing, and she joined him.

They spoke of small things, as friends do, and when he rose to leave, he took her hand. "My mother would agree with you. In fact, you are very like her." She stood, but he kept her hand folded in his. "I will think of what you said." He shook his head. "It would not be a simple thing to accomplish in my line of work."

She squeezed his hand. "I've found anything worth doing is rarely easy." She searched his face. *If ever there was a time when Eric the hunter seemed a million miles away, this was it. He was just Eric.*

Then the hunter returned. He clicked his heels and bowed slightly. "Until we meet again." He left without asking her for an address or arranging another meeting. He just walked away.

Eric couldn't explain why he left Ana so soon. He almost turned back when he realized he hadn't made arrangements to see her again. *Why is she always probing deeper into my private affairs?*

His thoughts turned back to Marguerite. He knew most of the guests would leave this afternoon, following a late lunch planned at three o'clock. He glanced at his wristwatch. *It's 1300. I want to catch Marguerite alone before she leaves with her father.*

He shoved his hand into his pocket to fetch out the keys to the transport. He felt crumpled paper and pulled it out with the keys. The note to Herr MacKenzie. He stared at it as if it could speak to him. *My intuition tells me something's up with the Scot.* He shook his head. *Does it matter? He's most probably back in Hamburg by now. I have his girl, and he has nothing.*

But it mattered. He wouldn't let one more bit of deceit slip past him. Especially since the nun and children had escaped him for so long.

He started the auto, a new resolve taking over his thoughts. *There are too many unanswered questions about Herr MacKenzie. If I become more involved with Marguerite, I must satisfy myself they aren't conspiring against the Reich.*

Eric made it back in record time. He saw Herr Voss' driver washing the car and smiled. It was clear they weren't leaving before lunch. Eric knew which bedroom belonged to Herr MacKenzie. Within minutes, he stood before the door. The handle turned, and he slipped inside.

How odd it hasn't been cleaned. He wondered if the man was still on the grounds, but as Eric flipped open drawers and looked in the closet, he became convinced Laurie was long gone.

He turned to leave. His shoe caught on a small throw rug. When he looked down, he noticed the edge of a photograph caught in the fringe. Even with the drapes closed, he recognized a picture of a woman. He walked toward the light and studied the photo in the full afternoon sun from the window.

His breath caught. *Not Ana but it looks so like her.* He studied every detail of the woman in the photograph. *The hair is different; the clothes are foreign. It might very well be her.*

He ran a hand through his hair and began pacing. *I have to think. Could this be why Ana was always disappearing?* He paused and spoke one word to the empty room. "Spies?"

He'd heard how the British were envious of the Fuhrer's new order. He shook his head again. *I could picture Marguerite as a spy but not Ana. She's innocent. But how sure am I? She could be an excellent actress.*

His mind was full of questions and suspicions but no answers. He squeezed his eyes shut, wanting to put all the questions out of his head. He had to control his feelings.

I will find the answer to these questions, and Marguerite will be my first stop. Pulling up his mask of calm, Eric headed downstairs to find his lover.

Marguerite was in the garden, walking along an old brick path. She turned when she heard him coming.

Her smile seems genuine, he thought. *Let's see how she reacts to the photograph.* She extended her hand as he came near. He reached for her, folding her into a warm embrace. Or at least that was how he played it.

He whispered in her ear, "You are so beautiful today, but I think I like you best the way I saw you last night."

Her cheeks were blossoming bright pink.

"What is this? You are embarrassed, or are you regretting trading me for your Scotsman?"

She shook her head. "No, no, we were too different. It would never have worked." She smiled up into his face. "I think you and I are better suited."

He pulled her body closer, feeling her arch into him. He kissed her, his own body responding to hers. Eric meant to pretend the hunger. But without his permission, every part of him wanted to pick her up and carry her to his bed.

The world around them melted away, and there was nothing but the softness of her breasts and the firmness of her hips pushing into him. He felt like he was losing the power to resist.

Eric fought his way back to self-control and stepped away. She was breathless, wide-eyed with surprise. He could feel his mask slipping. The unexpected power of their connection had rocked him as well. She whispered his name. "Eric."

He had no words. Last night, they'd both had too much to drink. His memory of their union was a series of blurred images. This afternoon, it was clear his body remembered their evening together. He slipped his arm around her shoulder and turned them away from the house. "That was—" He couldn't seem to find the words.

She sighed her answer, laying her head on his shoulder as they walked together without words. When the stables came into view, he remembered the photograph in his pocket. He pulled it out to show Marguerite. She stopped abruptly, studying the photograph in her hand. "Where did you get this?" she demanded, her voice sharp.

"I found it in Herr MacKenzie's room." He watched her closely. *If she's involved in any plot, I'll detect it from her reaction.*

"That cheating bastard."

"You know who this woman is?" Eric kept his voice casual.

"Oh yes, but I can't believe he kept this with him all this time." She stared into the distance, seeing something. Her face revealed the pain of betrayal.

"Who is she?"

"His neighbor. I met her once when we were out at dinner." Marguerite shook her head. "A simple thing. Poor. Common." Her words trailed off.

"German?"

"Nein. A Scot." Her face crumpled. A large tear ran down her cheek.

Eric turned her once again to look at him. "But he came to you, Ja? Why would he do that if he had a sweetheart back home?"

Her face hardened. "I'll tell you why. He wanted to get ahead. Most of his classmates are serving apprenticeships. Not Laurie. My father hired him as a full-fledged engineer." Her posture was rigid. Her lips pressed together. He realized the depth of her anger.

A servant appeared at the edge of the garden. He looked at them hesitantly. "Excusez-moi, mademoiselle et monsieur, lunch is served."

Eric gave him a curt nod and waited for the boy to leave before tipping Marguerite's chin upward until she looked him in the eye.

"If MacKenzie hadn't been such a fool, you and I might never have found each other."

Her smile was tentative.

"And we are a good match. I don't plan on losing you or chasing after another woman."

He felt a warning at the back of his mind. *Ana offered me friendship, nothing more. The possibilities with Marguerite are intriguing.* He heard Ana's voice in his thoughts: "Is she a good woman?"

He kissed Marguerite with a forced passion, unhappy that Ana always asked him to look within. But as he pulled back, he had to admit, *What would an SS officer do with a good woman?* He searched the blue eyes before him and found an honest, open acceptance. *Perhaps that is at least a starting place.*

Chapter One Hundred Eleven

House on Latimer Square
Edinburgh
June 1937

God is God, Right?

God is God, right? Fiona dipped her scrub brush into the soapy water and brought it down with a splash onto the floor. Her arm became the focus of her worries. Not that the floors needed scrubbing, only that she needed to scrub them. But her thoughts came again without warning.

How will Terry let Laurie know they're coming to Rüdesheim? Pictures of Laurie being arrested and thrown in some dark place floated in the bucket of soapy water. But she plunged her brush through them and scrubbed all the harder.

As she came to the door of the connecting bedroom, she sat back on her heels and looked at the freshly scrubbed floor. *Almost clean enough for a toddler to play on. God, keep that family safe.*

She picked up her pail to dump the used water in the upstairs bathroom sink. It was time to rinse the floors and let them dry.

Please, Lord, keep them all safe. She stopped to look down the hall at the few remaining rooms. *Three whole days till they come home. These floors are going to be spotless.*

The cradle came that morning. It sat next to the bed in the big room. *I'd like to get a few baby things.* She reminded herself to be practical. She had to watch her funds. *I won't buy very much, but they'll need a few things to start.*

She found clean sheets and bedding in the linen closet, even a set of lovely pink ones for the girl's bedroom.

The bedroom she'd chosen for Katrine was clean and beginning to look welcoming. She had found a dressing table in one of the other bedrooms and dragged it over, but the room still needed some special touches. Something that will make her sigh with pleasure when she sees it. *I think maybe I need another trip to the shops. Katrine will need a hairbrush and some other toiletries.*

Glancing down at her mop and brush, she decided more floor washing could wait until the next time she found herself beset with worry. For now, her excitement was growing as she made everything ready.

Chapter One Hundred Twelve

House on Latimer Square
Edinburgh
June 1937

Alec Searches the House

Alec tested his theory about Fiona's movements. If he knocked and the dog barked, she came to the door. Of course, he had to remember to bring flowers or cookies as an excuse in case he found her at home. So far that had only happened on one late afternoon visit. She'd accepted his gift and his apology, but she didn't invite him in, and their conversation was short. Even that day, he returned after dinner.

All the subterfuge allowed him to make a very complete search of the house. Early evening was usually his best window. It wasn't hard to get away from work a bit early so he could rest before he went up to her house. His father already saw him as a slacker; there wasn't any benefit in proving him wrong. Alec could usually begin his search well before he lost daylight.

On one occasion, he slipped on the floor in a guest bedroom and almost fell on his backside.

"Bloody hell!" He grabbed for the edge of a bed frame. "Why would she be washing floors?"

He took a minute to look at the furnishings. *The bed's made up. I don't remember there being a cradle in this room. Everything's so clean.* He went back to the other bedrooms. *She's getting ready for something or someone, but who? You'd best step up your search, old boy, or you may lose the treasure for good.* He also realized he must have just missed her.

This evening, Alec found himself in the attic. As in most old houses, the attic was full of small rooms. Back in the day, these were the servants' quarters. Each room had a wooden bed frame and chest but little else. This part of the house was empty, just a few storage crates and a stack of mirrors and picture frames. Everything was dust free. *Our Fiona's been cleaning up here.*

He knocked on every wall, looking for hidden compartments. He plopped down in a chair. "Nothing. Bloody nothing."

The only place left to search was Fiona's bedroom. Alec hated to admit the captain scared him, but the fact that he'd avoided looking into those evil eyes was proof enough. Looking out the attic window, he realized the light was fading. Fiona's bedroom would have to wait for another day.

Chapter One Hundred Thirteen

Gamekeeper's Cabin

Germany

June 1937

Too Late for Changes

For a time, Laurie waited by the window, watching for Ana's return. *If there's good in Eric, I haven't seen it. She's a brave woman.*

He'd been playing with the children most of the afternoon. They spoke only a few words in English. His German made them laugh, so it must have been pretty bad. Still, they seemed to understand each other well enough.

Deter was an excellent hand at cards. *He's a quick learner. Maybe I shouldn't have taught him how to play poker. Then again, he beat me twice. It's enough to ruin my reputation as a decent poker player.*

After lunch, Gretchen surprised him by bringing a blanket and cuddling up on his lap. "Tell me a story?"

She's a sweet child. So open. To think she could have fallen into Eric's hands. A shudder ran up his spine. *Thank you, my love, for sending me to find these bairns.* He kissed Gretchen's blond curls and began the story of the selkies. Her head dropped to the side as she dozed off.

"I'll take her."

Laurie looked up into the warm brown eyes of Katrine.

"She'll nap for a good hour if I put her down."

Laurie stood, still cradling Gretchen in his arms. "Where should I set her?"

"Just over on her mat."

Katrine pulled back the covers on the small makeshift bed by the fire. As he lay her down, Gretchen snuggled into the blankets and sighed.

Katrine smiled. "She is such a sweet child." Then her expression became serious. "Herr MacKenzie, can we talk for a bit?"

Laurie noted the worried expression. "Aye, sure, lassie, but please call me Laurie."

He followed her to the small kitchen table. She had set out two cups of hot chocolate.

"Thank you. I love hot chocolate." He pulled out her chair and then sat across from her. "I know you must have many questions. I'm not so sure I'll have all the answers you're looking for."

"Where are we going next?"

"My grandfather owns a fishing boat. He's coming for us all in the wee hours of the morning tomorrow. And we'll be on our way back to Scotland."

"Ana said Gretchen and Deter have cousins in Scotland."

"Aye, Bernie is a friend of mine. He asked me to look for them. And it took a bit, but with God's help, I found them."

"But you got more than you bargained for." She bit her lip, fighting to get her next question out. "What will happen to Ana and me?"

He reached across the table and put a hand on hers. "I'm not offering you a place to stay. I'm promising to care for you and keep you safe as if you were my sister."

And as God is my witness, I mean every word. I may have gotten more than I bargained for, but I plan to take care of everyone God has given me.

He could feel her hand relax. They talked of Scotland for a bit and were interrupted by the noise of a motor. Laurie bolted to the window but turned back to Katrine.

"It's all right, lassie, just Ana and Etienne."

Before they were even through the front door, Laurie could see something had gone very wrong.

"What is it?"

Ana handed him a small handwritten note. It said:

Mac,

I hope you received my last note. My baby girl seemed to think it was time for her to come into this world. We missed the rendezvous with your grandfather and have come to Rüdesheim. I hope all has gone well. See you soon.

Terry

Laurie looked up. "But I didn't get the first note."

Etienne answered. "No, I asked the boy. The note came during dinner. He went looking for you at the table. When you weren't there, he asked the people you came with. Your young woman took the note, but an SS officer snatched it from her hand and read it."

Katrine put a hand over her mouth, her eyes wide with fear.

Laurie said, "Terry wouldn't have said anything specific. I'm sure of it."

"I saw Eric as planned," Ana added, "but he seemed distracted. I think he's interested in a fraulein."

Laurie felt his heart sink. *So, Eric is interested in Marguerite.*

Ana was saying, "We talked about her. If he'd been looking for you, I think he would have said something." She looked from face to face. "He didn't even ask where I was staying. It was like a gift from God."

Etienne added, "There is one thing more. The staff overheard the SS captain say they were staying in the area for a few more days conducting training."

"Shouldn't we wait until they leave?" Ana asked.

"I'm afraid it's not that simple." Laurie shook his head. "I can't get word to my grandfather. He's on his way down the Rhine just now. He will be there on schedule—so will Terry, his wife and children. No, we'd best stick to our plan. If the SS are training in the area, this lodge isn't safe, either. No, we must trust God to get us out."

Katrine's small voice said, "Isn't that what we've been doing all along?"

Etienne left, promising to be back at the lodge by two-thirty in the morning. "I can drive you all into Rüdesheim, but I have la comtesse and our people to protect. I can't be connected to your escape." They assured him they understood.

"One thing I can do is contact your friend Terry. It would be good for him to know where and when to meet you."

Laurie thanked him, and they talked for a few more minutes before Etienne left. There was nothing to do then but wait. And pray.

Chapter One Hundred Fourteen

Rüdesheim am Rhein, Germany
June 1937

We Can Only Do What We Can See to Do

Ana glanced up at the dark sky. Only a quarter moon, yet the wet cobblestones still reflected its light. *Thank goodness the people of Rüdesheim are all asleep. Even the dogs are too sleepy to bark.* She'd felt sad to say goodbye to this quaint German village. Now it felt sinister, as if evil were waiting to snatch her little ones.

"I'm tired." Gretchen rubbed her eyes and slowed with every step.

Ana whispered, "Just a little more, my love. You must stay quiet, Ja?" Gretchen nodded with somber understanding, her eyes hooded with sleep. It was getting harder for them to keep pace with the others.

As if she were calling him with her thoughts, Laurie turned back and in one motion scooped up Gretchen. Ana smiled her thanks. She readjusted the pack she carried on her back as they caught up with Deter and Katrine.

Laurie held up his hand, and the group stopped. They melted into the shadow of the building. They'd stopped in front of the toy store. Gretchen's small hand reached for a beautiful doll in the window.

Laurie pointed to a narrow passageway between the shops. "There's movement at the far end of that alley. See, just there."

Father, he's looking for his friend. Please help— Ana's thoughts were cut short by the sound of boots on the village street.

But Laurie's voice stayed calm as he whispered, "I think it's just a patrol. We'll wait until they pass."

He shifted Gretchen to his other shoulder and pulled a Luger from beneath his jacket. He looked her in the eye. "A wee gift from Etienne. No worries, I'm sure everything will be all right."

Ana said, "I think if we go back to the last corner, we can weave our way around them and still come out where we need to be."

They turned back but stopped. The roar of a truck engine resonated off ancient buildings. The rules of this game had changed. Ana slipped her arm around Katrine, who'd whimpered.

They heard brakes squeal as the truck came to a stop. It echoed off the buildings. They looked around, but where they stood, it was dark and empty.

Ana looked to Laurie. His head swiveled, and she realized he couldn't tell the direction of the threat.

When he turned back to her, he commanded, "Don't stop."

Ana said, "We can still make it. Just keep moving. We must be very quiet." Once again, the group moved along the darkened shopfronts. "Can you smell the river?"

Deter's voice quivered. "I can't see any water."

"Take a deep breath, lad. Smell the diesel and fish. That would be the fishing fleet and my grandfather's boat waiting to pick us up."

Ana encouraged the children. "Etienne said they were doing

training exercises. That's all this is, just training." Still, she worried. *If we're captured, this training will turn deadly for all of us.*

In the distance, they could hear men and dogs. She looked up at Laurie. Even in the poor light, she could see his eyes widen. *This is more than a patrol. It sounds like they're searching the village. Oh, Father, protect us all.* Ana thought of la comtesse and baby Tony. She prayed for all of them as they made their way past shuttered storefronts.

Laurie was walking at a steady pace, keeping them in the shadows but moving ever closer to their destination. He said, "Fishermen are leaving for the day's catch. So many boats, and one will take us to safety."

Yes, take us all to safety. But Ana's hopes faded with a shout from the east. She could feel evil stalking them. *Lord, we're so close, so close.*

At the end of the street, she saw reflections of the moonlight sparkling off the water. They had to backtrack past Dolfmeyer's fish market. At the corner, she smelled bread. *Is the baker up already? Will he hear us as we pass his shop?* Across the street was a large warehouse. Lamplight lit the waterfront. Ana reached out to touch Laurie's sleeve.

"There's a double row of train tracks between us and the water," she whispered. "Katrine, will you help Deter? We'll need to hurry, but be careful over the tracks."

Laurie said, "Go."

Their little group hurried across the wide esplanade that ran along the waterfront. *Lord, we are so exposed here, don't let them see us. If we can make it to the warehouses, we can find cover.*

Two hundred yards down the esplanade, an officer directed men in a search. She was sure it was Eric. Stunned, she held back. The realization of what she needed to do washed over her, but with it came a kind of peace.

Make me strong, Father. Protect my children and keep me strong to protect Etienne and la comtesse and all the others who gave us help.

The group had moved away from her, their destination in sight.

"Geh mit Gott," she whispered to her children.

She turned back to the noise of the soldiers. *Don't let Laurie and my little ones notice I'm missing until it's too late.* "Go with God," she said again. Her voice was only a sigh. "I love you all." *I wish I could hug them one more time and tell them they're all my children.* She wiped a tear from her cheek. There wasn't much she could think to do but cause a distraction and delay the search long enough for the others to get away.

Once, before she turned the corner, she looked after them. Her heart stopped as she saw a group emerge from the shadows. Then she realized Laurie had found his friend. As she turned back, she thought she heard the faint cry of a newborn. She smiled, remembering the little family had just welcomed a baby girl.

Chapter One Hundred Fifteen

Rüdesheim am Rhein, Germany
June 1937

That They Might Live

They huddled between crates stacked to a man's height next to the waterfront warehouse. Laurie peered around them, looking for Rab's boat. *It would be off a little from the other boats. Not enough to draw notice but far enough to avoid scrutiny.* He spotted such a boat at the far end of the docks. He was turning to let Ana know all was well when dark shadows moved toward him. *God, not when we're so close.* He wondered for an instant if he could kill someone. Gretchen snuggled into his shoulder, and he realized he would do murder to protect this little girl. He chambered a round into his Luger, ready to fire.

An Irish accent said, "The word is Captain Moonlight."

Relief washed over him. There was only one person with the Gaelic wit to speak an old Irish password.

He grinned. "Is there ever an Irishman who isn't ready for rebellion?"

Terry seemed to materialize out of the darkness, his four-year-old son Richard in his arms, followed by Lydia carrying a baby in a bundle of blankets.

"Not likely, ye bloody Scot. Not likely."

"Well, glad you could make it, mo chara."

Terry wrapped his arms around Laurie in a hug. "Good to see you too, my friend, and we almost didn't, thanks to a beautiful little girl." He looked back at his wife. "Ahead of schedule but a darling all the same."

As if on cue, the infant let out a small cry, but her mother rocked her back to sleep.

Terry's voice grew serious. "Where's your grandfather's boat?"

Laurie gestured to the far end of the wharf. The fishing fleet moored alongside docks that extended like fingers into the water. Activity around all the boats was increasing as they readied to go out for the day's fishing.

The last quay lacked the action, but the boat moored there looked like the Elspeth. The lighting was poor at that end as well.

"I was thinking the boat at the far end must be Rab."

He turned to introduce Ana to his friend, but she was gone. He looked behind them and glimpsed her figure as she turned to go around the corner.

"God, no. What is she doing?" His voice was gruff. "Terry, move them down the warehouses toward that last boat."

All humor was gone from Terry's voice. "Where are you going?"

"We've left the sister behind." He was certain Ana had turned back of her own accord. *But why? Why would she do that when we're so close?* Laurie couldn't fathom her reasons, but he was sure as hell going to find out.

His voice cracked with emotion. "Keep to the shadows. We'll have to stay on the river side of the warehouse."

Terry gave him a double take but moved his family down the dock.

Laurie put a hand on Deter's shoulder. "Follow them. Understand?" The boy moved out behind Lydia. Laurie put the sleepy Gretchen in Katrine's arms, hoping she didn't look back for Ana. His one thought was to get everyone aboard while he searched for the little nun.

He waited for the group to move off before he turned to where he'd last seen her. Something else caught his eye. Two hundred yards down the esplanade, an officer stood in the street shouting orders to the men. The light from a streetlamp shone on his blond hair and slim form. It was Eric.

I think I know what she's up to, but I can't let her do it. He looked back at the group as they disappeared into the shadow of the warehouse.

Laurie moved with as much speed and stealth as he could. He caught sight of Ana as she passed under a streetlight. She was moving away from the water. Away from her precious children.

She must have heard him coming because she swung around. "What are you doing? Go back. Get them out of here."

He grabbed her arm as if to keep her from running. "What are you doing? You can't think of sacrificing yourself? Not after all you've been through. Not with escape right here."

"He's looking for me. Me. Not you. If I give him what he wants, they won't be searching for my kinder." Her face was strained and tears sat in the corners of her eyes. But there was a change in her. Determination. *God, she knows what she's walking into. Where does that kind of bravery come from?*

She put a hand over his. Her features softened. "Don't you understand, Herr Laurie? God only asks us to do what we can. I can do this." The words were spoken with such conviction, but he couldn't accept them.

"No, it isn't right. You're coming back with me while we can still get away."

"And if we are caught? Who will be implicated?"

His grip loosened. "What do you mean?"

"If I am caught, I'm not connected to the comtesse or your Marguerite." Her eyes were on his, and he realized she was giving him a moment to let what she was saying sink in. "If you are caught, many more people will suffer. Are you willing to take that chance? Trade my life for theirs?"

Emotions roiled through him. How could he leave her, but how could he risk so much? It didn't feel right.

"Laurie, it's God's plan to bring you here and get those children to safety. To do what you can."

The soldiers were coming closer. They both froze at the sound of an infant's cry. Somewhere dogs barked. Time was running out.

"Go with God."

He knew what he had to do, hating that it had come to this. Laurie reached for her small hand, still resting on his arm. *So like my Fiona's.* He kissed it lightly, saying, "If they arrest you, I can make inquires through the church."

She smiled sadly and moved off.

He retraced his steps and caught up with the group waiting for him by the last quay.

The Elspeth's motor was purring away.

He moved his people across the dock to the waiting boat. Rab's face broke into a beautiful smile as they emerged from the darkness. Laurie felt like he was seeing the face of God. The same hand that had taught him to fish and that had held him as a small lad now reached out to help them all aboard the Elspeth. Little Gretchen didn't even wake as Rab reached to take her. Katrine looked back after the last of them boarded.

"Where's Ana?" Her voice was thin and high.

Laurie grasped Katrine's hand even though she tried to pull away. Her body tensed, ready to run after Ana. With one great lunge, Laurie caught her around the waist and heaved her up to Rab's mate Kevin.

Laurie looked up to Rab. "It's so good to see you, Grandfather."

Rab jumped down beside him and folded him in a warm embrace and then looked past him. "Where's the wee nun?"

Laurie's words felt grim and final. "She's not coming." He looked through tear-filled eyes at his grandda. "I went after her but—" *How can I let her do this?*

A transport filled with soldiers sped past them down the esplanade. "She wouldn't come, I—"

Everything in him wanted to run back and rescue Ana. He looked at his grandfather. "How can I leave her? Maybe I could have helped her." He thought of the happy young comtesse and her new baby boy, Etienne with his wonderfully French outlook.

Shouts sounded in the distance and boots pounded the cobblestones, not toward them but in the direction of the little park. Laurie's body went rigid. One shot rang out.

"God, no. I have to help her."

"No, son. No, you can't."

Laurie knew his grandfather was right. He knew the children were everything to Ana.

The fishing fleet was moving out from the docks.

"We need to leave with the fleet." Rab cast off the mooring lines, and they climbed aboard. The Elspeth began motoring upriver.

"No, laddie, she's done what she could to get those bairns to safety, and you'll honor her by finishing the job."

Guilt washed over Laurie. He wanted to lash out at Rab, but no. *That was something the old Laurie would do.*

He looked over at his little band of refugees. The first face he saw was Katrine's, her eyes bright with tears. She mouthed the word, "Why?"

He came to her and folded her into his arms. "She turned back, lassie. She saw the soldiers and turned back to give us time to get away."

Katrine buried her face in his coat and sobbed into his shoulder.

"Why? Why did you let her go?"

His heart accused him. *I let this happen.*

He didn't tell her about the shot. It was better to have hope that Ana was only arrested. Laurie tilted her tear-streaked face up to his.

"She did what she could. We'll honor her courage with our own and allow her this sacrifice to help you all get to safety."

He kissed her forehead. Rab slipped a blanket around Katrine and guided her down the steps to the ship's cabin.

He couldn't stop thinking of ways he could still save Ana. Rab came back to stand and watch the shore with him.

"When we get clear of the town, slow and I'll go overboard. I have to find Ana. I can't leave her alone."

"Nay then, laddie."

There was a loud ruckus in Rüdesheim. Shouts filled the night.

Rab looked up to Kevin, who'd taken the helm. With an unspoken nod of his head, he gave the order. Within minutes, they were motoring out into the deep waters of the Rhine. From the shore, they'd look like just another fishing boat. Laurie stood on deck watching the lights of the village. Rab came to stand with him. He pointed to the cause of the disturbance.

"Ana. She's still alive." Laurie could see her as she walked into the light. The uniformed men surrounded her. They were yelling. Her head was bowed in submission. Not to them, he knew. Her submission was to a higher authority. Then she was out of sight as they led her away.

Rab put his hand on Laurie's back. "There's nothing you could have done."

You're wrong, Rab, Laurie thought. *There's one last thing I can do.* He prayed. *I'm not used to talking to you, Lord, but if you can help Ana, I'd be grateful.*

He heard her voice as they'd talked the night before. "Laurie, haven't you discovered yet? We can only do our small part. The bigger picture belongs to God himself. We just have to do what we can."

Laurie knew the little nun had done what she could see to do. She'd protected the children until the very end. Now he'd become part of God's plan to get them all to safety. He turned away from watching and scrubbed a hand over his face.

"Ye should sleep, laddie."

"Not yet, Grandfather." He looked toward the German side of the Rhine. "Not till I know we're out of German waters."

Rab handed him a mug of hot tea. "I thought you'd say that."

Light was breaking over Germany. The dark waters of the Rhine turned steel grey in the early dawn. The river curved north as it rounded a bend, leaving Rüdesheim far behind them.

Much later, with the open sea before them, Laurie made his way down below deck. He stopped on the stairs to look at all the people God had rescued. *God's plan had a high price, but to save so many souls, that was something.* He felt more at peace.

The passengers were curled up in the cabin wherever there was space to lie down, children and adults exhausted, tears of loss cried out. They slept deep. Laurie thought he heard the baby wake but even she soon settled.

Chapter One Hundred Sixteen

Rüdesheim am Rhein, Germany
June 1937

That You Might be the Man God Meant You to Become

Eric jogged toward the little police station. They were using it as a makeshift headquarters for their training exercise. He called to his friend Michael. "I heard a shot. Did one of our recruits misfire?"

"No, he didn't hit anyone. He got excited when he saw someone running down the street."

"Lord, we'll hear it if we wake the whole village."

"I don't think so. It seems our training has turned up a criminal." Michael's tone was playful, even taunting. This late-night training was his idea. Michael had told their commander it would be good practice for the men. Eric yawned.

He thought about Marguerite, probably already back home. "If it wasn't for you, we'd be back in Hamburg, you moron." His friend had been responsible for getting him this position. *So far, it had opened many doors for him, including one bedroom door. So, humor the man,* he told himself.

"Come, Eric. I think I've caught the little bird you've been hunting, and she was right under your nose."

Eric followed him into the harsh light of the police station. A young woman sat in a chair. Her back was toward him, but he would have known her anywhere.

"Ana, what are you doing out so late at night?" He moved around to her side and saw a purple bruise darkening on her left cheek. "I know this woman. She's a village girl. We are friends." His tone was angry and accusatory.

Michael cut him off. "She is a catholic," he sneered.

"What difference—" Eric couldn't finish his sentence, seeing what the officer pulled out of a satchel.

"She says she's Sister Ana from Saint Thomas near Mittenwald." Michael held up a rosary. "She was carrying this with her." There was an unpleasant smile on his face.

Eric grabbed it from his friend. He looked from the rosary back into Ana's deep-blue eyes. The first thing he saw was regret. Not fear or guilt.

"What does this mean, Ana? Did you know all along I was looking for you?" His face twisted with anger. "How could you do this?" He stuffed the beads in his side pocket.

"You never spoke about looking for a nun, but yes, I came to know you were looking for me." Her voice was gentle. "I always said I could only be your friend." She still wore her heart on her face—warm, caring.

"Where are the children?" Eric's demand was explosive.

She flinched a little at his tone but only said, "They're gone."

He was furious. He wanted to strangle her.

"You lied. All this time you lied." He knew his friend was finding this situation amusing, but he didn't care. "You said—" He realized she'd never said she was anything but a friend. As quickly as the anger arose, it fell away.

Michael broke in. "These holy women are nothing but whores for the priests. You know this. Everyone does."

That Michael could look into those eyes and see sexual perversion made Eric sick with fear.

He knelt in front of her. "Tell them what you were doing here. It will be all right. Just tell them."

Ana smiled sadly. "I told you. I was looking for you. Now that you've caught me, you won't have a black mark on your record, Ja?" He was aware of the men in the room watching them. "I wanted you to know the truth." A tear rolled down her face. "I always wanted you to know, but I had small ones to protect."

He drew back as if she'd slapped him.

"It wasn't you." Eric shook his head. "No, I would have known."

His friend had been pacing. "By God, Eric. You've caught your nun." Michael stopped, looking down at Ana. "We have ways of making you talk. You will tell us where those children are."

Eric's mind was racing. Thoughts ran wild through his brain, and with each twist and turn, his emotions rolled from one extreme to another.

Michael grabbed Eric's shoulders. His voice was gleeful. "She's right. This'll clear your record."

A young soldier came through the door. Clicking his heels, he gave the expected salute. "Heil Hitler."

"Well?" Michael seemed eager to get on with the interrogation.

"Some children were seen getting on a fishing boat."

"Did you go after them?" Michael demanded.

"Nein, mein Kapitän." The sergeant drew back in fear. "The fishing fleet was leaving. There are so many boats, we thought it was just one of them." The man spread his hands. "They are long gone by now."

Eric stood looking at Ana. Relief washed over her features, and it made him all the angrier. "You betrayed me."

She shook her head. "No, Eric. I befriended you."

Her eyes—they're clear. Honest. No. The woman is a liar. But even as the thought formed, he knew it wasn't true.

She looked him in the face. "I knew what you'd done. But I saw—I hoped—there was some good in you." His reaction was swift. He slapped her other cheek. Her head rocked back with the impact.

Eric looked at his hand and at the sweet face before him. He remembered his own mother looking at him with love shining in her eyes. He stepped back, but his friend was quick to take his place. He pulled Ana to her feet, shaking her like a rag doll.

"Where are those Jew brats?" Spittle hit her face with the force of his words.

She uttered one word. "Gone."

Another slap, and Michael let go of her. Ana crumpled onto the floor.

Eric looked into his friend's face. It was a mirror of the wolf, the same mask Eric wore when he interrogated the priest. He remembered the Jew in the woods. He was looking at the hunter as he had been the hunter—evil, feral.

Eric knew his friend was taken with the lust of the hunt. *As I would be.* And he knew too Ana was no longer a person to his friend. *She is prey. Before I can do anything to protect her, I must think.*

Michael drew back and kicked Ana's crumpled form in the stomach. She cried out and curled into a ball.

Eric yelled, "Stop." But the next kick didn't stop. It followed the first, matching both impact and aim. Before another kick could be launched, Eric stepped in front of his friend.

"Stop." He met the SS officer's direct gaze with a piercing glare of his own. "I will question her."

Michael sneered. "This witch has put a spell on you."

Eric held his ground, watching as Michael backed down. *You can't know your own reputation until you read it in another man's eyes. His friend was afraid of him.* The wolf recognized fear.

Michael's words dripped with contempt. "Have it your way. This woman's cast some sort of spell over you." He turned, but before he left the room, Michael said, "I won't let her ruin my career."

Eric was on his knees in seconds.

He brushed the soft black curls from Ana's face. "I'm still angry at you. Don't think you have any victory in this." But even as he spoke, the pain on her face melted his resolve. "Here, let me help you up."

She took his hand and stood. His arm slipped around her. He wanted to hold her, to comfort her. Still, everything within him railed at the betrayal he'd suffered at her hands.

She said, "You must be who you choose to be. I must also do what I think is right." The corner of her mouth rose in an attempt to smile with her lip swollen on one side.

"I can't hold the commander back for long." He spoke as if warning a child. "Tell him what he wants to know."

"And you do not want to know this as well?"

Eric thought for a moment. "I care about you more than catching a few Jews."

"Children, Eric. Just children. Innocent."

"Where are they?" he asked, his voice only a whisper.

"Gone." She smiled. "My job here is done, and I'm ready to go home."

"You won't be permitted to go home." He was affronted at her directness. "You couldn't have made it all this way without help. Come now, who has helped you?"

She shook her head, and he knew she would never tell them.

"I can't stop them from hurting you, Ana."

"I know." She reached out and touched his arm. "God only asks each of us to do what we can."

"I'm not like you, Ana. You see what I am."

A tear rolled down her face. "I see what God sees. The man He made you, what He wanted you to become." Her small hand touched his chest. "You are not the wolf. You still have a man's heart."

He drew his brows together. *How can you know I think of myself as a wolf?* He felt cold steal over his heart. He swiped her hand away and straightened his uniform.

"Michael's getting our commander. You had best stop playing these games and tell us what you know." As if on cue, his friend walked back into the room, his pistol drawn.

Ana looked down and slipped her fingers around the end of her rosary. She drew it from Eric's pocket.

Without warning, Michael fired once into Ana's stomach. Eric jerked with the weapon's report.

Everything seemed to slow. Eric looked down at Ana. The rosary beads tangled in her fingers. Her eyes were still on him as a bright plume began just above her skirt. She seemed to crumple into herself. He reached out to catch her. They slid together to the floor.

This can't be happening. He looked up at his friend, unable to breathe. "Why? She was just reaching for her rosary."

"You should thank me. She's already done enough damage to your career." Michael turned with the casual air of a man done at the office. "Besides, the commander would only have tortured her. She's better off dead."

And he was right. Eric had known what was coming. He just hadn't let himself go there, but ... better off dead?

She was looking at him. Innocent. Pure. A child's trust. The blood was everywhere, spreading out from the small circle onto the floor. A part of him knew she would be gone in a matter of minutes. The blood was carrying her away from him forever.

"God didn't take your mother from you, and He's not taking me. I've given my life that you might be the man you're meant to be."

His eyes clouded with unshed tears. His throat clogged,

choking off his words. And his heart, once cold and hard, now seemed to stop. All the smug, superior rhetoric failed him.

She is a person. Brave. A protector. She knows who I am, and she cares about me. He reached out to touch her cheek. "Ana."

"Remember..." Her eyes focused just behind him. A sweet smile touched her lips. He felt her last breath caress his face. She was gone.

Chapter One Hundred Seventeen

The North Sea
June 1937

The Elspeth Comes Home

The smell of food coming from the galley roused Laurie. He looked around at the sleeping travelers. *They'll all be awake soon.* He made his way above deck. He found Rab at the wheel. They were in the open sea. The air was fresh, full of hope and the promise of home. *And Fiona, he thought. I can't wait to see her.*

"We're free for now at least." Rab raised his voice above the sound of the engines.

Laurie turned to see Rab's face. "What do you mean? Surely, we're past German jurisdiction."

"Oh, aye. But it's not the Germans we need to worry about the now. We're smugglers, lad. Not French wine or fine silks. We're smugglin' people. Jews."

Rab took his eyes off the sea and gave Laurie a direct gaze. "It's our own people we need to worry about. Your friends have nay passports. They canna enter the country legally." His face was lined with the gravity of what he was saying.

"I've arranged to make port in the gloamin'." It was that wonderful time between full on night and the last soft light of day. "I'll radio ahead for some of my lads to meet us. We'll be needin' an extra motor car to get everyone back up to our hoose. It's a risk, but I see nay way around it."

"What would they do if they stopped us?" Laurie hadn't thought about getting the children past customs officials.

"They could send those children back to Germany."

"Rab, they can't. It would be as good as putting a gun to their heads."

All we've gone through just to end up losing them. Laurie's inner voice sounded panicked. *It's not possible—not after Ana's sacrifice.* He stopped, took a deep breath, and said, "God didn't bring us all this way for that to happen. No, it will be all right. I'm sure of it."

Rab looked at him with a piercing gaze before answering. "Nay then, I ken yer right."

Laurie slipped his arm around Rab's shoulder and gave him a hug. *I never want to go back to the old me. Never.*

The seas had been choppy, but they still made good time. Once, they passed one of her majesty's ships patrolling the waters off the coast of northern England. Rab waved, but the Elspeth wasn't stopped. To all the world she looked like an innocent fishing boat.

The passengers and crew of the Elspeth were excited by the time they motored into Leith harbor and tied her up at the slip Rab had readied before he'd left. Just as he'd said, his lads were there with large coats and an extra motor car. The coats went onto children and Lydia to make them look as bulky as possible.

Terry helped his wife into her coat. Brushing the blond curls up into a stocking cap, he kissed her nose. "Beautiful as ever."

She smiled and brushed a tear away.

"Are you sad to leave Germany far behind?" he asked.

"No, you crazy Irishman." She shifted the baby into his arms. "I'm happy that my children are safe, far away from there." He hugged her with his free arm.

"I'm happy too, luv."

Laurie watched them, his throat tight with emotion. He missed Fiona. "I'm coming to you, my love," he whispered.

Chapter One Hundred Eighteen

Latimer Square

Edinburgh

June 1937

The Waiting is Finally Over

Fiona looked out Rab's sitting-room window for the tenth time in the last hour. *It's nine thirty. If all went well, they should be home soon.* She was ready. Beds were made up at her house. The afternoon and evening had been spent preparing food at Rab's house. She stood watching the traffic on Queens Road. Cars came and went, but none turned in at Latimer Square. It was getting late. Fiona caught sight of her reflection in the window. She still had a scarf tied around her hair, and the rumpled old dress she wore was dirty from a day of cooking. *There's one more thing to do before they all arrive. I'll change into my blue dress and the pendant from the puzzle box.*

Tam wasn't happy about being left behind. "Och, laddie, I'll be but a few minutes, and I can manage better if you bide here."

She hurried up the square to her house, unlocked the front

581

door and sailed up the stairs. Everything looked like a dream. She thought, *Nowhere but Scotland has the gloamin'*. Her room was bathed in orange light.

It took only a few minutes to find her favorite dress and change. She plopped down at her dressing table to run the brush through her hair. The face in the reflection looked so pale.

You goose, there's nothing to worry about. Didn't Rab send word with his mates? They're all safe. She pinched the color back into her cheeks. Before she left her bedroom, she stopped for a moment in front of Wee Geordie. His face came alive in the soft light. His eyes held her transfixed, so full of love and understanding.

"What if he doesn't feel the same? What if he's changed his mind?"

Her lip quivered, and she bit it, waiting for her captain to speak. But, of course, he didn't. He just looked at her as if she knew better than to say such a thing.

"No, you're right. He's a good man. I know he loves me, and I love him too." She lifted Mairi's diary off the chair, but as she opened the book, she heard a car in the square.

He's home. She raced out of her room. "Laurie! You're home—"

The light was fading fast, leaving her entry hall in shadows. She stopped on the landing. Someone stood at the foot of the stairs. "Alec," she whispered.

Chapter One Hundred Nineteen

Latimer Square
Edinburgh
June 1937

Hellos and Goodbyes

There was no sign the harbormaster even noted their arrival. They were away without incident and before long pulling up in front of Rab's house.

Laurie was out of the car before it stopped. He was up Rab's steps and through the front door before anyone else opened a car door. Tam hopped around him, yipping with joy. Laurie called out, "Fiona." He ran to the back of the house. The kitchen was full of great smells. It was clear she'd been getting ready for their homecoming, but she wasn't there.

Up the kitchen stairs two at a time. He raced down the hall, looking in every room, calling out her name. Apprehension settled in the pit of his stomach.

What if she decided she didn't want me after all? He stopped at the head of the stairs. Rab and the lot of them were coming in the front door. The entry hall was crowded as they all peeled off their coats and stocking hats. Laurie came down the stairs, searching to see if Fiona was among them. No.

"Rab, where's Fiona? She's not here. Was she expecting us to come to her house?" He could hear the panic rising in his own voice.

Rab patted Laurie on the back. "Nay then, I told her ta bide here, and I can smell her cookin'. She's most likely nipped up to her place for something."

Laurie had his hand on the door handle when they were all startled by a loud knock. He opened the door again to reveal Bernie and his mother.

They came in and stood, looking at the children. Laurie shook Bernie's hand. Then he turned to Deter and Gretchen. "This is your aunt Trudy and your cousin Bernie."

They all stood, waiting for the stone-faced children to respond. Then, God bless little Gretchen. She walked to her aunt and said, "You look like our mamma."

Trudy stooped down and hugged her niece. "That's because we're sisters."

"Do you know how to make streusel like Mamma?"

"Ja, and blintz and all the things you love." Trudy wiped tears from her eyes.

Little Gretchen reached up and kissed her aunt Trudy's cheek, saying, "Don't cry. The Nazi men can't come here. You are safe."

Deter hung back, his serious little face appraising his relatives. Bernie stepped forward to offer his hand and said something in German. For the first time, Laurie saw the child locked in Deter's little body emerge. Deter's face crumpled, and Bernie wrapped him in a firm embrace. He hefted Deter into his arms and came toward his friend.

"I can't thank you enough." He stuck out his hand.

Laurie shook it. "I'd say thank God, 'cause we wouldn't have made it without His help."

Bernie jerked his head up, giving Laurie a double take. "If you say so, then it must be quite a story. We'll get the bairns home. But I'll be taking you for a pint soon. Then I want to hear all the details, aye?"

After all the thank yous, the children were gone.

Terry gave Rab a pat on the back. "It smells fantastic in here."

"Aye, it does that. Let's get something ta eat for you and yer family."

Rab led the way back to the kitchen. In two giant steps, Laurie was at the door. He reached for the handle once more. He wanted nothing more than to run up the street to see Fiona. The sound of a soft sigh stopped him.

He closed his eyes and took a deep breath—not wanting to be distracted from the goal. Another sigh pulled him back. It was then Laurie noticed Katrine looking out the window. She pressed her forehead against the glass as she watched the children drive away.

She said under her breath. "They didn't even say goodbye." Tears rolled down her cheeks.

He couldn't turn away from a heart so broken, not even to find Fiona. He put a hand on her shoulder and said, "So much to take in. They're just children being carried along. But not to worry. You'll see them soon. Bernie is one of my closest friends. We were at university together."

She wiped her cheeks. "It's just that I've lost everyone." She gulped in a sob. Then the torrent started.

"No, you haven't. No. You've just started a new life with a new family." He put his arms around her in a loving hug.

Katrine hiccupped. "Who would want me?" She could barely get the words out.

Luckily, Rab had come into the room with some hot chocolate. Laurie guided Katrine to the big easy chair by the fire. He hadn't realized Tam had been at his side all along. The little dog jumped up on Katrine's leg.

"Och, Tam, doon with ye," Rab scolded.

"No. It's—it's all right." Katrine scooped Tam up into her lap, rubbing her hands through his fur. Tam gave her cheek a welcome kiss and curled up.

"You see, Tam lost his friend, and now he's come to love his new family. Rab and I and Fiona will be your new family." Laurie knelt next to her chair. "Things will get better. You'll be safe, and someday you'll be happy again." He knew she didn't believe him, but perhaps over time she would see. *That's my promise, God. I'll take good care of Katrine.*

Rab pulled up a chair and sat with Katrine before the fire. He looked at Laurie. "The lassie and I will be all right. I ken yer wanting to see yer Fiona. Go along now."

Laurie touched Katrine's arm. "I'll be back with my Fiona in a wee bit." She nodded, her hands stroking Tam's black coat.

Chapter One Hundred Twenty

House on Latimer Square
Edinburgh
June 1937

A Man Could be Capable of Anything

From somewhere above, Fiona called, "Laurie?" Alec stopped. *Damn girl, always ruining things. Not supposed to be here. She's never in the house this late. Only one room left to search, and she has to come home.* He came to stand in the half light at the foot of the staircase.

"Alec?"

He made his voice light and amiable. "There you are. I knocked. No one answered. Thought you might be at the back of the house. Did you know you left the door unlocked?"

"I was just leaving. Laurie's coming home tonight."

He could feel his blood boil. *One room left to search. Her room and now she says Laurie's coming home.* All his hopes of putting Father in his place vanished. Lost with little hope of making it a reality. His temper flared.

The kind Alec spoke through his rage. "Oh, that's splendid. When do you expect him?"

She beamed with happiness. "Any time now." *Was that a declaration? Laurie will protect me. I've done nothing but befriend the poor waif.*

He put his foot on the first step. "How nice for you to have him back." *Well, he's not here yet, is he?* She still hadn't moved. *Perhaps she's afraid of me.* He took another step. Alec was careful to keep a pleasant smile on his face. *This could be my last chance to search her room.*

"And don't you look lovely? You know, you should be more careful. It's dangerous to leave your door unlocked," he scolded lightly, taking two more steps. "What about my father's hired man?" He was three steps from the landing. "A man like that won't stop until he has what he wants."

Alec stood on the landing. Fiona backed away. "I was just thinking we should have another look for the chest." He knew desperation laced his words.

"I told you I don't care about the war chest."

"Brave words. But you know when something is that important, a man might be capable of anything." *Laurie can't have what is rightfully mine.*

The upper hall had an eerie, misty half-light quality. Details blurred. The door to Fiona's room was a few feet away. Fiona was the only obstacle standing between him and his treasure. Her expression of confident defiance angered him beyond reason.

The voice in his head shrieked, *You stupid girl! Think you can cut me off after I've been your friend?* He made a sudden grab for her arm. She yelped when he caught hold of her.

"What are you doing? You're hurting me. Alec, let go of my arm."

Her fear was empowering. He felt something in his head snap. It was as if he was watching the other Alec from outside his body. He forced her to the stairs. She was struggling to release his grip on her arm, but he held on all the tighter, feeling his fingers dig into her flesh.

"No, let go. What are you doing?"

Someone with his voice said, "No one will know any different. They'll think you fell."

She pulled away, shaking her head and backing into the shadows of the upper hall. "No, Alec. What's wrong with you? Why are you doing this?"

He wasn't listening to her. Instead, he caught sight of movement behind Fiona.

Cold rushed at him from her room. He could smell the sea and a whiff of something sweet and musty. Decay. Something dead.

In the misty half-light, a figure took shape.

He stood with his mouth agape.

"Something's wrong with you, Alec." Her voice sounded a long way off.

The white film wavered, then slowly materialized into a tall, broad-shouldered man. He wore the clothes of a buccaneer. The spirit's flared jacket moved with a non-existent breeze over black breeches and tall boots. Long, black, curly hair framed his fierce face. Cold dark eyes bore down on him. The Black Captain took shape.

Alec yelled, "Get back."

Fiona took a few steps back.

Alec pointed an accusing finger at her. "Tell your captain to back off, or you can join him."

As she took another step away, she seemed to move through the apparition. Now the captain stood in front of her.

The ghost wavered. He could see Fiona right through the figure. Then the captain solidified into a man.

He's so real. When the captain advanced two more paces, Alec heard the weight of him as his tall boots thudded on the floor.

He retreated to the edge of the stairs.

"Alec." Fiona said his name like she was talking to a child. "You're not yourself. Come away from the stairs."

"Who does she think I am if not myself?" Alec's face contorted into a sneer. "You don't know me. No one knows me, not Father, not you, no one." A blinding rage possessed him. He wanted to shake her.

The captain faced him down.

"You're dead. You can't stop me."

Fiona cried, "Stop it. I'm not dead. I'm right here."

He heard the scrape of metal as the captain pulled a broadsword from its scabbard. Light glinted off the blade as he swung it in an arc, holding it before him, ready to do battle for Fiona.

Alec threw his arms up to block the attack and stepped back, his weight shifting, but to a foot that found no solid floor.

The captain's image drew back, regarding him with something akin to sympathy before it evaporated.

The front door opened. Alec flailed his arms and twisted, trying to stop his body's backward motion. As he fell, he glimpsed Laurie in the hall below.

It all happened in slow motion. Fiona lunged to grab for him, but he was already tumbling down the stairs. The last thing he heard was Fiona screaming.

Laurie stood over the prostrate body. Alec's head was caved in on one side, and his neck bent at an odd angle. Laurie looked up at the landing. Fiona's hands were covering her mouth. She shook, her body wracked with silent sobs.

Alec's face was frozen in a death mask of terror, his eyes wild and open, his mouth drawn back with fear. Laurie checked for a pulse. Alec was gone.

Laurie ran up the stairs to catch Fiona as her knees buckled.

They sat together on the floor of the upper hall, and he held her while she wept.

"Are you all right? Oh, God, it looked like he might pull you down with him. What happened?"

She buried her face in his shirt and sobbed. "He was trying—trying to kill me."

I've come all this way, and I could have lost you. "Did he hurt you?"

"He was trying to kill me. Alec was trying to push me down the stairs."

Fiona's eyes rose from the fabric of his shirt to meet his. Her dark lashes welded together with tears. Her beautiful eyes gazed at him, tortured by grief and shock. "He wanted the captain's treasure. I think he was angry that I wouldn't help him find it. Is he…"

"Yes, he's dead."

They both looked down as the blood from Alec's head slowly spread on the bottom step.

"Why was he so afraid?"

She looked up at Laurie. "He said something about the captain." They turned toward the upstairs hall. It stood dark but empty.

"I'll have to call the police."

This wasn't the homecoming I'd imagined. But she was safe in his arms. He didn't want to let go. Not now. Never. "Can you stand?"

She nodded, and he helped her up. They wouldn't go down the staircase. They wouldn't look at Alec. He slipped his arm around her, feeling her warmth. She was his. Her head rested on his shoulder as they walked down the hall to the kitchen stairs.

Chapter One Hundred Twenty-One

House on Latimer Square
Edinburgh
June 1937

Ye Have Yer Lad Now

Laurie made two calls—the first to Rab to explain what had happened and to warn him to keep their guests out of sight. The second brought the police to Fiona's house in short order. But it was hours before the constables were through questioning them.

Alec's father arrived looking old and grief-stricken. He muttered, "I was only trying to get him to take charge, be a leader." Perhaps the old man had loved his son after all.

Laurie handled everything. He talked with the police, relating what he'd seen as he came in. Rab came up to ask if there was something he could do and to tell Fiona everyone could stay with him for the night. Then he wrapped Fiona in a warm embrace.

"Ye have yer lad to look after you, but if ye need me, I'm only a few steps away."

She cried again, holding this strong old Highlander to her with a fierce grip. Laurie put his arm around her, and the three of them stood together.

Later, after the body was taken, Laurie went to make her a strong cup of tea.

She wandered back to the entry hall. Blood still covered the bottom step. She went to find her scrub bucket still sitting in the butler's pantry. The soapy water was cold, but it would have to do. She needed Alec's blood off the stairs, especially before she brought guests home in the morning. As she scrubbed, Laurie came in with the tea. "Take the tea, lassie, and I'll clean up."

"I just need his blood off my stairs." She looked up at Laurie, tears pooling in her eyes. "He wanted me to die here. It was all about the war chest."

She watched him work, feeling strength from his nearness. Her world was coming right again. The cold from those awful moments when she struggled with Alec was receding, replaced by the warmth of having Laurie home.

Chapter One Hundred Twenty-Two

House on Latimer Square

Edinburgh

June 1937

War Chest

Laurie knelt to scrub the stair. Only a sticky film covered the stone. Most of the blood had disappeared down a crack where the stone bottom step sat beneath the riser. The soapy water followed Alec's blood trail and disappeared through the opening. He stood and kicked the step with his shoe. It moved.

Fiona asked, "What is it?"

"Alec's fall dislodged this step. I'd best mend it before someone—"

He saw a shudder run through her body and didn't finish his sentence, realizing how close he'd come to upsetting her all over again. "The tread stones fit into a groove. I think it's an easy fix."

He pulled the step back to make sure it lined up with the groove. But something caught his eye. "Hold on here. There's something under the step."

He stopped, drawing a deep breath. "What's this?"

She moved to the step above.

In the hollow under the tread stone sat a dusty old wooden box.

Laurie moved the stone step back and set it on the floor.

"Could it be the war chest?" she asked.

"I thought it would be the size of a sea trunk, not a shoe box." His tone was doubtful.

"The captain said he collected jewels and coins from the Highland chieftains. I don't think they were a wealthy lot."

They stared at the small chest. But neither of them made a move to pick the box up. With a crooked smile, Laurie asked, "Do we want to know? It seems it's brought bad luck, at least to Alec."

She looked at him for a long moment. "Greed brought bad luck to Alec. And Prince Charlie, for that matter."

"Right." Laurie brushed away the thick layer of dust.

"Oh, my," she said.

The wood was dull with age, but beautiful carvings adorned every side. It bore a silver band spanning its lid. Even the blackened silver clasp was carved in old Celtic designs. She could tell it was weighty as he lifted it out of its hiding place and set it at the foot of the stairs.

"See?" he said. "It's missing the piece in the center. Could be a lock with a missing key."

Fiona's hand went to the pendant she still wore. "The shape is the same as Wee Geordie's compass rose pin." She slipped the Celtic knot pendant off her neck and handed it to Laurie. "I think it's the key."

He hesitated. "Are you sure you don't want to open it yourself?"

"Will it change anything between us if it's empty or full?" Her voice was small and tenuous. "If it changes how you feel about marrying me, I don't want to open it at all."

Laurie met her eyes with a steady gaze. "Not on your life. Rab used to quote a piece from the Bible to me. He criticized my desire to be successful with it so often I know it by heart."

He closed his eyes like a schoolboy trying to remember his lesson. His voice was rich and mellow as he said, "For where your treasure is, there will your heart be also."

When he opened his eyes, she could see her deep love for him reflected in his face. His voice grew husky as he said, "You are my treasure. I need no other."

She leaned forward to kiss him and then pulled back just enough to say, "You are my treasure, too. But if the captain meant us to find this, there must be some good it's needed for. It makes me wonder how many more bairns we could smuggle out of Germany with the captain's treasure."

Laurie chuckled. "Never thought I'd say this, but I'm looking forward to a simple life with you by my side." He drew his brows together with the thought. "That's what I want, but I'm not sure what God may ask me to do about all I've seen in Germany."

"That's what I want too, but you never know what He has planned." She added, "Those are worries for another day. Go on, open the chest."

He nodded and slipped the chain off the brooch. The carved silver wound around a compass rose in a never-ending pattern. Laurie held onto the brooch and matched the winding knots to the indentation in the silver lock. He turned it, and a latch clicked. With a deep breath, he opened the lid. It was indeed a treasure box. Gold and silver coins crowded together with precious gems. "Ooooh," they said in unison.

Laurie held up a large ruby, and there were old necklaces, plaid pins and bracelets covered in jewels.

"The coins must be ancient." Fiona studied one in the light. "I can make out the date of 1717, but the rest is in a foreign language." Her eyes twinkled with each new discovery.

Laurie grew quiet, his voice so serious. "I suppose if I ask you to marry me as soon as we can, it might seem like I'm after your fortune."

A smile started at the corner of his mouth and spread across his face.

She laughed. "Not on your life. I'm not letting that stand in my way." She threw her arms around him. They kissed again, a long deep kiss full of the promise of more to come.

They were both breathless when the kiss ended. Laurie spoke first. "Your tea is cold. Let's go make another cup."

They walked away, leaving the war chest on the floor where Alec's body had been just an hour ago.

Laurie asked, "I have one request for our married life?"

"And what would that be, my love?"

"Can we move the Black Captain's painting down to the front room?"

The smell of the sea washed through the room. Fiona imagined her Black Captain smiling as she said, "I think he'd understand."

THE END

Acknowledgments

To my daughter Sheilla Christine Hagedorn, my cover and interior art designer: You amaze me with your creativity. I so appreciate your help and encouragement.

To my writing buddies Melva Timm and Liz Visser: I couldn't have written this book without you. Your critiques were always insightful. You encouraged, instructed, and enlightened me. You are both great writers and good friends. Thank you so much.

About the Author

I think we learn best through the stories of others. We see ourselves in their lives, imagining how we'd react. I explored my mum's life in Scotland during WWII. You can read about her adventures in *First Life*, available on Amazon or on my website. Mum lived through bombing and helped to catch a serial killer spy. And second sight was often part of her history.

What's it like growing up with a mom with the Sight? It's not just the glimpse of the future or a warning of danger that makes you listen closely. I think it's a real sense that life is so much more than we see with our natural eyes. She taught me to listen to the whisper of the God she loved and depended on.

Her faith fueled my own. Looking back, I never felt alone. I always carried the expectation that something amazing was just around the corner. "Watch for it, Wendy. You don't want to miss what God has for you next." I grew up in Seattle, met my future husband in our senior year of high school and later married and had children. My husband indulged my love of animals with cats, dogs, and horses over the years. I was a Highland dancer, a painter, and a writer. As a volunteer in many roles, I've met lots of wonderful people, and I've been grateful for every moment I shared with my husband and family. Yes, an ordinary life but rich, rewarding and full of twists and turns I never expected.

What am I doing now? Watching for what God has next for me.

Follow me at wendymutton.com for news and updates.

The Compass Rose Journey Continues

with Eric's Story

Wolf's Cub

Footsteps in the Dark

Edinburgh, Scotland

Dec. 19, 1937

Only half-past six and the streets of Edinburgh were empty. Laurie drew in a frosty breath and exhaled a foggy cloud. He flipped the collar of his overcoat up and pulled his fedora down over his forehead. Every surface reflected the sparkle of newly formed frost. An inviting glow from the Tolbooth Tavern tempted him to go back inside.

 A year ago, he might have done just that, but life had changed him. He was eager to get home to the warmth of his new wife. He couldn't believe how much he loved her, and his heart still raced when she looked at him with such love in her eyes.

His footsteps echoed off the old cobblestones. He set a steady pace up the Royal Mile toward Old Town. The buildings lining the street hadn't changed in hundreds of years. They leaned over the walkway, watching him pass. He could stroll these streets with his eyes closed. Edinburgh was his home. Gratitude filled his heart that he'd escaped from Germany with the children in his care. He'd rescued them from the Nazis' new world order and its oppression of all non-Aryans.

At the corner of High Street and Cockburn, he stopped for a moment. The unmistakable tapping of footsteps came from behind him. He shrugged off the sound. Only the memory of all that German subterfuge could make him imagine something sinister in another man on his way home.

He turned right down Cockburn toward New Town, listening for those other steps but hearing only the echo of his own. At Princes Street, a few autos passed him, leaving tracks in the frosty street. The snow dulled the glow of the lampposts, but the lights from neon business signs illuminated his way. He stopped again, pretending to be interested in the display of menswear in the Marks & Spencer window. There it was again. Two steps, then a halt.

The last time someone had followed him it was by order of an SS officer by the name of Eric Braun. The personification of the perfect Aryan male. Braun was a man without a moral conscience. Evil.

He glanced around, trying not to be obvious. Another man stood in the shadows a hundred feet down the road. Laurie shook his head. This was ridiculous. He waited to see if the man would move closer. After a while, the figure started walking his way. The dark shadow now looked harmless. Not sinister or threatening. Laurie smiled as the man walked with his hands in his coat pockets. More of a stroll than aimed at a destination.

Laurie's greeting was friendly. "Out for a walk on the town?"

The man stepped into the light spilling from the display windows. He was indeed very like Eric Braun. Blond hair in stark contrast to a black overcoat. *Another cookie-cutter Aryan.* Or maybe it was still his imagination.

"Herr MacKenzie. Back in your homeland, all safe and sound, Ja?" The German accent was unmistakable.

Laurie's breath caught. Anger coursed through him. They dared to follow him even here in Scotland? He snapped, "Who wants to know?" His hands were already clenched, his muscles tight, ready for a fight, but he held his ground and his temper.

"My name's not important. I'm only the messenger." The man's mouth turned down in disdain. "Voss trusted you with some very secret information."

"What, you mean those fly bombs?" Laurie tried to hide his thoughts, remembering how he and his co-worker Terry Mulligan had sabotaged the project. "Fantasy, never work."

"Oh, but you're wrong, Herr MacKenzie. I'm here to watch you.

Remember, you signed an agreement not to talk about your work at Voss.”

“Who would I tell? They’re junk, I tell you, not worth the breath to talk about.”

The man edged closer. “If you say a word, you’ll lose that pretty wife of yours.”

Laurie saw the gleam in his eyes. The same expression he’d seen on that Eric Braun character. A wolf on the hunt.

“Touch my wife and you’ll lose your life.” He added with menace, “Scots don’t make idol threats or make war on women and children. We aren’t part of your master race. We don’t mind being savages when it comes to protecting our own.”

The German took a step back and turned on his heel. A black car moved out of the shadows at the curb. Before getting in, the bloke swung around, saying with a casual air, “Oh, and tell your friend Herr Mulligan. One word from us and things will go badly for his family. Aren’t his wife and children German? A simple matter to deport them back home. Back to Germany, back to us.”

Laurie stood alone on the empty street as the car rolled past him. A bone-chilling fear for the ones he loved settled over him.